What HAROLD ROBBINS says about THE DEAL:

'Much like Dante reporting on Inferno, it takes an outsider to see what Hell is really like. Donald Zec's viewpoint of Hollywood in his magnificent novel THE DEAL, is one that is both exciting and erotic. My congratulations to Donald for a great achievement'

THE DEAL
Donald Zec

NEW ENGLISH LIBRARY/TIMES MIRROR

First published in Great Britain in 1978
by New English Library

© 1978 by Donald Zec and Anthony Fowles

First NEL Paperback edition May 1980

NEL Books are published by
New English Library from
Barnard's Inn, Holborn,
London EC1N 2JR.
Made and printed in Great Britain by
William Collins Sons & Co Ltd, Glasgow

45004411 4

Prologue

There was a desert wind blowing that night. All day it had blown. Hot, dry, choked on its own dust, it had swept up out of Mexico and on unimpeded across the long empty miles of grey, scrubby wasteland. A rasping wind. It rasped first against the paint-peeled clapboarded houses that unsurely marked the desert's edge, the beginning of the coastal strip. Its force unspent, gathering stinging momentum it reached the cities of that coast. It rasped against the buildings, the windows, the doors of San Diego, Long Beach and Los Angeles.

A hot breath from a bad side of the world it rasped against the nerve ends of the people in those cities. It blew grit under their skins. It made a night of old bad thoughts where men with tract housing mortgages brooded in their dens about the good ideas they'd always meant to get around to and now it was too late and, let's face it Harry-boy, the worst day's work you ever did was getting married to that dumb-ass dead-weight spreading at the hips. And in the kitchens, the same wives hated the greasy water from the dishes with an increased passion and thought with bitter, satisfying longing of young men's bodies and, well, never mind that now but, oh! and then screamed at those goddamned kids. In the dreary high-rises the thousand upon thousand loners stared at the four walls of their solitude and felt that loneliness more achingly. In the bars, the bars on Pico, say, and Western and on Franklin, the trade was down. Who the fuck wanted to go out some place this kind of night when your skin itched like an un-clean arm-pit and the electricity in the air was like it was making your teeth curl? The trade was down. But the brawls were up. It was a night for showing that smart-mouth plenty, fella, and right now while there was room to swing a punch. It was a night to pull a knife or hope to Christ you would avoid one.

Scouring, rubbing old sores raw, the wind kept on. Only some-where out to sea, meeting cool air from the Pacific, did it at last, in turbulence, abate. For the gritted, buffeted land there was, as yet, no hint of let-up, no indication of relief. It seemed all one, part of the stinging landscape when, mid-evening, the tremor ran gently down the coast. The wind had gotten to the rocks too, it seemed, and the earth, its own skin crawling, was shifting uneasily in search of comfort. In Los Angeles the newly rising buildings swayed slightly with a rhythm different from that of the whipping palm trees. Across the Valley lights snapped on and off in patterns uncharacteristic of the hour and people went out on their porches to call nervously to each other until the hot wind drove them in again. Off Long Beach, a rolling tanker had leaked some black overflow into the basin and fucked the beaches. In their pinched retirement homes senior citizens tediously remembered the big earthquake that flattened out this place when they were just knee-high and said that on a night like this, you bet, most likely anything could happen.

The filling station stood inland one hundred miles and some the nearer to the hot wind's source than Long Beach. A shack of a place set on the intersection of a dirt road into nowhere and a shimmering desert road of pitted pavement and squelched rabbit bodies picked at by the birds. Two pumps, the wild-cat company's showy logo, long since sand-blasted into obscurity along with the 'Regular' and 'Supreme', provided it with some sort of reason to exist. If, for example, for Christ knows why, you were heading for the Springs from Temecula, then you might, you just might, pull into the dirt half-circle and, as the dust cloud swirled up all around you, bang on your horn to get someone to gas you up and fill your water-bag. Maybe if you were desperate you'd try to find some shade and walk on over to the second no less lovely building where a blistered sign – wooden this time, you'd notice – hung the message 'General Store and Fountain' down from the underside of the two-by-four verandah.

That would be the day. You wouldn't chance that sort of drive by night. Leastwise not on a night missing the usual desert coolness and with the hot breath of the wind driving the world toward the edge of violence.

But one car came that night. The dipping, disappearing pinpoints of its headlights ceased to come and go. They grew steady, widened into beams and a mounting noise machine-gunned across the empty land. Then, with a suddenness shocking after the long build-up and its muffler certainly needing work, it was skidding to a halt close to the pumps. Its lights went out and then its motor. It rested quiet and dark as the dust settled.

In the darkness of the shed from where he'd watched it, Carl Ukinski swore.

'Shit,' he repeated.

He put down the can of Blatz and wiped his mouth. A gust of wind rattled against the side of the building. Shit, he thought, let it lay. There's something I don't like. I need dough but I don't need any kind of dough that bad. But at that moment a hard rectangle of light fell across the tire-tracked dirt and his wife's shadow filled its middle.

'Carl!' she called. 'You there?'

'Shit!' he said again. He grabbed the beer and took a pull and set it down a second time. He stood up. The gun was in the house. He took a tire-iron down and stuffed it down inside his coveralls.

'Carl? Carl?'

Leery, drunk, he pushed the screen door open and went out toward the car. Instantly the sweat upon him was dry in the hot wind.

Shit, he thought, a clapped out De Soto five years overdue for the scrap-heap. A make they don't bother making no more. A junk-heap on wheels. Shit, a two dollar sale if I get lucky. He glanced to his right. Leaning against the door, arms folded, his wife was still silhouetted in the doorway of the store they lived behind.

'Okay Norma, I got it,' he called.

She did not move or answer. More than ever he wished he had the gun.

He all but stopped and turned to go get it. But at that instant a door of the dark car flung open and as the interior light came on he could see the men inside. Jesus, he thought, greasers, meatballs. Wet-backs as like as not. Son-of-a-fucking bitch!

Three of them. As bad as he had feared. Two up front, one in back. Hopped up to the hairline, you just bet. He'd just better go get that gun. Only he didn't. Somehow the action of the car door opening, this young punk stepping out, had locked him into keeping on.

'Hey, man,' the young punk said, 'we ain't got all night, you know.'

His accent was heavy. His dark eyes glittered.

'How many?' Ukinski asked. The other two were sliding out of the heap.

'Fill her up,' the young punk said. 'Supreme.'

He hesitated, looked at them and found them looking at him

hard. The certain knowledge he would not get paid drove itself into his stomach. Once more he nearly stopped. But it was way too late. All the same, he had to make some kind of stand.

'This car don't need no Supreme,' he said.

'We like to give it the best we can.'

The other two were watching him. They had the same hard eyes. The same age. The three could have been brothers. The furthest one slammed shut his door.

'Fresh out of Supreme anyways,' he heard himself make out and felt the wind gust grit into his face. They had their backs to it.

The young punk grinned. 'It all goes man.' The wind dropped. In the lull Ukinski heard the footfalls of the other two as they moved off to left and right in back of him. They were double, triple, teaming him. He daren't call out to Norma. But maybe the dumb shit of a broad would have had the sense to go find the gun and . . . He sneaked a glance. But no. The stupid, fucking bitch was still there in the doorway, her brain between her legs, as always, shit-full of fucking 'True Romances'. And oh Christ! Now she had the kid with her! Christ, he'd better slip them the Supreme.

But the young punk was moving. He was shrugging and nodding in an understanding way.

'Reg'lar'll be just fine,' the young punk said.

Ukinski moved over to the pump. He lifted the nozzle from its cradle and flipped the lever across. He was coming away with the hose when he saw something that stopped him in his tracks. The two others were making for the door from where the light spilled out, and where Norma and the kid were standing.

'Hey, you guys! Where you think you're going?' he heard himself call out.

'You got coffee in there, maybe?' one of them called out.

'We're closed up,' he said.

The wind whipped cruelly at his thin yellow hair and flicked it stingingly into his eye. He brushed it back.

'Maybe we find something, huh,' the man called back. They were still walking on.

'I told you already. It's too late,' he said and then he said no more. The first of them had brought down something hard upon his head. Across a few seconds of eternity he felt more pain than he had ever known and seemed to hear someone, perhaps himself, scream from a place far away. There was a corridor of black and at the distant end a door of shining light. Two figures were turning in the door to hurry out of sight but in the corridor two other shapes were leaping forward just as rapidly.

The hose had dropped out of his hands and now, slumping down first to his knees, he fell across it. He did not know of this nor of the look of gleeful shock lifting the dark features of the young man whose blow had splintered his skull. His brain had started haemorrhaging and there was nothing else that he would ever know.

The spill of light had not stretched as far as to the pumps, the car. It had been hard to make out just what the hell was going on. But the moment the three men had gotten out of the car the sense of menace, the scent on the hot air of violence hanging in the night had kept her rooted in the doorway. She had no will to move and no desire. Fear of the moment when that violence would find its bloody climax in an act was neutralised within her by the fascination as to how. And by hope. Sweet God, just let them kill him, she was saying to herself, just let them kill him and I'll promise I'll be good. I swear. Please God, please God! Over and then over.

'Momma, what's happening? Why you standing in the door like that?'

She did not hear him. She was hypnotised by her own fears. She feared that, oh God, they just might not kill him. Beat him up bad but not kill him. That thought paralysed her. She did not hear the boy. She had no awareness that he had come to stand by her, yawning, his eyes still heavy with sleep. Her eyes were on the half-seen shadows of her husband and the men. Even when two of them began to walk toward the store she still stared fixedly upon the man she prayed might die. An animal knowledge told her that at any second now on this hot night her prayer might be fulfilled, delivery come with one sharp spurt of blood. She watched. Her son watched too.

The blow fell. For that frozen moment pleasure was at the centre of the horror she knew distantly she ought to feel. Guilt thrilled through her. She did not know it but there was on her face the same look of awed and disbelieving satisfaction as on the face of the twenty-two year old chicano who had struck the blow. She even smiled. In that instant she had the unconscious courage of her malevolence. Then her son had screamed. And as her husband silently sank down, Norma Ukinski screamed too. The spell binding her was shattered and, screaming, she was free to be washed through by total terror. Two men were coming at her and they'd killed her husband and now they must kill her. Turning she blundered back into the store.

In that sudden release of action she crashed against the boy. He was sent sprawling. Silent after his one scream he had been starting forward blindly towards his father. Blindly because his eyes held only bulging horror. As blindly she hit into him and, dressed only in the hand-me-down work-shirt that served for his PJs, he was sent sprawling to the floor. She never felt the impact. Her back a mile wide for their guns, their knives, she floundered through the veil of nightmares toward the distant phone. She knew she'd never make it and then, almost there, remembered how slow that must be. The gun! She swung towards the counter and, Christ! how slow that was! Forever! Oh God! the screen door going, oh God, please God! sweet Christ, just let me—

A fierce, bruising weight was driving hard into her legs. She crashed towards the rising wooden floor. All breath went from her and pain shot through her shoulder, knee and hip. Her nose and mouth were grazed. The back of her skull felt as fragile as an egg.

'Uh-huh, lady,' she heard a close voice say.

Instinctively she tried to squirm around. And was allowed to. A weight was on her belly. Thick hands held her arms. She stared at inch's range into a flat, hard, young and savage face.

She made to scream. The heel of a hand across her mouth snapped her head back to the floor and now all she could see was rafters, and the smell of sweat and dirt replaced the heavy and unnaturally sweet smell she had caught on the man's breath. She thrashed from side to side. Hopeless. But now, as if from habit, the other hand had moved to squeeze her breast. It moved away. She felt her blouse pull tight then rip. The hand slithered the bra cup aside. She felt the warm air on her exposed flesh and then the sharp pain of the nipple being plucked.

And she knew she had a chance. Old memories of her alley days came to her aid. Without too much effort she let herself go limp. She licked at the rough hand. It came away and she could raise her head and even try the look she'd always had.

'Hey, Paco! Take a look at this!' the man called out. 'It ain't so bad at that.'

There were steps. She twisted her head sideways. Another man, or kid, slimmer, sharper than the one astride her, stood looking down. He whistled like she could've bet he would.

'Hey, that's a nice one she's got there,' he said. 'I wonder if she's got the other.'

The hand groped at her other breast.

'Oh sure, it's here okay,' the first one said. She could feel him getting hard.

'She's pretty young at that to go with that old guy.'

'That's right. Hey, are you his woman or maybe his little girl?'

'His kid sister,' she heard her thick voice lie. It seemed the better chance.

'Then how come you got a ring?'

'I was married once. Some no-good.'

'And how's about you, honey – are you good?'

'Hey, listen,' she was saying throatily, 'I know a trick or two, you know. Go easy on me now, I'll show you boys a real good time. I swear—'

The screen door crashed again. They turned their heads and she raised hers. The first one out of the car was standing there. The bare light made his slicked black hair gleam shinily and match the highlights in his purple bowling jacket. The staring face between seemed only dark. Shock had set it rigid. The dark eyes were fixed on visions that the mind could not take in.

'That guy,' he said. 'He croaked.'

'Jesus Christ!'

'Tony!'

It had never occurred to her he hadn't. But a second time she felt the thrill. And fear. The squat one had twisted up and off of her but that was only for the minute.

'We just said "hit him"! That's all we said.'

'I know! I know! That's all we did!'

'You hit him too hard!'

'I know I hit him too fucking hard! That's why he's fucking dead!'

Silence.

'So what we going to do?'

'Do? We're getting out of here! That's what we're fucking going to do!'

The slim one had said that. He rushed now to the bar and to the till. He rang it open. When he saw what there was in it his breath came out in a long hiss.

'Jesus wept!' he said.

But the third one, the one in the bowling jacket, was looking straight at her. He seemed very young to be a killer but maybe not in such a place on such a night as this.

'She's seen us,' he said in a flat voice and she felt the panic rise.

'Listen,' she said. 'I never liked him! I never liked the guy!

He kept me here! He used to keep me here and wouldn't let me go! Listen, I'll trade you. I'll do a deal! Go easy on me and I'll tell you where he keeps his money.'

The slim one's head whipped round.

'Where?' the squat one said.

'Listen, I got a better idea. I could be good for you boys.'

She licked her mouth and half got to her feet and made quite sure her breast was hanging full. The squat one liked all that, she could be sure.

'Take me with you,' she went on. 'I won't tell. I wouldn't tell. Just fix it so's I can git from here and I'll—'

'Mommy!'

It seemed a giant's wail. All four adults turned toward the child that everyone of them had quite forgotten. On the edge of the harsh light he was sprawled sideways on the floor and trembling like a dog. The front tail of the long shirt, part of the boards nearby, were dark with moisture. Pushed up and half-supported on his thin white arm, white face streaked dirty with tears, he stared over at his mother with eyes as wide and ghastly as those of the murderer. It was the squat one, though, who first recovered. He took a forward step.

'Shut up, kid,' he said, 'or I'll kick your teeth in and you know for sure I will.'

Now the mother found her voice.

'He's just a kid,' Norma Ukinski began, 'He don't know from nothin'. We can leave him and—'

'Lady, the money! That money! Where'd he keep it?'

'Quick! for Chrissakes, quick! Or I'll come across—'

'Right there! Right where you are. Down underneath in an old tin marked "Sugar".'

Abruptly the squat one laughed. And then, sending the can lid drumming crazily upon the counter the slim one was feverishly shuffling the money Carl Ukinski would not trust the banks with. Now he began to giggle. His button eyes stayed like a snake's but as he flourished the curled green bills from waving arms his laugh shrilled like a girl's.

'Five, six, maybe seven C's,' he said. 'Come on, let's go!' He was stuffing the can inside his windbreaker.

'Hold it!'

It was the one by the door who'd spoken, the one who'd struck the blow. He turned to face the woman fully, seeing her it seemed for the first time.

'How many people come by here a day?' he said.

'For gas? Ten, maybe. Maybe fifteen.'

'In here?'

Her breast flopped as she shrugged a second time.

'Five maybe, tops. I don't do but coffee and if they ask—'

'Paco, Luis. Go bring him in here.'

'Jesus man, you hit the mother-fucker. You go—'

'I know I did and that's why I don't want to look at him!'

Either he was their leader or his deed had brought him status. They pushed the screen door open and went out. The wind blew louder. The dust swirled and the door shut after them like somebody had fired a shot. The killer seemed not to hear. Aimless suddenly, he took five or six steps into the store.

'Boy,' he said out loud. 'Boy, what a dump.'

And he was right. The centre of the room randomly stacked with smaller hardware items on cheap racks and faded cards seemed more a stock-room than an effort at display. Cheap skirts and pants for God-alone-knew-who sprawled from the boxes. Only some storage bins behind the counter and the bar itself held any residue of quality. Dark wood, mahogany perhaps, with lighter golden strips, they had been craftsmen-made an age ago, before the war of '42 for sure.

'Used not to be like this,' the woman said as aimlessly. 'Mine used to be up a ways.' She stiffened. Through the moan of the wind there was the tread of boots. A scraping at the door. The killer looked away but, spellbound again, she as deliberately could only watch. There was a muttering. The door was grabbed open a little way, caught on the return swing by a boot low down. The boot hooked the door back wide again and then the squat one's shoulder worked inside and jerked and then, as he came in, the body kept the door ajar.

They brought it in head first, face down. That way, the lank, sparse hair hanging down, it was easy to see that the blow, striking home, had gashed open the surface of the skull it cracked. Blood oozed in the light and, just once, dropped down on to the boards.

'Dad! Daddy!'

This time they did not hear, pretended not to hear, the boy. But as he scrambled to his feet, still shaking, now sobbing out loud, the squat one halted and turned his face to him. Even so, the boy stepped forward a short pace.

'You want you should end up like this?' the squat one said.

'I don't care! I don't care!' the boy screamed. He started in to run toward the corpse. The one in the purple bowling jacket whipped round. A full force backhand blow caught the boy across the face. Its impact drove him spinning back and off his feet into the wall. Blood spurting from his nose, he collapsed, whimpering.

'Where you want this?'

The one in the bowling jacket motioned to the counter.

'Behind there.'

The two men swung and heaved. The slim one was late letting go. The body never looked like it would clear the counter. It went twisting slantwise through the air and crashed face up, slack-jawed among the levers of what once had been the soda fountain. The counter seemed to shake and dust rose up. There was a trickling sound.

'Dad! Dad!'

'Well go ahead! Finish it! Get him down behind!'

The slim one vaulted up on to the bar. Savagely, and many times, his boot thudded at the corpse. It slid, it moved. Finally, with one last crash, its staring eyes were lost to view.

The boy had seen his father a last time.

Only the slim one could see the body now. Still on the counter he looked down in back of it. Once more he started laughing. Once more his voice slid up into a high-pitched giggle. His pointed cowboy boots pushed at the fountain's levers as if they were the keys to some strange musical machine.

'Hey, man,' he said, 'you wanna—'

'Come on,' the one who'd killed cut in abruptly. 'Let's git. Get the woman, Luis.'

'Hey, Tony! You know what you're doing?'

'No I don't know what the fuck I'm doing! All I know's we're getting out of here right now and taking her and stealing us another short!'

'Okay, Tony.'

'And Paco. Grab the kid.'

The squat short one moved in on the boy who cowered but did not struggle. He stooped and with one arm between his legs hoisted him across his shoulders.

'He's pissed himself,' he growled.

'Let's go.'

The slim one dragged the woman by the arm. The wire of the the screen door scraped at her and then she was out with them in the wind, covering her breast as best she might with her free hand.

The store was silent once again. Almost silent. Occasionally still, the sound of something dripping splatted through the rising and the falling of the wind outside. It came from behind the bar. It was a long, long time since anyone had bought an ice-cream sundae there. But no-one, Norma Ukinski least of all, had thought to clean the syrups out of the dispensers. Across the chest and the face of Carl Ukinski, lime and blueberry and strawberry syrup were splotched into a rainbow. Close to the head, raspberry would be almost indistinguishable from the spreading blood congealing with it on the bare boards. All awaited the morning that would bring in the heat and the flies.

When the boy had been standing with his mother in the doorway looking out toward the pumps he had not been certain if he was awake or still asleep. At first he thought he was awake and had gotten up from his mattress even though he hadn't wanted to go to the bathroom like most times he got up at night. Then he had not been so sure. He had not had any pants on like it often was in real bad dreams and even though he knew that this was really bad and something terrible was maybe going to happen he'd all along thought pretty soon he would wake up. A part of him kept thinking that he should run out and help his father or maybe shout or something but he didn't run out or shout because in dreams your legs would not move forward when you ran and no-one heard you scream inside the dream. They only heard you scream outside the dream and then his father came to him and talked the dream away. Only this time for the first time his dad was in the dream so maybe it was real. When the other man came up behind his dad with the dark thing in his hand he knew that it was no dream and was more scared than he had ever been. He knew he ought to yell, run warn his dad. But though he knew it was no dream he still could not believe it was all really real. It was not happening. Then the man knocked down his dad and then he knew it was all happening and suddenly all he could do was scream. And part of his scream he knew was screaming because he had not screamed before. He hadn't helped his dad. Too late he'd started out to but she had knocked him to the floor and then the men had burst into the store.

One of them had had a knife and cut the phone wire just like on TV. The other one had thrown his mommy down and sat on her until she went real still. For a moment he thought she must be dead but there then was a ripping sound and the man was touching what mommy called her peaches when she was joshing him the way he didn't like. He knew that that was dirty and he ought to do something. But he was more scared now than he had ever been and shaking so he couldn't stop. And all ashamed. Although he hadn't wanted to go to the bathroom he'd peed himself. It all came out before he knew. It didn't seem like he could do something while he was all ashamed. If he stopped shaking and stayed very quiet they might forget all about him and not notice the damp stain on his shirt. Only he couldn't stop and then his mom had said she didn't like his dad and talked of leaving him and he'd been scareder still and screamed out loud and hoped his dad would come.

For a moment, when they'd bought his dad inside, he thought that he was still alive. His arms and chest had swayed from how they carried him. Then he'd seen the blood stuck on his head and known his dad was dead. He'd felt all sick like when they ran over the yellow dog and he had tried to run and say how sorry he was he hadn't shouted out and it was all his fault before his dad was gone away completely. But the man who'd hit his dad had hit him too and the pain to his face was so terrible and so awful bad he thought that he was going to die and join his dad inside that white and spinning light. And he'd been still more scared because although he loved his dad he didn't want to die. But the blood from his nose had dripped on the floor and he had seen it and known he was still in the store and when he swallowed it was all salty from the thick blood in his throat and he wondered if that meant that now he'd choke and he had gone all dizzy.

Then the short man had picked him up. His thick arm had gone right up between his legs and hurt him, but he'd been too frightened to cry out and, besides, the man had told them all he'd wet himself. He'd started to feel bad at being out the house with just his nightshirt on but they had thrown him in the car and it had started off.

He'd been in the back seat with the thin man, the one who had the knife. His mommy was up front between the other two. The car bumped and bounced a lot and made a lot of noise and he thought maybe that they would push him out and he would die that way. Except if that was what they'd do why was his mommy in the middle and not next to the door like himself? Maybe they'd just do him. His mommy had said to leave him behind. When he tried to take a look outside the thin one pushed him down. He lay curled up and still from then, so scared he thought he might be sick. His heart was hammering and he could still taste blood. The car was going real fast now and bumping even more. If they threw him out he'd die and if they stopped to do it, his dad had warned him plenty of times how dangerous it was wandering off into the desert by himself.

It was not quiet inside the car. The motor made that noise and the three men were shouting at each other. They were fighting about which way they ought to go. Fighting like his dad and mom would fight. He couldn't understand too much. One wanted to go down to Mexico but the one who'd hit his dad said everyone would look to find them there and he was driving. He said something about some other place but the fat one said that was crazy too. They were all smoking. Even his mom. The air inside the car got sweet and thick and soon he felt real tired. He tried to stay awake in case they threw him out but they were going pretty smoothly now and it was harder all the time to keep his eyes from closing and, funny, for the first time since the men had come he didn't feel afraid no more about what they could do.

He woke up again when the car stopped. For a moment he didn't know where he was except he knew he wasn't on his mattress. Then in a great icy rush he did remember and his heart began to beat like it would burst and he wanted to scream out. But luckily he didn't quite and hadn't moved and so he stayed as still as he could manage and hoped his dad would come. Then he remembered too his dad would never come. That made him moan out loud but as he did his mother spoke.

'Alright,' she said, 'if we're going to do it, let's.'

She got out of the car with one of the men up front. That made him just as scared as he had ever been before he'd fallen asleep. His mother had left him like she'd said and the men still in the car would not want him around. When the car started again he felt sick to his stomach and felt so bad because he wanted to go to the bathroom once again but didn't dare to ask. But the car stopped almost at once. Doors slammed. Rough hands grabbed him and dragged him across the seat so he hit his shoulder hard upon the door. His bare feet dragged across some stones. Then he was lifted high and carried out of the warm night into a room. He was thrown down so hard it hurt into a wicker chair.

He'd never been in one but knew what kind of a room it was from watching TV. It was a motel room. What he didn't know was that it was just as scuzzy and as cheap a no-questions-asked-folks place as could be found in the backside of Orange County.

All he knew was that it smelt of dust and that the light in the one bulb was orange and all dim.

There was one bed inside the room no bigger than his mattress except that it was raised up a ways from off the floor. His nose ached and the cane in the chair bit into his bare skin.

He watched his mother carefully in case she'd tell him what to do. But she didn't look at him. She looked real scared. She had a hand up to her throat holding her torn clothes and she was looking at the bed and at the men, then at the bed again. Suddenly she made a funny noise and ran toward the door. But the short man got in her way and hit her and grabbed her as she twisted round. He put his hand over her mouth and the front of her blouse came down again.

The thin one got out his knife. He held it just in front of her wide eyes and they got wider still. Then with the point he flipped the cherry on her peach.

'Mommy!'

It was hard moving up and out of the chair. The quiet one in the bowling jacket grabbed him right away. The one with the switchblade turned around real fast. Like a snake his other arm shot out. The hand caught his willy hard and squeezed so hard he wriggled but that made it worse.

The man held the knife up close where he could see it. His face was burning because he felt ashamed but when the man lowered the knife and he could not see what he was going to do with it, it seemed the blood all rushed into his knees. He tried to struggle but the other held him tight. The thin man tugged his willy.

'Listen, kid,' he said. 'Another peep out of you your pecker gets cut off. You hear?'

He tried to nod.

'Put him in the can.'

The quiet one shoved him in the bathroom. He looked at him. He had funny eyes. The most horrible eyes of all.

'You stay here. You stay put. You stay quiet,' the man said.

He was pushed roughly back against the wall. The door closed. In the dark he sat down on the toilet to cry as quietly as he could. For the first time that he could remember he was feeling cold.

It was cold in the bathroom as well as dark and pretty soon he started shivering. Keeping quiet was not such a problem, though. There was a lot of noise outside. He could not understand the words but the men were arguing again. When they had finished he had stopped his crying. It went real quiet, then he heard laughing and some quiet whistles and the springs go as somebody got into the bed. It was quiet again and then the springs kept going like somebody was jumping hard and somebody was panting and somebody was laughing and kept calling out. He thought he heard his mother half call out but it was hard to tell.

There was more quiet, then angry voices once again. Maybe somebody hit somebody else. He heard the bed start boinging once again. Maybe if he was quiet . . .

As quiet as could be he crawled across the cold tiles of the floor and reached the door. He reached on up and found the knob. As slowly as he could he opened the door until there was a crack and he could just look out. He didn't understand all that he saw at first but after a while he did.

The quiet one with the scary eyes was sitting on the chair. He had no pants or boots on. Just a shirt. His legs were brown except for down the side of one where it was white and shiny from a scar like some long centipede. He couldn't see the thin man anywhere but when he opened up the door a little more he saw the short man sure enough.

He had no clothes on at all. He was on the bed and his bare ass was stuck up in the air. He was on the bed but on top of his mother. She was all doubled up. She had her white legs wrapped round his thick brown back. She was panting and groaning as the man moved up and down.

For a moment he thought the man was trying to hurt his mother in some special way but then he knew what he was really doing. This was the dirtiest thing of all. Charley Twomoons had told him all about it once when they'd been hunting lizards. It was called fucking. It was what men did to women with their willies and it was just about the dirtiest thing that you could ever do. A strange feeling he liked ran through him. His stomach seemed to go all warm and soft and for a moment he felt giddy. In a way the man was hurting his mother because it was his way of making her all dirty. He was holding down her arms. There were shining streaks of sweat running down his sides.

The boy saw something else. By the bed there was a table of yellow wood. A square bottle with water in it stood on top next to a cut up lemon. By the lemon was the thin man's knife. If he ran fast enough he could pick up the knife and stick it in the short man's back before he could get up. The boy grew tense. All he need do was run real fast and then he'd stab the man. Only — each time he'd tried to help before they'd grabbed him just as soon as he'd moved. There were the other two. They'd get him. They'd cut his willy off. He was too small to help and, anyways, his mother was the one always getting sore. She'd not tried to help him. She said to leave him behind. She was always saying there were things she could've done if she'd not been dragged right down by him. You were supposed to love your mommy just like baby Jesus but maybe he didn't like Norma too much. There was something kind of funny about what they were doing to her that sent this pins and needles feeling up and down his back.

His mother gasped much louder now. Like her legs, her arms were now around the short man's back. Her hands began to beat and scratch and claw.

'Yes! Oh, yes! Oh, yes!' his mother panted out. Her head turned fast from side to side like it was being hit. The man was stretched all straight like he was doing press-ups. He was panting too, grunting like it hurt.

'Yes! Oh yes!' his mother screamed out loud. 'Oh, lover! Oh yes!'

He remembered that. He hadn't understood it then but one time when his dad had hurt his foot and gone to San Diego he'd heard it in the night when Uncle Al had come to stay. This was just the same. Suddenly, with utter clarity, just how he'd never know, the boy knew that his mother liked all this. She'd enjoyed what was being done to her.

They'd stopped, grown quiet. He was sprawled across her now. Face down. His dad had been face down as well but his chest had not been pumping up and down like the short man's. It had just swayed from the way they carried him.

His mother moaned. The thin man stepped suddenly into view. He had nothing on either. There was thick hair all around his willy and that was thick as well. If the man looked up he'd see the opening in the door. But he flicked the short man on the bed.

'Hey, amigo,' the boy heard, 'let's move it, huh!'

As slowly as he'd opened it, he closed the door. He let go of the knob. There was more noise from the bed. He crawled across the floor towards a corner and remembered he was cold. He started shivering again. He pushed against the walls and hugged himself. It wasn't fair. They were all grown-ups. There was nothing he could do. All he could do was wait and hope that all of this would stop and go away.

He'd been asleep again. When he woke up there was a grey light in the bathroom and he could see. This time he knew at once just where he was. There was a brown-black cockroach inching along the bend where the side of the bathtub curved into the floor. He watched it for a while and realised that he was still alive.

He felt like ice. He tried to move a little and found he was so stiff and sore it hurt. His nose was sore. He touched it and it smarted and felt twice as big. His top lip was swollen too. And now he truly wanted to go to the toilet real, real bad but was afraid to because of the noise that would make. He could hear no sound.

His heart stopped. His mother had left him! Or they'd killed her! He was all alone! They'd gone away and left him all alone! Or they were all there still outside just all asleep. He couldn't tell. He couldn't hear no noise but that was nothing much. He'd have to go and look. If they were all asleep maybe he could sneak outside and find some help.

A second time, hurting his knees, he crawled towards the door. He opened it a hair's breadth wide and saw no sign of anyone. Wider. No one. Wider. Someone, his mother, was huddled in the bed. But no-one else. The three men had all gone. Only . . . his mother didn't move. Yes, he was right! They'd killed her too.

Holding his breath he watched to see if he could see the side of her face move. He thought maybe it did, but he'd been wrong about his dad. He got up on his feet but did not dare to move.

'Mommy,' he said. 'Mommy?'

An eye opened and looked straight at him. It blinked.

'Oh,' his mother said. 'Oh.'

She lifted herself up and shook her mussed up hair. It was a kind of red colour mostly.

'Oh,' she said again. Then she remembered to be nice. She half-raised the bedclothes. She smiled.

'Hey, Junior,' she said, 'come here.'

He ran across the room with joy. He was so happy that halfway across he started crying yet again. But differently. He squirmed into the bed and held his mother tight. She jumped and moved away.

'Jesus!' she said. 'You're like an ice-box.'

It was true. He could feel how cold he was by how wonderfully warm the bed was feeling. And his mommy still had nothing on. He tried real hard not to touch her anywhere until he had warmed but it was difficult because it was a narrow bed and sloped toward the middle. He hung on to the side. After a while he moved against his mommy and this time she didn't mind. He put an arm around her.

'Wish I had a lousy cigarette,' she said.

At home she always smoked when she got up. Now that he had feeling in his leg again there was a sticky feeling lower down the bed.

'Mommy, are you alright?'

'I guess.'

'They didn't hurt you, Mommy?'

'Those punks! Cheap stinking punks!'

'They did hurt you?'

'No. I'm okay. Hush now. We'll get up in a while.'

Pretending to turn over he twisted high and lifted up the bedclothes. His mind froze at the uncomprehended horror of what he saw. His stomach lurched into his mouth and with no effort he was sick.

'Jesus fucking Christ! What the hell you think—'

'Mommy, mommy, they did too! There's blood down in the sheets. You're bleeding!'

'What? Oh . . . oh, that's nothing, Junior. That's something you'll understand about one day when you get older. They didn't hurt me none.'

She didn't seem to mind his being sick. She turned and hugged him tight as tight could be. She didn't seem to mind the blood either.

'Listen, Junior,' she said. 'This is going to be our little secret. We won't tell anyone about what's happened, huh?'

'Not anything? But mommy, daddy's dead.'

'Oh, yes. We'll get up real soon and go tell the police about what those sons of bitches did to him. But afterwards, when they brought us here, we won't tell the police about how long they stayed. We'll just say they brought us here and left us and left right away.'

'But mommy—'

'Now you say that, you hear? You hear? You promise? Junior, you're going to promise me that you'll say what your mommy tells you now, now that's right now, isn't it?'

He began to cry again.

'Daddy's dead,' he said. 'They killed Daddy.'

Frighteningly, she began to cry too. She held him even tighter, rocked him. Her skin smelt sweaty.

'Those punks of kids,' his mother cried. 'Greaseball bastards. I won a beauty contest once. People said how beautiful I was.

Not just pretty – beautiful! People said I had a big career ahead of me.'

She cried some more.

'I could've been in movies,' she said.

That morning the air was still and clear. The wind had whipped the smog to shreds before, at last, it had blown itself right out far over the Pacific. Yessir, it looked like it would be a nice one. That's what they were saying on the breakfast newscasts where the minor havoc that the wind had wrought provided the lead story right across the Southland. Hundreds of thousands of plain folks could set out to have a real nice day, now, heart-warmed by the added glow of hearing how that tree went right on through the roof, this car was blown clear off the 101. The few unfortunate other fellas set untold numbers of their neighbours up real well.

One story that didn't make the news for all its potential for good cheer. Not on radio or TV. Not in the papers. Nobody was in a hurry to report on how two patrolmen acting on instructions had driven out someplace into the desert and found a stiff, some veteran. There were other stiffs that morning a lot closer to home. Let them have the PR.

The two patrolmen knew. The ambulance team knew. Some of the force in the mean redbrick precinct house in a mean grey suburb on the heel of East LA already knew. A woman had come in dragging a kid even more beat up than she. She blatted out some story about some chicano punks and how they'd knocked off her old man. It was the last thing that you needed on the night shift half hour before your relief.

Now some hours later two men in suits sat in the second least unlovely office in the precinct looking bored. One who was short and dark and good looking sat behind a desk. The other who was lanky sat in a chair leant back against the wall. He was grey in a way that seemed tired, and ugly in a way that seemed cruel. The one sat at the desk had a typed report in front of him. He sighed into the stale air.

'Where'd you say now?' he said.

The other jerked his head toward the barred and painted-over window.

'Out there somewhere,' he said. 'Holed up in East LA. With their kind, you know.'

The dark man smiled a little. It was a pleasant smile.

'I know,' he said softly. 'If she's telling the truth.'

'You think she is, Osuna?'

'Pretty much — Gregg. Not all. A lot went on in that motel. We got the sheets.'

'We ain't got any charges but homicide and attempted kidnapping.'

'They'll do.'

'We should've had the doctor take a look up her.'

'Maybe. I don't know what the hell she thinks she's got to preserve but she's sure goddamned set on preserving it.'

The detective named Gregg leaned further back in his chair.

'You believe her when she says she wouldn't recognise them punks?' he asked.

Osuna smiled the gentle smile again.

'No.' he said. 'But you know how some folks think that we all look alike.'

'That's right,' Gregg answered quickly with an equal malice. 'Know what? When I talked to her, first thing she asked was were there public funds for looking after widows made this way.'

'Figures,' Osuna said. He glanced down at the papers and sighed again.

'Okay,' he said, 'we'll wrap it up for now, I guess. We'll just talk to the boy.'

He flipped a switch. After a few moments silence in the stale impersonal office, shapes moved behind the frosted glass door and it was opened. A uniformed policeman showed in a white-faced boy, with eyes like lead. He was wearing a police shirt and trousers turned up inches at the cuffs. His feet were bare.

'Jesus!' Osuna said, 'that nose! Hey, you feeling alright, son?'

He felt tireder than he'd ever felt but that was alright because it made his aches seem far away. He nodded.

'You want to sit down? Here, son.'

The man behind the desk got up. He came around to give him a chair. When he'd come through the door his heart had missed a beat because he'd thought it was the short man who'd carried him and been on top of his mother.

'Here, son. Sit down.'

He shook his head. It was better, maybe, to stand.

'You have something to eat?'

He nodded. He'd had donuts and milk and later bacon and hash-browns. The man was back behind his desk. He looked down.

'Okay, then, Paul,' he said. 'We'd just like to ask you a question or two. Mainly what we'd like is have you tell us how it was after those two men took you and your momma into the motel.'

He just looked straight ahead at one of the tall green closet things. He'd already been asked this by one of the policemen in a uniform, but he'd kept his holy promise and not said anything. These were policemen too, he knew, even though they had no uniforms. They were detectives like in M Squad on TV.

'Just think a while, then tell it like it was. Take as long as you like and then just tell us in your own words. Whatever comes to mind.'

He just stared straight ahead. He had no underpants and the trousers that they'd given him were itchy up and down his legs.

'Okay then, Paul, here's one I think you know. What is the name of our new President?'

The name was Kennedy, he knew, but he just kept looking straight ahead. The best thing was not to talk at all. The man asking questions got up from behind the desk and moved to where he had to look at him. He smiled.

'How old are you, then, Paul?' he said. 'Why I'd just bet that you were — let's see now – why, seven I would bet.'

It was a nice friendly smile and Paul thought that he might like the man but he seemed very far away and Paul could tell from how he asked the question he already knew that he was eight. He looked back at the man but didn't say anything. The man slowly shook his head.

There was a scraping sound, and very fast, the other man was reaching out at him. A huge strong hand had grabbed him by the shoulder and shook him so the room went up and down. The fingers dug into him like iron and the new pain was very near and not at all a long, long way away.

'Hey, Gregg!' the other man said.

The big cruel man paid no attention. He put his face down right in front of his own. He had thick lips and long yellow teeth and his breath smelt real bad.

'Listen, kid,' he said. 'You're in big trouble if you don't talk.'

But he had promised that he wouldn't talk. There was all blood in the bed.

'What happened in there, huh?'

The man shook him, hurt him more. He'd better say something to be polite.

'Don't know.'

'Gregg! Knock if off!'

'Your mother's all bruised up! You know that don't you? They beat up on her, right?'

'Don't know.'

'They got her in the bed and did things to her, right? Funny-business things!'

'Don't know!'

The other, nicer man did something very fast he couldn't see. The big man's hand let go and the big man went sort of falling back on to his chair. He started to get up real fast but then sat down again. He rubbed his side. The smaller, nicer man was standing close to him.

'You shit-heel,' the big man said. 'I won't forget today, Osuna. A cheap greaseball protecting his own.'

'About your speed, third-degreeing kids.' Osuna said.

The funny thing was he still had on the smile. He turned right round to Paul.

'Sorry about that, Paul,' he said. 'Tell you what. We won't ask you any more questions.'

He put an arm round Paul and gently walked him over to the door. That was funny too. He looked just like the men who'd come last night but didn't act like them at all.

'What we'll do,' he said, 'we'll do a deal. You don't want to talk, okay. I'll pretend you can't remember.'

Remember. He could remember every moment from the time they hit his dad. He could see their faces just like they were there. He would see them always, alone, in darkness.

'You go back on down and try to get some sleep, now,' the nice man was saying. 'I just want to talk to your momma one more time and then we'll have a real fast police car take you to your aunt. Maybe the officer will let you sound the siren.'

He tried to smile but with his swollen lip it hurt. He just nodded instead. The man opened the door.

'Lou,' he called out.

One of them in uniform came over to get him.

Osuna shut the door again and went back slowly to his desk. Gregg glowered at him. Bested, he would not let it alone.

'I still say what that snot-nose needs is the flat of someone's hand on his bare ass,' he said.

Osuna sat down.

'Wrong again, Gregg,' he said.

He looked down at the papers in front of him and picking up the report slipped it into a manilla folder.

'Two things needed,' he went on. 'I need a new partner.'

He paused, smiled at Gregg sweetly and then stopped smiling.

'The kid – poor little bastard — needs a shrink.'

chapter one

... actor seems sadly out of touch with role and director, misfiring on six of his eight basic looks. It is left to new find Paul Madison to make the one strong impact in the brief but potent role of the bull-fighter whose infatuation for Lady Cliff is the plot's flash-point. Madison seizes his chance with style and spells it out that he's a comer. His brooding, dark good looks suggest brain as well as bed. He comes on with more polish than anyone this reviewer can recall since the late Monty Clift stole *Red River* out from under big Duke Wayne. The other plus is the smart lensing by Powell. Using a low-key ...

Variety

At first glance only the almost sub-audible whisper of the air-conditioning broke the room's cover. On first hearing, rather. Tom Leonard smiled as he corrected himself. It took a while – a half-hour maybe – to sniff the cool and filtered air and understand that the room was about as authentic as a sound-stage set. Impeccable, of course, but phoney as they come. A set was infinitely more honest.

The carpet was authentic English Wilton. The table let it be known it was Sheraton. The chairs, imported via the same London agent, were reproduction of rare finesse. The chaste, sole picture on the wall – a charcoal by Lautrec – tipped the balance towards the genuine. Jesus, thought Tom, only the eau de nil paint on the walls, discreet naturally, is good old domestic USA.

Oh, and the books of course. They were the real giveaway. They might be housed in a genuine English secretary-cabinet – made in London on the Salem pattern – but the two-hundred-years-dead craftsman must be revolving in his grave. *The Encyclopaedia Britannica*, *The Great Books*, morocco-bound and gold-tooled copies of the works of Dickens, Thackeray, Hal Wallis, Jerry Wald. Presentation scripts that ranged in time from Dore Schary on through Frankovich and on to Di Laurentis. For a moment Tom had a flash-back to his Rhodes scholar days. He caught a vision, clear with total recall, of his Oxford tutor's room. Draughty, high-ceilinged, the door finger-marked by those who'd sweated in and out. The floor a heaving sea of books despite the shelving three-sides round the room. He remembered the huge frayed chairs which only needed metal straps to make them look as lethal as they felt.

He sighed. He was well used to the room and waiting in it. It was the memory that, obscurely, depressed him. Not so obscurely. To banish it he gave himself something to do. He got up from the table and letting down the slant-front of the secretary, fixed himself a Campbell's. He'd postpone his real drinking until a little bit later when he would be seeing Manny at The Two Other Maggots a short block away. As he raised his glass, he caught sight of a movement in the glazed panels of the secretary's upper half. Automatically he converted the upward movement into an ambiguous toasting to himself.

Well he wore pretty well. The face, with thirty-eight years behind it, was still a youngster's. The contacts helped, no question, but there was still a symmetrical neatness about his features that called to mind an early Tony Randall. Too much to tell the truth. That Ivy League fresh-facedness took some working at sometimes. When it got rugged there were times he had to come on really strong to show he was no kid, no dude, and screw it, that was him. He had never felt the need to go the love-bead route taken mostly by clapped out producers shit-scared of the young Turks who had come from TV or the top agencies, to take over the studios. He had watched them at the discos, their chains and mystic signs bouncing on the dyed hair of their chests, wondering what would hit them first: a coronary, or reality. So he'd stayed Brooks Brothers Yale, which he knew pleased Lyndon.

He tilted the glass and drank. As he did so Lyndon Oates came in through the door behind him.

'Sorry, Tommy. Jesus that fucking Constantine,' he said. 'He thinks because he's married to my ex somehow I'm obligated to push that fucking bitch. That's how a faggot thinks.'

'He keep you long?'

'Forever. Finally I just got up and left. I told him. We do PR for the present. We do PR for the future. For the future 'special-ly. But history we leave to the opposition.'

'How old is Frances now?'

'Jesus, how should I know? Twenty-nine going on thirty-three. Seen *Variety*?'

Tom moved to the table, kept his voice casual.

'Sure.'

'Yeah, sure. Sorry. When's our boy due in?'

Tom looked at the hands of his old-style watch.

'Forty, forty-five minutes,' he said. 'If he's on time.'

'He will be, believe me. And good enough. Hold your fire a second. I need a drink.'

Oates moved to the converted secretary and reached for the platinum jigger. A spruce, fierce little man. His head was elegantly bald, its tan joining with the smooth side-hair, the trim dab of a military moustache to suggest distinction. The thrusting nose gave purpose to the face, direction. It had directed Oates from Omaha, Tom knew, and law grades best forgotten, to a one-third partnership in, and effective control of, clearly the most powerful PR agency in Hollywood. The suits from Saville Row, the ties, the shirts, the shoes from Jermyn Street were more than just an English-loving front. The Anglophilia denoted a mid-West boy's enthralment with a lifestyle he could never confront without feeling inferior. Enthralment – and way deep down, hatred. Oates filched his style from his spiritual opposites. He did it extremely well and it took you a long time to penetrate down through the incisive shrewdness to that hatred, but in the end you knew the man for reproduction too, Tom smiled inwardly. The wives and mistresses and five-hundred-dollar hookers could testify to that too.

It had taken Tom some years to sink his awareness down that far. By that time he was well-established within Oates, Becker and Rimmer as number two to Lyndon Oates whom, along with himself, he increasingly disliked.

Oates had been doing frothy things with a battery-powered blender. He swung round now holding a whisky sour. He sipped it, set it down.

'Okay,' he said. 'From the top.'

Tom sat down at the table, took his notes.

'You're not going to like it.' he said.

Oates ceased the pacing he had begun, swung round a second time.

'Tommy,' he said, 'how many times? Just fire me all the facts, I'll tell the lies.'

And you will, you will, Tom thought.

'Okay,' he said. He smiled and made sure before proceeding, that Oates smiled back. They both had to be on key.

'Our boy's a local, a pretty much home-grown product. Born the back of nowhere, around San Diego back in '54. Wrong side of the tracks. Wrong side of everything. Father died when he was still a kid. The mother upped and ran off with the next thing in pants and parked the kid on a sister out in Annaheim.'

Oates had been pacing, turning, evenly.

'Alive?' he asked.

'The sister, no. The mother, I don't know yet. She ditched her meal-ticket real fast and from then on her trail gets cold. But probably she is. She was only around eighteen when she had him.'

'We gotta know.'

'We will. I got Bergman working on it.'

'Okay. Go on.'

'Education – Thomas Jefferson High. Quiet boy for a while, apparently, then blossomed. Stand-out letterman by eighth grade Track, basketball, football. You name it.'

'Girls go crazy about the way he walks?'

'I imagine. And no problems there. Stanley swears the boy is straight. He knows better than to bum steer us on that. If you get what I mean.'

Oates nodded.

'And?' he said.

'Er – the kid then parlayed himself into some kind of jock-strap scholarship at a Community College, er, Occidental. After a year he was picked up by USC for their football squad.'

'When'd he start fooling with theatre?'

'Right about now. My guess would be he found out he wasn't quite tall or fast enough and started thinking way past All-American. He must have realised by now that if his looks could get him chicks they might just get him parts so he started majoring in the Theatre Arts.'

'I hope he didn't waste time in that Cinema Department they got down there.'

'Don't knock it. It threw up George Lucas.'

'And don't I know it! What I mean – those kids come out of there, they try to tell you how it ought to go. You know. A little knowledge is a dangerous thing.'

Learning, Tom thought.

'Anyway,' said Oates, 'let's hold it there. See what we can do.'

He moved back to the secretary and sipped at the whisky sour.

'Hmm,' he said, 'I don't think we'll screw with any of that bringing him in from the Virgin Islands shit or making him a runaway from the cultured East . . . I got it. I got the start of it. A local boy, right? Okay, we'll home in on that. Anaheim. Perfect. We'll give him a summer job in Disneyland, popcorn stand, let's say, and he's got this line of patter he's worked up and one day old man Disney himself walks by, hears him at it and is so impressed he comes on over, congratulates him and tells him one day he's gonna make it big. That was his inspiration and then on—'

'I'm not sure the dates check out, Lyndon.'

'So who does Arithmetic? Well maybe not.' Anyway, we can still—' Oates was pacing again.

'And kind of corny, Lyndon.'

Oates shot him that fully frontal smile of confidence that is the press agent's best badge when faced with triumph or celebrity, disaster or uncertainty.

'Probably right,' he said. 'Yes, we'll low-profile it. We'll make it seem a natural, *local*, evolution. He was raised in LA so he just naturally supported his local industry. Graduated if you like. If it had been Detroit, it'd've been cars. But he knew he had a talent. Had ambition. All along he used football to buy his training. He could've played pro ball but movies always had the edge when it came down to it.'

'The Bob Wagner touch.'

'Right. We'll say he did his own stuff with the bull in *The Shadow and the Sun*. Did he, by any miracle?'

'With that budget and schedule? Come on! When did that faggot of a producer ever risk an interest?'

How easily I do it, Tom thought.

'Right. Except in bed. But who's to say he didn't? And oh, we'll make him an orphan. He *had* to play his way through college, see?'

'Hold on,' Leonard said. 'He may not want to be an orphan and his mother may not want to be a corpse.'

Oates laughed. 'If making the prick a superstar means he's an orphan, Tom, we can take care of the fine print later.'

'And the mother?'

'Your department. What about his credits?'

'A summer up near Denver. Then nothing for quite a long while. He'd got himself some agent at this time that nobody has ever heard of. Quirk. Ralph Quirk.'

'I don't believe it! That schmuck! Never mind. It's better,

actually. We don't need any ten-cent kibbitzers getting into the act. So now?'

'Back in LA. A one-line part in the new *Star Trek*.'

'Might be useful.'

'And then his break. He copped the lead in that VW commercial. You know, the one where there's this young apprentice and he has to go through all the—'

'Oh, *that's* the guy! Hey, Jesus, Tom, I hope to Christ that we can sit on that.'

'I think we can. We've sat on tougher things. Look, I've got these stills here. You want to take a look before he comes.'

Oates was not that interested.

'When he hits big that's maybe something else again.' he said. 'Maybe.'

'That's where Stanley spotted him – with that East-side intuition he flies by—'

'He says!'

'—and reached out for the phone. He sprung him from this other clown and it's the key role in *The Shadow and the Sun* and tomorrow the world.'

'That fucking Stanley. I hate him but I love him. Okay, let's see those stills.'

Tom slid them across the warm expanse of Sheraton. Oates shuffled through them in no time at all.

'Yes,' he said. 'He's got it. DeNiro quality. We've gone past Redford now and all that wholesomeness. Your girl-next-door wants someone who'll go on a while after she says 'Stop, you're hurting me!' He looked at Leonard who had heard it all before. 'End of seminar,' he said uncomfortably. He finished his drink.

'Listen,' he said. 'We got a basis here. What say we bring Ginny in and have her take down what we've kicked around?'

'Fine—'

'Oh,' Oates gestured with the sheaf of stills. 'This Madison – not his real name?'

'Nope. His real name is Ukinski.'

'Wouldn't you know it? Well, looks like that Quirk did him one favour, anyhow.'

There was no desk in the personal office of Lyndon Oates at Oates, Becker and Rimmer. The atmosphere was of the age of Walpole, Chatham and at a stretch Benedict Arnold wearing thin, and Oates was clinging to what was left. Tom Leonard liked the Sheraton table. It was the only touch of class, of reality, in the place. It pointed up the massive snow-job they were about to lay on their new client.

The outer office was not required to ape the postures of Oates' executive suite. Big as a badminton court, screamingly lavish even by that part of Wilshire Boulevard's realty values, the decor was Tijuana Mexican, chain-store Californian. Matt-black wrought iron, ox-blooded leather chrome and frosted glass proclaimed that you could not accuse the company of having taste, good or bad. There were three desks for three flesh and blood secretaries, two of whom were conspicuously absent.

Susi had been seconded to Palm Springs where for two weeks, Monday through Sunday, she had been the ageing Seamus Rimmer's handy Girl Friday. It was a perfect arrangement. What the perspiring and over-scented Mr Rimmer could not manage to do for himself of nights, Susi, in a fair imitation of a geisha turned hooker, did expertly for him. Then rinsing her mouth she would make the phone calls in which she reiterated her promise to Mrs Rimmer that he wouldn't overdo things and that his heart pills would always be in his pocket. Ginny who looked Latin in her lushness but came in fact from Worcester, England, was in taking dictation from Mr Oates. Her genuinely phenomenal typing and shorthand speeds were almost as valuable to her as the mileage she extracted from cutely correcting the inevitable American mispronunciation of her place of birth. 'Wooster' she would purr through accentuated lips. Celine had heard she was into sado-masochism with a freaky group in downtown Los Angeles, and bore, somewhere, the bruises to prove it. Celine was obliged to know such things at Oates, Becker and Rimmer.

Celine was the sole possessor of the inch-thick, shag-piled field that moment in the afternoon. She was a classic fine-boned beauty of a type that once would have seen off Gene Tierney, but now made do with imitating Faye Dunaway. Tall, thin, elegant, legs up to her armpits. Eyes grey rather than blue, hair driftwood silver rather than blonde. Her breasts were just feminine enough to support her policy of no bra and most often, cashmere suits. Entering a restaurant, a bar, or hotel lobby she knew, just like royalty, that all heads turned. She also knew, unlike royalty, that 'Jeeze! Look at that ass!' was the standard reaction of bellhops and other connoisseurs. She was twenty-three and like the girls with whom she shared the room, a technically superb secretary-cum-personal assistant. She greeted clients with a finely poised display of deference and arrogance. 'With this broad you'll never know who's screwing whom!' This from a writer-client who would not be favoured with that dilemma. Celine worked flexi-time. Occasionally moonlighting, at Oates's request, with selected patrons, she gave a versatile performance. Every ecstatic groan, whether she was making it or faking it, was the soundtrack of success. It was well understood that it was all in the day's work. If some ageing patron came through the hard night with proof of some still existent ego and maybe the lingering triumph of a climax to show for it, good for him and for Oates, Becker and Rimmer. Syndicated columnists preferred items from this delicious source to anything they got daytime from the studio 'planters'. If editors knew from whence these items came, they had no complaints. Just envy. Anyway, go argue with one hundred and seventy six outlets coast to coast. The word was, among several rock groups and not a few solo stars, that given first some claret and maybe a steak Tartare at a restaurant in the *Bistro* class, she'd come on with the best French hot and cold this side of Reno. She knew she was well worth the fat salary they paid her. When Oates told her that the accountant had noted sourly that she was on an assistant vice-president's salary, Celine flashed back, 'Tell him I do more than lick stamps.'

She was at her desk calculating with a Texas Instrument with just that ice-queen air when the door opened and a young man stepped in.

'Hi,' he said. 'Paul Madison to see Mr Oates. Reception said to come on in.'

The wide-lipped smile she turned on him was polite and civilised, beautiful and unfriendly.

'Mr Oates is expecting you, Mr Madison,' she said, 'but you're a little early. He's in a meeting at this moment. If you'd care to have a seat and wait.'

'Thanks.'

He was wearing Levi's and a Sears work shirt which had been tailored to fit tightly at the waist.

'In fact I'm smack on time,' he said. 'But as I'm meeting Stanley Markovitch I guess I will at that.'

His returning smile was no less beautiful. No more friendly.

He sat down on the couch that she had indicated. A chrome frame supported space for five to sit on light tan pig-skin. He threw one leg along it in a fair imitation of a crotch-shot for a glossy centrefold.

'What's your name,' he said.

She smiled.

'Celine Whittaker,' she said. 'And Miss Whittaker to you.'

He smiled. She was glad she'd made no effort to supply him coffee.

Affecting not to, she looked at him. Having had two trade passes for a preview of *The Shadow and the Sun*, she had recognised him instantly. Not that she'd ever show it but he was better in the flesh than on the screen. She was taking in every bulge and every muscle. And she knew he knew it.

He was just short of tall. Dark. Dark-haired, that was, and tanned but with blue eyes. The combination seemed, half-literally, electric. His forehead was high and the mouth a natural actor's, wide, expressive. It could be savage, poised, witty, delighted at any given turn. Too much, almost, you would have said except that the face was rescued from the pretty-boy by a strong hint of thinness and by a nose knocked faintly out of line.

He caught her eye and she realised she had been looking openly. She pressed the Constant button and went on with her work. The head would have seemed large but for the width of the shoulders. That was your classic young stud of a hopeful. Those and the slim waist and hips which more than anything, she'd like to bet, would've first caught some casting director's eye. There was no hint of padding in his crotch but the tight Gucci belt hinted of ridged muscles down a flat-board belly . . .

She felt in her own belly a sense of something warm and melting and was chagrined at herself. Her love of it – the moaning, clutching, kicking, the dark-golden pleasure of the thrusting within her – had become too dominant these days. Her mother had said she'd be a bad girl but thank Christ she'd never been a pro. Otherwise . . . Hell! She tried to think of the old farts who couldn't get it up, the super-studs who creamed in nothing flat and bored you the long hours with tears and replays of their therapy. No use. The image of the dark young presence lounging in faded blue upon that field of tan was too pressing for comfort. Well, she was not Annie Roundheels to sprawl legs open on her back the moment some cock-sure macho son-of-a-bitch . . . Only . . . She swivelled slightly on her chair as if in doing so she could dismiss the moistness that her thoughts had generated. As she did so she caught a blur of movement on the edge of vision. Then he was leaning forward, looking down at her across the desk. He did not blink and eyes held hers with assurance.

'I figure your name isn't Celine,' he said, 'no more than mine is Madison. And you're no more a snow queen than you're a ten buck TJ hooker. Something we both know. You may be sitting there like you're all on ice not fixing coffee but you and me both know you got the hots for me. And if not sweetheart, why not?'

Rarely lost for words she opened the grey eyes in blank astonishment. Her mouth tightened on a gutter phrase rising in rescue to her lips.

'I'll pick you up at eight,' he said. 'You'll recognise me. I'm the one with the hard on.'

The tan-leathered door whooshed open. The heat was off as the large shape of Stanley Markovitch loomed in. She knew she had nodded. Just the once.

Markovitch smiled in a way that could have had no meaning. 'Paul, sweetheart. Angel,' he said.

'Good afternoon, Mr Markovitch. I'll just see whether Mr Oates has finished his conference.'

The door to the inner room was opened. Oates stood on the threshold.

'Stanley, baby,' he said, 'And Paul. Paul Madison. Come right along in, young sir. I've been following your progress from afar with a keen interest and I want to say right now that I'm delighted we're the ones doing the lift-off.'

Madison smiled to reveal snow-capped dentistry. Oates shook his hand with best professional warmth but, as he led the way back in, did not quite try to put his arms around the young man's shoulders.

There were miniatures of British regimental flags and drums upon the coasters. If, like Madison, you drank tequilla old-fashioneds, the bright red-coat colours, the blues and golds, swept pretty swirls of rainbow patterns up into the liquid through the glass's base. By now the coasters had soaked up their fair share of punishment.

It had all gone thoroughly by the book, Tom was thinking. Oates had made most of the conversational running with his urbane line in coarse anecdotes and bitchy trade-talk. Yes, it was quite true Shelley had had to get to the judge and it was only after the girl had changed her plea . . . Markovitch had chuckled often. He always did. And so did Oates. It was part of the ritual of Hollywood horse-trading. You can hide anything behind a laugh – like suspicion, guilt, or a medium-sized lie. Occasionally he seized the opportunity, obliquely of course, to puff the virtues of his latest rising star. Then, with the tide of the Glenfiddich running strongly through his veins he stopped pussy-footing.

'Lyndon,' he said, 'you and I are both in the talent business. If I didn't think Madison had it, believe me I wouldn't be wasting your time and drinking your Scotch. Lyndon, I haven't felt such a genuine excitement since young Newman hit it in *The Silver Chalice*. Lyndon, this young man's talent is going to earn him more money than he's ever heard of.'

'I'll drink to that,' Oates said easily.

Liar, Tom Leonard was thinking automatically. *The Silver Chalice* was maybe the worst film Hollywood ever put together. Still, congratulations, you old mealticket collector, you've got the drums beating nicely, nicely thank you.

He stared at the agent. His appearance fascinated him. The florid, not quite flaccid features, stood out startlingly from the brushed-back snow-white hair. It was quite impossible to say finally whether the unnatural pinkness came from sun-ray lamp or booze or a masseur's fingertips. The effect was of pink rubber run to baby-fat. Lightly glazed. It made a glaring contrast along-side Oates's Burmese Colonial teak.

Tom sipped his rye.

Oates was winding himself up now. Big with the big finish he was even allowing his perpetual smile of all-things-to-all-men bonhomie to fade. His voice was taking on the resonance of a slightly more accredited professional – a senior attorney, say, briefing a Congressman. A well-arrived behaviourist servicing the carriage trade from his consulting rooms on Cannon Drive.

'Paul,' he was saying, 'you'll have gathered from this breeze-shooting session it's not our style here to mince words. I'll come straight to the point. I've been looking at you and I like what I see. I happen to agree with Stanley. I think you've got what for me is the most exciting quality in the world – potential. I think you've got what America wants – looks but looks with awareness.'

And a twelve inch dong, Tom Leonard thought.

'I can give you my solemn oath,' Oates was saying, 'that you can't go anywhere in the world and entrust your career to better hands than Stanley's. And to ours. The scripts you come to pick, the re-writes that'll be necessary, the directors you'll work – or not work – with, the other performers you'll play against – you'll find his experience in these fields, his decision-making perspective great. I mean shit hot.

'Paul, let me lay an old movie cliché on you. The director goes over to the girl extra. He looks at her. "Open your legs, honey," he says, "and I'll make you a star." Paul, that's what we can do for you here. Not a star. A superstar! All you've got to do is lie back and enjoy. What do you say?'

Unselfconscious, casually at ease in the formal chair, he had known as well as any of the three other men that he'd made the right kind of vibes in the room. He shifted his shoulders slightly, smiled, ducked his head in a way that wasn't deferential.

'I never argue with geniuses,' he said.

He has got something, Tom Leonard thought. Contempt. They're right as they always are. People will line the blocks to see those eyes look out at them in Cinemascope and tell them that they don't add up to a row of beans. The more that face says it doesn't give a shit about all those jerks out there, or those chicks with their tongues out, the more they'll care and love him.

'Good,' Oates said. 'Good. I had the surest feeling you'd be alongside us. No messing, huh?'

He pushed his chair back, rose on his neat, English-shod feet. The silver buttons of his blazer winked randomly in the chandeliered light as he began to pace. He paused and briefly laid a hand on Markovitch's plump shoulder. Too much polish on his nails, Tom thought.

'Stanley is dead on,' he said, looking sharply at Markovitch for appreciation. 'You can get the world by the tail. Money . . . cars . . . the right houses, good paintings . . . we take care of all that—'

You missed one out, Tom thought.

Oates now studied Madison carefully.

'Of course we'll want a couple things in return.'

'Like what, captain?' Madison's smile, like the 'captain' was a matter of how you read it.

'Obedience and discipline.' Oates knew his brief. He was less priestlike now. The money odour was filtering into the suite. For all its heard-before crassness, Tom Leonard still found himself admiring. It took a champ to spill out the phoney baloney with such conviction. He was the NFL coach of the year. Yep, he would whip this talent into something mean and utterly unstoppable.

'But when I say obedience I do really mean it. First off, you throw away your old life.' He grinned at Leonard. 'We've just constructed a new one for you. Here.'

He gestured at the sheaf of papers.

'Paul Madison's there. Hope you like the beautiful sonofabitch.'

Madison didn't move. Oates, less surely, went on.

'What we do Paul, is tell you how to move. You go to the shows we say. You eat at the joints we say. You wear the clothes we say and buy them from where we say. If you like what we say, well and good. But if you don't, tough shit, you still do it. You do it, Paul, because we know all the best routes. If we say "go to this premiere with some beat-up broad carrying third-degree syphilis you do it because we know there's some mileage in it for you. If we set you up in a Pro-Am tennis game with the biggest faggot on the circuit, you go! And you smile going and you smile when we're taking the publicity stills, and you smile when Rhona Barrett sits across from you at lunch, and you smile when some fan grabs at your crotch or asks you to write Paul Madison across her tits. On the way up you do every frigging interview going from *Oskosh Bugle* to *Washington Post*. Then, God willing, when you're at the top, we cut off all communication. You pull a Redford and we let the bastards come to us.'

'Who do I ask when I want to go for a leak?'

Madison had put the question with one foot up on the Sheraton.

Interesting, Tom thought. Lyndon's gone too far this time. He's just lost his man.

For perhaps four seconds silence shredded the room's elegance. Then smiling easily, Madison brought his foot down and shifted his weight in the chair.

'No sweat, Mr Oates. I dig the routine, and the bread. I guess we're cooking on the same burner, gentlemen. You want discipline and obedience, you got it. Just lead me to the promised land and watch my smoke.'

No problem with your timing, either, Tom Leonard thought. Or nerve. Two years you'll have it all.

Madison stretched one arm lazily forward toward the thin sheaf of papers

'Mind if I make my own acquaintance?' he said.

'Sure Paul.'

'Sooner the better, after all.'

Tom reached out and slid the top copy across as Oates sat down again. He pushed the carbon over to the agent. Both men commenced to read. The silence in the room was fractionally gentler now, but speculation beyond the air conditioner's power still hung heavy in the atmosphere. It was time, Tom thought, to earn his keep.

'You see what the British government says it will do for film production over there?' he said.

Without taking his eyes off Madison, Oates blew air out of his mouth derisively.

'Those dumb shits,' he said. 'They had it and they goofed. Well, they deserve all they get.'

Markovitch looked up from his reading.

'I was over there two weeks ago,' he said. 'I tried to tell them but . . . like you say, what can you say?'

'Not a single solitary thing,' Oates said, 'Hey, listen Stanley. I meant to tell you. You've got to give me the name of this new trichologist of yours. He's taken five years off you, I swear to God—'

'Yeah, off my gross life-time earnings too,' Markovitch grunted. 'But that's fine, that's okay. If you've got an ego, what the hell.'

His eyes dropped back to the paper, then came back up fast as Madison casually tossed his set back down onto the table. One beat and then he nodded.

'Uh-huh,' he said. 'Fine. Not too much different, I guess. I guess maybe that's the trick.'

For all the difference in their settings Oates's and Markovitch's smiles were mirror images. Madison smiled boyishly.

'Just maybe one thing I think we'd maybe better add,' he said.

'What's that, Paul? What did we leave out?'

The smile grew even shyer. The head dipped apologetically.

'Well . . . why don't I just go ahead and add it and you see what you think. You know, kind of put it out on the stoop and see if the cat licks it. You got a pen or something on you, Tommy?'

Tom didn't miss Madison's hint of insolence even as he smilingly offered him his Parker.

'Real nice pen,' Madison said. The silence came back into the room as in large script he added something to the third and final page. He wrote fluently, Tom saw, without the slightest pause.

'There you go. You just forgot that,' he said.

Still smiling he pushed the paper back over to Oates. Oates gave him back a no less gentle smile. He took his time gathering up the sheets, dropping his eyes.

Come on, thought Tom, you're pissing yourself to find out what he's put down and you are fooling no-one.

'How's Brenda, Stanley?' he said.

The agent reluctantly dragged his eyes away from Oates's face.

'Fine, just fine. Er, she sends her best,' he said.

Oates coughed.

'Paul,' he said, 'this is no use to us of course. We can't use this. But can I give you my assurance that I think I appreciate the point you're trying to n ake.'

Madison got up.

'I thought you might,' he said. 'You don't have to use it.'

'We have an understanding, then?'

'Oh, sure.'

Oates's beam was like a well-aimed ten-kilowatt.

'Wonderful,' he said. 'Just wonderful. I'm sure nobody here will ever regret it for a moment.'

He gestured with the paper.

'As for this – well, it's best to know, of course.'

'May I see that please, Paul?'

Markovitch had turned two thirds of the way to puce in trying to seem cool. He read, turned back to pink and turned reproachful slightly bulbous eyes toward his client. He laid the paper face down on the table.

'And anything we can get you, do for you right away,' Oates was saying, 'you let us know.'

'Well – there is one thing.'

'Try me.'

'How about a bungalow at the Sunset Ritz for tomorrow night . . .'

'Why, certainly, if—'

'And some company by way of room service?'

Oates didn't miss a beat.

'Why not tonight?' he said.

'Tonight I got me something else going. Well, gentlemen, I guess that about wraps it . . .'

It was Madison who led the drift doorwards. Tom stood but did not follow. Oates saw the lasting impression of the parting handshake as his own prerogative.

'Hey, Paul,' he was saying, 'tomorrow I have to fly up to the Springs. How'd it be if you gave my Rolls a little airing this weekend? She's been laid up awhile and I reckon she could use the exercise.'

Madison paused in the doorway.

'Fine,' he said. 'Always wanted that experience as well.'

Madison had turned.

'Tom,' he said, smiling and flicking a hand. Tom noticed that the edge of contempt was, for that second, sheathed. He nodded back.

'Bye, Stanley,' he said.

'Ciao.'

'You want to take a look. She's parked right around,' Oates was saying as, shutting noiselessly, the closed door brought instant silence.

He paused, then took the one pace necessary to reach the paper. He turned it over. At the bottom of the reconstruction of his life Madison had added just two sentences.

When I was a kid I saw my daddy murdered by a bunch of grease-ball punks and then I saw them gang-bang my mother. That was real and all this sucks.

Tom sighed. He sat down and took another snort knocking it quickly back. I don't doubt for an instant but that's true, he thought. Oates is right. It's better known. I'll have to get to the mother and talk just as soon as Bergman comes up with something on where the hell she's at now.

He stood up. So Madison was going to shove it home that he was his own man. Well most of the young studs were compelled to make that stand. Usually you could nod and look them in the eye and nothing more would come of it.

The itch to succeed and lead the sweet life, their totem-pole of insecurities, gave you all the leverage you needed to keep them in their place. If one or two of them got up to two and a half million for ten days work and went right off the scale, well, you could leave them to say 'Up yours!' to the world. Nobody cared by then. They'd stopped being actors or stars even, and were just rare animals. It was nonsense then. And there was always another pretty face coming down the turnpike.

Some, of course, were trouble all the way. Too insecure for their own, or anybody's good. Too take-charge and screw you. Started believing their own publicity. They took their cues from a Streisand or McQueen and made the world stand in line, and jump. Madison . . . well Madison looked like he just might turn out to be a pain in the ass of royal intensity. That contempt thing. The cobra touch. It was great for the broads – and the grosses. But deep inside Tom knew there would be no peace at night. If the gang-bang incident were true, Madison would be fuelled by something more savage than merely wanting to chop Oates down to size. They might be into shrink territory with this one. But then . . . he might not last six months . . .

He moved to the door. As he turned down the rheostat to zero, the loosely woven oatmeal drapes were last to lose their colour. Suddenly the place looked drab. As cold as a disused hangar.

He opened the door and went out and, unusually, Celine looked up and smiled at him.

chapter two

Exec vice-prexy Milton Rosner confirmed at a press conference yesterday completion of major casting on Magnum Fawcett's upcoming lensing of America's No. 1 bestseller *Curtain*. Scooping the pot all young macho Hollywood had been bidding for, relative newcomer Paul Madison gets catapulted up there alongside already slated Barbara Lemerle and Jack Preston. 'We're all enormously excited,' Rosner said. 'This boy has a magic that is just perfect for the role of Johnny Silvano. It's a magic that will confirm him as the most exciting fresh talent to hit this town for years.'

Madison took his bows as to the manner born. While the hired praisers beamed he turned on all the cool charm needed to get that Redford-style magnetism over on the cameras and the nation's breakfast tables. He is built well, walks tall, and if his impact on the gossip hens yesterday is any yardstick, Rosner could be on a winner. Lensing of the $8 million movie begins ...

Variety

Los Angeles real-estate values being what they had become, Magnum no longer owned a single square inch of studio floor-space. The high-rise buildings dressed with the Savings and Loan company logos stood up now as black-windowed markers to the long-dead studio system and Hollywood's shot-gun marriage to television. Just about due a Silver Wedding anniversary, Tom Leonard thought. Maybe they'll tinplate the Oscars this year. He turned right off Hollywood Boulevard and changed down to give his 633 a little exercise on the upward curves of Laurel Canyon. The accelerating Munich engine dispersed the last fading echoes of guitar flower power and Joni Mitchell that had haunted the parched, sage hillsides when he'd first come to the Coast. Within moments he was easing down into Van Nuys. For their studio work Magnum were renting from Universal out at Burbank.

He was waved through the studio Checkpoint Charlie and on

into the VIP slot as royalty might have been. He turned off the engine, nodded an ironic goodbye to the air-conditioner and braced himself. For a few seconds as he crossed the alleyway between two stages the sun smashed down on him with full uncorrected heat and, unscreened by tinted glass, blinded him. He groped at a half-seen handle, pulled an unnaturally heavy door. Then he was inside waiting for his eyes to accept the gloom.

Christ, he thought, I'd recognise it anywhere. If I were blindfolded and a giant hand picked me up and set me down in some sound-stage somewhere, anywhere, I'd know it by the smell. That musty, dusty, kind of mealy-mouthed smell made up of – what? The sad sacking of the sound-proofing on the walls. The swirling motes reheated time and time again by the arcs, the babies, the inkies and all the other lights that danced above. Sawdust, plaster and paint. Old, for the most part. Yesterday's. Last year's. Oh, yes. The smell of old dreams, old fantasies and old ambitions. A factory dealing in dreams has more durable ghosts than one manufacturing ball-bearings.

He could see now. He began to pick his way cautiously across a dark cable-strewn no-man's-land holding centre stage in the vast hangar of a building and towards the incongruously small patch of light and activity in the far-off corner.

Some forty or fifty people – camera crew, soundmen, grips, electricians, name it – surrounded a replica, painstakingly authentic, of the boothed section of a New York bar. Most of them were standing idly, talking softly, while nothing much was happening. An inner knot of four or five were huddled at the table central to the actual set. From somewhere else a sharp shout went up.

'Put in a half-single, Harry.'

'Coming right up.'

Feet on the gantry overhead spilt more dust into the atmosphere as one of the electricians moved to fine-tune a light. Tom shivered. That was another thing about sound stages. The temperature. As you forgot whether it was day or night outside you always felt a little too cold out of the circle of light; a little too warm within it. Well in the background now, he paused on the outer ring of onlookers. A young assistant director whose name he didn't know looked sharply up then instantly modulated his features into recognition. Tom frowned inwardly as he smiled back. He ought to know the kid's name. He had a week ago. Knowing names – and the numbers that went with them – was two-thirds of his job.

'Okay, gentlemen, we'll try it this way round.' Arthur Schneider, the director, was breaking up the huddle. He and the camera-man moved away to reveal Madison sitting in the booth across from Dennis Curtis. The clapper boy moved in and blocked his view again. Tom automatically registered they were up to take seventeen. Safely in shadow, he winced. Seventeen takes and still fumbling. It was going to be a long day.

'Quiet everyone,' a loud mouth shouted. 'Here we go!'

A bell rang. The focus-puller checked a last fast tape measurement.

'Turn over!'

The clapper boy squared the board to camera.

'One hunder and twelve, take—'

'Hold it loves! Hold it please!'

From behind the clapper boy it was Dennis Curtis.

'Cut it!' Schneider gave the command. He looked hard at the continuity girl who sighed at the world. The clapper boy, case-hardened to artistic foul-ups of these sort, prudently moved out of the line of fire. Schneider bustled forward with a bad imitation of concern. 'I take it we've got a problem,' he said to Curtis. 'Fuck all actors,' he said to himself.

'I'm sorry to be a pest, love,' Curtis said, 'but I've just realised that if I start off with the glass in my left hand – so – there's no way I can lose it in time to suit the action to the word on my "peanuts" line. You do see, don't you?'

Schneider never for an instant lost his gentle smile. He nodded sympathetically. He stood all of five foot two.

'I think love, that if you do it as we just – as I understood it – agreed, put the glass down on Paul's "Playing God because you couldn't play the second fiddle", you'll find I've left you a perfect-ly free hand for the peanuts.'

The sweetness and light of Schneider's tone carried instant translation. If, my dear sir, he was saying, you could manage to be a fraction less so fuckingly incompetent we might cease wasting the valuable time of all these genuine professionals and get this eight-million-dollars' worth of investment back on schedule and the road. Schneider knew this to be what he had really said. And so did Curtis. He blinked. He was, Tom knew, fifty-three, but make-up and a toupée made him around forty.

'Did we say that, Arthur?' he said. 'Oh, I'm so sorry. I didn't—'

'I guess that may have been my fault, Arthur,' Madison inter-vened. 'I kind of think I threw Dennis by putting my own glass down just before he should down his.'

Slouched against the false wall of the booth Madison had

seemed handsomely apart from the flak. Now the obviousness of his lie did not detract from its graciousness.

Curtis clutched the face-saver.

'Yes, maybe that's what confused me,' he said.

'Okay, thank you, Paul, I think that was it.'

In dark turtle-neck, denim jacket, Madison shrugged.

'Got it now,' Curtis said. 'Shall we have another bash?'

'Why not,' Schneider smiled. There was ice in his voice and Tom knew that the completely shaven-headed director was soured at Madison for stealing out from under his own ego a plum off-camera scene.

'Here we go then! Quiet, please!'

They went into take seventeen. Tom began to relax. He had no specific purpose in being on set other than as neutral observer running a quick check on Madison or, at the very worst, if the boy were out of line, riding a little discreet herd on him. But the actor's behaviour was shrewdly on the nail. The traffic was all in the other direction this morning. Even as Tom thought this, Curtis clumsily transposed a line.

'Cut!'

They went again. Tom could find it in him to feel sorry for Curtis. Ten years ago, having hit big in England after a decade of comedy in English variety and radio, he had landed the lead in a mid-period Neil Simon. It had been a smash. Hollywood and the world had been his for the taking. But he'd been hard to cast. He was not goodlooking, not ugly. Just anonymous. It was an all-purpose face which lent power to his unerring mimicry and versatility in a comic style that the experts said compared well with Peter Sellers at his best. He had now joined, for tax purposes, that band of English emigrés who, Tom noted with some amusement, spoke with anguish about their love of the old country ... from their million-plus mansions in Bel Air or the Holmby Hills. They were either aggressively Cockney which the natives no longer found quaint; or they fulsomely adopted all the schticks of tele-celebrities, kissing panellists, contestants, bandleaders and presenters with a passion. And Curtis was no exception. In two years he had scored three pictures, two wives, and one coronary. This last had kept him out of movies long enough for him to grab this role without demanding his usual big percentage of the gross. They had bought him as much for his accent as for anything else.

He was playing a Broadway critic, Clive Barnes in everything but name. And in England, when the movie finally opened, Curtis could have stepped-up billing. He could be flown over to boost the pre-premiere puffing with a guest-shot on Parkinson or whatever passed for Johnny Carson and Dick Cavett on his side of the pond.

'Cut!'

Madison as the young actor trying suicidally to win a public apology from the critic had fired-in his disgruntled lines perfectly. It was Curtis once again who'd fluffed.

'My nose alright?' he was asking. 'I have to tell you it *feels* shiny.'

Bud Eastman was immediately in there. The quick, flurry of his powder puff could not mask Curtis' visible nervousness. The golden heydays when he could burst into the Beverly Wilshire in the boringly predictable outrageouness of cricket pads and gloves were long, long gone.

The riggers, grips and electricians who'd seen it all before muttered 'bullshit!' or looked at the morning trade papers to see who was filming where or screwing whom. The tools in their work belts seemed to make them a jury of the elect. The silent collective sneer was coming through all transmissions.

'Cut!'

Madison had been a carbon copy of his previous excellence. Once more it had been Curtis, overlapping this time, who had blown it. It wasn't easy. He was going for Barnes's speech impediment – riding to orders, obviously – and Schneider was hoking up what was essentially a dialogue scene by playing it very tight. The positioning of the glasses was critical. In Cinemascope their ice cubes would look capable of holing the *Titanic*.

'Arthur, love. Could I make a little suggestion?'

'Go ahead.'

'Well, I do think it's this first long speech that's throwing me. Even when I'm through it I've still got my mind's eye on it, if you know what I mean . . . Well love, we have got that bit haven't we? Several takes. What I was thinking was, if you could just change angles and come in on my next—'

'Denny, please,' Schneider cut in. 'Can I just ask you one favour. Let me do the driving, eh? Really? Just let me call—'

'Oh, sure, sweetheart, sure. Only I just thought—'

'Denny, I need that speech to give me time for my zoom in. You see, Denny – if you don't mind a brief fill-in on the art of directing – this is a scene potentially dead visually unless we bring a little zip into it. There's a risk here we'll lose the pace I know we'll have coming out of the third reel. And if we lose pace and you lose your audience all these nice people around here won't like you one bit. No intellectual pretentiousness, old love, but pace is what film is all about.'

Or significant non-pace, you faggot sadist, Tom Leonard thought. He had never heard the sweet reasonableness of Schneider's voice laced with such venom. It was curious. The wrestler's skull belied the soft voice but completely betokened the ambitious ruthlessness Schneider deployed behind people's backs. Even more so, it indicated, Tom thought, the obviousness of the man's film style. He had made some ten features all of them shot as if they were beer commercials – 'Zoom in tight as the tab is pulled'. But give the cock-sucker credit, zooms were what Joe Public thought made a good film. And Schneider had another plus. Employing verbal terrorism and ingratiation in equal parts, he could draw the best that his players could give. It was a bad day if they didn't hate him. There was already one Oscar holding down his collection of gay erotica, and *Curtain* would have so many angles going for it he must be in with a chance of racking up another . . .

Curtis had taken the lecture badly. He had not grown angry but even more obviously uptight. As he made to protest his togetherness with Schneider his gesturing hand up-ended the highball glass. Cold tea spilled across the table as the prop man raced in. Curtis on reflex had jumped half to his feet and edged out of harm's way.

'Oh, I'm so sorry. So sorry. Do forgive me,' he went over the top by way of an apology.

'Arthur,' he said, 'my throat. It's a little tight. Perhaps . . .'

Without waiting for the director to speak, he moved to where his stand-in and unofficial valet stood in the ring of onlookers. The man's hand was already sliding into the pocket of the cashmere topcoat he was carrying. It was he who led Curtis into the shadowy, twilight-zone centre of the stage where, dimly but certainly perceived by all, Curtis's head snapped smartly back three times as he pursued mastery of his part at the bottom of his flask. Schneider sighed loudly. If that prick goes on taking that stuff, he thought, it's going to be Errol Flynn all over again. I'm going to have to provide stage furniture for him to lean on, and a pot to piss in. Shit him. 'Don't worry, Denny,' he said.

Madison had not moved. The more Curtis screwed around, the more secure he felt. Charmingly young, darkly, devastatingly handsome, he had relaxed casually at ease – Patience in a bar booth. He had time on his side. And balls. And Oates, Becker and Rimmer.

'Ready whenever you like, Arthur,' Curtis was back, speaking in a voice too clear and small, too precisely controlled. 'So sorry, Paul.'

Madison smiled boyishly.

'Forget it,' he said. 'Who's crying over spilt tea? So what the hell? We're up to take twenty-eight but we're still going to get it in one.'

Curtis' smile had genuine gratitude in it. Oh, baby, if only all the stable were like him, Tom thought, I'd be in clover. Well maybe not. Maybe then I'd be pounding sidewalks.

'Okay. We're going again! Stand by, everyone!'

They went again. And again. Again. Each time Curtis fluffed. Madison's performance was not deviating by an eye-lash. Voice, expression, movements were impeccable take to take. Curtis was struggling now to place two words accurately the one after the other.

Tom could feel the technicians' irritation and restlessness crawling all over him. Eyes rolled to heaven. Groans were loud and the language was straight out of a losing ball-team's locker-room. Hunger was also playing its part, Tom knew. They were close to lunch and the half-hour before on any set always took eighty clock-watching minutes.

But Schneider was inflexibly gentle-voiced. As patient as a Gestapo interrogator.

'Once again, please, gentlemen. Right away.'

'Camera reloading. Five minutes please.'

Schneider spun round.

'You don't have another full magazine?'

'Not at this rate,' the assistant cameraman said. 'We figured to reload during lunch.'

'Oh, for God sake!' Schneider stopped at that. He read the danger signals well. The message, clearly transmitted, was, 'Don't ruck us because your frigging actor has ballsed up every take. You want a dispute you can have one, baby!'

'Okay, five minutes,' Schneider conceded. 'I want to look at the next set-up anyway.' Curtis grabbed at the reprieve. He walked towards his flask expertly imitating the crab-like walk of Groucho Marx. The continuity girl laughed.

'You'll need a refill soon,' Curtis's gofer whispered.

In the darkness Tom Leonard decided he was glad he was not

starting out in the movies today. Too many permanent decisions being made by the temporary help. Harry Cohn may have been a monster, but he did make motion pictures. Not deals. He would have taken Curtis's balls off after take five, and ridden hard over Schneider. He remembered the story they told of Humphrey Bogart being dangerously stalled by a young actor who couldn't speak his lines. 'I need a little time to warm up,' the green-horn explained. 'You do your warming up in your own time sonny, I'm walking' said Bogey. That man had class. Style. Now ex-hairdressers call the shots, and the money comes from biscuit-makers, lettuce growers, or from dubious sources who launder dirty money in Europe before shipping it back to the coast. For all that, *Curtain* was bound to be a smash. It had the dead-certain chemistry of Barbara Lemerle and Jack Preston which hit the world where it liked it most. In the crotch. Sure the story had been worked over so many times before. It reached back to *Golden Boy*, was brilliantly re-furbished in *All About Eve*, acquired some added venom in *The Sweet Smell of Success*. For today's seventies-going-on-eighties it had been given a top dressing of modish soft-porn. Rosner, of course, had ordered 'no beaver shots' more at the dictate of his wife than of his own prejudices. 'When *The New York Times* shows pubic hair we'll put it in our movies,' he declared at one board meeting. Everybody dutifully applauded the gem including a producer who muttered, 'That still gives us plenty of tit and ass to play with.'

But you had to hand it to the Oates-Markovitch team. It was a brilliant move to slam Paul Madison in there, rough-shod over a dozen better-known faces. He had almost as many lines in the script as the two stars with their names above the title. More, he had the face, and the unmistakeable body-language that grabbed millions of women as stealthily and as potently as a hand sliding up in the darkness. Unless he fell flat on his face, Tom figured, Madison would hole out in one. But he wouldn't fall on his face. Along with his looks and build, he had the competence. And a menace which Leonard couldn't measure, though it was power-fully registered on his own inner Richter-scale. If there were some rough edges, a combination of skilled direction and smart editing would construct a creditable performance. Especially in the part of Johnny Silvano.

There was Oates's brilliance. Madison would superimpose a rugged, if blurred, fidelity on the role, of a punk kid whose ability as a fighter leads to his being discovered as an actor and who then claws and screws his way – almost – to the top. For millions, Madison would be Silvano in the way Dean had been *the* rebel without a cause, Brando *the* wild one. Millions had read the book and Magnum were still sending station-wagons down to Pickwick each week to grab still more copies and maintain it at No 1 on the best-seller lists. Books can be made as well as stars. What would clinch it for Madison would be the crucial sequence where, the lead role of the season in his grasp, he refused to play ball with a homosexual impresario's dramatically explicit advances. That was the best of the top dressing. The virility and the ultimate return to a kind of integrity would have Madison-Silvano coming out of the picture like heroes. He'd be able to write the pay check for his own next role. Able to light his cigarette with Federal portraits of the president whose name he'd borrowed.

'Cut!'

The camera reloaded, they had gone again. Again, unbelievably, Curtis had failed even to stagger through. This time, as people sighed with every obvious intention of being heard, he had stood up.

'People,' he said, 'it's getting boring keep having to apologise. Therefore I'll drop it. Arthur, my dear fellow, why the blazes don't you yell at me like a normal man – I'd at least know where I was then.'

Deciding attack was, if not the best, the only defence, he had, Tom thought, achieved a measure of tattered, actorish dignity. He waited now with everyone else for the storm to break.

Schneider gave it two beats. 'My forbearance, chum,' he hissed politely, 'is due to my awareness that largely owing to your own unaided efforts, this motion picture, employing the talents of some two hundred others, is three and a half days behind shooting schedule.'

The voice had not risen. Tom remembered Schneider had started as an actor himself. He wanted the crew with him.

'And I know,' he continued, 'that if I start spelling out to you what I feel about actors who can't seem to handle lines, let alone . . .' he checked himself on 'their liquor' '. . . their props, then more than shit will hit the fan. Are you getting my drift?'

'Perfectly old sport,' Curtis smiled. 'In fact I get it so well, I have decided . . .' his voice rose to reach the furthermost technicians aloft, '. . . to permit you to go ahead and fucking shoot without me.'

He marched off, his face reddening beneath the make-up. As

grins, embarassed, openly gleeful, were exchanged, Schneider held his fire. Then he took command.

'You heard the man, folks,' he said. 'Lunch. Back in one hour.'

'Lunch! Back in one hour!'

As the first assistant director bellowingly echoed the instruction bells rang and, lights clunked off, Schneider casually lit two cigarettes, handing one to the continuity girl.

'And so it goes,' he grinned. 'We gonna grab some food and a couple of beers?'

She smiled back. 'I have to watch my figure—'

'You eat, I'll watch it! Quite a session with our friend.'

'You handled it beautifully,' she said, knowing that when all the versions of the incident got back to Rosner – the boss man had informants at all levels – Schneider would earn the most points.

Tom shifted his gaze to look for Madison. He saw instead Schneider bearing down on him.

'You saw all that?'

'Yes.' Tom said.

'You know we weren't going to get that shot whichever way I played it?'

'That's the movie business,' Tom Leonard said, hoping that banality would stop the director pitching into a solo of self-justification. It didn't. Two egos had been on the line. Schneider was determined that his was the one that didn't show the bruises.

'You know me, Tom. I'll do anything to get the best out of actors. Eat shit if necessary. I'll compromise ten thousand times a day to bring out the best fucking movie we can get. I only ask one thing in return. You know what that is?'

Leonard sighed. Of course I know what it is, you prick, he thought. It is the standard lament of every director going back to de Mille.

'Discipline.' Schneider declared.

Bang on, Leonard noted to himself.

'But this Curtis is a real one-off,' Schneider snarled. 'Behaves like he shits pearls. Who needs it!'

Tom gave a brief, all-purpose nod. Who needed any of this self-justifying crap anyway? He saw Madison moving towards them. Relief.

'I'd better grab a sandwich.' Schneider said. 'Can't fight temperament on an empty stomach!' He threw a friendly salute at Madison and disappeared in the darkness of the set.

'Tom, how're you doing sweetheart?'

'I'm in good shape. You okay?'

'Oh sure.' Madison laughed. 'You make the cabaret?'

Tom frowned. Madison was speaking too loudly for safety. A couple of electricians were wheeling a 5-kilowatt lamp well within earshot.

'Yeah. I saw the show.' He spoke softly, with a sideways glance at the crewmen

'You're on to a winning game, Paul. You handled the situation like a champ. You go on playing that way and you'll have nothing else to do but count the money.'

Madison abruptly jerked his hand.

He led Tom away over more cables, past a randomly abandoned back-projection screen into a far corner of the stage. Half a dozen young-old men, extras called to populate the bar in long shot, were yawning collecting their thoughts, their newspapers, their packs of cards, from the ball-pen area in which they'd just slept out the morning. As if on cues, they each smiled and nodded at Madison and Tom. It was a formal tribute from the last in the pecking order.

A kind of feudalism, Tom thought. They know we have the power, the percentages and the muscle. The serfs paying homage to the gentry. It sickened him. The motivation of this town was fear, fuelled by greed. And as the elevator went up you passed hate on all floors. It is all too fucking easy, that's the curse. Just a question of latching on to which way the public is jumping. One minute it's disaster movies; then the supernatural; then wars in outer space; God knows what the next genius will come up with. Yesterday's schmuck is today's biggest-grossing producer.

So you smile back at the bit-players and look like you mean it. Any one of them could be signing your pay check tomorrow. Christ, fear was getting to him too. He looked at Madison. No sign of fear in this actor. For all his rawness, Madison looked almost arrogantly intact.

The studio lights had now clicked on. Madison turned to face Tom fully. Tom was startled. The relaxed charm had vanished from the lean, young face. Instead the blue eyes blazed lighter, and the jaw-muscles were knotted with anger.

'Now listen, Tom,' Madison said. 'I can keep on like any country boy from now till Hell freezes over. But I want you to make me, here and now, a promise.'

'Sure.'

'I want you to give me your word that in no picture I ever do after this one, will that washed-up, washed-out has-been Curtis have a part.'

'I don't actually think, Paul, after today, that that's a problem we're going to have to face. But . . . sure!'

Indignation had caused Madison to pace a few steps, come pacing back again.

'Schneider I can maybe use.' he said. He's a phoney on top and deep down, if he has a deep down, but he's slick and he's bankable this year and that I can use. But Curtis – that's bad news, friend!'

Tom tried to stay poker-faced. Madison could either be totally trusted to keep his nose politically clean or, through smart-ass manoeuvres all his own, bury it up to his ears in a shit pile. No easy way with this one.

'What is with this English Mafia anyway? Curtis is behaving like he's made you an offer you can't refuse.'

Tom laughed. 'Ego-trips by actors are par for the course. English ego-trips are just a bigger pain in the ass that's all. Anyway, all you have to do, Paul, is to steal the picture from him.'

'Yeah, well I guess I can handle him. Faggy directors are something else.'

'You mean Schneider propositioned you?' Tom was amused.

'All but! I swear if he'd had another gin and tonic the other night he'd have grabbed my balls and kissed me.'

'You mean he didn't? He usually gets around to it by take fourteen. How you getting along with her ladyship, and big bad Jack?'

'Her – pretty good. I can see she likes to call the shots and crucify the hired help. But that's her style. Him – I kind of dig but I don't want to move in too fast. Like I'm begging for favours.'

'Good thinking. All the same Lyndon thinks pairing you with him will pay dividends. Looks good to be coming out of the Preston stable.'

'You mean stud farm.'

'I was coming to that. Lyndon arranges . . .' he thought 'procures' more accurate but less smart, 'the action for Jack. There are a couple of chicks he's lining up for you both to get you into the circuit so to speak.'

'All that's part of the service from Oates, Rimmer and Becker?'

'Sure, as long as you keep it cool and don't damage the beautiful image. Which reminds me. You've remembered the party tonight at Barbara Lemerle's pad?'

Madison turned a direct, unguarded grin on him. 'Our hero crashes the big time!' he said. 'Forget! You have to be kidding!'

'Everybody who rates big'll be there. We've fixed your partner. We should get some mileage with the trades and the fan magazines. You'll want to know who, and what, and where.'

Paul Madison had a sudden uncomfortable vision of himself as the manipulated man. It passed just as swiftly. He gave Leonard a mock salute.

'I'm listening, colonel.'

'Lyndon has fixed for you to take Christy Roberts. She's class and a great piece of ass.'

'Is that the . . .'

'Girl in the new Seven Arts film. We have to figure out the right chemistry for the party routine too. Be nice to her. It'll pay.'

'Ten-four. Does the fine print say I can bang her? I mean . . . don't want to screw up the Master Plan!'

There it was again. Another left-field vibration. The feedback from Madison needed a constant monitoring. A trained ear might detect under all the intelligent, relaxed co-operation, the faint ticking of a time bomb.

He was uncomfortably aware that Madison's easy grin was the same one he'd smiled across at Curtis.

'Personally,' he was saying, 'I'd just as soon have the black chick Lyndon fixed for me to celebrate the day I joined you.'

'She do things for you?'

'Skin like velvet. Nipples you can put your eyes out on. Body scent like you can't believe. Say, we going to eat?'

'Yep. Let's go.'

They had reached the padded door. Tom's protégé, his meal-ticket of the imminent future, sighed luxuriously as he followed him into the drab corridor.

'Hallelujah!' he said. 'Come sundown, a four-day break in schedule. God willing.'

Then they both saw Schneider and Curtis together. The director had his arm around the actor's shoulders. Curtis kissed him. On the lips.

'Holy shit,' Madison said.

Star-kissed, the lights of yachts reflected in the black velvet waters of the night, the Monte Carlo yacht basin lay spread before them through the open window. Tom Leonard stared down on the toyland shipping, trying as he sipped his rye to calculate its combined value. Noiselessly, Monte Carlo faded out and, dazzling, with the daylight bright at its summit, Fujiyama loomed high over a Japanese wall. Then as silently as the shores of the Mediterranean had disappeared so Fujiyama stole away. And so did Tom Leonard. There might be more 'oohs' but he had already been to Yucatan and seen a big moon, rosy-gold with haze around, wedged helplessly in better windows than these. See two wall-projected holographs, he figured, and you've seen them all. Most people, invited over to this tennis-court-sized den to watch holiday slides, would groan 'Oh come on!' and roll back to whatever was the in-trick of the week. But tell them it was for holographs and at Barbara Lemerle's yet, and nothing short of a better offer would keep them away. He steered his way through an obstacle course of sprawled couples. The atmosphere was standard Hollywood aroma. Pot, sweat and perfume overladen with a hasty squirt from an aerosol odour-killer. He knew coke was around for the afficionados. A variety of other multi-coloured lifters and downers were to hand in crystal bowls, like salted peanuts. Maybe you needed these to watch holographs. Wait till some genius of a bitch pins down laser movie projection. Then nobody, but nobody, would go to a movie theatre. He pushed against leather and as he went out through the door the noise of the party proper babbled upward to meet him.

He looked down into the lower section of the split-level main room. The effect from there, the scale, was rather like the airport terminal at a large provincial city which had been taken over by an Italian Government design team, and peopled with two hundred of the world's currently rated Beautiful People. The Lemerle establishment was more honest that most in Bel Air. Modern, and therefore hideous in its expensiveness, it proclaimed that Barbara Lemerle had made it and could therefore flaunt it. It aped no Mexican hacienda, Loire château or Fairbanksian castle. It was contemporary Western-Hemi Anonymous, on a grand, bland scale. The sculptural best of chrome acrylic, leather, cane and the occasional antique piece, Tom knew to be more attributable to Barbara Lemerle's own chain-jangling taste than to the ultimatums of some designer.

He felt vaguely marooned. There was no percentage in trying to seek out Margot. Since she had announced to him that she was telling the world they'd only stay together until Charley got to ten pending their divorce. It was every girl for every thing in pants.

He'd done her no more service than chauffeur her to parties. She made her own arrangements for the journey home. That these invariably involved stop-overs en route no longer troubled him. He was supposed to be the joke, the sad, sad chump but it was infinitely sadder that, the wrong side of forty, Margot should be trailing her coat among the tennis pros, beach boys, actors, scarcely half her years. Only the latest, Julian Hadfield, had got through to his nerve ends. Hadfield had something. The screen-play with which he'd won a nomination had real class, ought to have won. A guy that age producing work . . . For a moment he felt the old familiar angst at someone else's success gnaw at the inner, private, part of him. But he had long ago learnt how to keep the spectre of his self-contempt a good arm's length away. When in self-doubt or sorrow, head for the bar. He pulled back his shoulders, started to descend the stairs towards the swirl of kitsch and kaftan.

'Hey, Tom!'

He looked down and round. The couple he had carefully negotiated on the corner of the stairs were a handsome young tele-stud and the new girl in from Paris.

The girl, dark, boyish, exquisite, smiled up at Tom a smile weighted with all the knowingness of main-chance impermanence. Her escort smoothed her tight helmet of hair.

'Hey' he said. 'Hear you're warming up some useful competition.'

Tom laughed. 'Ways to go yet,' he said. 'But pretty good. Maybe one day – well – who knows.'

The man darted his innocently wicked smile and the girl laughed not unprettily as if she might have understood. Tom nodded and moved down into the press.

'Yes, sir?'

He had reached the long well-staffed bar stocked with the routine ingenuity of a transatlantic liner. Now, confronted by the barman's question he was wary. He'd had too much too soon. Time to go easy.

'A Campbell's please,' he said. Often he had to explain but the barman had been hand-picked, like the guests.

'Yes, sir,' he said, reaching sideways, 'leave the angostura in?'

'Thank you, yes.'

He watched admiringly as with the throwaway self-conscious-ness of a Vegas dealer the Philippino deftly added ice and tonic.

'Lemon, sir?'

'Please.'

Without seeming to try, the quick brown hands sliced lemon wafer thin. Oh for one person here tonight who's not giving a performance, Tom thought. Everybody's an act.

'Thank you.'

He took the glass and the ritual over he must turn away on cue. He did so and at once caught a glimpse across the room of Barbara Lemerle talking to Sylvia Kilmartin. At once he went back on duty. If a star was in cahoots with the editor of her current movie it was going to be tough on even a sensationally-promising newcomer. The performance would receive no wider distribution than the inches square screen of one editing machine. The new sensation would be tomorrow's cutting room sweepings and the day after's has-been. He had work to do. Madison business. He pressed, grinning, through the crowd. Closer, he could now see that Dennis Curtis had made a third with Barbara and Sylvia.

'Tom, angel! Did you have trouble parking the car?'

It was Barbara's joke of East coast superiority always to greet him with outrageous New York mimicry.

'Took the subway,' he replied in kind.

'Smart, very smart,' she said returning his grin.

She had a reputation deserved down to the last shred of cold-blooded calculation of being a bitch-goddess. But she had talent, worked until all others had dropped and a nerve in him responded to her naked directness. She leaned forward to kiss his cheek and he noticed that even with so homely a gesture she instinctively favoured the left side of her face. Directors had told her it photographed better than the right. You could afford to ignore it only in sleep or in death. Market research had proved she was adored by millions. A studio publicist detailed to appraise those Arab eyes, the Euro-Afro curls, the swoop of nose and full mouth beneath, announced definitively; 'That's a fantasy image for jerking off on five continents!' When news of the accolade reached Barbara Lemerle she said, 'How nice. Tell him to be my guest.'

She gestured now towards Curtis.

'What do you think of this crazy Limey!' she said to Tom.

'He's been asking me to marry him now I'm back up for grabs. He's been trying to sell me on going over to England for the promotions on *Curtain*. Culture shock or not I may just do that.'

'Marry me?' Curtis smiled.

'Hell no. That would be all shock, no culture.'

'Beautifully put!'

'Go to England, I mean.' She turned to Tom. 'Denny swears he'd introduce me to the Queen.'

The liquor in Tom Leonard was working corrosively.

'The only queen he knows is the one he sees every morning on the set in the chair marked "Director"!'

Curtis's teeth dug into his lower lip. Barbara Lemerle laughed the fish-wife's laugh of which no speech coach had yet been able to rid her. Curtis, who had known such taunts before, backed off with a faint imprint of a smile.

'The Queen I had in mind is a personal friend, believe it or not. Her sister has come to my parties. But you won't see that in Army Archerd's stuff. Protocol and all that.'

'Bullshit!'

Barbara looked at Tom. 'Why don't you knock it off? What's the trouble, Margot leave you at last?'

'Margot left me at first!'

'You win some you lose some. Which cradle she snatching tonight?'

'Why, you want to make it a threesome?'

'Not my league, Tom, you know that.'

Curtis stepped in. 'My sole purpose in coming to this little bunfight was so that I could get Sylvia to put that final touch of magic on my superlative performance. Not that my work needs much embellishment but it would be nice to have the best editor in the business with me rather than against me. Do you read me my sweet?'

Sylvia Kilmartin rolled her eyes to heaven.

'Jesus, Denny baby, I treat every frame of celluloid as if it were a masterpiece. That takes in everything from the better class of cheap junk to Larry Olivier. And I've had them all. You, amigo, will get my usual tender loving care. After all I am supposed to be the best salvage merchant at the studio.'

Sylvia Kilmartin had been married for twenty-seven years. She had three grown-up children. She was brilliant and she could make the work of bad directors come alive, cut dud acting into magic. She knew she would have to labour hard and long over Curtis's slurred phrases by cutting to livelier business, or those gilt-edged stand-bys, Barbara Lemerle's breasts.

Almost as much as her talent – she had the awards to endorse it – her appearance had helped keep her safely afloat in what was still a man's world. She was a plain-Jane and she underscored it with a butch hair-style above old-fashioned spectacles. Like the cameraman and the make-up artist, she knew her value. And so did the stars.

'Sylvia, darling,' Curtis said, 'why don't you and I go to the nearest waterhole where I can tell you how much I really love you?'

She weighed that prospect against her empty glass. 'Okay, but why do all Englishmen have to talk out of sync?'

As they moved off Barbara confected a smile that leaned more towards malevolence than contempt.

'So that prick thinks that by touching up Sylvia she'll turn his last crappy scenes into a great performance. I've got the key shot there and if one inch of it is cut Mr Curtis's balls will be in the meat grinder! And on top of that I have to play midwife to your bright new baby, Madison.'

She looked directly at Tom, aware that the worst side of her ego was showing. 'I mean, okay, he's the new threat. But screw me, I don't see why . . .'

'I'll screw you any time,' Tom said.

It took her too quickly. Her words went into a holding pattern. 'No you wouldn't,' she said. 'You're too nice. You have too much class. You know something, Tom? You've been miscast.'

'Don't be too sure!' He was stung by her accuracy. As he lifted his glass to divert his annoyance he saw Paul Madison steering his date for the evening out onto the patio. Others were studying Madison too he noticed. All systems functioning.

'You're looking thin, Barbara,' he said. 'On you it looks good.' He thought he'd kept some honesty in his voice. He wondered if she knew that he knew she was eating enough for two. Eighteen months ago her career had been halted. She had become too fat. Despite all the faddy treatments the prospect of reverting to her basic type – plump New York Jewish broad – rolled over her. Then she had had a tapeworm artificially introduced. Lining her colon, growing, it had devoured everything within reach as voraciously as a sea-monster. It had also ensured the swelling of her bank account with every pound it slimmed off her.

But he must speak his piece for Madison.

'It won't be any skin off your famous nose,' he said. 'You're the girl. You're unassailable. It's Jack who's going to find out he's the midwife.'

'Oh, Big Black Jack knows that,' she said. 'A lot he cares. He's taking the money and screw the critics. While they're marking comparisons he'll be laughing all the way to the Crocker National. He's into production now and in a year he'll be king of his own mountain. He'll be playing with himself and holding a finger up to the world.'

'That's some trick!'

She laughed. 'They're teaching frigid women to do it now. Saturday morning classes in New York. Just watch teacher – and go man go!'

'Young Mr Madison – I guess you're right. I've got built-in protection. It'll be what he does next that counts. For the moment, with the Silvano part, he can't miss. Or do any harm. Just so I get fifty-one per cent review space.'

'You know you will.'

'The next thing he does, he won't miss either. No shit, Tom, he's got it. A lot more than my ex-husband whose name temporarily escapes me had – and he went most of the way up.'

'That's why we're running him, Barbara.'

She looked at him. 'That's another thing,' she said. 'Tom – I just said you were too nice. That you had too much class.'

He felt his face harden.

'Tom, right now you're running interference for Paul Madison. He's going to be a bitch like me. Another year you'll just be running errands. Quit, Tom,' she said suddenly, 'Quit Hollywood. Quit Margot. You can't be a gofer all your life.'

She looked him in the eyes, then on over his shoulder, and smiled from ear to ear.

'Jason!' she exclaimed. 'Wanda! You both look gorgeous!'

But Tom couldn't let it go at that.

'Barbara, sweetheart,' he called out in a public voice as she brushed past him. 'When I need a shrink I'll give you the sixty-five bucks.'

'For that money,' she flung back, 'you wouldn't even get a security blanket!'

He had a sense of undisguised grins at his expense. He pushed by more people and, nodding to more household names, went out through the open Cinemascope-sized French windows and onto the patio.

The air was still warm and soft, rich with the fantasies of all the lonely. Tom sighed his own breath into it. He looked up. No moon at all was fixed above the Bel Air. The square pool in the mid-distance seemed to float emptily up to meet him. Its underwater lights had washed it artificially pale blue. It shimmered, clean and pure. The Mexican poolboy picked off dead leaves almost as they touched the water. At the tables to the right, more people were grouped and, from still further beyond, non-acoustic instruments pulsed out an insistent beat.

Far off on a perimeter he caught a glimpse of a sleek movement of black and white through a pool of light. A red signal cut flashingly through the orange and the dark. Bel Air patrol or private security force. Law and order was about to see a rubber-necker or unauthorised photographer get his. Two people were walking up towards him now. Christie Roberts and Alan Rudolph had arms around each other. Sealed in their closed circuitry, the starlet hung upon every word with an intense expression of rapt dumbness.

He by-passed them and began to walk down from the mound which gave the house its unnatural elevation. It had cost a fortune to truck the soil in yard by yard. House and garden must have cost that bitch as much as she had netted for herself on *Pay Off*. More than he'd earn in his life. But as he came closer to the music and began threading his way through the Frank Brothers patio furniture and the names to match, he had to give Barbara Lemerle that she had not been falsely modest. Her party was not trying to play in the exclusive Grace Robbins league. The timing, no doubt, in part explained that. This was a simple affair because it fell slap bang in the middle of *Curtain*'s shooting schedule. She had had enough leverage to have Michael Heiffetz, her personal manager, get a two-week recess written in to her contract. One week would take her out to The Sands where, for her nightclub act she would receive what would be, for a month or two, a world record fee for a Las Vegas appearance. That was discounting the disc she'd cut. For the satellite hook-up to the Sporting Club, Monaco and the Princess Grace charity, she would, as the press releases announced, donate her services. The party she could afford too. On the face of it, the object was to see her off in style. The open secret was that it coincided with the last rites of her divorce from Erich Cornblatt, the erstwhile man she'd love for-ever. Trust her, Tom reflected, to get all the coincidences so beautifully organised. Banging her, he decided, would be like screwing a calculating machine or a praying mantis.

Oh, there was Madison! He was standing on the edge of a small circle listening to Buddy Boyle proving yet again that clapped-out stand-up comics never know when to quit. Madison drank deeply from a salt-rimmed glass as Tom moved to him and winked.

'Walk you to the pool, Paul?'

'Sure – and fast!'

'You've split from your action for the evening?'

'Yup. She's stupid and she's not interested in my balling her,' Madison said simply. 'Oh, don't worry. We got our picture taken here and there.'

He flashed Tom an easy, cynical smile. Tom noticed with approval that he had dressed very formally and with great restraint. His shirt-maker had cut out all the frills and the single-breasted tux lacked Beverly Hills's mandatory embroidery and fancy frogging. The effect was calculated to hit the young market and also turn on the matrons. There was the money market. As his hand came up once more to sip the Marguerita, Tom noticed that the dress watch was Piaget and probably white gold.

The smell of the chlorine reached them before they arrived at the pool, their collars and shirt cuffs fluorescent in the metallic glare.

'We re-making *Sunset Boulevard*?' Paul Madison asked.

The actor in him was obliging him to stare down Adonis-like at the far-off wavery image beyond his patent leather shoes.

'Right. As a musical. You get the Swanson part.'

'In a musical it'd better be Stroheim's. So – what, Tom?'

'Paul, I talked to Bergman today. We've located your mother.'

Madison's head came up and turned towards Tom. It froze into a marble nonchalance. His eyelids were half closed. Whatever lay behind them was as brittle and dead as volcanic lava.

'Don't tell me where,' he said at last.

'Well – okay. But she's alive and well.'

'I said don't. Not ever!'

'Okay, but—'

'Was there a need for me to know?'

'Forewarned is forearmed, Paul.'

'That's your department. I don't want to know.'

'Sure, Paul. Understood.' Christ, Tom thought – already he's talking like he thinks he's Redford. And already I'm replying like a schmuck.

'We've just located her,' he heard himself repeat. 'We've not made any contact. Those were my instructions. Right now she's probably no idea of where you're at but some day she'll open up a magazine and, whammy, figure there's a meal ticket somewhere out . . .'

D.—C

'Christ, I'm not reaching you! I told you not to tell me!'

Abruptly, without unfreezing, the tensed statue had been possessed. His arm came up and dashed the salt-rimmed glass splashing into the pool. Its spiralling contents wreathed lazily away. Tom stared fascinated as it hung translucently near the bottom. Then he looked back at Madison. The gesture had been so sudden and so charged with violence he had actually recoiled thinking to be struck. Had it happened? Madison had returned to his unmoving stance. But, yes, the glass was there slowly sinking deeper still.

'If and when,' Madison said, 'you get to her . . .' A sighing wind filled the long pause. 'Take care of it,' he said, 'and just remember. I don't want to know.'

This time, Tom knew, the better part of valour was a nod.

He reached towards Paul's arm, but did not touch it.

'You need another drink,' he said.

At last the eyes blinked and the too smooth, too tense face relaxed. Madison smiled and his hand sketched the ghost of an apology through the air. For a moment all the charm and composure flooded back. And then it was gone again.

'Stay on the bench,' he said. 'I guess that as of now I'm old enough to manage for myself.'

He turned and walked away.

Tom watched him go. So soon, he thought, so soon. He felt a black and sour annoyance clawing inside him. He had liked to think that Madison gave him less shit than he contemptuously dealt out to the others; that Madison acknowledged between the two of them some kind of we're above-all-this equality. No chance. The star in the making had just looked him straight between the eyes and diminished him. De-balled him – in spades. In perpetuity. Frankenstein was right on the button. You create them, animate them, feed them their lines, and they destroy you. The guy at Fox who said the inmates were taking over the asylum was the sage of the year. Barbara had set him up, Madison had put him down.

In the meantime he stood stock still and not by a long way nearly drunk enough. Alone, the night air colder now, he stared moodily across to the far end of the enormous garden. The hired group was playing soul. The music taunting him, he lurched away from the pool.

A familiar face shone into view. Its owner, an agent clutched his arm. 'Just seen your new boy. You got something big there.'

It was cold in the garden now to the point of unpleasantness. Almost all of the earlier loungers on the patio had regrouped around the indoor fireplace. Only a few earnest couples still remained quietly making play, or audibly talking deals. They had all given up the game of posturing like models in the glossy ads. The pop group had split. The outdoor bar staff were beginning to stack empty bottles and clink dirtied glasses with a mean professional explicitness.

Their hints were perceived but disregarded by Paul Madison. He thrust an empty glass across the freshly stained white tablecloth.

'Another,' he said.

Cigarette ash bowled across the cloth.

'Margarita, sir?'

'Si.'

The unnatural cast of the lights had turned the barman's thick features a sickly shade of orange. The malice in his eyes was unmistakable. It was the hatred of the underprivileged for those who have. The hatred of all those whose time was at another's beck and call. Paul Madison recognised it well. And enjoyed the recognition. It added savour to the thrill of triumph pulsing through his veins.

'There, sir.'

Madison took the glass from the Mexican and, for an instant, as the peon face stared insolently and unblinking into his, felt his thoughts slither towards the trapdoor in his mind. Earlier, Leonard's talking had pushed him there, abruptly sprung it open. He had glimpsed the nightmare darkness of the bottomless shaft down to the past. Perhaps to the future. Then with desperation, he forced the trapdoor shut.

He made another effort now. He spun on his heel and drank. The salt bit at his lips, the sweet mixture of tequila and triple sec slipped across his tongue as easily as syrup. It's like pussy straight from the bath, he thought, and knew he was himself again.

He stared up at the house set on the artificial mound. Silhouettes were blocked out on its brightly lit windows. His head knew it was cold but his body was still insulated by the liquor and a sense of exultation. He had them! He had it all now! The days when, his hands scalding, he had washed dishes down on Figueroa were gone forever. He had broken through! He was on to them! He had them by the balls. Their hearts, their minds would follow. And just whatever props he wanted. Well, he wanted! Tonight he'd ditched the automatic pilot and from here on in he was taking back from Life some fraction of what its greasy deck had so long sharped for him.

Behind the flicker of distant foliage, the lights of a departing car glided silently down towards the guarded gate. The movement stabbed him into action. He shivered, without looking tossed the drained glass back on to the table. He must go on in and see about getting laid.

It was not outrageously late. Only a small proportion of the guests had specific jobs to go to at the crack of the invading dawn. An actress or two, an editor, maybe a costume designer had probably upped and gone. The producers, agents, out of work directors and stars could bide their time. Tomorrow could start with a Bloody Mary around noon. The rest of the day they'd take as it came, or as it took them.

Madison surveyed the field.

Nothing. The crowded room had been cast by a good assistant director. The clusters were formed neat with no-one obviously shaken loose and cruising. The music had changed. A piano tinkled in a 'forties way and he had the quick impression that somewhere around he would see Bette Davis smiling up from the keyboard at Paul Henreid. He squared his shoulders. As he pushed through to the bar he decided, his thoughts running almost sinuously, that he had it in him to earn more money than Henreid would have dared to dream of.

'Margarita.'

'Yes, sir. Just a moment while I mix.'

He went on looking. The woman he was almost certain must be Tom Leonard's wife came by him tightening a stole about her shoulders. There was a tautness to her throat, her jaw, he didn't like but it obviously didn't phase the thin artistic-looking dude who was reaching the silk around her shoulders to help draw it further up across their bony ridges. Madison watched them to the door. Cradle-snatching. The guy was no older than himself. He must find out who the fuck he was.

'Sir. Your Margarita.'

'Oh. Yeah. Thanks.'

A group quite close to him laughed loudly. A woman pushed coquettishly at a man. The group swayed and his eyes, still scanning, were brought up short by a glimpse of a woman sprawled on the floor against the wall. He moved sideways. Now he could watch her with less foreground interference. Other people, men and women, were elegantly alongside chairs, settees, the better to stare up adoringly at the owners of the feet they reclined by. But the graceless, skid-row slump of this one's posture set her instantly and gracelessly apart. Her head sagged. Her eyes were closed. She looked like a fighter hit by two quick lefts to the body and a finishing right cross who'd never get his butt up off the canvas, his back off the ropes, without help. Intrigued, almost feeling he'd seen her before, Madison moved forward. In a thick-carpeted no-man's-land between two garrulous groups he paused, ten feet away, to look at her more closely.

She was brushing middle-age, and what had been firm was run to flabbiness. Her head was slouched sideways. The cheeks on her pallid face were pouches. There was tell-tale heaviness about the upper arms which protruded from the ill-chosen and, now that he looked, badly dated evening dress. A little apart, her legs were stuck directly out in front of her in parallel like a rag doll's. They'd been well-made, no doubt about that. And like the rest of her, blow the dust off, walk her to the light, and you'd have to concede there was still a touch of class. A sense that a thorough-bred, having stumbled badly, had been put too early to grass. But looking at her now, the thin straps of her elegant but scuff-soled shoes cutting into her insteps, made him wince. Christ! What a broad! Who the fuck let her in! There was a large dark wipe of dirt across part of the skirt and a moist yellowed stain centrally emphasised the slack thrusting belly beneath her thick-ened waist. Jesus Christ!

But as, fascinated, oblivious to voices to the right and left, he continued to stare, it slowly bore in on him that he was looking at the wreck of a great beauty. Middle-aged perhaps, but the skin was still of a whiteness to scorn the soiled cream of her dress. Classic bone structure still gave distinction to the thickness of the face. And the great sweep of chestnut hair was ageless. It was the better for its windswept tousledness and for the highlight streaks of grey she hadn't cared, most likely hadn't bothered, to match-dye. Memory nagged at him. From this angle the head was down and inclined away from him but it seemed to him . . .

Movement out into the edge of his vision. He shifted his gaze. A short bald man was edging along the wall. He held plates piled full with canapes high in both his hands. There was no way he could clear the spread skirt and stretched legs in one stride. He didn't even try. His gold-barred shoe trod on the nearest flare of dress. The other hovered blindly above the woman's shins. He tried to peer down past the load he was carrying, then half-stumbled. Mayonnaise, pimento, fell plop on the dress, wine splashed alongside. The woman stirred and half-raised her head. The mouth opened wider but the eyes stayed shut. After a second the lips stickily closed and the head lolled doll-like down again.

'Hey, mister,' a voice called. 'Where'd you learn waiting table?'

Madison sensed a fall of silence on the groups around him. The voice, he realised, had been his own. The short bald man was turning around awkwardly. He had tufts of wiry hair above each ear. Deep regular grooves on the forehead of his monkey face ended at what had been his hairline and his skull rose up above with disconcerting smoothness. A plate in either hand he stood now like a Soviet caricature of justice in the West.

'You talking to me?' he said.

'No-one else.'

The man's thick nostrils flared with his quick intake of breath. His arms quivered. For an instant it appeared that with small variation on the custard-pie routine he might let fly with a plate.

'You know who I am?' he hoarsely said.

Madison felt the pool of silence widen.

'I don't want to know the who,' he said. 'I already know the what.'

This time the hiss of breath was outward. Paul Madison stepped forward thinking to swing first. Then as the baboon seemed to back off, Dennis Curtis was standing between them.

'Steady, old chap' Curtis said easily. 'No point in putting up a black. I suppose we can still use that phrase these days?'

'You see what he did? He walked all over her.'

'I'm afraid that's always been our dear Judd's form ever since good manners went out of style. Anyway, let's face it, it's what she's long grown used to.'

'Who—'

'And there was a time,' Curtis said, 'when if she had flicked one eyelash Judd would have come crawling.'

'Who the hell is she?'

'You don't know? My dear chap. Look again.'

Madison stared down. The woman stirred.

'Christ, yes! Stella . . .'

'Exactly!'

As Curtis nodded a key turned inside Paul Madison's brain. Jesus! That broad, dripping with spilt mayonnaise was Stella Lang.

'You're kidding,' he said on reflex, but yes, he'd heard all the talk. He could see now it was true.

This time Curtis shook his head.

'I only wish I were,' he said. 'Heavens, I wish I were. But if you still can't believe it, go ask the Beverly Hills Police Department.'

'Why – what have they got on her, murder one?'

'It's no joke, my friend,' Curtis said quietly. 'She still lives in the palace Herman bought for her up on Mulholland. All alone. Bit of a relic now. She's broke. Oh, maybe a cook, a handyman. She gets lonesome. Three o'clock she calls up the police, tells them she's seen a prowler. There's no prowler. She's lonesome. She just wants someone to talk to . . . so, you alright now, chum?'

'What? Oh, yeah. Yeah. Thanks.'

'A pleasure.' He began to go.

'Hey, Denny. Really. Thanks.'

'As I already said – a pleasure. You can do the same for me sometime. Ciao.'

Curtis slipped away. Madison looked down on the drunken woman whom he now knew to be Stella Lang. Man! Ginger Rogers, Rita Hayworth, Ann Miller, Cyd Charisse, Stella Lang. Ask ten people with memories, which one had the most educated legs in musicals and six would have said this creature now at his feet. There was that famous story of the single take without a single later cut-in. And, solo, she'd been as big as Hepburn, Crawford, Davis. Until . . . what? Someday my prince will come, the old song went. Only this was a Swedish diplomat and he hadn't been much use to her.

Talk had resumed around him. Slightly to his own surprise he found that he had moved forward and was kneeling down. Tentatively he tried to ease the glop from off her dress. He could see now that she might once have danced in that dress. And these shoes. The mess really needed a knife but maybe his handkerchief . . . At a disadvantage as he crouched, he reached for it and as he did her eyes opened and she looked directly at him.

Her eyes were brilliant violet-blue, the whites bloodshot. For a long count of heartbeats they struggled to find focus but, before they found it he could tell she was not quite so far gone as the whole room must believe.

'A nice guy,' she said. 'A relic. Thanks.'

A river of drink was eloquently present in the huskiness.

'You heard?'

'Eyes shut to keep the fools away. Ears open to hear them.'

Madison said, 'Well – no damage done. Unless you would have preferred thousand island dressing.'

She smiled. An old sad tiredness hung about the corners of her mouth, old, old defeats were in her eyes. But generosity and the flawless lips still raised the smile to a rare pitch of beauty.

'Another reason for keeping your ears open is you get to hear when people want to buy a girl a drink.'

He was all but on his feet again when her voice reached up to pull him down.

'No,' she said. There was panic in the syllable. 'Don't go. What's that you've got in that glass?'

He told her. The lips this time stayed closed, only pulled wider to etch bitterness across her face. Her arm reached heavily up.

'Sweets to the sweet,' she said. 'Booze to the boozed.'

She made two grabs at the drink and he guessed she needed eyeglasses as well as sobering. The perfect mouth slurped noisily and the liquid was all gone. She grimaced with feeling.

'Ugh,' she said. 'Never could take that stuff.'

Again he made to rise. 'What would . . .?'

'No! Stay here. Buy my house instead – 's a big house. All empty now so you won't have long to wait when I move out. Take no time at all. Had to sell so many things. Dark squares on the walls where there were pictures. Modigh-yawhatyacallit and an iddy-biddy one by Degas which always reminded me . . .'

Her voice had trailed away just as moving away from his face her eyes had grown blurred again in swimming into the past. He looked at her now in a new way. The fullness that had spread the dancer's figure was ripely evident in breasts sagging far lower than in her lacy pin-up days. But with an added heaviness. He had a sudden vision of her naked in his bedroom. She standing in half darkness at the foot of the bed. He lying upon it. Those breasts would dip. But still curving round. The hair would be freer, tossed back behind her shoulders. Like the breasts, the belly would droop, curved convexly but that would serve to concentrate attention on the bush of hair in shadow on its under-rim. Within the flatness of his own stomach, deep at the base of his spine, he felt a quickening. There, where it mattered, he seemed suddenly charged, felt that slow, hot kindling in his flesh. He knew he wanted her. This frayed bag, naked, standing thick-haunched by his bed, would be a kind of ultimate. Luscious – no, not luscious but over-ripe and smothering, Yep, it could just work. It would have a kind of slushy ecstasy. Like sliding to a winning touchdown through a sea of mud.

'What's your name?'

He blinked. It was as though she'd read his thoughts – almost as if she'd sensed his pain at her wretchedness and spoken with distracting kindness.

'Paul Madison.'

She nodded. 'I read about you,' she said. 'Yes. Sure. I keep up. I've got a lot of morbid curiosity. They say you'll be real big.'

'We'll have to see.'

'Oh, won't we just. But if you make it, lots of luck. That's when you need it.'

Whether or not they saw him closely the eyes told him she had spoken without rancour.

'Look,' he said. 'How are you getting back to this big house of yours?'

She just looked at him. He wondered if she'd heard.

'I mean,' he said. 'You look to me like you could use a ride.'

The tightening of her face showed that she had heard him alright.

'How old are you?' she said.

It was his turn not to answer.

'Less than half my age. I'm old enough to be your mother. Well listen, kid. I wouldn't fuck with the guy who hired me, what chance you think you've got? I've been married to the best. Right out of the top drawer. I been married to a guy hung the way studs like you have forgotten. So what makes you think I need you. What makes you think I'd insult myself by letting you go tell your friends you had me for a one-night stand and all I charged you was a little company?'

There was rancour in plenty now. The disdain she had aimed at herself was now projected as savagely at him. He had a sense of people once more growing quiet behind his back and turning round to look.

'That wasn't the idea,' he quietly said.

'It was,' she said, 'and we both know it.'

Weariness came back into her voice and took away the edge of stridency.

'Go on,' she said, 'beat it. If it'll help you to think I'm sorry I yelled, you may.'

She closed her eyes.

He ducked his head. Slowly, giving the people just in back of him plenty of time to turn away again, he stood to his full height.

Now he turned. Nobody was quite looking him in the eye but the looks they gave each other matched their knowing grins. What the fuck? What did he have to lose? He turned back toward her.

'Lady,' he said, speaking loudly, 'you're flattering yourself by fifteen years. Twenty.'

Not opening her eyes, as wearily as ever, she had an answer.

'Up yours!' she said.

The surrounding laugh confirmed for him that what he had had to lose was the last word, and there was no coming back again. Empty-handed, he made tracks for the bar.

It had gone wrong. He had been kicked in the balls by an expert. He with his bleeding heart had been prepared to ride her home and screw her as a bonus, and she, no longer in a seller's market, had told him to go screw himself. That loud 'Up yours!' from this juiced-up broad on the carpet, was the put-down of the year. And she'd had an audience. A shitty one, but an audience. Well screw them too. One day the deck would be stacked in his favour and he would walk away the big, big winner. Now? Who gives a shit for these people anyway? Scratch them and if they bled at all they'd bleed Arpege and alcohol. He knew if he were prone and dying on a sidewalk, they'd step over him to buy *Daily Variety*. Well he would piss on them, in time. Now he needed a drink. 'Up yours!' Jesus, this room, it sucked.

To his left as people rose to go, he saw Tom Leonard sprawled in a chair. He was beaming with an alcoholic, motiveless grin. Perhaps he was just trying to be polite. Christie Roberts was leaning over Leonard, their heads close. Her silver sheath dress, her boy's chest, the slick of short fair hair sideways across her skull made her appear a hinge-jawed mannequin. It was not true as he'd implied to Leonard earlier, that he had propositioned her. He'd not even had the thought. Sure she might have been there for the taking. If a guy could get a hard on while she talked. She had the one-dimensional seriousness of the totally self-oriented. He knew that while his hand was trying to soften the going she'd talk on and on, as she had during the photo-call, of her 'master principles' her past triumphs, and, surprise, current plans. He knew that within minutes she'd roll over from a climax and ask him whether she should change her drama coach. Who needed it man?

Looking at her he knew suddenly what he did need.

Some little groupie chick two thousand miles from home and

two months over the minimum. Long hair down her back and jeans so tightly soaked to hug, you could see the outline of pressed open lips.

He cancelled his latest order for a drink and headed for the door. Fuck a formal leave-taking. He had no topcoat. He did have the money, his new credit cards in the wallet in his tux. Money in his jeans. Soon he'd be in hers. Whoever. Wherever.

Despite the low clouds, two bored jockeys were slapping themselves against the cold as he came out the main door of the house. They darted forward to offer to find his car. He cut them short by flicking a five dollar bill at their feet.

'Find it myself,' he said as they stooped.

Twelve minutes later he had the rented Cutlass traffic-jammed nose to tail in the slow crawl along the Strip. The sidewalks were just as choked with cruisers, loiterers. Beneath the neon, in the spill from the headlights, eyes caught other eyes, held or flicked away. Most of them young.

chapter three

. . . weather satellite showing a pretty nifty depression over Washington and Central Oregon. Signs are it's set on heading on down to the Southland, so better batten your hatches tonight, folks – it just could be a wet one.

KNBC News, Channel 4, Los Angeles.

Driven down, perhaps, by some lost Indian god, the rain beat savagely against the windshield. Tires whined. The wipers slapped out their bleared, their all-clear time. Lights dazzled towards him blurrily as they came on and then in a sudden rainslicked whoosh the dark shape of a car was by and gone. High on booze, the night, the girl, Paul Madison laughed out loud. They drove by night, right, and the rain made everything high-powered.

'Something funny?'

'Nope. Just feeling good.'

He did. Once again he could feel the frequencies of triumph pulsing through his veins. What if the party sucked? It was all his for the plundering without his having to join. Hollywood was laid out with its legs spread wide waiting for his rip off. Whatever he wanted, he could take. He was free, white, manoeuvrable. He had momentum. Control. Like the car storming on up the highway, he was driving straight through the middle of the game, piling up the yardage to whatever golden touch down he might care to choose. Control. Yes, that was the word. He'd use them all, control them, just as to its finest limits he controlled this car. Control was power and going places. He sensed the power now, racing through him, felt himself luxuriously dynamic. His spirits surged and, his own man, he carried his own charge.

The warm glow from the precisely laid out dash pointed up the wild, rain-lashed and incoherent darkness of the rushing night outside. There was fury in it and the red stripe was signalling a steady eighty-five and yet inside the car was total calm. It was as if from here, its eye, he controlled the storm as well.

Well-being filled him. He squirmed sideways to his right, extended his free arm further about the girl who, sour-smelling, pushed her slight weight against him. With the extra inches he thus gained, he could feel down to the barely chubby centre of her bra-less boob. She had the smallest nipples. She was that type. She was the type who has them almost hollow. As his fingers worked to make the left one proud, she wriggled harder into him but made no sound. Not even her breathing changed.

She was perfect. He had glimpsed her standing on the Strip alone, a little girl lost. Cops were up ahead running a possession search but there were none that he could see behind. He had wound the window down.

'Want a ride?' he had said.

'Where to?'

'Wherever you want.'

'Monterey?'

Why not? He had nodded. No further questions asked, she had got into the car and he had gunned away out of the traffic.

She was perfect. Eighteen, as she said. Wearing jeans, a denim jacket over a plaid shirt mostly unbuttoned. Her name was Cindy. When she'd made the token joke about dropping the last syllable if he wanted, he had responded to the total aptness of its awful obviousness. She was from Durango, Colorado, she said. Had friends close to Carmel. That was all. He had shut her up. She didn't know of him and he had shut her up before he knew too much about her.

She was perfect. Thin, dark-haired, sallow. She had the washed-out, only just feminised face of a Plains Indian brave. And smelled of sweat, of clothes kept on too long. Gamey. There was this sour, mean smell of gutter, peasant dirt that made her perfect.

'We have the radio on now?'

'Nope. I still like it quiet,' he answered.

It was far too late now to find a motel open. In a moment he would slow and look for a dirt road or some other place to park and give her one good and quick and dirty. In the morning they could find a motel. He'd put his money down and he would have her for the day and for the night if he still felt like it.

'Hmmmh!' She grunted as, unconsciously anticipating, he squeezed her nipple over-hard. The firmness he'd induced softened a touch as she shifted. Then suddenly he needed two hands on the wheel.

A lucky thinning in the rain had showed him through the clear fraction of the wiper's arc that he was right upon a sharp right-handed bend and late in setting the car into it. A pass of the wipers

later and a murderous dazzle of oncoming hi-beams had robbed
him of all sight. Blinded, displaced, heart lurching up into his
mouth, he steered from memory and instinct. For split seconds
he stared into the sun and then into a pulse of purple blackness.
It faded to reveal his lane right between his sights and he could
breathe again.

'Shit!' he said. 'Motherfucker.'

'What?'

Head on his chest, the girl had not even been aware. As his
pulse slowed he allowed himself some praise. Zapped from nowhere by some maniac he had kept his cool, still kept control.
It had to do with being young.

For a moment as satisfaction and relief washed through him
the image of a glass suspended in a depth of pale and artificially
blue water floated out of nowhere on to his inner eye. The image
troubled him. He sensed . . . He began to think about the girl
next to him and what he'd do to her.

He'd have her all ways. Time and time again. Once in the motel
room she'd not get her clothes on again for eighteen, twenty,
thirty hours. Even if he skinned himself alive he'd go until she
begged for him to stop. Now, driving, he felt the gathering
firmness straining at his thin dress pants. He felt a rich core at his
stomach's pit grow warm and liquid in the sweetest of all anti-
cipations. Slim like a colt, not yet a full-fleshed woman, she'd be
perfect! Arms about her like a wrestler, the wedge of his torso
pinning her, he would engulf her with his body.

The swell of pleasure was now intense enough against his cloth-
ing to be painful. His hands upon the wheel itched with a secret
sympathy. Their dryness put them and the whole dash-lit interior
of the car into a different world and time to the brutal rhythms
of the rain outside. Hell, Jesus, doing it in cars with jeans around
your knees, your boots still on, was no man's way to fly. And, hell,
why slow down their progress.

His right hand tugged at his zip, worked at the fly to his boxer
shorts.

'Wow!' the girl said.

'Okay,' he said, 'start paying for the gas.'

As unquestioningly as she had first gotten into the car, she
scrunched back in her seat to make room to bend. Her head came
down. Unerringly, the whole technique bespoke expertise on
familiar territory.

Oh yes, wow, she'd done all this before. And sweet Jesus, was it good. From deeper and deeper within his body the blood seemed to be rushing toward this centre of all pleasures, of the very world. The muscles flat across his belly were aching from the very strain of longing. Provocatively her teeth hinted the spice of danger.

'Don't stop! Don't stop!' he hoarsely said.

Jesus!

The blaze of headlights was total. He thrilled with horror at their head-on imminence. Instinctively he pulled the wheel full back to the right. Tires screeched as the girl screamed and a giant's hammer wrecked at the rear end. The wheel twisted his hands off it. White fence rose up in a hurtling slow motion and then crashed splinteringly away. The giant drove a fist into him that jarred the last bone in his body and the last breath from it. He was squeezed into thick wetness by a boot bone-crushingly across his back.

But still conscious. From somewhere he heard a noise gathering momentum. A slithering, tearing, crunching noise. A shrilly screaming noise. A splashing, steaming noise.

He was on a slope. Rain cascaded about him. He was on a slope, face down. Head up. Rain plastered his hair to his skull. It was hard to breathe. The noise had been somewhere below. He had to look round and down. He went to raise his head and liquid fire ran through him. His head slumped into the mud. It swam sickeningly. But his body knew it was not equal to the agony of throwing up. But there was something down there that he knew he had to see.

Face sideways hard against the streaming earth he somehow slewed his body partways round. He was on a slope, some kind of an embankment to the pavement up above. 'He came straight at me!' his brain screamed. 'He came straight at me.' He was on a slope. The slope ran down into a rain-curtained pit of darkness. A darkness where something gleamed with the reflection of two faint red lights like water. Car taillights. As he watched them they went out.

An enormous pain burned at his middle. His groan rose up the scale into a scream and then for a while as he passed out he was spared the pain of feeling anything at all.

He was falling, falling into nothingness. A nightmare. In a moment he would scream and his dad would come and talk it all away. No, not now. The man had killed his father and the pain was all from where the man had smashed his back against the wall . . .

He opened an eye. Blurredly it seemed to see a wavering pool of light. A boot, black, heavy, fuzzy, stepped into the light. Rain came slashing down between. Light crashed into his brain.

'Here's something,' a voice maybe said.

He began to mumble. Numbers. His memory told him he must above all else keep on with the number.

There is a providence that shapes the end for some of us. Begun at the right one, the endlessly repeated digits formed the number of Lyndon Oates's personal phone.

The phone trilled by Tom Leonard's head less than an hour after he'd laid it down to rest. Slowly, grunting, he came up the long velvet well-shaft of his sleep. Dry-mouthed he came to. For an instant he thought it might be Christie Roberts phoning to say, well, she'd changed her mind and why didn't he come over right away. But as he groped for the receiver he knew it wouldn't be and even if it were, her game no longer seemed worth his tired and detumescent candle. He made the pick-up in one try.

'Hello,' he said.

'Tom. Lyndon. Listen – trouble. Shit just hit the fan and unless we pull miracles it's going to be the edible variety.'

I don't need this Tom Leonard thought. Why am I doing this? He began to listen. His brain was taking information in faster than Oates was delivering it to him. He groped a pad towards him.

'Where?' he said. 'Give it to me again.'

Oates told him.

'Okay – I'll get on up there. Speak to you from there.'

He cradled the receiver, got out of bed.

'Son of a fucking bitch,' he said aloud. 'But he sure as hell needs me now. Let's see the cunt-head manage this one for himself.'

He dressed. He went out of the spare bedroom to his den and reached down his Olivetti portable. He didn't mean to but as he passed the master bedroom, in spite of himself, he took that look inside. By the dawn's early light it looked cold and grey as well as empty.

It was cold. As he felt for a topcoat in the hall closet he heard a car draw up outside. He waited. There were footsteps. A key turned in the lock. To give himself something to do, he was shrugging his shoulders into the coat as the opening door swung Margot into view.

She glanced at him, down at the typewriter.
'You needn't bother to write,' she said.
Outside, the car revved up and moved away.

chapter four

GIRL, 16, HEISTS CAR – DIES.
Following a Route One head-on crash nine miles south of
Pismo Beach last night, police authorities today recovered the
drowned body of Mary-Lee Foster, 16, from the wreckage of a
car stolen only hours before. The '78 Cutlass had plunged head
first into the swollen waters of Alonas Creek. The driver of the
other vehicle, killed instantly, was Ray Browning, 19, an Air
Force corporal from Vandenberg Base. Sheriff Finis Johnson
stated that preliminary investigation suggested the AMC Grem-
lin driven by Browning had crossed into the north-bound lane
of the non-divided road and the impact had forced the Cutlass
up over the berm.
    Also injured was Paul Madison, an actor, travelling behind
the stolen car. In trying to go to the aid of Foster amid last
night's torrential rain, Madison lost his footing and crashed
down onto the submerged car itself sustaining multiple injuries
and lacerations.
    'It was a brave thing to try,' Sheriff Johnson said, 'he's lucky
to be the one alive.'
    Madison, now 'comfortable' in the San Marino, Los Angeles
nursing home to which he was removed is reported as saying,
'It was a crazy play to go for but if I hadn't tried I'd have
wondered for the rest of my life if I was chicken.'
    The Oldsmobile had been stolen earlier the previous day
from the parking lot of a Lompoc supermarket . . .
                                            Lompoc Chieftain.

They were doing their usual good lunch. Tony Rivera was in a
good mood. The place was its usual booked-full self and no jerk
to whom Tony didn't care to play host had come in demanding a
table. Three kinds of restaurant in this town, he found himself
thinking once again. The kind where you go to eat. The sort where
you go to be seen. Sort where you go to be not seen and talk
business. My sort. Sort I prefer. Food's better and the customer
doesn't pay for some half-ass decorator's Ferrari.

The decor of his place on Camden was unpretentious, but the steaks were as good as you could find in town. It was as simple as that. In a lull between customer coming and going he stood close to the entrance with a sharp eye on the waitresses and their orders. Nothing he saw disturbed his sense of professional satisfaction.

Martin Cohen was talking to Mike Fortman. Law, insurance and show-business. Blend smoothly with a hint of bitters and cream off the dividends. Irwin Blacker made a fast, expansive point to a Haskell Wexler as he chewed. The college maybe needed finance for another scholarship.

'Tony. George Marks wants a booking for tomorrow night.'

Mario was standing in front of him. He looked like the waiter from any film you ever saw and his wise, tired eyes already knew what the answer would be. Tony Rivera shook his head.

'Not then. Not ever,' he said.

Marios nodded a quick dart of approval and went back to the phone.

At a far table sat Lyndon Oates, Tom Leonard, of course, and Stanley Markovitch. He had helped seat and menu them himself but his chief asset was reading the signals that they were in too serious a mood for passing banter. You'd say that they had problems. They were making a point of not being eavesdropped and beneath that neat, square, buttoned-down top dressing, Leonard looked bushed to hell.

'French mustard, sir?'

The waiter was serving the fillets and they'd stopped all talk.

'English,' Oates said.

Tom Leonard nodded he would have the same. He felt almost too tired to talk. The inside of his eyelids, his gut, his very scrotum all seemed made of emery paper. He felt as if he were enclosed in a belljar from which someone was suffocatingly pumping all air. Across the room not quite in focus, as if the glass dividing them was optically impure, he made out Tony. He felt a stab of envy. In his open-necked Ted Lapidus shirt the restaurateur seemed to personify a freedom from all care. His tightly curled, grey Italian hair, his hard-living playboy face placed him at the peak of good-living middle-age. He looks like a welter-weight champion, Tom thought, who knew enough in the ring not to get hurt bad and knew enough to quit the moment his legs started slowing and who's had five times as many women in his time as he had fights in his career.

'Tom!'

The waitress had disappeared and they had started up again. Irritably he turned his head. Why the hell couldn't they have all met up back at the shop?

'Tom, Stanley was trying to say he thinks it's a pity Paul's name was brought into this thing at all.'

Fatigue made him more direct than usual.

'As he's already said. And as I've already said he *was* in it – right up to his prick – and too many people saw him there. Now, listen Stanley, I was the guy went up there. I was the guy on the spot. I made my decisions and acted accordingly. I played the hand just about as well as anyone could the way the cards were lying. You can do better? Next time you go.'

'Hey, Tom – easy.'

Like a Colonial administrator at the club, Oates turned his hand in a quick, nervous semi-circle in case the native bearers might be listening. 'I'm sure Stanley appreciates that you did absolutely the best the circumstances allowed and that we're all very lucky he's got a client who's still viable in the market place.'

'Right,' Markovitch said. 'Hey, sorry Tom. I appreciate what you've done. I do.'

His florid face was close to a pink grapefruit colour from the strain of apology. Like an infant on the pot, Tom thought.

'Jesus,' Markovitch said. 'Thank Christ we were thrown clear.'

'We?' What we, Tom thought.

Oates abruptly snorted, laughed.

Markovitch's head jerked back with annoyance that his plural usage should be a target for derision. But Oates's mind was on on another tack.

'You don't wear safety belts in any car you're fucking in,' he said. 'Jesus! What a combination. One guy with his head squashed like a tomato dropped ten floors and one guy with impressions on his dick any dentist in town could work up a plate from.'

His serrated knife drew easily through the yielding flesh of his blue steak.

'Hey, what about the guy?' Markovitch said. 'The soldier? Are we—'

'Airman,' Tom said. 'Well, we're lucky there. We've been lucky so many ways considering it had to happen at all.'

'Any more luck like this I shan't need—'

'The guy was in service because he was an orphan. No next of kin. He was out on a forty-eight-hour pass and had been staying with his girl in Fresno. According to the cops he'd drunk himself

silly. Screwed himself thin. No time to sleep. Left it late leaving.
They figured he fell asleep at the wheel trying to make time. Anyway, thank Christ that's the way the Captain read it – says that
stretch is quite a murder alley. The military won't start throwing
shit. Raise too many questions.'

Markovitch was mopping his face with a handkerchief

'One thing, Tom', he said, 'I can't thank you enough for getting
us to Eichler so soon. He's still the best there is.'

'Hell,' Tom said, 'I knew we had to pre-empt him fast. I got his
clinic on the car phone on my way to the scene, told them to
put him on standby. Then when I saw Madison's face – mask of
the Red Death stuff – I called Eichler's assistant and warned that
they'd need more than a couple of Band-Aids.'

Markovitch looked unsure. He wiped sweat off his palms with
a monogrammed handkerchief.

'I don't know about this no-stitches business,' he said. 'I hope
to Christ Eichler's right. If the marks show it'd put Madison out
of business. What do you think Lyndon?'

'Like I said, Alex is the best in town.'

'If he uses stitches,' Tom said, 'however brilliantly, there'll be
scar tissue. That's what he says. And you'll see that tissue in
close-ups. The lacerations are total, but all superficial. Relatively,
anyway. The eyes are okay. Paul can't wash for two weeks and in
two more, Eichler swears, the cameras will be turning on him
again.'

'Yeah, that's the greatest stroke of luck of all,' Oates said.
'We've already got six weeks work from Madison in the can. It'd
cost us more than they pay McQueen these days to recast and
start all over.'

'How was Rosner this morning, Stanley?' Tom asked.

'Pretty burned up but not too much,' Markovitch said. 'He's
a realist, is Milton. Enough to know that this is one big insurance
claim we pick up on. By the way, he said he's gonna call you boys.'

Oates winced. 'I don't like summit meetings,' he said.

'We're okay on the insurance bit,' Tom Leonard said. 'Ted
Putnam knows we scratched his back last time. We're due a big
favour. How does this affect the shooting, Stanley?'

Markovitch consulted a suede-backed scribbling pad. 'As you
know they're shooting round Madame while she's giving it to
'em in Vegas. Schneider says he's bringing forward the Preston
stuff – there's a whole chunk of that – which means locations
now in New York instead of three weeks from now.'

'He's not admitting to it of course,' Oates said to Leonard, 'but the bastard is really delighted. He was four days down on schedule. Now this gets him off the hook.'

'That's nice,' Markovitch said, 'we have to have a major accident, pay the best plastic surgeon in Hollywood to repair the damage; our insurance premiums hit the roof, all to get Mr Fucking Schneider off the hook.'

'Cool it, Stanley,' Oates said. 'We just want the logistics, not the bullshit.'

Two red spots appeared high on Markovitch's cheeks. A rapid internal calculation however, persuaded him against a clash on status. First off they were all in the shit together. And soon Oates and Leonard would have to start explaining things to Rosner. He, Markovitch, had survived, made more money than he could ever spend, by taking crap from stars, producers, and now fancy press agents like Oates. In this town, survival was the name of the game. They had to face Rosner. Good luck!

'Alright, this is the play as I see it,' Markovitch said. 'The movie loses maybe only three weeks on its bringing-in date. With the contingency insurance and a bit of luck we may not lose our balls. Of course,' he added with a malevolent grin, 'there's all the below-the-line costs you guys are into, papering up the cracks.'

'What are we up to, Tom?' Oates asked, his tone by-passing Markovitch.

'Thirty – maybe forty. Excluding Eichler's fee. And he doesn't come Blue Cross.'

'Thirty, forty grand! Jesus wept!' the agent exploded.

'Come on Stanley! Do your homework. I had to get to the sheriff. And the half of his department who saw Paul's pecker waving in the breeze. I—'

'Will they stay bought?' Oates asked.

'Long enough. By then it's sealed off. We'll have the leverage then, and we can put on the pressure if it's needed.'

Reassured Oates nodded and returned to his steak.

'There was the editor on that local sheet – the car dealer I had to grab the other car off of. I had to put Madison in a different one from the girl's you see. The real car was rented via Magnum, thank God, so we got muscle there to see the paperwork comes out neat and tidy.'

'All the same,' Markovitch began, 'it hardly seems—'

'And there's the girl's family.'

'Oh yeah. Her.'

'Lucky again,' Tom said. 'A Mary C. Brown. Local. From Redondo Beach. I got to an elder brother. He's married, solid citizen. When he came down to the morgue to wrap up the ID. It seems she had a history of coming into LA this last year or so and making her little scene. He knows she'd used grass – is pretty certain she was into acid. And . . . oh yes, she was having driving instruction down at good old Calvin Coolidge High, so the stolen car angle holds up better than I thought, once we found out her real age. Christ, I was in need of a change of shorts by then, I kid you not.'

'How much to keep the brother quiet?' Markovitch asked.

'Nothing. Directly. He went for the stolen car bit so why jeopardise a genuinely held misapprehension?'

'Hell – no family's complete without at least one skeleton,' Oates said. 'That's right, Tom?'

Cunt, Tom thought.

'What I did,' Tom said, 'was make out Paul Madison had been told what happened in the ambulance; that he'd been touched by the circumstances and being wealthy these days wanted to pick up the mortician's tab and all that jazz.'

'We'll send a wreath in his name,' Oates said. 'No way he turns up in person.'

'And kill all "Actor-Hero" follow-ups,' Markovitch said as quickly.

'It's all in hand,' Tom said wearily.

'Did the brother take the money and run?'

'Yes, Stanley. He was human. Touched even. I also gave him Paul Madison, a local boy routine, almost a neighbour, and how he thought that if he hadn't had the breaks, well, gee, there but for the grace of God . . . I did it pretty well actually.'

He shivered. The room was maybe heavy on the air-conditioning.

'As a matter of fact, it may all turn out rather well,' he heard himself continue. 'No disrespect, gentlemen, to the dead, but right now, outside the trades, Madison's still pretty much unknown. "Paul Madison, actor" the paper said. Six months from now it'll be "Paul Madison the superstar".'

Without warning Oates leaned across to pat Markovitch less than softly on the shoulder.

'There you go, Stanley,' he said. 'I wouldn't say your boy was home free but I'll stake my reputation that's where he is.'

Markovitch choked from pink to crimson. From the impact,

Tom wondered, of Oates's hand or the concept of Oates having a reputation? He hid a smile. As if Stanley should worry. Or Oates for that matter. They were both clean. He'd done the dirty tricks.

Tom settled back into his chair, sipped some more Inglenook. Surprisingly, the weight of tiredness had left him. He could breathe more easily. For seventy-two hours he had buzzed around like a blue-assed fly but he had done a great job, had pulled it out for all of them. It was their asses he had saved.

He glanced around the crowded restaurant and locked eyes with Tony Rivera. There was no sense of distance or of separating glass between them now. He winked, smiled and flicked a hand in quick quasi-conspiratorial salute. There was no real reason. For a moment, conscious of work well done, he had a sense of honour about the way he spent his days.

'What do you hear from Columbia?' Markovitch asked Oates. He was talking loud now for the world to hear ...

Rivera waved back to Leonard. It was good to see the guy had come alive. Thirty minutes earlier he'd been looking like the nominee who hadn't won the Oscar and didn't know he was on camera. Now he looked human at least which meant the food and wine and atmosphere had got to him.

But twenty-five minutes later, as the three agents left, the restaurateur could only change his mind. Leaving between Oates and Markovitch the drawn-faced younger man looked like a soldier just kissed by his Don.

'Jesus,' said Mario to Rivera as the three men left, 'did you take a look at that Mr Leonard? A guy coming in here with a face like that – he can scare off half our trade.'

'Why do you think I'm in the food business,' Tony Rivera said, 'Steaks I can handle. Kissing famous asses twenty-four hours a day ... there's a customer there wants his check.'

'Mr Rivera, I meant to tell you, Stella Lang wants a booking. I wasn't sure whether you—'

'Jesus!' Tony Rivera said. 'She gives me grey hair. She just collected on this month's relief check?'

'I'll say thanks but no thanks, then, Mr Rivera?'

'Yeah. Do that.'

'Okay sir.'

'Hey, Mario!'

Mario was ten paces towards the bookings table.

'Yes sir?'

'Tell her okay.'

'Yes, sir Mr Rivera!'
'What're you laughing for – like I'm some kind of idiot?'
'No, Mr Rivera. It's just I already told her is okay.'

Milton Rosner's mansion in Bel Air did not descend to such
mortal requirements as having either a name or a number. This
was based on a simple principle. If you did not know it was his
house you had no purpose in being there. High up on a crest,
approached by a long sinuous driveway, it had been one of the
lavish homes Howard Hughes kept for his several stand-by
mistresses. In a way the two lifestyles, his and Rosner's were not
dissimilar. Both were rich, powerful, beyond reach, and ruthless
manipulators of lower echelon people. But unlike Hughes's
Rosner was no recluse. He relished confrontations, enjoyed seeing
other men squirm. A notice on the tall, wrought-iron gates
advised intruders that if the guard dogs didn't get them, the elec-
trified fences certainly would. The vast acreage of lawns, cedars,
Japanese gardens and tropical foliage was festooned with hidden
TV cameras which monitored anything that moved. The mailman
forced on a chilly morning to take a quick leak before the long
ascent to the main, white-pillared house, would be swiftly observed on all Rosner's eight TV screens, from the first furtive
unzipping to the final wriggle of self-adjustment. There was the
mandatory two-way speaker at the entrance into which callers
stated their name and business as obediently as enlisted men
giving their rank and number. Even by Hollywood's security
neuroses, Rosner's fortress seemed overly vigilant. But there were
special factors. In the early days, he had received the odd phone
threat on his life. As executive Vice President of the studio he had
siphoned-off, for his own purposes, chunks of money that were
legitimately due in percentages to producers, directors, and many
major stars. Since all film budgets required his final approval and
all cheques his signature, he could rip them off in a style that
made the skimmers at Vegas seem like amateurs. If other officers
of the company knew the what, and the how, of his operations,
they dared not speak. Rosner had masterminded three blockbusters which had taken the studio out of the red, produced a
total of nine Oscars and seventeen nominations, raising the stock
levels to a record high. When finally, events forced an enquiry
before a Los Angeles Grand Jury, Rosner had paid off sufficient
numbers of accusers to get himself in the clear. Now, five years

later, his personal fortune was said to be upwards of sixty million dollars. His art collection, which included masterpieces by Cézanne, Picasso, Renoir, filled eight rooms at the house. A much sought-after sculpture by Rodin had only recently been acquired from an associate in Paris. Or more accurately from the man's estate, the owner having committed suicide after failing to meet payment on a distribution contract with Rosner. There were threats of bankruptcy and ruin. The man had telephoned Rosner asking for a month's leeway. Rosner had replied in bad French that business was business. The man sent his wife and three children down to La Réserve at Beaulieu, put the muzzle of a Luger in his mouth and squeezed the trigger. Six weeks later, the Rodin arrived at berth seventeen at the New York docks, with a note from the widow as icy as the statue itself. 'Enjoy' it said simply.

Tom Leonard lowered the electric window nearest the call button at the gate. He reached out to press it, noticing – trust Rosner to rise above it – that below them all Hollywood was blanketed by smog.

'Christ, do we breathe that stuff every day?' he said to Oates.

'Night and morning,' Oates laughed. 'Why d'you think they call this Bel Air?'

'Who's this, sah?' the voice of the Japanese houseman sounded muffled, metallic, like the crackle of a pilot's radio.

'Mr ...' Leonard paused to observe the correct pecking order. ... 'Oates and Mr Leonard, to see Mr Rosner.'

There was no further word. The two gates swung open without a sound. The car moved forward a few feet, then paused to break the photo-electric circuit which beamed across their path. The doors glided back behind them.

'Does he know everything that happened?'

'Chapter and fucking verse,' Oates growled, his head back and eyes closed. He's got more spies, per capita, than Nixon had at the White house.'

'What do we tell him?'

'*You* tell him, Tom,' Oates said. 'Just lay it on him the way you told Markovitch at lunch. Jeeze look at those Dobermans!'

Three Pinschers, flat skulled, their black and tan coats hard and sleek, leapt on the car as it swung round in front of the house. Rosner, in a black turtle-neck under shiny black leather jacket, called them off. He was dark, thickly-built, with an aggressive forward tilt on his pointed-toe shoes as he walked.

'Hold off Rommel . . . get down Adolph . . . DOWN!' The dogs retreated, rubbing their hard bodies against his legs.

'Okay gentlemen,' Rosner grinned, 'the heat's off. Let's go inside.'

They took the two leather chairs placed squarely in front of Rosner's desk. A third, a turn-of-the-century dentist's chair with straps on the arms, testified to Rosner's fascination for some of the more exquisite facets of pain. The word was that he liked to be strapped naked in it and then taken from hand to mouth and on to a climax by an 'assistant' totally nude under her starched white coat. Leonard noticed the American flag, furled Presidential-style behind Rosner's head. There were no papers on the massive desk. On one side were two portable TV sets. One gave Rosner a round-the-clock surveillance of the entire spread. There was an auto-graphed photo of an English Lord whose charity had benefited by a flat one hundred thousand dollars from a Royal film premiere Rosner staged in London. The ageing peer had returned the gesture by introducing Rosner to royalty, and inviting him to his castle in the North Ridings of Yorkshire for some exclusive hunt-ing, fishing, and screwing.

'Marvellous paintings you have here, Milton,' Oates's tone was deftly poised between respect and friendliness.

Rosner glanced at the walls. 'Set me back a fortune,' he frowned. 'That Manet alone cost a quarter of a million.'

Leonard knew Oates couldn't pick out the Manet from the rest. And Oates knew Leonard knew. Rosner smiled. 'You can look afterwards. They're all labelled. Now let's get down to business. What's all this crap with Madison? I don't buy scandals, you boys know that.'

He stared hard across the table. 'I've heard a lot, I can tell you. And I don't like what I hear.'

Leonard glanced at Oates, who nodded back.

'It's all taken care of, Mr Rosner,' Leonard said leaning for-ward. 'It was hairy for a day or two but it's all in good shape now.'

'We have two corpses on our hands,' Rosner said quietly, 'I don't like that.'

'They're not on our hands I promise you,' Leonard said. 'If you want it on one sheet of paper; an American airman gets loaded, his car lurches over the divider, and hits head-on a hot automobile driven by a kid girl who's into pot and acid. Our man just happened by and comes out like a hero trying to rescue the girl. End of story.'

Rosner stared at Oates.

'That's about it, Milton,' Oates said.

'What about Madison?' Rosner asked. 'He got beaten up pretty bad didn't he? I got a lot of money invested in that face.'

'The surgeon stakes his reputation not a mark will show,' Oates declared.

'I don't go by reputations,' Rosner grunted. 'You can buy 'em and sell 'em. Is the bastard any good?'

'The best,' Leonard said.

'And what about Madison? He's quite a cocksman they tell me.' Rosner removed a cigar from a monogrammed humidor near the phone console. 'Bit early days isn't it for him to start screwing around with pick-ups, like Errol Flynn! Can't he do the decent thing and go for hookers?'

So that bastard knows it all, Leonard thought. Worse than a spy satellite. He probably knows which hand his chauffeur jerks off with.

'It's what I lose and what you both lose, we're talking about,' Rosner said, his tone cruder. 'You see all this?' he waved a hand towards the masterpieces on the satin-covered walls. 'I got 'em, like Avis, by trying harder. I'm not putting them in jeopardy bailing out some half-assed actor who likes to get gobbled on the freeway. I've had all the traumas I need. I'm relying on you both to put the lid down on this one. I'll pick up the tabs, you just make sure that everyone, including Madison, stays in line.'

'Don't worry, Milton,' Oates said.

'I won't,' Rosner smiled evenly. 'You worry for me!'

There were two controls for the television. One was the normal remote switch to allow you to efface Reasoner with Garner, Garner with Savalas, Savalas with Yogi Bear as you rocked around the dial without rising from your chair, in this instance, your bed. The other control, though obliged to make use of a lead, was more exotic. It controlled the electronic, hydraulic and Christ knows what else besides system set into the wall. Finger-tip pressure on a series of rocker buttons allowed you to elevate and swivel the set, depress the tilt of its screen to best suit your infirmity. A man at death's door, the soft black wings of Death beating at the window, could still, if he felt inclined, summon a last effort and go out with Mary Tyler Moore.

In this instance both controls lay neglected on the chrome and smoked-glass occasional table. The room, in eau de nil and mush-room, was reminiscent more of a crisp modern hotel than Doctor Alex Eichler's private clinic in San Marino, California.

Covered only by a single candy-striped sheet, Paul Madison lay propped up in the angled bed and reading. A half-invisible thermo-perspex shield the shape of a station-wagon roof was suspended some three feet above the surface of the bed. Allowing the sun streaming through the window to pass through to the patient, the device prevented the rays from escaping up again. Paul Madison was thus kept optimumly warm while being shielded from unwanted pressure.

His face was bizarre. Two thick strips of white plaster horizontally banded his nose to give him a touch of Chiricahua. The impression was intensified by the dun-coloured, unwashed roughness of the rest of his complexion. Scabs, flakes of dried blood and scurfed skin coated his cheeks and forehead. The face was a moon surface. At first glance. At second it was Martian. Beneath the scabs, alongside, the thin red lines of closing cuts formed an intricate tracery like the enlarged veining on the cheekbones of a drunk. None of the lines looked over-angry. Some had already begun to fade. By now Madison, Lyndon Oates, the assessing surgeon employed by Capital Insurance, were all alike in feeling convinced the features would heal blemish-free. For all three and, indeed, for many others, the consequence was of the highest importance. *Curtain* would continue in the making.

At a cost. A cost to Magnum Leisure of contingency monies running into seven figures. A cost to Paul Madison of an intolerable itching. The cuts had been sterilised and left. Unwashed. As the sour smell of his own flesh odour had mounted through his broken nose Madison had felt the urge to scratch himself becoming nearly unbearable. He had itched to get his hands on his face. A hair-shirt mask had been pressed on him. It required an iron resolution to keep his fingernails from raking at the scabs.

Eichler had offered to bandage his hands to prevent just that. Paul Madison had declined the offer. He had correctly anticipated that his itch for money would prove greater even than the urge to scratch. His control at the car's wheel had been somewhat sensationally less than adequate. His control over himself with a fortune still in the balance had been face-saving.

And not such a price to pay. A broken nose, five cracked or broken ribs, severe bruising, is a small fee to be asked for safe ejection, the odd one of three, from a fatal freeway car smash . . .

Reading had kept his hands full. Thinking preoccupation might begin at home, he had asked for the latest Jackie Collins. If Eichler's know-how was to maintain him among the beautiful people, he should perhaps run a check on what styles his life should imitate. Typically, a nurse had brought him the copy at once from the hospital's own best-sellered library. He had lain back to enjoy. Within thirty minutes he had hurled the book aside. It did not, he saw, suit his purpose. It was for outsiders, looking-in.

On impulse he had telephoned Tom Leonard. Two hours later a yellow cab had rolled to a halt upon the hospital's finely stoned driveway to deliver the collected works of Dickens. He had them stacked next to the crate of Jack Daniels, gift of Jack Preston which in contrast to the harvest-festival flowers from Barbara Lemerle he had elected to keep by him. The get-well-soon card from Arthur Schneider he had flushed down the john.

Previously he had read only one Dickens novel – *Hard Times*, a freshman English requirement. Now, eleven days later, he had read four and was now three-quarters of the way through *Little Dorrit*. It had been hard going at first, needing an initial effort. But that effort of concentration had been just his need. As his itching face begged for relief, he had gripped the book the tighter, willing himself into it. Then, a solenoid opening in his brain, he had become compelled. When he put it down on top of his script of *Curtain* the juxtaposition amused. 'Shit and pineapple,' he said. Yet he had not been depressed. They were not playing the same ball game, not in the same league, that's all. Meanwhile there was something compelling in the way that Dickens, fascinated by his own evil characters, let the dark side of his nature hang right out, as far exposed as any psyche on a Beverly Hills couch. The good guys were more troublesome. Nobody, for fuck's sake, could ever live like that, but yet there was a touch of class to their—

'Well, here we come again!'

As she well knew, the nurse looked like an ad-man's idea of a blonde air-hostess. But it was with an inward sigh of annoyance that he laid the book aside.

'Ninety-eight point four on the button,' he said in anticipation.

'Uh-huh,' she said, 'not today. Doctor Eichler thinks it's time we took a look under those bandages. He'll be right here. In the meantime, I'll just soften them up a little.'

In a uniform more tailored and less highly buttoned than would have been the case in Los Angeles County General, she came towards the bed. She held a kidney bowl in one hand and foil-wrapped sterile gauze in the other.

'Now just hold still there for me like that. That's just fine,' she said.

She leaned across him. For a moment, as he stared down at her breasts, a delicious, heavy scent of musk seemed to rise up from the cleft between them to overcome the sweat-sour stink of his own skin. Then the far cruder smell of some kind of spirit swamped everything. He felt it soak through the tape and moisten the bridge and sides of his nose. The rest of his face itched with a persistency trebly enhanced.

'All rightee ... there you go.'

She removed the whiteness of uniform and cantilevered flesh out from under his nose. As his head naturally came forward to follow her retreat, his eyes were diverted by the bulk of Alex Eichler entering through the opened door.

'Paul, my friend,' the surgeon said, 'how does it go, then?' The cadence was exactly that of an agent. Or better, Paul Madison thought, with the Swiss Alps accent, more like a producer's.

'Pretty good,' he said. 'I'd still give my right arm for a good scratch.'

'So. You are left-handed, then? Let us see. And I shouldn't joke. You have been a good boy to let well alone.'

Eichler approached to take his look. He was of average height but stocky. He had a peasant, potato face saved from being ugly by the lightest of bright blue eyes and, a profusion of tight, natural curls to his dark hair. The face radiated eagerness. The overall effect was of a rather charming, winsome little boy whom many a fine lady might care to mother. The little boy, Paul Madison knew, had been raised in poverty and was now a millionaire.

'Good. Very good,' Eichler said. 'The itching I keep telling you is a very healthy sign. Two more weeks, I promise, your skin is like a baby's. Now – the nose.'

He had a less charming bosom than the nurse's. And short stubby arms, the classic thick squat hands of a surgeon. Or wrestler. The first time Madison had been in any shape to talk, Eichler had appeared to deploy his effortlessly engaging bedside manner.

'You know,' he said, 'when I was a boy in Zurich, everyone said I looked like a butcher. So I thought if that's what I'm cut out for, hell, I'm going to travel in style.'

He was about forty-five with the silken charm tooled to bolster film-star vanities. Behind it, a calculating mind ensured his fat fees were shrewdly invested to take care of old age or the odd malpractice suit. Paul Madison wondered at what stage in the good doctor's career he foresook healing and the more pertinent demands of the Hippocratic Oath in favour of re-treading the rich and the wrinkled.

'Good,' Eichler now said, 'good.'

Like a barber he produced a small pair of surgical scissors from his tunic. He did something deft with them. With only a fraction of the pain Madison had expected, the cut bandages were stripped from about his nose. Very gently Eichler's fingers brushed along its length.

'Good,' he said again. 'In fact, perfect. You know picking the glass out of your face was nothing. Just patience. But setting your nose so that it exactly matched the photograph they gave me . . . that is where I earned my fee . . . Your nose has been broken before in the past, by the way. Did you know that?'

'Yes. I knew that.'

'That's why it has that shape and why it is difficult for me. But I have done it beautifully. Look.'

A mirror flashed in the nurse's hands. Paul Madison looked first at the band of horizontal paleness left by the plaster, then beyond that at his nose.

'It's really me,' he said.

'Still a little puffy. But that will go at once now. Here, I will remove the little bits of stickiness the paster left. Hold still.'

Eichler took the bowl of spirit from the nurse. He began to sponge at the residue of plaster.

'You know,' he said, 'I – oh, Janet, perhaps Mr Madison would like some coffee. I'll handle this if you could fix it. Thank you.'

The nurse left the room.

'You know,' Eichler repeated, 'I lied to you. I really earned my money by not operating on you.' He winked. 'There is a story if you can be discreet.'

'Sure.'

'I mention no names but some years ago a woman was brought to me. A well-known actress. Her breasts, her shoulders, her neck, her face were a mass of fine cuts. Some not so fine. There was in town then, and he still is, a famous producer, somebody who learned his trade in Budapest. There were times, it seemed, when he could only get his jollies, as you would say, by taking a razor blade to the woman and working slowly across her. You under-stand?'

D.—D

'Sure. Nice guy.'

'Charming. And a bad film maker—Well, this woman. I made a professional error. I tried a certain amount of patchwork. After she left here she could go about only in high-necked gowns. Her career was partially saved by cosmetic make-up but she herself had lost her appetite to be a star. She is now dead. An overdose or bad mixture of drugs.'

'Who was she?'

'No names. The next woman this gentleman provided me with, I did nothing with at all. She recovered quite perfectly. As, I repeat, will you. I am now the world's greatest Boy Scout.'

Absolutely aware of the effect his expertise and boyish charm combined to give, Eichler winked again.

'I'll see you tonight,' he said, glancing at the Jack Daniels as he rose to leave. 'I'll need a drink. I've got six pairs of tits to raise between now and then!'

'It's a date,' Paul Madison grinned.

He settled back against the bed. The bridge of his nose now felt perceptibly lighter. He fought back a temptation to sneeze. After a while he reached for the Dickens once again. But before he did so he had allowed his mind to run upon the little proclivity Eichler had just given him an insight on. There was something in the image of a woman's torso, naked and razor-cut, that excited him as much as it disturbed.

'Were you asleep?'

'No. Just closing my eyes and having a sexual fantasy.'

'It's on the house, but don't get too excited.'

His nurse had come back into the room. She stood by the bed, the door half open behind her.

'Could you take a visitor?'

'I thought I was off-limits to callers.'

'You are.' Her nervousness showed. 'This one's persistent. He's a reporter. From the *Examiner*.'

Madison felt a gut tremor that he knew was more than an unease. Fear. What the hell was going on?

'What does he want?'

'Wants to talk to you, I guess. About the accident. You're quite a hero you know. You should see the papers.'

'Screw it, I've got nothing to say.' Irritable, he hauled himself up against the pillows. This was Leonard's department. Where is he anyway? What's the point him pulling me out of one heap of shit only to land me in another. Mustn't panic though.

'Have you heard from Mr Leonard?'

'He phoned about an hour ago to say to call his answering service if I wanted to leave a message.'

'That's great!'

The nurse glanced at her watch. Celebrity or not she wasn't going to get caught up in this hassle.

'What do I tell him?'

'Christ, I don't know, anything you frigging well . . .'

'Mr Madison?' The young man, suede jacket over smart levis stood in the doorway wearing the too-bright smile of the professional intruder. The nurse, angry now, made to bustle him out. 'I'm sorry Mr Madison, I specifically told him . . .'

'That's okay,' Madison said, 'he's doing a job . . .' The actor in him noted reassuringly that his voice sounded casual, almost friendly. 'You can give us ten minutes. If he's still here after that call the Fire Department.' They watched her leave, sharing an appraising wink as the white butt-end of her disappeared behind the door.

'Okay friend. You're breaking all the rules. But make it painless. Too much talking at this stage could fracture the remould.'

'I understand,' the reporter said. 'It's just that we don't get too many actor heroes in Hollywood these days. Trying to rescue that girl from that blazing wreck was one hell of a thing to do.'

Madison's face twitched slightly. He was sweating now. He felt the truth oozing out of his pores. He decided on the double bluff.

'Just did it for the publicity,' he said and they both laughed.

'Maybe. But didn't you figure those gas tanks could blow any second?'

Madison felt the sweat clammy on his face and on the dressings. There were rivulets of it on his neck and spine.

'It was all so fast,' he said scrabbling for words, 'I just did what anybody else would have done.' Christ this was awful. Fuck off, man! Where the shit is Leonard!

'Even so,' the reporter pressed on, 'you had plenty to lose going down those wrecks. Not many actors would have taken the risk.'

Madison rolled his head sideways. Lifted a Kleenex from a pack and saw his hand was shaking. 'What can I say. It's done. It's over. Don't let's make a big deal out of it.'

The reporter smiled. 'Sure. I understand. I won't push it.' He got up. 'I have to tell you, Mr Madison, movie stars are not usually my bag. But it's been a pleasure, and a privilege.'

The nurse stood threateningly in the doorway. 'Okay, I'm off,' he said. She followed him out, gently closing the door behind them.

Madison closed his eyes, sank back against the pillows. The tautness left him. He shuddered.

Oh shit. Oh God!

That this was Southern California summer made not a shred of difference. The fire blazed up as it would do for each day of the year. Memorial to the unknown actor, Tom Leonard thought. Unknown hooker. Going down the list, memorial to the unknown writer. The fire in the open grate of the lobby to the Beverly Hills Hotel. The outer shrine of the high temple.

His steps sinking in the thick greenness of the carpet he made his way across the vastness to the Polo Lounge. A bell-boy crossed his path. His long Scandinavian face was parchment yellow and scored with wrinkles well up to the receded line of his faded hair. He bore the inevitable first name on his lapel. Freddy. As inevitably Tom Leonard wondered where, in what rest homes, what cemeteries, were the child stars of yesteryear.

To his left three ageing women stood on the fringe of blue-rinsed argument. Only the expensiveness of their costumes and the genuineness of their jewellery redeemed them from the category of crone. Playing his private game he ran an eye over them. It was always fun to see whether they were just rich divorcees, mothers of stars, ex-star mothers, or beautifully preserved veterans like Barbara Stanwyck or Gloria Swanson.

'Good afternoon, Mr Leonard.'

As he adjusted his eyes to the darkness of the Polo Lounge's noon, the Captain was upon him noting down his name.

'You wanted a booth I believe, sir.'

'That's right. I'm expecting a Mademoiselle Forrestier.'

'Ah yes, sir. The young lady from *Elle*.'

'That's right.'

'She's not come in as yet, Mr Leonard, but if you care to come this way I'll make sure she's brought to you. Victor!'

'Thank you.' He followed the waiter through the medium noise level of lunchtime Hollywood small talk. No doubt wanting the trip, La Forrestier had swung it. Otherwise she could have stayed at home in Cannes and saved the fare. She could as easily have caught him and all the others in the lobby of the Carlton during the fourteen-day crap game that they chose to call a film festival.

'Anything to drink, Mr Leonard?'

'Johnny Walker – Black Label – on the Rocks.'

'Yes sir.'

She'd doubtless be young and probably beautiful and he hoped she would. But in the meantime he could have another of his meaningless jokes.

He glanced toward the patio area beyond the windows. At the white wrought-iron tables a predominantly female clientele ruminated over their Diet Salads or Tortilla Specials and – just cheating a little, dear - chomped between-whiles on the courtesy celery and olives set out on each table on beds of crushed ice to give an edge to appetite. The concurrent verbal crudities were less immediately apparent but, he reflected, would probably possess a more lingering after-taste.

'Mr Leonard.'

He brought his vision back to gloom and foreground. A waiter was at his table not with a tray and glass but with a telephone.

'A call for you, sir. A Mr Oates. Will—'

'Okay, I'll take it.'

Courtesy of Pacific Telephone Company and a jack, the waiter hooked the phone into the world.

'Tom? Lyndon. You alone?'

'Yes Lyndon, I can talk.'

'Fine. Listen. I just got back in. I have—'

'Good trip?'

'Huh? Oh, fine. Tubby says to say hello.'

'Hello, Tubby.'

'Tom – I have to tell you I'm not too sure you did such a good job covering on our mutual friend's attempt at skinny-dipping.'

Common, not mutual, you common upstart, Tom thought.

'Oh?' he said.

'I have to tell you. Milton's passed on to me a stack of letters. They're on my desk now. Most of 'em have got it right. They're full of the most terrible accusations. Jesus – there's one here talks all the time about our boy as the Chappaquiddick Kid. Now, if—'

'Did they spell it right? Look – how many letters, Lyndon?'

'Er, twenty, maybe. Twenty-five. It's—'

'Lyndon. Something I have to tell you. You're losing your sense of perspective. Twenty-five. Is that all? I mean that's nothing. But nothing!'

'It's twenty-five, maybe thirty people – with friends, friends they talk to – who realise—'

'Lyndon, you know damn well that in this town like anywhere

else only weirdos bigots and faggots write letters. Who gives a shit anyway? Listen, I can't talk. It's like Grand Central. We're in good shape. Forget it.'

'All the same—'

'Lyndon, if we've only got twenty-five letters in we're laughing all the way to the Oscar ceremony.'

'Tom – will you for fuck's sake stop interrupting me! . . . Tom, you there?'

'Still here, Lyndon.'

'I wish I was as sure as you. In any case, here's what we do. I think. When does our boy get out?'

'Two days. Maybe three.'

'Remember the invitation to that kid's hospital thing way out at Riverside? Is that still on?'

'Not for him. We nixed it weeks ago on account of his schedule.'

'What date was it?'

Tom spun the tumblers of his mind.

'It was a Thursday. It's . . . day after tomorrow.'

'Fine. Get him back in there, will you. I don't care who else they got. Get the fucker out of it and get our boy in. Call up the superintendent or matron or whatever they have. The mayor. Use the accident as a reason for the availability and talk money. Much as it takes. A donation, right.'

'Right. A donation.'

'Name a bench or a ward or something after him.'

A shit-house? Tom wondered.

'And see it's covered big. Up to local TV. You may be right, I hope to Christ you are, but from where I sit we can badly use a Mr Clean campaign before this whole thing snowballs.'

'Oh, I'm sure we won't use it badly, Lyndon. Anything else?'

'Isn't that enough?'

'I'd say so but I was just wondering if there—'

'Tom, I have to tell you, I'm not sure—'

'Got to hang up, Lyndon. Our French connection just came on the line. Talk to you later. 'Bye.'

Pissed off, he cradled the receiver. There was no Mlle Forrestier approaching. Only the waiter with his drink. He sipped it sourly. He fished in his inside pocket for the book of numbers.

Two minutes later he saw the Captain unmistakeably gesturing towards him from across the crowded gloom. As he rose to his feet, his heart sank to his Church shoes. At thirty paces he could tell that Mlle Forrestier was short and plump and middle-aged, ferociously efficient and equally as butch.

The door to the eau-de-nil and mushroom private room was opened and the patient on the candy-striped bed looked up from his book. A nurse, looking, as she well knew, like an adolescent's image of a backing singer for Diana Ross stood grinning at him with quite perfect teeth. Her uniform, a dazzlingly white contrast to her skin, was a little shorter than the recommended length at training college.

'You got a visitor,' she said. 'A lady. Okay?'

'No such animal,' Paul Madison said. 'But okay – who?'

'She said to surprise you.'

'Young, blonde and stacked?'

The nurse grinned again.

'None of those,' she said, 'but if that's what turns you on I'll go get a rinse.'

As she turned away Madison watched the long sweep of slender legs Eichler seemed not to require to be stockinged in white. In bitter-chocolate they were classic and for a moment, imagining them muskily tight about his neck he felt his spirits lift beneath the candy stripes.

The door opened again and another woman came in. She was far from young, and podgy in a coat two ways beyond belief. It was mink – incredible in the seventy-one degrees they'd given it on TV. It was an aged mink – soiled, stained, matted in places, balding in others. His blood froze. With heart-stopping certainty he knew that if, in any second, the woman removed the great lemur-like eyes of her sunglasses from her puffy face, he would be looking for the first time in a decade and a half at his own mother. His hands tightened on the book as her own hand came up to the glasses. Rigid and aghast he was powerless not to look. She removed her glasses and he found himself staring straight at Stella Lang.

'Well,' she said, 'I could always step back outside and try coming in again. Alternatively I could step back outside and keep on going.'

'I'm sorry,' he said, 'I thought you were somebody else.'

He relaxed, slumped back into his plumped-up pillows. He could feel sweat standing out on his forehead, trickling down the centre of his chest into the crepe bandaging.

'A guy you knew from Kansas City?'

'Huh?'

'Never mind. Mind if I sit down?'

'Oh yeah. Sorry. Sure, go ahead.'

She did that, and fumbled in a purse new and stylish once upon a time.

'Mind if I smoke?' she asked.

'Christ, no.'

'Want one?'

'I don't. Never have.'

She grimaced. 'Smart,' she said. 'I do. You know once in a while they still play my version of "Once In A While".'

'I like your voice. It's full of old sins.'

'That's a brand I've used a lot.'

'I don't have fire.'

'That's okay.' She lit her cigarette. Inhaled. When she tilted her head back to exhale the ghost of old beauty came into the room a second. And left. In broad daylight the ravages to face and body showed painfully. More so when, as now, the chin was raised proudly, oblivious to the rest of her which resembled a mudded, torn-off cover of a years-old magazine.

'Shit,' she said. 'I can't think of a thing to say now. I always used to be this way in hospitals I suddenly remember. I didn't have a thing to say to one husband when he was stretched out dying after his plane crashed. But then I didn't have anything to say to him the day before or the year before, or the second day after we got married.'

'You could try a "How are you coming along?" '

'How are you coming along?'

'Don't even ask.'

For the first time in their acquaintance she smiled with instant and complete spontaneity. The violet and bloodshot of her eyes looked suddenly straight at him from behind the swollen lids.

'Don't worry,' she said, 'I'm not going to ask you what really happened. I've known what lay behind too many handouts in the trades to do a thing like that . . . Jesus, the stories . . . I guess I should've let you take me home at that.'

He found her impertinent.

'So why did you come?' he asked.

'Partly that. Because I didn't let you . . . You said I was presumptuous. Later I gave you the benefit of the doubt on that. Now seeing you in a bed I know I was right in knowing what you were thinking . . . When you getting out?'

'Day after tomorrow.'

'Over the wire?'

'Roco got to the Governor, see, I'm getting a full pardon, see.'

'Let me guess— Jimmy Durante.'

'Right.'

'There's not too much damage I can see from here.'

'It's nearly all gone. I was leaving the end of the week but there's some charity stunt I have to make a show at.'

'There would be.' She laughed loudly. 'But, like I said, I don't want to know.'

'Will you for Christ's sake—'

'I'm sorry . . . Truly. I wanted to be nice because I finally remembered you were nice to me. You know, trying to clean up my gown. You were the first new person to be nice to me since, hell, I don't know. Since the Dodgers played in Brooklyn. That broke a rule. No-one new is ever nice to me. And damned few old. Just one or two, maybe, who're real old.'

Without warning she had begun to quiver. Now it was she who was locked by tension from within.

'I can tell there's some Jack Daniels in the house,' she said.

'Help yourself.'

She rose, took the bottle and glass from his bedside table and poured generously. As generously, she drank. There was no gagging, shuddering. Hard and businesslike.

'Watch out,' she said. 'I'm already bloated and blowsy. This'll bring out the screamer or the suicider. I never know which way the bitch will jump.'

'I knew someone who kicked that habit once,' he said.

'He stopped drinking,' she said. She wagged a finger at him. 'Stay clear of old movies and their lines,' she said. 'You can't live your life by them.'

'Yes, ma'am.'

'It doesn't work like that – booze. Don't have romantic fantasies that you met me and smiled and I was springboarded up on to the wagon. I wasn't. I won't be. No more than I'll be twenty-three again. I need the stuff. Chemically I need it. Only—'

She paused as she poured another.

'Only?'

'Only it's killing me. And I'm afraid to die. If there is a – well, never mind that. Part-reason I came was it's been so long since I was this side of a hospital bed . . . I thought maybe it wouldn't seem so grim and maybe I might go off yet some place one last time and try to get myself dried out. I find it is, though. Grim.

Maybe I'll just stop all by myself.'

She drank again and as quickly.

'Mañana,' she said.

'Tomorrow always is another day,' he said, 'and look what happened to her.'

For a different reason once again she didn't quite shudder.

'I know,' she said quietly. 'I can't bear that side of me. The one thing I had most of all and more than any of them was true class and now . . . now I couldn't be the stooge to a Mexican knife-thrower . . . Now I don't have mirrors in the house.'

She downed the empty glass and pulled the bedraggled mink tight about her as if in the actions she would forthwith begin a brand new life.

'I'll go before I get too loaded to drive,' she said. 'Thanks a final time.'

He shrugged. 'Anytime.'

'I got lonely, you see. I couldn't bear that either and—'

'Yes. I know. That goes too. Come around – any time.'

She paused in the doorway. Oh God, he was thinking, she will.

'Getting strapped down on beds comes really high,' she said. 'I've got to sell my house. I really do. It would be nice to see it go to someone like you. Somebody with class.' She laughed. 'Well, less bad!'

'Stella. It's not like you think. I don't have that kind of class. Your kind.'

'Oh yes. You do. But be original. Try keeping it.' She took a step towards him back into the room. He was afraid she might stay. 'You didn't mind, did you?' she said.

'I told you. Anytime.'

With some return to her long vanished style she put the shades back on and, not looking at him further, made a clean, fast exit. He stretched back in the bed. He tried to figure if he'd really been as bored towards the end there as he'd seemed to be. He had used her name, he'd noticed, as if he had some right. He had noticed. She had not. Had maybe not. Oh, Christ, she had. 'Come around' he'd said. Jesus, he shouldn't have acted kind. He could be saddled with her forever . . .

On her knees, straddling him on the bed, the nurse arched her body backwards as in the darkness she began to moan. From where he lay, hands supporting the small of his own back the better to aid his efforts, the view was steeply up the shadowy, foreshortened perspective of her body to the peaked horizon of her dimly outlined breasts.

Strong as he was within her and excited, it pained his strapped-up chest to work too fiercely. He had no wish to dislocate the knitting joins to his several broken ribs. Nor did he wish to tear the stitches to the scar which they had all agreed Eichler would deliberately incise some five inches diagonally under his right nipple. It might one day add an extra frisson felt by all the little girls in Oshkosh when they saw him up there nude. But right now the tensing of his chest caused it to hurt like crazy.

This girl here was eager enough to take on the whole state of Wisconsin. Head back, the sinews of her neck stretched taut as it thrashed from side to side, she was lost to everything including the post-operative condition of her patient.

Something began to gather answeringly in him. It would not take long now. He struggled one arm free and pulled her lips down to his. And with that gesture it occurred to him that for some moments he had forgotten which one of them she was.

'Darling, oh darling,' she began to say.

It was over. In the let-down of the aftermath he seemed to hear an echo in the room.

'Somebody with class,' it said.

London was wreathed in the thick opacity of Victorian fog and law. He turned the page.

'Oh my God!'

He looked up. For the split second he expected to see Stella Lang. Instead, the open doorway framed Kurt Geisler. The burgundy suede valise in which he carried his instruments was genuinely set off to advantage by the powder-blue of the jeans he held it against. Cuffless and widely flared above his seersucker casuals, the jeans were of a second-skin tightness about the thighs and the unnaturally bulging crotch. He wore three chains about his neck. Two, outside the semi-see-through cheesecloth were silver and bore cabalistic signs. The third, in gold and shorter, was a stylised dog-tag. It nestled in the opening of the shirt on chest hair thick and silky-grey and curled beyond the art of nature. It was a dog-tag you could hock and live a year on.

'Well!'

Indignation was written across the coarse-pored homosexual

face bringing a hint of flush to its normal flat pallor. Indignation made him toss his head and shake the stiff quiff of blonde hair no less coarse in texture and, for one of his profession, surprisingly crudely dyed.

He advanced on Paul Madison.

'Well!' he said again. 'Stanley said to prepare you for tomorrow, but just look, your hair, the state it's in! What have they been doing to you! I'm going to be here half the night!'

chapter five

... The match for Miss Lemerle's fireworks comes from the no
less brightly blazing newcomer Paul Madison. If Fowles's
screenplay gives the devil the best lines, the pyrotechnics of
Madison's abilities more than do them justice. It's a superbly
ambivalent portrayal. The charm and intelligence never quite
conceal the truly vicious mix beneath of menace and brutal
ruthlessness but always seem that touch more genuine than a
mere mask. When in a compelling and daringly original cli-
mactic scene Madison-Silvano saves his soul by turning his
back on all that his ambition has driven him to (but not on the
producer who wants to give it to him!) we feel that his talent
must win through for him ultimately. He exits like a proud
Shylock – to be heard of later. As better believe, will Madison.
It's good, too, on the bouquet front to see that Dennis Curtis
has lost none of his guile ...

Esquire

'MADISON AV'NUES TO STARS'

Variety

The music pounded at you from so many sides it ended up by
starting from the centre of your brain. Not bothering to conceal
the gesture, Paul Madison lifted the joint up to his lips and
inhaled deeply. He had the way of it by now. A month earlier the
sheer physical mechanics of smoking had left him coughing,
spluttering. But, an actor mastering a strange art for the role –
piano playing, fast-draw technique – he had worked on it in
the occasional privacy of the bungalow at the Beverly Hills Hotel
to which he'd temporarily moved up. Success, they had told him,
was absolutely confirmed by the rough-cut of *Curtain*. It was time
to savour its sweet smell. And the sweet things it did.

There was a steel guitar on this track. It was uncanny. He
seemed to hear, to see, each individual note it made hanging
separately in his mind like a gleaming bead of oil floating in water.
And yet at the same time each individual shimmering bead was

threaded to the next in a necklace that seemed to run away from his mind's foreground into the deep perspective of infinity. He could hold the whole melodic line, beginning to end, start to finish, in his head even as he ranged along it examining each single note three dimensionally and quiveringly alive against its black velvet backdrop.

The disco was scarcely less dark. As he sat watching, the press of gyrating bodies seemed to swim from out of the smoke into his forehead and out again. They were dim shapes, sexless as to themselves; in aggregate a twisting mass of sexuality anticipating the varied releases that a few more hours would bring. In the thick darkness you could smell the musk of sex above the marijuana, could almost reach out and stroke it in the air. 'Champs' had no light show but spots concealed somewhere brought everybody's teeth, shirt-cuffs, collars, kaftans out in a phosphorescent blue-white sheen. Black-tied or beaded, negro or other, nobody escaped their sudden pin-points against the blanket of the dark.

Milton Rosner had taken 'Champs' over for the night as a place to go on to after Chasen's. He had taken Chasens on for the late evening as a place to go on to after the premiere of *Curtain* at the Pantages.

One way or another Paul Madison had had a ball. Two days earlier, after long horse-trading, Oates had finally given him the go-ahead to sign with Rosner for his next one – *Cold Turkey*. There is no creature on earth more euphoric than an actor, the hottest thing in town, who has a sure hit premiering, a star role lined up and no need for the moment to get up at first light. The wind this night was wholly in his favour.

For Mr and Mrs America out there on the bleachers the Pantages' showing still contained the ghosts of premieres past. Searchlights had blazed away, criss-crossing skies. Police lines had held back rubber-neckers. Arriving to their shrieks, their to-be-depended-on applause, with Lauren Hayworth on his arm, Paul had stood alongside Jack Preston and Barbara Lemerle while the cameras snapped, crackled and whirred.

He had gone into the theatre with Preston and Lemerle slightly ahead of him. The status ritual, like the credits above the title, had to be just as strictly observed in public. But since new blood is as vital to the media as it is to Hollywood, they had pushed a microphone under Madison's lips, and he had said all the right things. With a little help from Leonard and some grass. The beneficiary of the charity premiere was the Cedars of Lebanon, the celebrated hospital of the area which, in superlative luxury, handled the coronaries, ulcers, paranoias and critical delusions of the famous. More specifically the money – a hundred and fifty thousand dollars was confidently expected – would go to the hospital's Nuclear Therapy Department where they were chasing a new cobalt monster aimed at prolonging the more embattled livers of its noted clientele. Madison stood under the lights and declared that as a newcomer – pause for a deferential shuffling of the feet – it was a privilege to work on behalf of so distinguished a project. Then he paid humble homage to the talents of his two co-stars – a smile now to Lemerle and Preston – and naturally 'to a distinguished director without whom his own performance would have been . . .' Bang on. But then, as for the first time, he had entered the theatre to sink ankle-deep into its foyer carpeting, the whole stage-managed charade had momentarily got to him. The magnificent, excessive garishness of this temple to the idols of the 'thirties brought home to his gut that he was standing in direct line of descent to Gable, Cooper, Bogart and Tracy. There was an ecstasy to it that made the adrenalin surge through him. For that moment, at least, he could banish visions of a freeway and of the police markers where the two bodies had lain.

The euphoria persisted some two and a half hours later when the end credits rolled to sustained applause. It went on well after the final fade to black, the bringing up of the house-lights. People were on their feet cheering and clapping wildly. Not all of them briefed beforehand. The follow spots carefully positioned inside the auditorium blazed on and pencilled their way to the strategic seats. Lemerle had risen to an ovation. She had led the applause as Preston rose. When he, Paul Madison, stood up the tumult of applause had crescendoed to a new peak. Preston had winked across at him. Barbara had blown him kisses and put on a happy face.

Later, at Chasens, the euphoria had flowed through him as freely as the real champagne, the synthetic congratulations. The napery had gleamed immaculately, the spotless glasses shone with a hypnotising brilliance. Look into us beyond the highlights we reflect, they seemed to say to him, and you will see the future written on the air we hold. But soon they had been brimmingly overfilled with liquid and the table-hopping had begun. A stream of second-team well-wishers homed in on him. Veteran freeloaders, they had dived into the trays of drinks one second from blast-off and were now too loud, too flattering, too much. He'd grinned and borne it charmingly.

Others more weighty had come across. Rosner himself, neat,

dark, dapperly self-controlled had taken his hand and with locker-room affection punched him once on the upper arm. He had given one short, approving nod.

'Nice,' he had said. 'Real nice job. We'll be talking, huh?'

Paul Madison had nodded and smiled back his one totally sober smile of the past two hours.

'That's the first time you've smiled tonight and meant it,' Lauren Hayworth had said.

He had turned to his dinner companion.

'Wrong,' he had replied, 'I just didn't mean that in a different way to the way I didn't mean the others.'

For a moment both their smiles were genuine, his as well as hers, but Oates, across from him, had frowned. As J. U. Carpenter, his newly-assigned accountant had come over with Dan Webster, Magnum's head of distribution, he had felt a sharp needle of disquiet pierce his well-being. What was the point of taking them for all they had, if you had to go into the dance they led you? That was what a voice inside him asked. All in good time was his answer as he drank some more. What price Gable, Cooper, Flynn or any of them now? the ice-dark voice persisted. Is it for that – for *that* – you eat this shit?

'Why, Lauren! What a fantabulous gown!'

Another tour of duty. Christie Roberts had come over. In her habitual silver, slender as a wand, she was like a moon-pallid imitation of Mia Farrow. Miraculously Lauren Hayworth was contriving to be gracious without resorting to female-talk flattery. Madison was puzzled. Christie Roberts had come as far as she had on a vibration of anti-Hollywood Establishment off-handed-ness. She was hip or pseudo-hip aiming for whatever cult fame remained for flat-chested unwashed-looking stars of films that won French prizes and never got their money back. Now here she was discarding denim for diamonds and knocking on the doors that led to caviar and dolce vita. The doors already opened to him. I'm a more honest whore than she, he thought, as he pushed his interior charm button and with seemingly uncalculated casual-ness bent to kiss her.

'Sweetheart,' he said, 'you look choice enough to eat.'

She almost brought the laugh off.

'I had to come over, Paul,' she said, 'just to apologise. I . . .'

'Apologise? Baby, you've –'

'I knew you'd be good. Okay, you know. I had just simply no idea how good – that you'd be absolutely great. I'm just speechless with admiration, Paul, I mean that. I mean, to be so technically

THE DEAL 113

sure in such an *extroverted* part, I mean, oh wow! I mean introverts, good introverts yet, still a dime a dozen, but to project such
a conflict of motivations . . . too much, Paul!'

He had grinned and borne it.

'You know,' she was saying, 'I'd be fascinated, just fascinated
if maybe sometime we could get together and talk about it. How
you approached the part. You know, discuss what . . .'

'My bed is always open,' his devil prompted.

She was ready for him this time. Her eyes looked down, waited
the requisite pause, looked back up and fully into his.

'I'll remember that,' she said.

'So will I.'

Happy, pretending to be, she kissed him and left.

As he sat down, Lyndon Oates had sneaked round on the blind
side to replace the evil voice in his head by a live one at his ear.

'Maybe now's a good time to go make the big presentation to
Sylvia,' Oates said. 'You bought the stuff I suppose?'

'Sure, Lyndon,' Madison said tapping his breast pocket. 'I
don't forget the rules of the game. Some you fuck, some you
flatter, some you bribe.'

Oates gripped his arm. The force of it matched the flash of
malevolence in his eyes.

'You're talking too loud for comfort, friend. Let's cool it, eh?'
Then he smiled. 'What was all that about?'

'What was all what about?'

'Christie Roberts. Laying it on you a bit?'

'Oh her,' Madison shrugged. 'Just telling me I was brilliant,
how marvellous I was. And maybe sometime there'd be a bonus
waiting for me between her legs.'

'Well just so's you know, her people are hot for her to get the
girl in *Cold Turkey*.'

'Oh Jesus, no! You've got to be kidding! You just have to be!'

On reflex, as if the idea would be less painful if he were up on
his feet, Madison rose and moved off. Oates kept him company
two paces.

'Find Sylvia,' he pressed. 'Strike while the broad's hot.'

'Yeah, right, I'll do that,'

Satisfied, Oates fell away to divert to a nearby table where Jack
Preston sat talking business cheek by jowl with a producer. He
hovered close enough to hear the producer's urgent pitch to
Preston. 'I can get you a million up front – plus, Jack. Seventeen
days work and you're pissing on them!'

Oates's eyes closed in disbelief, yet believing it. They're all fucking mad. A million – for what? He glanced towards Madison weaving between tables with the assurance of a two-times Oscar winner. How long will it be before he figures he's in that class? But you had to hand it to the cocksucker. He had style. People looked, no question about that. The problem is, he knows it. That's when the fuse begins to burn.

They were all looking at Madison now. It had been a great premiere and Madison carried the sheen of it . . . away from Preston and Lemerle. He had seen Alex Eichler at a distance, close to a blonde-burnished showgirl three inches taller than himself. Alex had flicked him a fast private wink, his head nodding in the direction of the girl's high and mighty boobs. The message was clear. All my own work. Madison turned from artifice to art. He moved in on Sylvia Kilmartin. She sat with her two assistant directors, Jerry Carson the production manager, and various family at a table close enough to the top brass to reflect Rosner's respect for the skilled mechanics of motion pictures. The essence and not the ego of motion picture making.

'Hi,' Paul Madison said. 'You all deciding it was nearly worth it?'

'I always enjoy them when they're over,' Carson said. 'And then the next day I remember that I'm out of work.' His weather-beaten face, lined with the years of location shooting from African safaris to Wayne Westerns in Mexico, made clear it was more truth than joke.

'With this one under your belt, Jerry,' Sylvia Kilmartin soothed, 'you won't have problems. Good production managers are hard to find. It's actors who don't sleep nights. Isn't that so, Paul?' It was a big laugh with the midnight editions already heralding 'a thrilling new talent'. So Madison grinned too. 'I've got other things to keep me awake at night.' He moved closer to Sylvia Kilmartin, signalling private business.

'You wouldn't care to come into my office for a second,' he said, smiling politely at the other guests.

'Sure. Will you excuse me folks?' She rose, allowed Madison to steer her to one side.

'Well, Paul, you've got me. What's the problem?'

'No problem, Sylvia. Just wanted to make a short speech. Seriously . . . I wanted to say a big "thank you" for a great editing job. Really.'

She looked at him drily.

'Apart from that, did you enjoy the play Mrs Lincoln?'

'No kidding. You were brilliant. Though candidly from me to

you, I thought Schneider did everything on that zoom camera short of working it up Lemerle's ass.'

For an instant a gleam crept into her calm, cold eyes. A mean and matching smile spread across her broad, butch features.

'The Editor's Section of the Academy of Motion Pictures Arts and Sciences has a technical expression for such a phenomenon.'

'Oh?'

'We call it jerking off.'

He had laughed out loud.

'You should have seen the director's first cut,' she said. 'Twice I got motion sickness. The zoom lens! Directing died the day after they invented it.'

'I've no grouch,' he said. 'You left my stuff nearly as good as I delivered to the camera.'

'Modest sonofabitch, aren't you,' she said with a return to dryness. 'The times Tom Leonard found he had to just stop by the cutting room. He was nursing every frigging shot of yours. He's really pushing you, you know.'

'I guess it's his job.'

'I guess it's his job.'

'Save your tears. In any case he was wasting his time. You were okay. Really. I earned my money on this one putting some changes of pace into the beast. They're there now, but they don't come from anyplace else but me.'

'You did a fantastic job on Curtis.'

Not displeased, she nodded in brief acknowledgement of her craft.

'Yes, I did,' she said simply. 'Right now about a dozen people know it. Including him. A month from now they'll all have forgotten and he'll be the first . . . Ah well, that's the old editing game for you . . .'

'Sylvia, I'd like you to have this. My sort of personal Oscar.'

She looked at the slim black box.

'Pearls?' she said. 'Oh Christ!' It was with a sharp edge of hostility. He blinked.

'Open it and see,' he said.

She did so. The antique Chinese peacock hair-ornament stared back up at her with an exotic refinement two centuries away from Hollywood.

'Why!' she gasped. Pleasure had now taken away her breath. 'It's lovely!' Embarrassed, reddening, she stretched clumsily up and pecked him on the cheek.

'Sorry I was snide,' she said. 'Lyndon's always had this thing, thinking pearls are a girl editor's best friend.'

'Me . . . I'm not the same kind of animal. You wanna know the truth? It was pearls. I hocked 'em and bought that instead.'

She looked at him. For a moment show business was gone and she was a gratified dumpy lady smiling shyly at a grown-up son who'd just been becomingly honest.

'I don't know what to tell you,' she said. 'I should tell you; don't change your ways. You can go a long time around here without running into genuine class and style.'

Their common reality came back to her.

'But let me warn you too,' she said. 'Keep your personal statements private. If you want to get ahead. The public ones always turn out to be luxuries. And luxuries, remember, are things you can't afford.'

'You can afford anything if you're rich enough.'

It was a false note. He had destroyed the intimacy between them. Her face visibly hardened. She knew it.

'Hell,' she said by way of apology. 'Pay no attention. I always played it a little too safe to be quite comfortable with myself.'

'Sylvia – promise me you'll cut my next picture.'

'A pleasure, kind sir. If the fates and the smart money allow.'

He threw a mock right cross at her and, less than clumsily, kissed her on the cheek.

'See you around,' he said.

He returned to his table to find Lauren Hayworth rising.

'Want to walk me to the car?' she said.

For the first time that evening he realised how casually, how elegantly, stunning she was looking. Without effort she seemed to project the patina of refinement. He felt a sudden quickening urge to knock her from that perch, to rip that sea-green fall of dress off her, dirty her.

'So soon?' was all he could manage to say.

She flashed a smile of dazzling naturalness at him.

'Paul,' she said, 'your people and my people thought it would be a good idea if we made tonight's little shindig together. I have to tell you the thought of meeting you intrigued me. That's why I went along with it. I also have to tell you I enjoyed myself. You were great up there on the screen and meeting you, was . . . well, no hardship.

'Thanks. But—'

'So, for the moment, see you around, yes? A girl has her own life and particularly she has a photo call at eight-thirty tomorrow morning.'

Shut out, he had regained composure and charm.

'Alright already,' he said. 'Never let me come – between a girl and her Art. I'll walk you to the car.'

There had been an appreciation in her second smile which he had not known whether to feel good about or bad. But returning to his table he had this time been caught right in the centre of Jack Preston's sights. He had received a broad, tough-luck grin of horny complicity. Twenty minutes later Preston was over at his table.

'Smoke one of mine,' he said.

They were expertly tailored and, aroma apart, could have passed for cigarillos.

It was a night for grins and smiles. Preston's now, was broad and a little toothy, lop-sided, curiously coarse.

'Shit,' he had said, 'I'm no ways near being properly crocked. It's time, wouldn't you say, to beat it on down to Champs.'

So, in a hooting, tyre-screeching convoy, they had done so. Preston had traded in-jokes with a police acquaintance on Wilshire to offset their disturbance of the peace, and then one of the sweat-suited parking jockeys was scrunching himself into the BMW 633CS, which, on Tom Leonard's advice, Paul Madison had bought to replace the rented Cutlass. It would be a custom-built Mercedes next. 'Champs is happy to be in *Curtain's* Corner', said a banner on the canopied marquee. Whooping it up before the resentful gaze of the car attendants, a jostling pack of them had waded in to take their ringside seats around the disco. From the four corners, from inside their heads, the music pounded at them. Eichler seemed somewhere to have lost the well-stacked blonde, who, if professional ethics had permitted it, would gladly have stood in Macy's window on Broadway to plug Eichler's hand-reared mammaries. Paul Madison wondered where she'd gone, and with whom. Perhaps she had to be back in her coffin by midnight. Eichler had joined him at a table temporarily all-stag after Preston had beaten off the amateur hookers who had found the nerve to move in on them.

'Let's wait for the pros,' he'd recommended. He waved now to a young moustachioed actor who had made it big, faded, and was now having a triumphant renascence on TV, his series being picked up for the fourth time. It meant that his ex-wife, wherever she was, and the three kids, whoever they were, could go on living in the style their lawyers had insisted upon when they'd gotten around to carving him up. Other superstars in the Newman class – that actor had excused himself on the grounds that he never went to premiers – milled around ostentatiously trying not to be noticed. 'Just your plain ordinary folks!' Preston said, the light adding malevolence, to the grin he threw at them, 'coming on down here to show us all they aren't Hollywood establishment, but proving they're into as much bullshit as the rest of us.'

He waved again. As he did so, Paul Madison took the chance to look at him again. His interest was renewed by this sudden black flash of bitchery. He also had the intense, comparing observation of a Number Two figuring out the stratagems needed to become Number One. There was something perpetually ratty about Preston's face. It had a used look. A dirty look. Dirty, he decided, in the sense of permanently seeming to need a good wash. Whether he had make-up on or not. If you let your eyes float on the music and the pot and held them very wide open, not focusing, you could see a chimp face just under Preston's face waiting its moment to come out. But, also a hint of Bogart. That must have been part of his fantastic success. That and his savage individuality. Talent too. And the impression he gave the world's millions of being his own man . . . Madison blinked and squeezed his eyes back into focus. Yes, Preston was irrecoverably on the downward slope into middle-age. The furrows across his forehead were probably even beyond Eichler's skills and the hairline was erratically advancing up the skull. It was only a half-inch or so as yet. And as yet Preston was hot enough and secure enough not to give a damn. But it was an open secret bets were being laid around town on when he'd first show up with a hair transplant so good and subtle you'd have to look three times to check it wasn't the real McCoy.

Now, abruptly, he turned his head and seemed to look straight through Paul Madison's eyes and on into his thoughts.

'Hey, look here!' Preston snarled, 'Something bugging you?' The eyes, red-blotched, spelt danger.

The younger actor braced to throw the quicker punch but found a drowsy weakness at the centre of his fists. So, what the fuck, his uninterested brain seemed to be saying. I'll let him hit me first. It's no big thing. But Preston didn't hit him. He was, Paul Madison realised, not looking at him but on beyond towards where people made their way into the disco's main cave. Swivelling round himself, floating a little, it seemed, Paul Madison followed the direction of his look and thought.

Four women, not quite associated together or acknowledging each other were about to make the scene. Three were white, all were tall. They wore evening gowns that, if not from Saks, were from I. Magnin. In the subdued light with its phosphorescent overtones they looked stunning, superlative, whatever your dream of fair women might be.

'Hooker time!' Jack Preston said, with a rich college boy's enthusiasm. 'I guess that's for me. I'm feeling dirty tonight and I'm feeling lazy. I guess I'm going to play me a little pro ball. Can I interest you gents in a little fancy combination, now?'

He was rising to his feet. Paul Madison put his brain in gear but somehow the clutch was jammed. Maybe it wasn't such a good idea—

'Very kind of you, Jack,' Eichler was saying, 'but me – I do believe I'm spoken for.' He smiled his apologies.

'Paul, baby?... Ah, well, happy dreams ...'

And Preston was gone. Without finesse he went straight to the first woman. From the far side of a long way away Paul Madison saw him grin his twisted smile, saw the hooker look appraisingly at him as if he were a nobody and the choosing were all hers. Then dancers jerked between.

I should have gone, Paul Madison thought. I meant to go. I wanted to. But he felt very happy where he was. The music, the bead of oil, had swollen to surround him and enclose him. It was warm inside and at the still centre of the driving noise, peaceful. He watched the dark silhouettes, the sudden flashes of kaftan through a telescope that made them very far away but did not make them small. A thought floated at him. I own you all, it strangely said. For a second, he believed it.

Something weird began to happen. A bubble formed inside his head close to his right ear. It swelled then, noiselessly, without feeling but yet quite certainly, it burst. The string of all the other beads was dashed away. The film of oil encasing him was gone. The music was pounding at him beat by single beat. The swaying, thrusting dancers were right on top of him. He was thirsty. He drank at random from a nearest glass and, whatever it was, it seemed to be alright.

He heard a laugh. A happy grin was broadly spread across the plastic surgeon's boyish, potato face.

'Yeah?' Paul Madison asked.

The grin widened.

'You know, Paul my friend,' Eichler said, 'I've just been keeping score. To the best of my ability to judge in this light there are at this very moment eight of my tits bouncing around out there.

There is beyond question a prime example of one of my reconstituted butts. A butt lift, that is. One of my best jobs, actually, although I say it myself.'

He laughed out loud. Curiosity lanced into Paul Madison's brain like a laser. It had thrown the switch. All was crystal clear and hyperactive and he had gone from zero to a hundred in nothing flat.

'Like who?' he said at once.

Eichler's smile was no less wide but it had changed.

'Oh, no,' he said. 'Paul sweetheart, plastic surgery is like having a mistress. You don't talk about it. I'm paid as much for my discretion as I am for my expertise. That's ethics!'

'Screw ethics!'

'Can't afford to my good friend. This is the deal I make with my clients. There are three actors topping the ratings right now, who but for my knife, would be ruined on the first close-up. Professionally speaking I've kept them alive. Sure, its a conspiracy. Take away their looks, show the pouches, lines, and the dewlaps, and they're dead. And they'd be even deader if everybody knew. You wouldn't want that?'

'Yes please!' Madison laughed.

'I extend this confidentiality to all clients, including actors who do dangerous things in automobiles on freeways!'

'Okay, don't tell me. But did you really mean that? There are four broads out there you've pumped up into the Bunny Girl league?'

'More or less. To be clinical, one I have re-shaped, another I sort of augmented. The other two were straight lifts. I must say they look pretty good from where I sit. It really is amazing,' Eichler mused, 'the craving women in this town have for physical perfection. I have to thank God, and the media for that. The magazines, newspapers, television, keep hammering at everybody, "you've got to look like this to be desirable. Are your breasts the right size? Are your ankles trim enough? Does your ass say sexy things as you walk? Because if not, you're not going to make it." That, Paul, is what keeps us all in business. It is what you call a great rip off. But I don't complain. We're all hustlers here. To be crudely cynical every raised tit or butt buys the gasoline for my private plane, or gets me the number one hooker in the whorehouse.'

His throat was growing hoarse from the effort of shouting through the noise. 'We're getting serious, friend. We're losing orgy time.'

A shadow falling across the table cut short Eichler's naughty boy delight. But instantly it was restored. Paul Madison looked up. Towering above them, mysteriously returned, was the statuesque blonde he had seen alongside Eichler in Chasen's.

'Ah, my dear,' said Eichler simply, 'You're back.' He did not stand up. The blonde, impassive, seemed not to expect it. An ice-queen, she sat herself in the chair that had been Preston's. She wore no wedding ring Paul noticed. He tried to remember if she had been one of the hookers that had caught Preston's eye. If she was not, she could have been their kissing cousin.

'This is Bobby,' Eichler said. 'Bobby – Paul.'

She deigned to acknowledge him.

'Hi,' she said. 'Alex, I'd like a drink.'

More inevitably than usual, given the past conversation, Paul stared at her breasts. They were magnificent and, courtesy of the shoe-string supported black silk dress exposed down to their aureole's sun-rise top. Only their very fullness, tautening the silk, gave the nipples token modesty. Twisting in his chair to locate one of Champs' black waitresses in stylised ring gear, Eichler intrecepted Paul's look.

'Ja,' he said, 'I know what you are thinking. But wrong, my friend. Bobby is a self-made girl. Yes, my dear?'

Bobby didn't rate that worth answering. It was her raised slenderness of arm that brought the waitress. The music had stopped. As they re-ordered their drinks, Paul was aware of the dancers suddenly lost for an occupation. Awkward and gawky as they stood in a silence almost as deafening as the noise, waiting for the music to crash down on them again. Instead a rheostat was tweaked somewhere. The level of light came up dangerously close to allowing you tell a five spot from a twenty. There seemed to be a kerfuffle of technicians doing things with microphones on the suitcase-sized stage diagonally across the floor. A follow-spot jabbed on and a fat-faced man with crinkly hair was suddenly up, head and shoulders above the crowd.

'Ladies and gentlemen, your attention, please,' he said. 'A very important announcement . . . Well, two very important announcements. Firstly, let me say on behalf of Champs how delighted we are to be hosts tonight to the cast – Mr Jack Preston, Mr Dennis Curtis, Mr Paul Madison – to all the cast, technical crew, friends and freeloaders of what I know is going to be a great, great movie; Milton Rosner's *Curtain*— We hope you're having a great time, folks. And if you're a new friend – well now you know where we are.

'And now, my next important announcement. And this is something. Ladies and gentlemen, you all thought I just forgot the name of a mighty big star now. I did no such thing. Because I tell you, that here tonight at Champs, Miss Barbara Lemerle has consented to repeat for us, for you, part of her recent sensational Las Vegas cabaret performance as featured on RCA. Ladies and gentlemen – if you could just fan back a little to the side there, that's right – ladies and gentlemen, Miss Barbara Lemerle!'

There had been yelps of glee, rebel yells, cheers, clapping. All had sounded genuinely spontaneous. By now, Paul thought, the crowd was up enough to manage without cheerleaders. The applause died. Absolutely nothing seemed to happen.

'Folks,' the now invisible man said over the PA, 'if you could just make a little room up front here . . .'

Shuffling, falling back to the table areas, sitting on steps, kneeling on the floor, the kaftans and dinner jackets, denims and suede-leather cleared a space. Five indifferently and variously dressed backing musicians shuffled up on to the stage to a spatter of applause. Acoustic and base guitar, tenor sax, trouped themselves in front of drums and electric organ. They tuned a little. Fell silent. People waited, were mainly silent too. Christ, Paul Madison thought, they've been paid to wait around and see if Madame felt like she maybe cottoned to the feel of this audience and if she'd maybe like to do her act. Well, if she delivers, she'll have the *Reporter*'s gossip columns all to herself the next few days and wipe out the lead I've got on review inches. Shit. But what the hell. Maybe it shows she's desperate.

The acoustic guitarist seemed to get a cue. He nodded. The combo crashed into sound. Simultaneously, with a fast rush from nowhere into the spot, Barbara Lemerle was on stage and, as a vocal group slipped discreetly into a half-lit background was off without introduction into an up-tempo arrangement of 'Behind Closed Doors'.

The pitch of her own voice was better calculated. From the first note, with the first piece of gesturing business, more suggestive by far than anything she would have done public, she conveyed that because she was among friends this was the real Lemerle. I'll be leaving the odd stop in, won't shift to overdrive, the pact she offered said. But I shall promise more control, something therefore rarer.

Paul Madison listened carefully to see how she'd make good that marker. She did well. She did very well. She had voice enough, was musician enough, to have no need to fear any live performance.

She sang Negro, of course, smokey, harsh, simulating the cracking of notes against vocal chords made brittle by cheap liquor. Flawed only by the sense that it was all coming from the outside. Her beat might ride and skip that vital fraction off the laid-down beat to keep you hanging but the harshness had no sense of cold, or back-alley in it. No sense of four bare walls squaring in hopelessness, a sad night washing up to a damp porch to say tomorrow would be just the same. She sang Nashville. But the core of her belting tone lacked Joplin's trash desperation. Her notes came secondhand. Always you had an image of a black disc going round, her seated, ear glued to a vast loudspeaker, taking notes. She could offer finesse, technique and as camouflage for emotion, the chutzpah of an all-black backing group, two guys, two girls.

She maybe did forty minutes. The last twenty-five or so Madison hardly took in. His attention focussed on the tall girl on the right end of the group.

She was on the edge of a rim of light. As she swayed with the routines, she was in, was out, of its pale wash. When she was in he felt as if something had torn in the soft pit of his stomach.

She was tall, yes, with hair worn full and straight back off her forehead. It set off to maximum advantage the slender length of classic, goddess face. The length of nose, the definition of cheekbones and perfectly proportioned jaw were Nilotic. An Egyptian queen. The full width of mouth was made generous and lovely by a knife-edge demarcation between lips just less than full and the brown skin of her face. The eyes were wide apart and had something of an oriental hint of softness and of angling upwards from the flat planes of her cheeks. She moved like a dark flame. She might be all beauty and still part animal. The thought intensified the sharp ache at the pit of his belly.

Lemerle's planned, calculated impromptu had finished. She went into the three mandatory encores. The applause was long, exaggerated, overlapping the numbers in the familiar act of showbiz looking after its own. There was genuine admiration too. Also a fair showing of the need for ego to bathe in reflected stardom. That was all he had made out. His girl, as he already thought of her, seemed to be heading for the tables up against the furthest wall. The lights were dimmed, a bass thunked quadrophonically and bodies were already writhing in the shadows.

For some uncharacteristic reason he made himself wait five

minutes. Then, with a vague shout at Eichler and the fatuous Bobby, he was on his feet and edging through the weaving couples.

'Hi, Paul, how you coming?' Proud of his slack-breasted chick, the assistant cameraman clamoured to be recognised. He nodded a smile back. A kaftan twisted around and Alan Carr was jangling chains in poor time to the beat.

He shimmied past a couple, found himself partnering a surrogate Bianca Jagger.

'Paul Madison I do declare!' she lilted. Swiftly, not so impersonally, she kissed him.

'Nothing for it but to tell you you were wonderful,' she said. And she was gone. He side-stepped smartly into an island of non-movement. Two more steps and without loss of limb he had negotiated the crossing. He haunched his shoulders to settle his tuxedo and began to look for her. He saw her at once. She was beyond another press of people seated at tables in a booth against the wall. She was looking straight at him. Then her head turned and she was looking at the man she sat with. Shit, he thought, what did I expect?

He began to work his way through the barrier of densely crowded tables. People looked up resentfully as he brushed by expensive hairdos and precarious toupees. Almost all, identifying him, converted bitter, hostile looks to smiles of sheepish sycophancy. Cocksuckers, he thought. A young man whom he hadn't seen before looked up and a half-second too late, set his Afro-framed face into a rigid mask designed to deny all recognition of superior status. Shitheel, he thought, but had no time to enjoy his own ambivalence. He was almost at the booth. His pulse was actually accelerating. He found that it was extraordinarily important to discover whether, close up, she was as lovely as his imagination, pot, and bad lighting had made her out to be. He raised his eyes. Once more, unblinking, she was staring straight into them.

And she was even lovelier. Near to, he could see the soft brown, sheened and shadowed complexion was flawless. Her face had that rarest of things – perfect symmetry that did not bore but confirmed the exquisiteness.

Exquisite. Held by the flat darkness of her eyes he stood confronting her and realised ten heartbeats past the point that mattered he was lost for words. He was tongue-tied like a freshman fraternity-boy faced without warning by his chosen sex-fantasy made flesh. Against the background din the failure of his personal silence dinned about his ears. Whether from irony or comparison, it was she who broke the spell.

'I know,' she said and blinked. 'You just had to come across and compliment me on my singing.'

Her voice was low and soft but clear. There was nothing of ethnic or accent in it and he knew that it had been trained.

'Not quite,' he said. 'Not even close, if I try being honest.'

He risked a quick squeeze on his charm trigger. There was this other guy sat to his left. But now was not the time to look away from her.

'What a nice smile,' she said. 'Tell me. What do you think – did I sing the high line or the low line?'

'I wouldn't begin to know,' he said. 'I just know your vibes from across the room to me, zapped me between the eyes and said you were twenty-two carat, Fort Knox beautiful.'

What the hell was this other guy! Who was the star?

'Quite a line of yours for openers,' she said. 'But you've won first prize.'

Her lips stayed fluidly chiselled but mockery and wit gleamed in the suddenly no longer passive eyes.

'That means,' she said, 'you get to sit down here with us and buy some more drinks.'

'Paul,' he underplayed. 'Paul Madison.'

'I know,' she said in neutral. 'I saw the papers. My name's Sam. This here is Jerry.'

'Hi, Sam. Hi, Jerry.'

She sidled deeper into the C-shaped booth. Madison smiled, edged in beside her. For the first time took in her companion.

To his surprise, and annoyance, the man was neither of the two male singers from the group. He was younger. And, in a charcoal grey sports coat over a light grey roll-neck sweater, about as handsome as she was beautiful.

'Hi,' he said, 'how you going?'

There was something almost Ivy League in his appearance. The hair was clipped short and the moustache matched its neatness. He had a large head but the look of guarded tightness to the skin across cheekbones gave his face a contained and compact air. He was a lighter brown than she.

'Pretty good,' Paul Madison said. 'What are you drinking?'

The man – Jerry – shook his head. He signalled, managed to attract a passing waitress.

'Yours?' he said.

'Er, I'll just have a beer.' He still had that thirst.

'A Coors – okay? – and two gin and tonics.'

His surface style was white, but unlike her, his voice went back home to Watts.

'You see the picture?' Paul Madison asked.

Jerry shook his head.

'Uh-huh,' he said, 'we're just here on account of Sam's gig. Or she is. I just snuck in for a look around. Word is, though, that you steal the piece.'

Paul Madison shrugged. 'It's a sure-fire part,' he said. 'Everything plays to it.'

He was finding it hard to choose words. Jerry was offering him a wary politeness well short of four-lettered hostility and let's settle this outside. If it came to that they'd be well matched. He felt his stomach muscles tensing at the prospect of a feint, a duck, the stepping in to plant a short one in the gut. That was where she'd hit him. He turned to her.

'How do you rate Lemerle?' he asked.

'Nearly as good as they keeping telling her she is,' she said. The beautiful enigma of her face relaxed into a smile she could have used for collateral.

'She leans on it too hard,' she said. 'They all do these days. Since Billie Holliday it's all been downhill.'

'That's a long time ago.'

'Yes, it is.'

'How long you been singing?'

He knew they were being eavesdropped.

'Oh . . . years.'

'You like it?'

'Don't dislike it.'

'Is it all you do? What you want to do?'

'I'm an actress first. When I get to be. Singing's steadier and pays the bills. I wouldn't get so far soloing.'

An actress! A little rank-pulling and he could be home free! To disguise his glee he turned to Jerry.

'How 'bout you, Jerry?'

The guy still projected that hint of intense control which promised future violence.

'Me? Oh hell, I work for a living, man. I'm an accountant. In business for—'

The waitress had returned. She dipped to deal the drinks

around. Paul went for his dress wallet but Jerry, peeling bills at her from a roll had easily beaten him to the punch.

'Okay,' he said, 'I do believe that we asked you to come join us. Relax.'

'And I thank you, sir,' the waitress said.

'Cheers!'

They drank. Jerry was looking hard at Paul.

'Listen,' he said. 'A policy statement. You didn't come over here to talk to me. You came because of her. Isn't that right?'

Below the table Paul Madison clenched a fist. He kept a half-eye on the gin and tonic opposite in case it should be thrown.

'Don't mistake me. No sweat. It's understandable. What guy wouldn't want to? But how many would try? I respect you've tried. And, like I say, no sweat. Sam's a free spirit. Her own soul. If she digs you – and if I read right she does – well, fine. Like who am I?'

He paused, reached for his glass and drank. The reasonableness seemed stretched to breaking point between the comic and the threatening. He downed the empty glass.

'So,' he said. 'Okay, Sam?'

Paul Madison turned to look at her.

'I guess,' she said evenly. 'A movie star yet.' All in a monotone. Was she so cool? Wasn't she straining to suppress her own excitement? Wasn't she—

Jerry had stood up. He was not huge but from that angle he was a big son of a bitch. But all he did was nod. 'Okay,' he said, 'Have a nice day.' He moved away, disappeared into the press of dancers.

Paul looked sideways again at Sam. Her looks were staggering. Each fresh glance blew on the furnace.

'Well,' he said, 'what do I start to say?'

She moved swiftly on round to be able to more naturally face him. Her gaze was still on the dancers.

'That Jerry,' she said. 'He should thank God he doesn't pimp to make his bread . . . You want to dance?'

She was exquisite. She was exquisitely sensitive. It was impossible to make an error. All competitiveness, all fear of losing status had long been soothed away. He swam on cool instinct at the bottom of a transluscent pool.

When she had let her dress fall to her feet and stood, rising from its silver sea, he had caught his breath with a delight that was totally new to him. It was the long length of inward curving waist that was her ultimate perfection. The breasts, not large, were high and roundly firm, their distinct nipples central on the outer swell. Then came the long sweep of brown, light and dark shadowed, that glistened down to the smoothness of her limbs.

He had gone to her, she had received him, without preliminary. The rhythm had been one for both of them, its climax caught, given and taken in a crash of shared crescendo. Only then had come surprise. Her hands, angel wings before, had raked his back at the moment of shrieking triumph.

Afterwards, kissing him softly, she had fallen back and smiled.

'I do savage a bit when I'm having a nice time,' she said. 'I should have maybe warned you I'm a screamer but sometimes a guy gets led . . . I've been in places, apartments you know, where to make love where you can be heard, I've had to have a pillow on my face.'

Now, later, he was angled above her on the length of his extended arms. To look at that fineness of slender face, the black swan's neck's dissolve into the straight line of shoulders was visually to feel a stroking of desire. He had this! Possessed this!

But, wait. Softly . . . Ah, she was not moving a muscle outwardly. But sure, yes, she was. His body was suddenly teased by a faint thrill of current. She tightened. The current tingled more sharply. Panting now, holding himself from crashing down in greedy violence, he kept quite still. The sweetness now ruled him. It welled, gathered and, in a second past the unbelievable, exploded outwards in a pulse of ecstasy.

'Gott! Ah, Gott! Gott!'

He twisted his head. On the adjacent bed of the bungalow's large room Eichler was finding his own easement in the snowy tracts of Bobby.

chapter six

It's 'musical houses' would you believe, up in them Hollywood hills. Ms Lang – remember? – is finally abandoning her legendary pad where the best carousing took place this side of Errol Flynn, in pursuit, we imagine, of instant liquidity. The new incumbent who's been over enough times to know where the bottles are buried, is the town's currently hottest tip for Oscar nomination, Paul Madison. Maybe he figured it for the simple life though the word's out that a certain black warbler has been singing for her supper there, of nights . . . A new twosome clinching it at the . . .

Gossip International

The house was old. Built in the twenties. Mexican in style and, since the materials and the labour come from south of the border, authentic enough. Its outer walls were two feet thick; it had many windows but small; it had verandahs, loggias, ramadas. It didn't really require the air-conditioning system which in any case was obsolete going on defunct. Even at the high noon of summer thick timber beams the length of the main first-floor room presided over a perpetual coolness.

It had negligible security. Just a gate. Not even a full fence. They were supposed to be working on that. And the grounds. The lawns, the gardens, were as rankly overgrown as the central patio was withered and choked up. Every morning now two Toyotas would disgorge their truckloads of neat Japs and equipment and in a parody of Iwo Jima that still gave him a bang, Hirohito's buck-toothed bandits would come swarming up the hill.

The inside, he had given instructions, was not yet to be touched. He had had it cleaned, of course, and fumigated. The dust, the cobwebs, the mildew and all the other more dubious crud had all been taken care of. But he'd resisted all the pressures put on him by friends, as they were being called that season, to hire an interior decorator. He was prepared to have truck with the Jap gardener's restoration capabilities. But, snip purchase though it had been, he'd be fucked if he'd leave the feeling of his house to the self-indulgent, no-expense-spared mercies of some failure in another walk of life. Names had been urged upon him of men two blocks away, in New York, in London, in Rome. But furnishing his first-owned home was a pleasure he reserved for himself. He'd seen their handiwork all over Beverly Hills. Huge marble and stucco palaces hideously over-ornamented. Bought by millionaire pop-stars demanding instant 'Hollywood' and pissing in the pool.

In the meantime he enjoyed its sadness. Stella Lang had not lied. In every room light, melancholy patches on the walls blankly announced that here had been a painting traded for Vodka, there a mirror smashed for reflecting the result. Pieces of furniture had been remembered after their departure by the marks they'd scuffed on the walls. Some rooms had been totally bare. He liked to wander through their emptiness, fill in his own imagined scenario of their past. Only the servants' bungalow nearby had been done over. It was now as bright and shiny as a next year's auto. Like every other Hollywood king, queen, or young pretender, he now had a 'man'.

This was another necessity they'd urged on him. It would be useful to have someone to press pants and figure out alibis. He had not said 'no'. Lyndon Oates just happened to know just the man.

His name was Tibor Pal. His age was set down on the paperwork as being sixty. But he seemed ten years, fifteen, younger. He had a full head of straight-back fair-grey hair and a pale, sharp-featured complexion. He wore a grey suit and gave off an overall impression of grey self-containment. Unmarried, he had worked in a similar capacity for various of the golden names now being trodden underfoot around Hollywood and Vine.

'Tibor has several years' experience of working professionally as a chef,' Oates had said on his behalf. 'He doesn't cook, he cuisines. He gravitated to Hollywood, he says, because in the old country he actually worked in movies. Isn't that so, Tibor?'

'Yes, sir.'

For the first time in the charade Paul Madison had felt a stir of genuine interest. He asked his first question.

'What did you do in the war?'

The expression didn't change but the pause was just discernible. 'I made Art films.'

That clinched it. If they wanted to sic their boy on to him he could think of nothing more appropriate than another collaborator.

'Well . . . everything seems . . . very satisfactory,' he had heard himself saying.

Now, at evening, on the ridge of Mulholland, all Hollywood spread out in view before his newly-acquired windows as if also for the taking, he sat alone. He sat marooned in the grande salle on the island of creamy-white sofa that had so far been one of his rare, necessary purchases. Just discernible in the waning light an opened script of *Cold Turkey* lay disregarded on the cushions. Close to it were details of an Oregon housing development his accountants had pressed him to sink funds in. He hadn't energy for either. He had the blues. He hadn't even energy to get up, go over and switch on a light . . .

Blues. Maybe he got them out of the air. What was his house had been hers. Her twilight ghost was perhaps hovering infectiously there in that dusky corner, was gently there on the edge of vision as he turned his head. Perhaps she softly sucked on his energy to feed her own . . . But no. Stella Lang was still alive. Far as he knew. There was no ghost. This was just bad grass. With a sudden surge of violence he leant across to stub the joint uncaringly out on the bare flagstone of the room's original floor. What the hell! It wouldn't hurt the blue-grey stone. And there was plenty more where that came from.

He knew what his trouble was. He wasn't blue because he was alone but because he was without Sam. She wouldn't say why or where or anything but she had cut him dead for this one night. In doing so, he realised, she confirmed he'd built up an addiction. The unbelievable, smooth slimness of her body pressed to him, moaning beneath his hand, was something he'd become dependent on. With her not there, the room was five times larger.

Shrilly, knifing through the dusk, the square skull of a phone bleeped whitely at him. Tibor had switched it through. His heart leapt like a teenage girl's. He reached down to the floor again and lifted the receiver.

'Is that the Madison—'

'Sam?'

'Er, hello? Hello?'

'Yes, hello.'

'Is that the Madison residence?'

'Who's asking?'

'That is Paul, isn't it? Paul, I know I shouldn't have but naturally I have your number – Paul, this is Celine.'

'So?'

'Paul, I'm not very good at this sort of thing. I don't know

what I've done. It's been weeks. Paul, could we maybe . . . could
I come over maybe, or something?'

'What for, Celine?'

'Paul! Don't. Paul you must know how I'm eaten up with
wanting you. Inside, Paul! It hurts Paul, listen . . .'

'Aren't there any Scottish pop stars in town tonight, Celine?'

'Paul! I had to. That was . . . business!'

'No business like it.'

'Paul – I'm begging. Please Paul . . . Paul, I've got nothing on –
I'm wearing nothing. Just perfume . . . Paul? . . . Oh, please Paul!
Please let me come over!'

He hung up. For a moment the image of the thin, pale,
Dunaway-type beauty down on her knees for him had tugged
at his lust. But in the odd times he had let her pinch-hit for
him in the last few months he had run the gamut of humbling
her ice-maiden arrogance. He had bent her every which way, and
she had screamed at times. Even when he had raised his hand to
slap her bruisingly about, there had been dark enjoyment thickening beneath the bruising of the shock . . . Better to hang up.
For all her pretence toward class she was queen of all the mer-
cenaries and he had mined that vein of cheapness past enjoyment.
Cheap, mean scents came off her in the end. She was a pale
shadow of Sam.

Sam! He wanted her sweet richness! But tonight.

He tried her number. The pulsing brought him no reply. But
it had brought momentum. He pushed the button on the house-
to-bungalow squawk box. There was the sense of an open, invisible sound window.

'Yes, sir?'

'Tibor, get out the car, will you. The X1-9. I'm going out.'

'Yes, sir.'

He closed the circuit. That would be something. He'd go take
a little cruise down Sunset.

Those same evening moments Samantha Montgomery lay staring
at the ceiling of Jerry White's bedroom, a naked arm's length
away from the owner. The sound and fury of their love-making –
her sound his fury – had subsided to an after-death silence. Colour
and nakedness apart, they could have been husband-wife effigies
above a medieval tomb. When, finally, she spoke it seemed to
mark an increase in the lack of motion.

'This thing, Jerry,' she said, 'I'm not sure it's working out.'

'What thing?'

'This Madison thing.'

The hint of discord to come made him twist up and round and, the spell broken, she turned her head towards him.

'What other thing is there?'

He ignored that, went back to her first remark.

'So what way is it not working out?' he said.

'Oh, Jerry, I don't know – it all seems so goddamned oblique.'

Passion made him shout.

'Well, for fuck's sake, woman,' he said, 'of course it's oblique. Look, we gave up wearing Afros and carrying assegais – all that Swahili shit – long years ago. I mean I may still live down here because it's going to be my ward but all that roots stuff is like crap. I mean it's worse than dishonest. It's counter-productive.'

'Jerry, we've been through all this—'

'Damn right. And we're making it pay off. Forget that revolution shit. That's for dying in jungles or ghettos. Right here, right now, the route to power is through the system and that's the way it's going to happen for us. But it takes bread and influence and clout and in this town, this country even, Madison's a passport to all them things.'

'You make him sound like one of your correspondence courses.'

'Sometimes you've got a dirty mouth.'

'I'm sorry, hon—'

'What do you mean – it isn't working out? You're getting noticed, right? Mentions in the trades?'

'As his companion. "Thrush", they say. That makes me sound like a disease.'

'You're up for a *Rockford Files*. He's said he'll fix a screen test for Magnum.'

'Talk's cheap, Jerry.'

'You mean he won't?'

'Oh . . . I guess he will . . . Jerry – none of this is what I meant.'

'Oh?'

'Him and me. I think it means something to him.'

'You made a list of those other names in the trades? Maybe you didn't have paper enough.'

'Them. Most of them are moonshine . . . I don't know. I think maybe I get to some kind of spot in him.'

He stirred again now, levered himself up on the bunched muscles of one arm. Handsome, self-assured or maybe not, he looked at her.

'Like maybe you mean it means something to you,' he said.

She was silent.

He bent forward and across her. With his free hand he began to stroke the long length, the intimacies of her body.

'Is he good?' he said.

She was still silent.

'Come on, baby, I can take it . . . Is he good?'

'Oh, for Christ's sake, Jerry, don't pretend to be so goddamned cool all of the time.'

His hand pushed into her and tightened meanly.

'He is good, isn't he?' he insisted.

'Jerry, for Christ's sake! What do you want me to say? Yes, okay then, he's good. He's all stud, Jerry, is that it? That what you want to hear? Wind him up and let him wail and, Jerry, you wouldn't believe it, he's fucking marvellous!'

The hand twisted savagely. She refused him the pleasure of hearing her cry out. As savagely he had twisted himself up onto his knees on the bed. Jealousy, the thought of her with someone else, had physically aroused him. She stared at him. She was not sharing his excitement.

He reached to the shelf at the bed's head and brought his hand back holding the heavy tumbler filled with Scotch. For a second she feared violence but tossing his head back he merely drained it in one fiercely prolonged gulp. He smashed the glass down heavily.

'Then we'd better save you for the white sonofabitch!' he said, thickly. He swung off the bed.

In a moment she heard the vicious hiss of the shower begin to run but she lay still and did not go to soap him.

'Kurt, will you for Christ's sake turn that blower down or something! I can't hear myself fucking think!'

'Doing it fast's the way to do it! Oh, very well—'

Reflected in the mirrored cabinets that ran the entire length of the wall, the hairdresser grimaced before flicking a switch. The whirr of hot-aired noise about his ears abated. But for an instant, there, the sharp catty claws had been clearly apparent protruding from the soft pads of faggot fat. Geisler's complexion and dyed hair were both as outrageous as ever. Christ, he looks like a soft, fat Clint Eastwood, Paul Madison thought.

But he'd better say something in the way of a peace offering.

'Sorry, Kurt,' he said, 'but I'm not used to receiving folks like some fucking Louis or another.'

Kurt Geisler sniffed.

'Oh that's okay,' he said.

'No, let me say again that we're the ones that should apologise, Paul,' Tom Leonard said, 'for barging in like this.'

He and Frank Martelli sat either side of the barber's chair Paul Madison had caused to be installed in his own bathroom. They would have formed some kind of a triptych faintly reminiscent of a Christ hanging between the two thieves had it not been that a cabinet opposite Martelli was ajar and had bisected his reflection into a two-ways-facing distortion. The lawyer was sitting on the closed cherry-wood lid of the bidet. He had the eagle-eyed sharp features of an early Spanish grandee and his grey-white hair, receding to the sides of both his temples, had been expertly brushed with that effect in mind. As Kurt Geisler paused to clip an invisibly disobedient hair, Paul Madison looked sideways at Martelli's double-header of an image and privately congratulated the mirrors on their accuracy.

'You boys doing alright on your drinks there?' he said.

'Well, just a touch—' Tom Leonard said.

He got up from the rim of the half-sunken bath, also encased in cherry-wood and in the shape of a vat you'd tread grapes in. He reached for the crystal decanter of Bourbon on the closed top of the john.

'How about you, Kurt?'

'Not while I'm working,' the hairdresser snipped.

'Okay, Tom,' Madison said, 'you didn't just stop by on the way to the airport to check on whether I was into toupees yet. What is it?'

In the mirror Tom Leonard did a Tony Randall wince. He wouldn't have done that face to face, Paul Madison thought.

'You're not going to like this,' he said. 'I got word this afternoon that, no ifs or buts, Milt Rosner's gone solid on Christie Roberts for the girl.'

'Well, thank you for that great fucking bulletin!'

'Please! You must hold still for me!'

'But – I mean, she's dead. She's dead behind the eyes.'

Tom Leonard swilled liquor around the bottom of his glass. 'You can sort of see it,' he said. 'She's got that kind of vulnerability – you know, the sort that makes you eager to see that she gets hers. In a way, you know, she's right for it.'

'Vulnerable – Shmunerable. Is there nothing our people can do?'

Tom Leonard shook his reflected head. He was wearing a

double-breasted blazer and a tie that made you think of yachting clubs.

'Frank?'

In a confusion of images, the lawyer shrugged. 'She's got a contract. Word is she came pretty cheap.'

Madison gave an ugly laugh. 'They all do. Jesus – what about the nude scenes? I mean, Christ – she's built like a surf board.'

A debator acknowledging a point, a fighter slipping a lead, Tom Leonard ducked his head.

'I guess they've got something pretty tasteful in mind there,' he said. 'Like we're still going for a mass audience. Maybe Franklin figures the sight of a slip of a girl will make all the women feel superior. Maybe he figures a lack of boobs'll make her masochism all the more pathetic.'

'Maybe he's after the gay vote.'

The scissors snipped at his ear again.

'Christ – I'd rather pay myself to have it rewritten black and go for Samantha Montgomery.'

Tom Leonard's voice and looks had an edge.

'Don't be silly now, Paul,' he said. 'Nobody knows her. She couldn't draw her own folks. Don't rush it there.'

'Rush it! How much longer before this screen test actually gets—'

'It'll happen. Just give it time.'

'Time! Sure! My sweet Christ! Christie Roberts!'

Tom Leonard reverted to his head-shaking and sighs.

'Well, there it is I'm afraid. She's locked in . . . there's another—'

'Oh, on the subject of undesirable little blondes. Could you tell Lyndon I'd like him to let that Celine go?'

From the chair he saw Martelli and Leonard exchange a fast, unguarded look.

'Well, I'm—'

'She came through with a few bangs in the line of duty, right. Now she thinks it gives her rights. Privileges. She's calling me at all hours.'

'She shouldn't do—'

'Damn right!'

'She shouldn't do that, Paul. But, well, I don't know how Lyndon would feel about letting her go.'

Oh? So that was partly it. Maybe that's why she'd transmitted a sour, bleak after-taste.

'You know – he's kind of, er, attached to her, I guess. And Seamus Rimmer sets a lot of store by her.'

'Boot her up to the Springs or New York or someplace.'

'We don't maintain an official, er, office at the Springs, Paul . . . you know that. Look, it's just the chasing you, right? Tell you what. I'll take her out to lunch and tell her you're strictly off her limits. Out of her league. Verboten.'

'. . . alright. But make sure you tell her it's from me.'

'Oh I will. Don't worry. Look, Paul, Frank has to make this Chicago flight so maybe—'

'Jesus, Frank. Times you go to Chicago I don't know why you don't have a personal pipeline.'

The Spanish aristocrat grinned and for a second was a wolf.

'Business is there, but pleasure's here,' he said. 'So I like commuting.'

'Hmph! Family business.'

'Now, now,' Martelli said dismissively. 'Reason I'm here is business. Coast business. Your business. Something else I don't think you're going to like very much . . .'

'Well?'

'It's your mother. She's wised up who you are. She's started to smell money. That's bad.'

Tom Leonard saw Paul Madison lock rigid. His hand, extended on the end of the chair arm beyond the drape, grew visibly whiter as the force of his grip drained blood out of its surface. Sensing the tension, electric, almost as visible, flowing from his client, Kurt Geisler had frozen in involuntary sympathy. A tail comb still poised in his hand, he took a half-step back. A potential for violence was suddenly ricocheting around a bathroom that would never see a cockroach.

'Well?' Paul Madison said.

'Well, we—'

'You can take care of it, can't you?'

'Yes, of course. But we need your signature.'

'Oh?'

'Two things to do. We—'

'I don't want to know! Just—'

'Just listen a second, dammit!'

Frank Martelli had less need to pander to finer or worse feelings than Tom Leonard. He stared at Madison with a fierce irritation. The actor moved his lips and swallowed.

'Alright,' he said, 'sorry.'

'She's in Phoenix, Arizona. A little too close to home if she wants to play dirty and come calling. By all accounts the guy she's with is a real meanie. He's her fourth husband, by the way and I'd guess—'

'Come on! I don't want a book!'

'Okay. What we do is set her up with a house in Corpus Christi. And an allowance. In case there's any comeback that gets public later on, it's better—'

'There'd better not be.'

'There won't. But it's better PR-wise if her pay-off cheques come in the legal form of a settlement from you, her devoted son.'

'Cunt!' The roar had bellowed out of Madison with, it had seemed, an extra-human force. Martelli looked at Leonard with a genuine alarm and was answered by a look of quite real fright. Leonard gave a quick palms-downward flicker of one hand. The mirror caught it.

'Sorry. Not you guys,' Madison said. 'Something I was thinking of.'

Or had seen in the mirror from long years ago.

'Make you jump, Kurt?' he said.

'Well, I should think so!'

'Sorry.'

Martelli coughed.

'The accountants say the most effective way to fly tax-wise is to set up an associated subsidiary company to your enterprises in your name linked to hers and there—'

'How many signatures you want?'

'Two.'

'Give me two blank sheets of paper and I'll autograph them both.'

'Well – I can do a little better than that.'

Martelli produced two closely typed documents of some six pages each from out his briefcase. He flipped over each to the last page where a pencilled X stood above a dotted line. He produced a fountain pen from the inside breast pocket of his dark worsted suit. He closed the briefcase, put the pages on it as Madison, arm emerging from the dark mustard drape, scrawled two signatures.

'Okay,' he said.

'Thank you, sir,' Martelli said in mock servility. 'I don't think we need detain you any longer from your toilette.'

He put down the case and looked at his watch.

'Jesus!' he said, 'and we'd better fucking well not.'

He juggled the documents back into flat order. Reached again for his briefcase.

'Excuse me,' Kurt Geisler said, 'I think you've picked up—'

'Oh, I'm sorry. But they do rather look alike, don't they?'

'I think mine's a little gayer.' Geisler giggled at his own temerity.

Tom Leonard set down his glass as Frank Martelli picked up the correct briefcase.

'Must run, Paul,' he said. 'Talk to you tomorrow.'

'OK. You guys find your own way out?'

'Oh, sure. 'Bye now.'

'Hey, Tom. Sorry I hollered.'

'Aw, forget it. Ciao!'

'Ciao.'

They were gone. Letting out a deep breath, Kurt Geisler stepped forward to complete his handiwork.

He had agreed to be seen around with Christie Roberts. Lyndon Oates had laid it on him with the familiar coating of bullshit and apple-sauce.

'We have to promote her, Paul baby. We got to make it look as though you're banging her and liking it.'

So he had followed the ritual dance created years earlier with the young pretenders fashioned in the likeness of a Rock Hudson, Tony Curtis, or a Robert Wagner. They were paired with the current hot numbers in the studios then launched on premieres, parties, stunts, and important conventions. It was a parasitical process in which all the participants fed on each other. All got a fair leavening of publicity; the studio, the stars, the producers and the movies. Sometimes the double-acts actually ended in marriage. Most often they just slid resignedly into bed. Hell, we've been scheduled together for the evening, they're picking up the tabs we may as well go for the five-star service! Oddly, though he felt she was there for the taking, Madison had seen her off most nights with a brief 'thank you and goodnight'. She was too classy and coltish for his more immediate requirements. And she talked too much. Mostly about her father who had the largest stock holding in a vast conglomerate that was more a dynasty than an industry. It was obvious, because she gave him a score of variations on the theme, that anything Christie Roberts wanted, she could have. Papa had told her that. 'He hated my going to Hollywood,' she had giggled. 'Doesn't like actors!'

And then he discovered he was being tailed. He had dropped her off at Malibu and had noticed that the white Dodge behind him had kept at a regular distance all the way along the Coast Highway and had turned with him on to Sunset. He had stopped to get some gas expecting to see the Dodge streak past. But it had stopped too, the driver's face briefly visible as he lit a cigarette. Madison drove more slowly. This way he could confirm if the guy really was tailing him. Also it gave him time to think. He thought back to the freeway accident and visions flashed uncomfortably through his mind. No, that was over and taken care of. He made another turn and stopped at the news-stand outside the Beverly Wilshire Hotel. The Dodge stopped too, at precisely the same seventy-five feet distance. It was late. The lights had gone out at the Brown Derby opposite. It was dark too at the vintage car showrooms at the corner of the next block. Madison put a quarter in the machine, lifted the lid, and took out a copy of the a.m. edition of the *Examiner*. The man had got out of the other car. He looked around a hundred and fifty pounds. A thin, flat swathe of hair swung forward on his forehead. He flexed his shoulders and pulled the roll-over of his sweater up under his chin. Madison felt the pressure building up at his temples. He walked almost lazily to the other car. At five paces he paused. Each man measured the other. A taxi, its roof sign lit up, slowed down, and getting no signal, shrugged onwards.

Madison spoke first. 'You looking for someone?'

The man hunched his shoulders, thrust his hands deep into his pockets. 'Maybe.'

'You followed me from Malibu,' Madison said quietly, 'and you been tailing me all along.'

'Well don't let it get you . . .'

The blow took him without warning, on his neck just below the jaw. He fell back on the car, spittle dribbling down from his mouth. Now Madison had one knee at his groin, a hand forcing his head hard on the car's roof.

'Now listen, you prick, I got no time. Unless you want me to stuff your eyeballs up your ass you better come through with some information. Like who put you on to me, and why.'

The man gurgled, groped down to a hip pocket and pulled out a bill-fold. Madison looked for the ID increasing the pressure on the man's head and groin. 'Je-sus Christ . . .' was as much as he could choke out.

'Private eye, eh,' Madison said easily. 'Now look, chum, I'm going to quietly take the hooks out of you and you are going to tell me what this is all about. Okay?'

The man nodded.

'You going to be smart?' Madison added pleasantly, forcing his knee further into the man's crotch.

'Yes!' the man managed to screw out.

And so Paul Madison had learned that Christie Roberts's father had decided to check on the company his daughter kept.

'You got his phone number?'

The man was glad to scribble it down.

'You got a home to go to?' Madison was almost kindly.

'Yes.'

'Then I tell you what you do. You get into the car, you go home, and tomorrow you unload this particular assignment. I get nervous when I'm being followed. You dig?'

He pushed the man into the car, slammed the door, and waited for him to drive off.

The Japanese houseboy said he was sorry but Mr Roberts could not be disturbed at this hour. Madison said, 'You tell Mr Roberts it's urgent. Concerning his daughter.'

'I don't think he will like...'

'I think he will. You just tell him this won't wait till morning.' Madison heard a click as Christie Roberts's father took the extension.

'Who is this?'

'Paul Madison. I've just taken some sharp corners off one of your spies on Wilshire. The one you had on me tonight from Malibu.'

'Oh he's been on you much longer than that, Mr Madison.' The voice was too calm. A hint of cultured, well-honed menace.

'Well what the fuck is going on!'

'I will tell you precisely what is going on Mr Madison. I'm taking out a little insurance, that's all really. When anything very close to me, like my daughter, is involved, I want to be sure that...'

'Who the fuck do you think...'

'No let me finish. I just like to be sure that no harm, of any kind, comes her way. She wanted to go to Hollywood. Well, personally I regard you all in that trade, excuse my frankness, as whores and charlatans. But Christie's heart is set on it so I go along with it. But I've had you checked Mr Madison and to tell you the truth, I don't like what I hear. The name is Ukinski isn't it?'

The nerve-end touched, a momentary paralysis left Madison without words.

'No matter,' the voice said softly. 'I wouldn't like you to think I am a snob. But there were other . . . er, incidents, which fill me with some concern. You see Madison' – the 'Mr' had significantly been jettisoned – 'Christie has certain problems of her own. The analyst, the best there is, I promise you, has made it clear that a major emotional crisis at this time could be very dangerous.'

Madison had hardly been listening. He had been projected, brutally, to a scene long since buried under the progressive laminates of success and Oates's instant charisma. The vision, like the fastest shutter speed on a camera had clicked open infinitesimally. Then shut. But in it he had seen blood, death, and heard a woman laugh when he knew she should have screamed.

'You checked up on me,' he said at last.

'That shouldn't worry you, Madison. I check up on everyone.'

Slowly Madison put the phone down on its cradle. He switched on the remote control, latching on to the last third of a late, late movie.

Little of it infiltrated the looming barriers of his mind.

A naked arm's length away from its owner, Samantha Montgomery stared up at the ceiling of Paul Madison's master bedroom.

It was wooden. Tongued and grooved cedar ran evenly from right to left in restful, expensive simplicity. Beyond the screens the windows were open to the evening and its breeze blew the fine lawn curtains upwards like pale flags. After the turbulence of a short while ago, the cool quiet felt delicious. Then, chanting a gasping ecstasy, she had climaxed beyond all imaginings.

Now, he moved. He scrunched down sideways on the waterbed to lay the flat of his head across her belly.

'Soft. So soft,' he said. 'Do you know you smell quite differently after than before. Kind of sweeter.'

She laughed.

'Well,' she said. 'I guess we could certainly say there's a change in chemical constituents – before and afterwards.' She laughed again and her stomach gurgled.

'Well, well,' he said. 'Sounds like Niagara.'

'That was the water-bed.'

'No, it wasn't,' he said.

'How'd you know?'

'Oh I keep my ear pretty close to the ground.'

They both laughed, were both quiet.

'When do you start shooting?' she asked after a while.

'Week next Monday.'

'I shan't be able to see you so often then.'

'Sure. You can come around the set.'

'No. I won't. I wouldn't like that.'

They were silent again.

'Does it burn you up,' he said. 'That I'm working? Big. Famous. You're a—'

'Nobody. No. Not like that. I'm happy for you because you're beautiful and I love you.'

He did not change position by a hairsbreadth but she felt his entire body tense.

'I do, you know,' she said softly. 'And it isn't just this – the screwing. But you don't have to worry. No strings. No demands. You don't have to love me.'

'Maybe I . . .'

'You don't even have to speak.'

She didn't want to force him to her on her terms. She worked to bend their talk.

'What burns me,' she said, 'is being shut out from so many parts. On account of being black. I don't sing so well, I know, but I get by because I've got that black girl image. But I act pretty damn good. And I'm shut out . . . Know what I want? I want to play Hedda Gabler, Phaedra, Lady Macbeth – I want to play them because I know I can and I want people to come not because it's different like seeing a dog walk on its hind legs but because I'm good. And you know what burns me, lover? It's knowing that even if I did, I'd never know. I could do Hedda Gabler at the Lincoln Centre and everyone might come and clap and stomp and shout but I still wouldn't know if it was all for me or some uppity spade got up on her hind legs.'

'Yes you would,' he said. 'You've got brains to know you would and know it while you're doing it.'

'Have I?' she said. 'I wonder. When you've never made it big you can't help but wonder all the time whether you're maybe not so hot.'

'And when you do it all seems so ridiculously easy. Such . . . such a waste,' Madison said.

'Yes? You feel that? Really?'

He made no answer.

'One thing,' she said. 'I may not try to look or come on like Angela Davis, but one thing's for certain. I'll be fucked if I'll settle for the token nigger in this week's soap opera!'

'Forget it,' he said reaching for her.

'No,' she said. 'Not this minute.'

She rolled away. This time she was the one who got up first to shower.

His part in *Cold Turkey* involved him in research. As the piano-playing protagonist who started out a heroin addict he needed to give accurate portrayals of the highs, the lows, the experiencing of withdrawal pains, that getting hooked could bring. Once, with Lyndon Oates who seemed to know him, once alone, he had had a couple of pleasant lunches with a broad-faced narcotics dick from the LAPD. The second time the cop had looked at him with a shrewd smile.

'You don't want to mess with the stuff for real,' he'd said. 'If you want to know what's good for you just keep on the grass. But if you ever have trouble getting it up and keeping it, climb on to her after a couple of sniffs of this. At your age I guess you'd be shooting for a straight ten in a row.'

Quite openly he had pushed an envelope across the table. It had contained two or three teaspoons of a fine white powder.

'What is it?'

'Secret recipe. Nothing dangerous. If you like it and want some more you call me up.'

It had been suggested that he go down to the tank and see some of the young hop-heads coming in. He'd made excuses. He could do that scene from memory. He had gone out to Palas Verdes and visited a charming and anonymous large house. He'd put an eye to the spy-hole of the cell there and as he shuddered at the scream-ing, gagging, foetally-clawed-together scarecrow in its corner, made up his mind never to use that powder except down his john. Driving back in his new Corniche he had found his thoughts running upon Stella Lang. Booze wouldn't be so bad now, would it . . . ?

In the event he found out most about addict behaviour one

evening with Eichler over a couple of whores.

The second thing, was playing the piano. What the fuck, why pussy-foot around? He had had Magnum send up a Steinway. And two tutors. The one was a stiff-corsetted lady of advanced years and some two hundred pounds. But a wit – a brilliantly lucid explainer. With her he began to learn the piano from square one. He found he had some flair, that he enjoyed it. He had enough finger dexterity still, unconscious ability to count, to translate his first readings into something quite acceptable in a beginner.

But Hank Wells came in too. The slim jazz great was doing the score and laying down the sound-track recording for the film. From him he was to learn some passable approximation of the fingering for when, in the studio, before a gutless piano, the cameras would start to roll to playback. He was with Hank working to a tape-deck stride version of 'Don't the Moon Look Lonesome' when from the corner of his eye he saw the light on the phone flash. Well, Tibor would get that. It was switched through to him and that's why he got paid.

'Mr Oates, sir,' he said. 'He said he'd rather prefer to talk with you.'

Sieg Heil!

'Okay. I'll take it here. Excuse me, Hank.'

'Hello, Paul sweetheart?'

'No-one else. How you coming, Lyndon?'

'Fine. Just fine. Listen – can you talk?'

'Oh, I guess.'

'I got some sort of bad news.'

'Oh?'

'I wanted you should hear from me – before anyone else felt like laying it on you.'

'What's happened, Lyn ...'

'So I thought rather than run up—'

'For shit's sake, Lyndon, what's this all about?'

'It's the campaign, you know, for the Oscar nominations. We've been asked to pull the plug on ours. That means on you, Paul.'

'But you've been pushing me all week in the trades. "We respectfully recommend to Academy members the brilliant performance of Paul Madison" and all that shit. What happens to all that?'

'Listen, Paul, baby. There's been the usual horse trading. You know, you scratch my back, I'll scratch yours. A lot of it. You know we're slugging it out with *Rat Trap*.'

'So?'

'They want to go for the "best actor" slot for their man but they're prepared to leave the field open for "the best supporting role".'

'Meaning me.'

'Well that's not exactly eating shit, Paul,' Oates's tone hardened.

'I'm not eating any of it, Lyndon. No way! Listen, the press, the television, all over, have been saying I've got the edge on the "best actor" nomination!'

'We can take care of it, Paul baby. I tried, believe me, I tried. But that's the way the big boys want it played. We have to go along with it. I swear if I have to go down on my bended knees that you'll get the big guns next year for *Cold Turkey*.'

'Promises, promises—'

'I give you my word, Paul. Listen, it's early days. Be patient. It's only a year.'

'And my frigging career.'

Paul, you can see. *Turkey*'s a one-part movie. *Curtain* wasn't and *Rat Trap* was in line ahead of you. It's as simple as that, Paul. I mean, like what am I supposed to do?'

'Tread on a few heads.'

'Paul. I know how you must feel.'

'Do you?'

'But I deserve better from you than that.'

'Yeah, well . . . maybe. Yeah, okay, Lyndon – sorry.'

'That's okay. It's a rough one sweetheart. I'm just glad you see how it must be.'

'Okay. Another day, another dollar, maybe . . . Hey! Jack isn't up for anything now, is he?'

'Oh no. He had his crack a couple of years back and this time – well, what did he have to go to bat with?'

'Nothing, I guess.'

'Dennis Curtis is also up for supporting, actually.'

'What? Fucking what?'

'We're not behind it, Paul. Some of those guys at the Academy are suckers for an English accent.'

'Lyndon, you've got to be kidding! This is a put-on, right? Dennis Curtis! Dennis take-one-hundred-and-fucking-ten Curtis!'

'Paul, I swear to God, I was never—'

'Is Sylvia up?'

'Sylvia?'

'Sylvia Kilmartin, the editor, for Chrissakes.'

'Oh, her.'

'You know she saved Curtis from being a big, big joke and . . . I . . . I just . . . Lyndon, I need a drink. Lyndon I'm going to do something I never did to you before. I'm hanging up. Okay, I'll talk to you to morrow. 'kay?'

'Paul, don't whip the messenger who got stuck with—'

But Madison slammed the receiver down. He did it with such violence that for a second the glow-worm light flickered on as between life and death. As he looked up Hank Wells was closing the Steinway's lid. He looked at Paul from above the endless pockets of violet rimmed beneath his eyes. 'I figured that'd be about it for today,' he said.

Not long after the phone rang again. He answered it himself. It was Jack Preston.

'Listen,' Preston said eventually, 'I hear you play a pretty mean game of tennis.'

'So-so,' he said. But that was true. He had never majored on the game but he had the reflexes, the build. He had a ball-player's co-ordination.

'So listen, then. The smog count's down today. Stop being a one-man clan and come on over. We'll knock us some balls and maybe crack open a virgin or two.'

Like the summons to the Oval Office, the Court of St James, or the Vatican, the invitation was a landmark.

So did he obtain entry into Hollywood's innermost circle.

Even by Hollywood's exacting requirements, their forty-eight hour spree enjoying the best hookers and high-life on offer, had been a triumph. It had begun at Preston's home, in style. There had been a set-piece duet between two black girls on the Mexican rug in Preston's den. They had writhed over each other from all points of the compass, and as they climaxed, one raking the other's back with silver painted fingernails, Eichler roared 'olé!' while Preston went over and kissed them both appreciatively on the buttocks.

That had been the curtain-raiser. Afterwards, when joints had given way to more sophisticated stuff brought over by Eichler, they, the five of them, had launched themselves upon the sexual goodies which Preston had commandeered for the revelry. Madison and Eichler were being pleasured by three of the girls, a novelty introduced by Preston with his usual crooked grin, 'always carry a spare, friends!' He himself had taken to his own bedroom with one of the black girls, a stewardess on an African airline. The studio, alert to the possibility of cheap location facilities on what they still called the dark continent, had persuaded Preston to be guest of honour at the party celebrating the airline's inaugural flight to LA. He had presented each stewardess with an inscribed watch paid for jointly by the studio and a Japanese watch company, and then banged this particular one rigid that same night at the downtown hotel where the crew had been accommodated. She had told him that she believed passionately in total, uninhibited sex and had proved it by inviting him to take her any way he pleased, after she, of course, had enjoyed her own tricks. At the end of it all, Preston felt mauled inside and out. He murmured appreciatively and swore he'd always fly her airline. When he had invited her for the weekend she had eagerly consented, and brought a like-minded friend with her.

This one was hand-operating the handsome actor-turned-independent producer, Walter Bygraves, on an air-bed in another room. Married and cuckolded twice, Bygraves now lived from hand to mouth. Whose hand and whose mouth was largely a matter of whim or recommendation. The fifth member of Preston's group was Dave Sutherland, a bronzed giant of a stuntman, bodyguard and procurer, indispensable for the whole jag. He had taken unto himself a Hungarian actress named Magda whose predatory appetite in sex was so fierce only someone like Sutherland, who received ten thousand dollars a time for say, allowing a building to fall on him, could cope with her.

When finally all five men had, in Eichler's expert judgement cocked themselves numb, Preston gave each girl an envelope containing five hundred dollar bills, and had them swiftly spirited off the premises by his driver. It had then been Eichler's idea, that Sunday morning, to get his pilot to fly them to Lake Tahoe. They leapt at it with the enthusiasm of drunken salesmen at a convention. They had reeled out of Preston's Rolls at LA airport, and tumbled into the plane yelling jokes at the pilot. He turned round from his seat and forced a smile. Eichler, attempting decorum, raised his hand.

'Gentlemen,' he boomed, 'you will please adjust your seat belts. You will not smoke, or jerk off during take-off.'

He smiled benevolently at the pilot.

'Okay Bill, it's all yours.'

And now, some hours later, they were sprawled out in Eichler's white-carpeted living room, the bloom of several successive Bloody Marys high-colouring their faces. Sutherland had passed out, and lay curled foetally near one leg of Eichner's grand piano. Beethoven's Für Elise lay open on the music stand above it. It was one of the few pieces Eichler could play with any competence. A party piece. He played only two bars that morning before Preston effectively murdered culture for the day.

'Fuck that, Alex,' he said sourly. 'Wrong time, wrong music, wrong fucking audience.'

Madison laughed. 'Don't shoot the pianist, Jack, he's doing his worst!' He could afford to be good natured. He felt elated in this company. It was top-drawer stuff. Bygraves, who had taken out his hinged, tortoishell spectacles to read the Sunday edition of the *LA Times*, was one of the most successful independents in the business. It was one thing to be called in to his office to discuss movies. Any leading actor can get into that. But to be invited in on this level, privileged to see Bygraves with his pants down and pecker up, was the ultimate accolade. Madison felt hooked to the generating current of real power. Here he was right in the inner circle. Better even than having 'fuck you' money. When you flew around in the company of Bygraves and Preston, the message was clear. You were 'A' class material.

Bygraves tossed the paper aside. 'How's the meat market these days, Alex?'

'Flourishing thank you, Walter,' Eichler said. He frowned. These pricks enjoyed nothing better than to denigrate his work. He looked coolly at Bygraves.

'But then we're all in the cattle business aren't we? What would some of your meat look like if I didn't improve upon it?'

Madison laughed. 'Oh boy!' he groaned, winking at Preston.

'No, it's a fact,' Eichler said, his fifth Bloody Mary and third straight vodka launching him beyond recall. 'It may just be meat to you . . .'

'But it's pussy to him!' Preston brightly interjected.

It was a word to take the heat out of any argument.

'Also true,' Eichler conceded, eyes gleaming. 'I have to admit that like you, gentlemen, I enjoy certain fringe benefits.'

'You mean you get first bite at any tit or ass you raise?' Preston asked, impressed.

'Frequently. And that includes some of the most famous breasts in Hollywood. You would be amazed at some of the er . . . talent

I have had access to through the medium of my profession. You must understand that when they see what I have done for them, they are full of gratitude. My clinic provides a wonderful opportunity for them to express it, too.' The thought excited him.

'Sometimes I feel people in this town do not fully appreciate the work I do. Sure some South African doctor can do a transplant and everybody says it is a miracle. But how many lives have been enriched by this procedure? None! How many have been given a new joy, a rejuvenation by this piece of simple carpentry?'

'None,' Preston said, stoutly, nudging Madison.

'On the other hand,' Eichler declared loudly, 'I make fading women bloom again, I make their bosoms proud and firm, the nipples hard and . . .'

'This I really gotta see!' said Madison.

'And you may, all of you,' Eichler declared. 'It would be an experience for you. You would have a new respect for a much maligned profession. I have no objection at all to your looking over my shoulder so to speak, to be in at the very moment of re-creation.'

'No thank you,' Preston said. 'I like my meat hot and alive, not cold and hand-sewn on a slab.'

'Chicken,' Madison said.

'I'm with Jack,' Bygraves said. 'If there's silicone in the tit I just don't want to know about it.'

Madison moved over to Eichler, put an arm across his shoulder. 'Seems like you lost your audience, Alex' he said. 'But I'm a fan. You know that. I've always wanted to see how these retreads were done. I'm not called tomorrow. Whose boobs you got on the slab in the morning?'

Eichler closed his eyes groping for the memory button in his overcast mind. 'Ah, yes – but . . .' he frowned, 'nothing sensational really. I've got Christie Roberts coming in for a standard breast-enlarging procedure. I don't think it's your . . .'

'Hold on, Alex!' Madison's brain jolted on reflex. 'You said Christie Roberts?'

'Yes. The studio told me they want, as they put it, a little more meat on the bone.'

An idea had sprung into Madison's mind through some diabolical trap door. So this spoiled broad was getting her boobs pumped! Well, he wouldn't mind getting a ringside seat on that! Her father had warned him off. The analyst had said she must avoid emotional pressures. Fine! But that had nothing to do with her boobs. He'd been leaned on by an expert and it disgusted him. Seeing Christie Roberts half-naked under the knife, wouldn't swing the advantage all his way. But it opened beautiful possibilities.

'Alex,' Madison said, 'you got a deal.'

chapter seven

. . . Also out, Christie Roberts to some hideaway in South Carolina to relax, recharge batteries and maybe sort of sneak up sideways for the part of Ginny in *Cold Turkey*.

Hollywood Reporter

The preliminary flight instructions having crackled through from Burbank Control Tower, the Bonanza wiggled its wings slightly and began the long, flat trajectory of its descent in to the Los Angeles basin. The smog was heavy that morning. Like a plague of Egypt, like the opening nasty of a routine sci-fi thriller. It was spread in layers of excretory browns and leperous yellows across the sprawling amorphous town blasphemously called 'The City of the Angels'. Here and there tall thin rectangles of black, aluminium and glass rose up out of the sombre haze, to ensure that bank, insurance, or movie presidents at least could breathe unpolluted air in their executive suites. At ground level it got into the eyes, the throat, had sent disgruntled matrons scuttling to Miami and Frank Sinatra to Palm Springs.

'Look at all that shit we have to live in,' Alex Eichler said. 'Put in some research on lung transplants and you could end up owning three of these babies.'

Eichler grunted. He made a small adjustment to the controls.

Backyard swimming pools three thousand feet below ceased to wink up at them provocatively like blue-eyed high-school teasers, and soon they had cut down into the brown morning twilight.

Eichler shifted moodily in his seat. He grunted again.

'Listen, Paul,' he said, 'I don't know about this thing. Monday morning's a lot different to Saturday night up at Tahoe. With four bare asses playing tag and everybody having fun. Monday morning I'm Doctor Alex Eichler, MD.'

'Oh, come on, Alex, what's to go wrong? What you got to lose?'

Eichler drew in his breath sharply.

'Jesus,' he said, 'what have I got to lose, he asks. You ever been poor, Paul?'

'Sure.'

'Real poor?'

'Sure.'

'Then you got a real bad memory. I have to tell you. Do you have any idea what it's like working nights in a steel mill? Have you—'

'I reckon—'

'Have you forgotten how fuckingly boring, monotonous, tired-making it is to be poor? Doing everything the hard way. Everything. Keeping warm. Keeping clean. Keeping half-fed. You're up to bat for something all the time, twenty-four hours a day. You're an American. Maybe you never knew the sort—'

'So what has this got to do—'

'I'll tell you what this has got to do with anything. The hours, the weeks, I stayed awake studying to qualify when all I wanted to do was sleep for ever. An effort of pure will. Young man's will. I don't think I could do that now. I know I couldn't. You know what I'm afraid of more than anything?'

'You'll make a mistake.'

'Right. I'm the best in town. I am. I work hard. But I'm human. I play hard. Maybe one day I make a slip. I have some bad luck and give someone a bad scar. Well, with the malpractice laws it would be goodbye Alex. I deal with influential people and influential people talk. United Press, maybe, would pick it up and – whoof! – I'm gone overnight . . .'

'Listen – how do you think Rosner would be feeling right now if he knew the star of his current twelve-million-dollar movie was hanging up in the sky in a single seater plane with a private pilot in the driving seat?'

'That's different. He—'

'He'd shit himself, that's what. Can me, most like, if he found out.'

'Yes, but—'

'But I trust you, see. I figure you could maybe do the same—'

Burbank came crackling through with an adjustment. Eichler's thick forearms made the necessary correction.

'Well, Alex, if you want to go back on your word and chicken out,' Paul Madison said, 'I'll understand. And no bad feelings, I swear.'

For twenty seconds they flew in silence.

'Well, I tell you, Paul,' Eichler said, 'I gave you my word and you are my friend and I don't go back on my word to friends. I guess I just want you to appreciate the extent – the personal, psychological extent – I'm putting my head on the block for you.'

'Alex, I do appreciate it. Truly. Remember it's not just rubber-necking. I got a reason for all this. And it'll be okay. You coached me fine and when it comes to getting a part down I'm the fastest read in town.'

'For both our sakes I hope so. A barred plastic surgeon coming at you with a scalpel is not a test of muscle you should want to face.'

'Which way do we play it – you're thinking of taking me on and—'

'No! I daren't tell my assistants. They're good guys but maybe they get drunk one time and talk or, they get jealous more like, and really talk. Competition will make them nervous and nervous makes jealous quicker. No . . . you remember I told you she's into all this primal scream shit . . . ?'

'Yes.'

'You come as her shrink. One of them, whatever. You insisted on being present, I shall say, to satisfy yourself that my surgery is not going to induce a personality change detrimental to your patient. And she insisted and so on. Okay?'

'Okay. Got you.'

Eichler heaved a worried sigh.

'Come on – you'll piss yourself laughing the next day,' Paul Madison said.

They had been brought in very low. The freeways were beginning to swim up through the dirt-cloud swirl. Movies had rendered the view cliché, robbed it of scale. The system was merely an elaborate toy layout in some rich kid's playroom and when he flipped a switch the scurrying models would immediately freeze. It was animation from a high-school science film. Corpuscles were rushing oxygen to the big nexus of an interchange. It wasn't real.

To their right, the white HOLLYWOOD sign in the hills of the same name picked up a little tarnished sunshine and seemed to fake a smile saying 'Cheese'. The same sun washed over the high-rises on Wilshire and Sunset, extending westward with the full symmetry of pocket calculators. Immediately beneath them, apartment buildings, bungalows, shacks, duplexes littered the hill-sides in an eyesore of dirty pastel shades. Whoever had laid them out had been bored, half-hearted. They weren't real, either, Madison thought. But the thought cheered him. If they were not real they were easier to own.

Eichler leaned forward slightly and pushed a button. He began calling up Burbank for final instructions.

An hour later Paul Madison was covering his nose and mouth

with a sterile, paper-disposable face mask which, had it not been for the efficiency of the air filtration system in Eichler's Mercedes, he might well have been grateful for during the ride from Burbank to San Marino. The mask was his pass into the operating theatre of Eichler's hospital. He and the plastic surgeon were alone together in the preparation ante-room next to the theatre. Eichler had just taken him through scrubbing up.

He turned to Madison a capped, masked face made commonplace by countless episodes of hospital soap-opera.

'Okay, now listen,' Eichler said. 'She's already had a hefty dose of relaxant. She's drowsy. But she's not out. You stand in the corner where I tell you and keep your mouth shut. Understood?'

'Understood,' Paul Madison said thickly through the moistening mask. 'Got you.'

Hands held up needlessly but from force of habit before his chest, Eichler approached the stainless steel and glass doors to the theatre like a priest about to bless a congregation. With a just audible whoosh the doors slid apart. Paul Madison followed his leader into the harsh, polished, metallic and curiously inhuman room.

Two nurses, two of Eichler's assistants, were in attendance. Christie Roberts was spread out on an operating table supported by one thick, chrome, hydraulic column. Above her, the huge inverted egg-poacher of an operating table lamp hung cocked at a crazy angle. She was bare to just below the navel. The table was quite flat and in consequence so was she. Her breasts pulled up and sideways by her pressed back shoulders would not have allowed you to mistake her for a boy. Not on a close second look. They were very slight. The left one seemed to have virtually no nipple at the centre of its pale, faint aureole. Paul Madison was put in mind of thrusting his hand down into a plaid shirt while a car sped north and reaching for—

'Doctor – if you'd like to observe from there,' Eichler said.

Paul Madison nodded. 'Thank you,' he said in his Philadelphia voice.

Christie Roberts had heard Eichler's Salami-thick accent. She turned her head and smiled up towards him.

'What's up doc?' she said in a voice straining hard for the offhand. Eichler laughed good naturedly so that you would have thought him genuinely amused.

'We'll soon have you up' he said, 'and about again.' He held out his hands as he spoke and a nurse, black, white-masked, helped him on with his gloves with the effortless snap of familiarity. Charlene, Paul Madison remembered. She's not dressed for fashion-sense here in the slaughter-house, he thought. She never had need to sample her boss's skill. Christ, though, I wonder if—

'Let me just remind you this whole thing will take no more than an hour, tops,' Eichler was saying. 'This evening you'll be on your way home. I'm sorry not to have been with your during your preparation but I was required rather urgently at my hospital consultancy overnight. The main thing, eh, is I'm here now. Now – thank you, nurse – we just inject this little, er, thing, so, and just lie back, relax and see if maybe you can't go to sleep.'

The actor in Paul Madison was put on his mettle by the casually vibrant bedside sincerity Eichler had spontaneously injected into his voice. He did the bit so well you less and less believed he was also qualified to take a knife to anyone. At any moment now someone would yell 'Cut!' and the DP would grab the chance to move in and check his light-reading.

As if reading his thoughts, Eichler now turned his head prepared to play out the little fiction of their scene – as he conceived it.

'Now, doctor,' he said, 'just to repeat my reassurances. Formerly the traditional technique was to make an incision here under the breast and insert the silicone implant by this means. This, of course, resulted in a scar. The patient might look fine in her bikini but in her bedroom – well, there was this giveaway, yes? My approach is to go down through the nipple. I make a small curvilinear incision and elevate the breast to make a nice big pocket. I insert the implant and close the nipple. Nowadays silicone manufacture has become such a fine art that what we insert is totally inert and I therefore prefer my method to the alternative of inserting a bag with a self-containing valve and filling it with a saline solution. That way you can have leakage problems. I prefer the gel. It means less follow-up work for me and far more important, being out of sight and out of mind, minimises your over-riding concern – psychological after-effect upon the patient. A patient whom, ah yes, you see, is already well anaesthetised.

'Here, in this instance, of course, on the left here, we have another condition which has probably caused Miss Roberts more distress than anything else – an inverted nipple. She doubtless has been unable to wear various of today's fashions and so on. Well, happily, I shall deal with two birds at one stroke. I shall seize the nipple so, with this clip and pull it out. Then with a knife here at its base I sever the fibrous tissues pulling the nipple down by a stab-incision. I then put a purse-string suture around it until the nipple has healed in this position. A few weeks later I shall cut it away and I promise you your patient will be thrilled.

'Right, Ben, if you're quite happy, we'll—'

Paul Madison cleared his throat. He found he was sweating in the over-light room and his knees felt faintly weak as if he was back making his first entrance in a college drama production. But it was time to make his grandstand play. Having come all this way he had to grab a vital extra in the way of yardage if his game plan was to pay off.

'Excuse me,' he said hard on the throat-clearing which had halted Eichler. 'Excuse me, but – excuse me nurse—' He had stepped forward to the operating table on the opposite side to Eichler. He could feel his pulse accelerating but he thought he'd kept the Philadelphia accent steady. And what the fuck could Eichler do about it now?

Unbidden, but not daring to look Eichler directly in his eyes above the mask, he quickly extended his hands and in the manner he had perfected two nights previously upon a no-longer-apathetic Bobby, began to manipulate the breasts of Christie Roberts. They were dry and their lack of fullness made them hard to grasp. He sensed Eichler's body and possibly that of the assistant next to him grow tense. But neither spoke. To head off any protest Madison covered the silence with his own false voice.

'As I'm sure you well appreciate, I have absolutely no question in my mind as to the rightness of your procedures, Dr Eichler,' he said. 'What concerns me is that Miss Roberts is of very slight proportions. Has been so, of course, for all her adult life. It would be unwise, would it not, to, er – over-compensate for this slightness now by, er, something way over the top. The psychological adjustments then necessary might well—'

With an intake of breath as sharp as any scalpel, Eichler had cut him off. For the first time he dared to confront the surgeon's eyes. Their light blue – lighter than his own – had drained down to a grey gleam of laser-like malevolence. Hatred fuelled by betrayal and fear, by the need to play silently along shone from them with a dangerous intensity. Madison removed his hands yet even as he did some final trick impelled him, to flick an index finger against Christie Roberts's left breast. She would not feel it, yet he'd know that he'd done it.

But Eichler was not altogether silent. There was scope within the charade for him to syphon off some feeling.

'Really, doctor,' he said, 'I really am surprised to hear you bring up such a matter at this so late a stage.'

Iciness had replaced his jolly American twang with something approaching Hollywood Gestapo.

'The aesthetic consideration is always my prime concern,' he disdainfully went on. 'I have had no fewer than three consultations with Miss Roberts prior to today – partly to explain the basic technique of the operation and familiarise her with it but above all to impress upon her that I would only consent to surgery enlarging her bosom proportions to those consistent with and aesthetically matching her shoulder width, her waist size and so forth. I am amazed that she had made no mention to you of these consultations.'

'Dr Eichler, I must—'

'I took Miss Roberts through my range – my illustrated range of prototypes. I am amazed she makes no mention of this. If you but turn your head you will see the configuration we are decided upon!'

Paul Madison dutifully turned his head. Hung on a wall-mounted and, for present purposes unlit, light-box was not the usual X-ray but a normal colour photograph, neck to waist, of a woman's torso. The box was positioned behind where he had originally been standing. Now, seeing it for the first time, he saw too that the breasts were delectable. Not gross but prominent – high, firm and centrally nippled. It was not quite a girlie photograph but in that antiseptic environment, three times as erotic. Even as his mind raced for improvisations, he felt a twinge of malicious envy that Christie Roberts should be about to benefit to such a roundly handsome degree.

'Dr Eichler,' he was saying, 'my apologies. I beg you to accept them. I did not, in fact, know of your previous consultations because, in part, as I think you know, I have only just returned from an international convention in Hawaii. Having said that, it would doubtless be to everybody's benefit if I now get out of your hair.'

Eichler's double-barrelled stare had not batted so much as a split-second eyelid.

'I think my colleagues and I would appreciate that, thank you,' he said.

'Very well, then.'

Paul Madison made for the electronically controlled door. He saw the eyes of the other nurse and one technician look questioningly at him but he could afford not to suppress the broad grin under his mask. It was coming home to him that he had success-fully converted *General Hospital* into *Mission Impossible*.

The doors parted and let him through. The outer room was empty, its sinks gleaming. His street clothes were in a locker-room beyond. But for a moment, human, he was compelled to turn and look back into the theatre through the glass set in the door. Charlene was just applying spirit of some sort to Christie Roberts's nearer breast. Eichler stretched out a hand. A scalpel was slapped into it.

For a second Paul Madison felt a universal queasiness threaten-ing to dissolve his stomach into total diarrhoea, once more un-hinge his knee joints. But the quickness of the stubby hands that not long before had been clutching the controls of the Beechcraft anticipated his emotions. They made a quick movement over the breast. For a moment the blood hesitated, then, the incision prised initially apart, began copiously to flow. The other nurse began to staunch it.

On reflex Paul Madison sucked in both breath and stomach. There was something in the sight of that soft flesh being cut into that made him feel high powered.

The phone he'd had Tibor switch through into the bedroom began to purr. He decided to pick it up.

'Yeah – hello ?'

'Madison – you're just one shitty son-of-a-bitch '

It was Eichler.

'Something troubling you, Alex, sweetheart ?'

'My Christ! My Christ! You realise how close you came to . . . to . . ."In his wrath Eichler began to splutter.

'Alex, baby, I thought I was very cool. Very professional. Know what I mean ?'

'Jes—'

'Ethical, yet. I mean when I touched the little bitch I did it just like you showed me how on Bobby. Talking of showing Bobby how, Alex, you like to talk to her ?'

He rolled over in the bed and placed the receiver against Bobby's heart. She started at its coldness but, high as a kite, grinned and made no effort to knock it aside. To make her heart beat louder he began to stroke her.

From the receiver came high-pitched sounds that were largely incoherent.

chapter eight

... Also cutting out the decor frills to put his money on straight-forward but superlative food is Cesar Giron at The Silver Peso. If Mexican's at all your thing, then the long haul down to San Pedro St is certainly rewarding. You won't find valet-parking but the wrong-side-of-the-tracks atmosphere offers a nice change of pace. Tables are covered in red check but you may find Burt or Ryan at the next one. We tried, and particularly recommend, the guacomole ...

Eating Out

'We'd better take my car,' Sam said. 'None of yours will have a snowball's chance in hell of making it through the night down there. Natives no like gringo affluence!'

That was true. The Corniche would be stripped to its underpants. The X1.9 would vanish, bones and all, to reappear unrecognisably the stretched pride of a Colorado Boulevard hotrodder.

'Okay,' he said. 'But I get to drive.'

'You get nothing,' she said. 'I know its tricks.'

'Well, screw you too, lady.'

'Later!'

They went out to her ageing Mustang. The door was firmly reluctant to open on his side.

'You have to lift it as you pull,' she said.

'You got to let me buy you something better.'

'Uh-huh. I roll my own.'

She moved them out. The magic-eye did its open sesame stuff and the check-point Charlie in Madison's newly installed fence swung its iron gates wide for them. The mounts for the closed-circuit, scan TV had already been set up and the wiring channels dug. The men would be back tomorrow to press on with it. The money was there.

They wound down through the dark bends towards Sunset. There was no screeching protest from the tyres. Like most Californian broads, he allowed, she drove well. He felt a vague irritation and was as vaguely pleased when a psychedelic VW bus lumbered out of left field to balk their progress. Sam braked but said nothing. She took her time before she overtook. Without the small mechanics of driving to occupy his mind, he found he was getting bored. He went to switch on the radio but her hand reached out to anticipate his.

'I don't like it when I'm driving,' she said.

He grunted. Her being in the driving seat had one thing going for it. He lit up a joint. Driving, he wouldn't have dared. He had had one fatal auto crash. Safe now he drew on it, leaned sideways to feel her warm arm on his.

On Sunset Sam turned left into the headlight dazzle of the heavy west-bound traffic.

They crossed Vine. To his right he caught a flashing glimpse of the Hollywood Ranch Market and just as suddenly he discovered he was in good spirits. The motion, the buildings, the sense of high-powered octane in the air combined to remind him this was his beat, his town.

They passed Hollywood Film Enterprises and the former stomping grounds of Old King Cohn; passed huge monolithic banks, the Children's Hospital. Diagonally right they were past where the Akron had marked the bargain-basement living of his student days. Now he could possibly buy their entire current stock with one fast autograph. Or the whole district. Skirting Echo Park they were running past stucco buildings whose bold primary colours, livid under the sodium lights, told of lost-cause Cuban exiles putting a last brave face on things.

Well, Paul Madison thought, put on a happy face is the name of the whole town's game. You use emulsion or Eichler or a PR agency. And the fashions came and went. In – out. Batista – Castro. Debbie Reynolds – Burt. The Factory – the Bistro. My God, he thought, I've been in the game just months and now I can see at a glance the strain on this whoremaster's face, round that cocksucker's eyes, as they fearfully wonder if they're losing face. Yesterday's indispensable, today's disaster. Hollywood didn't make musicals any more. Not like it used to. But, by Christ, it continued to play musical status-symbols!

And here am I, he thought, hot-footing it to the current fab fad place – the greasy spoon the wrong side of town where black, they say, sits down in uneasy alliance with brown, where rich white folk from Movieland come along to show that they're just plain. And cool. And committed. This week.

Sam had wound her window down. Air from the still warm night was blowing in to dispel some of his better mood. Still manic depressive, he thought as, off Sunset now, she drove past cross-streets running down into increasing meanness. They emerged into an open exposed-feeling intersection and jolted over rail-tracks. Sam made a few blocks more and turned off to the right down one of the mean streets. Two long blocks south past lonely warehouses and she was slowing in a stretch abruptly overloaded with parked cars.

'There 'tis,' she said. They got out into a night underlit and, with its warm air primed for violence, a setting for movie cliché. In every way it resembled a 'B' movie stake-out. The warehouse a half-block up the street was where the hooch was stored. At any split-second a Packard would come screaming round the corner on three wheels and men would spring up at the windows of the silent parked cars to rake it in a hail of bullets from their Thompsons. For a moment, crossing the street with Sam, Paul Madison was shrugging shoulders in a non-existent trenchcoat. Then, a cold breath of reality was blowing at the back of his neck. He felt watched. The movie-making disappeared. Danger in this time and place would be delivered by some Mexican mugger. Even now he couldn't swear that he hadn't heard from somewhere the soft hum of a window whirring down, the clink of metal upon glass. His back felt suddenly three miles wide. Christ, he would have to go into the bodyguard business like all the rest of the rich old ones on Beverly Drive and Benedict Canyon!

As they gained the sidewalk opposite, Sam took his hand and squeezed it.

'You know ABC did a series on this block?' she said.

'Oh yeah?'

'After two weeks they cancelled the block.'

He laughed with amusement and a relief that punctured the wildly exaggerated balloon of his movie-fed fears. For an instant, in a remote corner of his mind, he saw them for what they were. Childish. Then they had reached the restaurant.

Without the light that came from inside, it could have been a hardware store. No neon designated it a place to eat or picked it out from the handful of low-down stores that leaned against the taller commercial buildings in the neighbourhood. Light was only visible from the top quarter of a plain front window. The bottom section had been painted over a dark colour and it was only there that the place bothered to proclaim its name. A wagon-wheel-size peso had been stylishly painted on the darker field with the three words of the name running, in English, around its rim.

With the last three or four steps of their approach he caught a buzz of sound through the all-painted door and then, opening it for Sam, was assaulted across the face by a surge of light, of high-pitched voices and blurred movement. The joint was jumping and the contrast with the night outside was total.

'If people live with this,' Sam said into his ear, 'you know the food is good.'

'Two?' A short, stubby man in a DJ was abruptly accosting them. It was part of the radical chic at The Silver Peso that you couldn't make reservations. He had the negligent manner of a theatre manager who knows he had a long-running smash hit on his hands. Paul Madison nodded.

'Two we got. You want to go through right away?'

There was a take-it-while-its-going tone in his voice that Sam latched on to instantly.

'We have a choice?' she said.

The maître d' shrugged negatively.

'We got a bar,' he said. 'Sure you got a choice.'

'I guess we'll go right through,' Sam said.

He led them past the small horseshoe-shaped, non-Mexed-up bar into a narrow, surprisingly deep room. As he led them to a table about halfway down, Paul Madison experienced the ball-aching ritual of people casually glancing up at newcomers and at once freezing their stares into rigid looks of determined non-recognition. The men, now, mainly kept their eyes on Sam. Taking in the throwaway styles of the other clients, he was glad the two of them had opted for denim. Tailored they might be, but their outfits gave them the cool and common touch even while making Sam look more aristocratic, more of a Sheba, than ever.

The maître d' did his stuff seating them.

'Something—'

'A jug of Margaritas seeing we missed the bar,' Madison said.

'Yes, sir.' He put small, unfussy menus on the table.

A bus-boy came to clear away remnants of the last supper and lay covers for them. He got in the way of talk. Paul Madison looked around some more and found he had been right. Privilege was chic by jowl with the radical.

At a table across to the right Mort Sahl was talking volubly to a columnist from England who had been present at one of Oates's pool-side Sunday brunches a few days ago. Paul Madison felt a small stab of irritation that his memory bank could not compute the name but even as he frowned his attention was caught by a table further on where actors he knew but disliked were huddling. He looked away quickly before table-hopping should set in. He hadn't come downtown looking for any elimination contests.

A waiter brought the Margaritas. He offered Sam a silent toast and drank. The drink was so good it was almost worthy of her. He set his glass down, followed Sam in reaching for a menu, stopped. To his left, toward the end of the long no-nonsense room, three tables had been placed together to accommodate some six, perhaps eight, men. They seemed evenly divided, Mexican and Afro'd negro. In the centre, talking even more rapidly than Sahl had been, was Jerry White. Sam's guy that was. Her guy maybe that still . . .

'Hey,' he said, breaking into her selection of a meal, 'what made you think of this place?'

'You don't like?'

'No, it's fine. I just wondered how come you suddenly thought of it today.'

'No real reason. Several times I've meant to mention it. I used to come here with Jerry once in a while. Looking around it's got a lot more up-market since those times. Must have the flavour of the month.'

'You want to tell me that you're unaware that right now you—'

'Hey, look!' she said, interrupting him. 'At the bar! That face! If you had any brains you'd go right over and sign that face to a life-time contract. Jesus! He'd never have to speak a line.'

He followed the direction of her look. From the angle of their table just one bar stool was visible. On it sat a slight man, with, he had to acknowledge, one of the world's great faces. It had Mayan in it and Spanish and Yaqui and Questzalcoatl knew what else. He had high Mongol cheekbones that looked broken and made his cheeks two flat converging planes. They turned his face into a hatchet. The nose, broken, mended, broken again, was a thin, jutting additional weapon. It was a face that conjured thoughts of violence. And of men suffering. Paul Madison caught his breath. A muscle the size of a fist seemed to have dropped into the pit of his belly. It was squeezing and relaxing, squeezing and relaxing with a cold-hot churn of adrenalin. It was a face that conjured thoughts of a car bumping at night across a desert, of a man being brought in through a doorway face down and dead, of a woman—

He shut his mind to that and tried to do the sums. The man, staring with thick vacancy at the brimming glass of beer in front of him looked maybe forty. Too old surely. But . . . White scar tissue bisecting one black, slanted eyebrow to highlight the brown-yellow skin made it hard to set his age. Such a tough face meant a hard life which meant he could look older than he really was. A strange, dispossessing wash of insecurity swept over Paul Madison. He felt his balls seem to contract and try to crawl back up into his body as if in their own independent terror at the nearness of a man whose hands had once abused them with such coarseness. But was it the same? It really – truly – didn't quite seem so. And yet, and yet, one tiny part of him argued that logic tells you that on the law of averages the possibility existed. You've walked past them in the street, drawn up alongside them at stoplights. Why can't this guy be one? Quit being chicken and examine—

'Paul! Are you alright?'

He pulled his eyes away and back at Sam.

'Kind of feeling a little sick,' he muttered dully. 'Be okay in a moment. I—'

'Hi, there! How's everything?'

He had to drag his eyes round again and this time up.

Standing smiling by their table in a black polo-neck was Jerry White.

'Great, just great, Jerry,' Sam said. 'And nice to see you. You okay?'

'Oh, pretty good, pretty good,' Jerry White said. 'Paul.'

He held out his hand with an obviousness that could not be denied the halfway house of an answering clasp.

'This is still kind of my bailiwick,' he said. 'Seems like I'm in here most weeks trying to help solve the Third World's problems. Bunch of us are working away at it right now. Well – an iddy biddy local transit scheme problem right now, if you really want to know.'

I don't, Paul Madison thought. But in the meantime, you're just impressing the living shit out of your buddies, shaking hands with me, aren't you, cunt-face? He had a weird feeling, too, the guy at the bar was watching all of this. Could even hear.

'Won't you join us?' he said with flat unenthusiasm.

'Thanks, no, I got to get back,' White said with perfect seriousness. 'I just came over to say "Hi". I don't want to spoil – oh, say, there is one thing.'

He interrupted himself and his half movement away from their table with a double-take monumental in its studied deliberation.

You might have it about right to be a swell politician, amigo, Paul Madison thought, but an actor, I have to tell you, you are not.

'Yes?' he said.

'Well there's a little pressure group, to come straight out with it, I've been asked to associate myself with aimed at furthering the opportunities for non-white technicians in the film industry. Now, seeing as Sam, here, would seem—'

'Oh, Jerry, for Christ's sake,' Sam said. 'Let's not—'

'Okay. Okay. No sermons. I was just hoping, Paul, that maybe we could have a drink some time or I could maybe drop up to your—'

A volley of shrill, staccato cursing cut him abruptly short. It brought his head up and that of everybody else inside the restaurant round towards the door. Framed in the door was a teenage boy. Mexican. He wore a bright green bowling jacket. His mouth was working convulsively although for a moment the stream of garbage Spanish had stopped. Then, as vehemently, it seemed to begin all over again. It had only one target. One man. That man, the man with the face of an unsuccessful prize-fighter now presented his back to the restaurant as a whole. He had swung round on his stool to take whatever was coming, face on.

For a moment Paul Madison's own eyes blurred and the whole scene wavered in rhythm with the pulsing from his own stomach. If the man had become too old, this kid must be too young. And yet, even at thirty paces, there was a larger-than-life intensity seared upon his sweating face that seemed identical to the look of that one in a bowling jacket who'd—

'Get back!'

The maître d' had taken a step forward. Diverted from spewing out his monotonous torrent of abuse, the boy snatched at the inside of his jacket. The maitre d' stopped dead. Prudent, if he wished to stay alive. The boy's hand had come out holding a black cannon of a gun that seemed to dwarf his arm. He pointed it at the man and it was shaking in his grasp.

A woman screamed. The man at the bar's arm went flying backward and knocked his still full beer-glass spatteringly over. A moment later as he staggered back and upwards his stool had crashed down to the floor.

'No, Ramon, no!' he yelled.

Nothing happened. Boy and man were frozen motionless.

The beer-glass had rolled one way. Now with an insistence

deafening in the total stillness it began a drumming kind of rolling back. Towards the counter's edge. It hovered a second, another, at the edge then, shatteringly, fell. With its glassy crash there was the most enormous roar. The man was bodily slammed back against the bar. Blood already at the chest of his white shirt, he hung there, the beaten fighter on the ropes. Then, without resistance, he had crashed twisting backwards down to sprawl, in an ungainly tangle, face up, head hanging down, upon the legs of the stool he'd just upturned. Nobody so much as breathed. Blood came from his mouth. It ran speedily, almost merrily, across the ridges of his face and down to his right ear.

The boy was not looking at him. He faced the crowded diners. Then, in an optical illusion allowing them to blink he had darted through the door, was gone.

The woman, a woman, screamed again. Men shouted. Chairs scraped back, fell over. Paul Madison grabbed Sam's arm.

'Come on!' he shouted too. 'We're getting out of here!'

Quicker than most to his feet, he pulled her totteringly down an increasingly tight-packed aisle. An elbow went bruisingly into his ribs. He heard Sam moan. Someone had kicked his ankle hard. As he lurched through the stampede, Oates's dictum always to come up smelling like roses no matter what or where, had quite erased from Paul Madison's mind the queasy flashbacks induced by the sight of the Mexicans' faces. He side-stepped Sam around the grinning body. There was no doubt of death. Upside down eyes stared from out of hell. Peckinpah gets it wrong, he had time to think; it's all over before you know what's hit you. He lugged at Sam again.

Only in the place's tiny reception area did he pause. Suppose the kid was waiting just outside ready to slam five or six fast shells at them. Some of the customers had spilled out fast into the night. But there were no shots. He pulled Sam after him for one last time and through the doorway.

Air, cooler, struck him. He was sweating. And then light. A broad lightning flood of it. For a half-instant he thought he had been shot. Then as the world pulsed purple, violet, mauve before his swimming eyes he realised he had been. By a camera. He brought his hands up to shield his face. With that action it occurred to him that his other instinct might not have been wrong. A feeling their arrival had been watched.

chapter nine

...also back in from vacation Christie Roberts for *Cold Turkey*.
Also, let us not be slow to add for occupancy of her newly acquired Malibu beach pad that comes with mini-gym and I don't
know what else in the way of custom goodies. She sports a ...
The Celebrity

'Hey, maybe now I'm not so sure about all this,' she said nervously.

She had jumped at his personal call and invitation. She had
played up to him at The Two Other Maggots and later at The
Bistro. In the car she had let him know she'd given her house-
keeper the evening off and snuggled against him while, with
malice aforethought, he had kept his free arm from riding any
higher than her waist.

Now, as the door had shut out Malibu's Pacific Coast Highway,
he had closed with her and, in time, moved from exploration of
her revised breast to a firm pressure between her legs. She had
wrenched herself away.

'I don't know,' Christie Roberts said again. She groped for and
found a switch and flipped it on. Lights came on all over. Paul
Madison looked at her. The sleek slide of hair fell diagonally
across her forehead. She was wearing a simple white dress that
had got its gigantic price tag from its calculated, highly erotic
impression of being no more than an underslip. It showed off her
firm, high breasts. And with new ambivalent pride of ownership,
she knew it.

She flapped an awkward, indecisive arm toward him.

'Nutty,' she said. 'That's me. I guess I goofed. I just clutched
up. Again. I'm giving you bad signals Paul.'

He looked at her.

'Let me make a speech,' she said. 'Okay?'

He didn't help her out by speaking. Like an embarrassed little
girl she swayed from side to side on anchored feet.

'I'm an actress,' she said. 'Okay? Maybe not such a bad one

either. Pretty good, even. A little over-taught perhaps. I don't know.'

'So?' he threw at her.

'So. I wanted this part. Really bad. I wanted it so bad, like I could eat it.'

'Go eat!' he laughed.

'I'm serious, Paul.' Her voice rose. 'They said, my people, to go out and try to get close to you.'

'Good thinking,' he bantered.

She ignored him. 'They said it was important so I tried, you know. A couple of times. But believe me, it wasn't a part that I could play easily. Sure I wanted the part but it didn't seem I had to go grab it between the sheets. If I'm going to be anything as an actress that's one thing I have to prove. If I'm going to just be a great lay, well that's something else again. But if you really want to know, I'm terrified of both. Really scared of life. I have to force myself to go through the door of my agent's office. Scared of the commitment, terrified when I have to go out there on the mound and perform under a million eyes. I don't know where or why I picked up this great curse of insecurity but I was into it a long way back.'

'I'm in it, for the bread,' he said.

She winced but battled on. 'What I'm trying to say is that to-night is a mistake. My mistake. I thought now I'd got the part maybe we could meet on equal terms and I could be maybe myself and, well, not go, well, emotionally dead. You see . . . I love being touched. But I can only bear being touched by those I'm close to. Emotionally. And that's so few. I've not had many lasting relationships.'

'I don't believe that,' she said. 'You're too good. Some need has to drive that . . . Me . . . well . . . You had every right to expect, I know, after the way I acted earlier. It's just . . . well, I clutch up, go, well, frigid if you want to know. And now I guess it would be sort of cool for me to say "Thanks – sorry if I got the signals wrong" and cool for you to leave me now to sort it out.'

'I got a better idea,' he said. 'Let's go fuck.'

She blinked. She seemed not to understand. Then the coarseness seemed to slap her into matter-of-factness.

'I'd like to show you something,' she said.

She walked past Kandinsky reproductions hung on pine and out of the lighted area. She began to descend wooden stairs, her shoes clacking on each step. He followed her, knowing she was digging her own grave all the deeper.

On a small landing they turned a right angle. Moonlight flooded what might have been an enlarged squash court below them through a far wall of uninterrupted glass. Beyond the glass was a fall-away of sandy beach to the vast silvered-over eye of the Pacifi. It was a calm night. Long, even-spaced waves were rolling in, their crests rocking like the necks of swans in flight. Then she touched another switch and a mirror image of the room below splashed out to efface the ocean. He looked down upon walls and a floor of pine and the smoothly combining furniture and arte-facts of antique, contemporary, of two dozen schools and styles.

'With the compliments of my father,' she said with a hint of defiance. 'Don't worry. I chose it, but I couldn't afford it. Not ever. He bought it for me when I got the part. He's in printed cir-cuits. We've always had money. Too bad for me, maybe. Maybe. Come on.'

'Yes, I know about your father,' he said. She did not seem to hear him.

From the bottom of the stairs she led him across the room. Looking back up he could see a gallery run in an L-shaped con-figuration around two walls. There was some sort of European chaise longue. And a Navajo blanket on one wall, a *Friends of the Earth* book on a low table.

'Here,' she said.

They were facing an otherwise blank wall of vertical pine boards. She reached forward to a brass ring the size of a dollar set flush into the wood about waist-high. She pushed and twisted it. A door in the pine opened and swung inwards away from them. Simultaneously a light had blazed on in a room of sorts beyond.

'What is it?' he asked. He had a glimpse inside of some kind of padding like on a chesterfield or gym-mat and for a moment, half-thrown, sensed he could lose the initiative.

'Go on in and see,' she said. 'It's okay.'

She led the way. He followed her and all but stepped back out again from shock.

The room was a padded cell. Literally. It was a cubicle or booth about five feet square. All four walls were covered with a quilted-but-not-buttoned-mattress kind of grey-cream padding. He prodded with a finger. It yielded a good inch. The material felt like a sort of softer canvas and looked glazed. In places it was scuffed and was slightly torn.

'What the hell's this?' he said.

'My scream box,' she said. 'My primal therapy room. Sound-proof. You shut the door, so. There's a lock gismo so.'

'This is one of those primal therapy shit rooms? You're into that? You lock yourself in and scream and kick and let it all—'

'Yes,' she said, annoyed. 'I do. And it's not shit. I use it very often and it's something very serious. I wanted to show it to you to prove I was serious too. I work things out in here. I wasn't being dishonest with you, promising what I never intended to come across with. I have problems relating. Not just with you. Not just with men. With people. All kinds of people. All people if you want to goddam know. Every day's a walk on a high wire.'

He thought her so insane that for a moment he was intrigued enough to postpone the night's objective.

'How's it work?' he said.

'I have a sense – always – I carry deep inside of me a load of feelings. Well, everybody does. When certain feelings come up in me, bad feelings I can't handle and want to repress, I don't smoke or take dope or drink which are things I used to do, I come in here and I begin to talk. And it usually leads me back to an old feeling, a feeling I wasn't allowed to feel as a child. A repressed feeling. And going through feelings I wasn't allowed to feel then is a very painful experience. That's why young people when they take drugs – acid – they can't integrate it. All their loads of feelings. The brain has a little gate and it flies open when that acid goes down and all that body pain comes up and they flip out. They can't integrate it.

'But I come in here and I weep a great deal and I scream and sometimes beat on the walls and kick and tear. Screaming comes from the pain that's going on, the pain I'm releasing that I've held boxed in defensively until now because, let's face it, I mean, the only way I've existed, we've all existed, is by having these defences, by being out in the world and by protecting ourselves the best way we could whenever any of these things were happening.'

She had stopped. For some time, thinking of what he was about to do, he had paid her words no attention. He could not credit she had led him to so perfect a setting; to so total a trap. Now he realised that, there in this claustrophobic sweat-box, she had stopped.

'When you come in here,' he said, 'are you dressed or do you have to be nude?'

Her eyes opened wider as if insulted by the sensationalist

banality of the question. But in that moment he had taken a step forward and seized the low neck of her dress. He half ripped the dress from her body. She gasped, recoiled, opened her eyes yet wider in the shock of rapidly decreasing disbelief. With three violent, tearing, whiplike lunges, he tore the dress completely away from her body as one might somehow tear a sheet out from a bed. She gasped again, stepped further back and now, pain and realisation hitting her together began to scream, not from psychic pain, but from dawning terror.

He hit her hard about the face and she stopped screaming. She shrank back again and stopped. She had cornered herself.

He looked at her. Eichler's expertise had required that she wear a strapless, front-fastening bra. The new style. Now matching nipples rode clear of it. She wore bikini briefs. Nothing else. With an element of feminine fear, she tried to cover herself with her arms.

'We . . . we have to work,' she managed to get out. 'You can't be serious . . . we have to work.'

He grinned.

'We do?' he said. He hit her again. 'So let's work. But listen, baby, I don't like being tailed by half-assed private eyes. And I don't like fathers putting the heat on, checking up on me.'

Her eyes scrunched up, puzzled and then frightened. 'He didn't find anything wrong . . . just about your mother . . . and . . .'

'Oh yes . . . my mother . . .' the strangled words came out on an endless sigh. And with the words flashed the taunting images. He had seen the woman, Mrs Ukinski, his mother, and she had laughed, and heaved, and fucked, and his father slugged to death, and here was this classy, undamaged broad telling him that they'd checked and found him clean. The thoughts had contorted every muscle of his face. As he raised his arm again her hands instinctively rose to protect her head. He grabbed the bra. With difficulty, jerking her back and forth, he tore it off. He tossed it aside. She made a sound that wasn't anything. Now she stood, arms at her side in the corner, like a sentry at attention. Until she saw him advancing. Then, fearful, she half-stopped to remove her pants herself.

He forestalled her. His hand drove down to grasp them at the centre and, as she screamed in terror and in pain again, he pulled furiously at them in a series of short, sharp jerks. The silk was of the finest, but eventually it gave.

'Please . . . please . . . please . . .' was all she now unwittingly was saying as she held both hands between her legs. He reached out a hand to her down-twisting shoulder and, grunting, threw her to the floor. Moaning, she stayed there while he undressed.

'Get up,' he said. She did so before he had to kick her. She backed again into the corner. Half-foetally sloping forward she looked at him to see what he would do.

'Stand up straight,' he said.

She did.

'Put your hands against the walls on either side.'

She did so.

He advanced upon her. She swallowed convulsively and tilted her bruised face upward, her head back against the walls.

Her fears were going to make it worse. He forced and she groaned, her body shuddering. She made to move away. There was nowhere to go. She grunted gutturally and her head snapped forward down upon his shoulder. He could move evenly. As if to ease his grinding weight, the pressure on her body, her arms closed round his back. Otherwise she was quite rigid.

And then, very soon, he remembered he had business as well as pleasure to take care of. He sidled his bare feet wider to set his weight more comfortably. He lifted his head from her shoulder to look at her and to his surprise found her regarding him with grave and curiously serious eyes.

'Please,' she said. 'Take me upstairs. To bed. Teach me. Properly. Please.'

He hesitated – laughed. He brought his right hand up to squeeze her breast. Her head jerked back with helpless pain. Once more, excitingly, he felt his wedge of athlete's body invulnerable. He brought his own mouth down, and teeth. She screamed again much shriller than before. He wrenched his mouth away and grasped her head with his left hand so she must look at him.

'Boy!' he panted. 'That Eichler doesn't lie. When you were stretched out there he told me by the time he was all through he could line up six whores and slip you in and no way could anybody say who had the real McCoy and who the silicone special. And goddam that sonofabitch was right!'

He hadn't taken his eyes from hers for a moment. The effect was gratifying. Beyond the stretched-wide dilation of drained fear and shock, he seemed to see a pin prick focusing of comprehension. Of pain shamingly beyond all she'd so far endured.

'. . . you . . .' she managed to breathe.

' "What's up, doc?" – remember? Remember the consultant?

In the corner? – Hey, you see that movie? – three guesses, sweetie. You want to know something? You'll never guess how much of all kinds of fun we had with you. Wahay! We sent the nurses out – oh, they knew why but what had they to say about it? know just what I mean? – and we went into every little nook and cranny of your skinny little lamb chop of a build like you were new and just unwrapped. Just like they hadn't sent the instruction manual. Did you just know—'

Abruptly she had thrown her head back and began to howl. It was not a woman's howl. Nor a child's. It was an animal's. A young lost wolf's perhaps. It was a cry that came from an infinite humiliation. For an instant the enormity of his success threatened to chill his blood. But then, a trapped moth, impaled still, her arms began to beat ineffectually about his back, on his shoulders and her splayed legs began to squirm against him. Writhing from shame and from the absence of all hope, she quivered against him.

He changed his grip. His hands shot down to hoick her off the ground. The driving ferocity almost kept her pinned fast. At last she heard him catch his breath exultantly and crow in triumph.

For a time, sweating, chest heaving, he held her fast and motionless. Then, backing away, releasing her legs, he let her crash downward to the jarring floor.

Whimpering, shivering, she looked up at him looming over her, gigantic and all-threatening at that angle, and expected to be killed. She found it was a matter of small interest.

He looked down at her sprawled in total vulnerability.

'Okay,' he said. 'That's one way.'

chapter ten

Following a family bereavement in Raleigh, NC, Christie Roberts has asked to be released from her contract on *Cold Turkey* which begins shooting interiors today. The studio announced that it has accepted her decision 'with considerable regret'.

AIP

He was in bed – his own bed – alone and already awake. He had already ordered breakfast from Tibor over the squawk box. While he waited a drowsy luxuriousness seemed to possess his body. It wasn't fatigue but something far more delicious. It was a sense of potential energy. That lazy, cotton-wool feeling that his joints could be converted, you'd better believe, into twelve-cylinder action the moment someone said the word. As, in three days time, somebody would. *Cold Turkey* would hit the floor the next Monday. That was when the heat would be on.

But he felt ready for it. If he'd played hard these past few weeks, he'd worked hard too. He had the part down in his head and all his preliminary talk with Slater convinced him that here was a director less concerned with jerking off his ego. The piano was moving right along as well. One steady hour a day after his workout and he was beginning to find he could get away with it.

Sun slanted diagonally across the bed and, a St Andrew bound for crucifixion, he stretched with utmost pleasure. More light was reflected from his dressing room mirror into a bright distorted patch on the warm red surface of his cedar ceiling. He looked on it with a simple satisfaction and gave vent to a long wakening yawn that seemed to fetch up from his very scrotum. He heard a tap on the bedroom door.

'Come in.'

Tibor entered. He carried a breakfast tray. He also carried some newspapers. Paul Madison sat up against his Turkish-style bolster and Tibor straddled the tray across him.

'So what's the good word, Tibor?'

'Well sir, you made the front page today, sir.'

'The front page! I did! *The Times*?'

'No, sir, *The National Enquirer*.'

No-one could have actually said that there was satisfaction, simple or complex, in Tibor's tone.

'Let me see!'

It was there, large and lurid, the re-write men clearly relishing this gem of a tabloid screamer. He and Sam were grainily spread across the front page along with three or four others outside the Silver Peso. 'Star Splits Slaying' was the banner headline over a text which made less of the killing than of the apparent closeness of Madison and the 'sepia beauty'. Murder, Mexico, innuendo and a movie-star . . . it had all the tints of a tabloid masterpiece.

'Christ!' Paul Madison exclaimed. 'Look how they made me look!'

By his custom-made standards he had cause for complaint. Slack-jawed, hair awry, pop and white-eyed, he had the bemused look of an idiot teenager who'd spilt hot chocolate over his fly on his first date.

'Look at me!' he repeated. 'Jesus! And look at her! She looks great!'

She did. There was no mistaking the note in his voice. Jealousy.

'They seem to talk rather a lot about Miss Montgomery in the article,' Tibor said. 'And the killing. Apparently it was political after a fashion.'

'Yeah, well, that'll be all, thanks. No. Wait. Get me Lyndon Oates, will you.'

'Yes, sir. Mr—'

'If you can't locate him, Tom Leonard.'

'Mr Rosner already called this morning, sir.'

'Oh yeah?'

'He said he'd like to see you in his office.'

'What time?'

'As soon as you could make it.'

'Why the hell didn't you put him through?'

'He said he preferred that I should not, sir. Will that be all, sir?'

He had met Rosner eight, maybe a dozen times before. Never to talk business. That was why the Oateses and Markovitches got their prime cuts. He and Rosner crossed paths at premieres and parties, and occasionally stood shaking hands before approved photographers. At such times Rosner was invariably low-profile to the point of demureness. None of the legendary maniacal ogreness of a Mayer attached to him. But he was not a studio boss. He was not the emperor of so many acres of tangible film stages and back lots, the contract owner of so many household names. His unobtrusively excellent good manners, his matching tailoring, bespoke a man whose rise was founded on accountancy.

There had been one bizarre incident. Paul Madison had been told to spend a weekend at Palm Springs. Oates had arranged his acceptance at the Racquet Club. Sam had been discouraged from going but when Madison burned both Leonard and Oates reminded him that he hadn't done too badly on their advice. But there would be adequate provision, black or white according to his taste, to compensate. Sunday he had been invited to a barbecue hosted by Rosner. It had been made clear to him that the 'compensation' should disappear from his suite along with the breakfast dishes. She would also just as smoothly disappear from Palm Springs, that transaction being handled with Leonard's customary expertise. There would be only one engagement before lunch. Attendance at an Episcopal Service.

Rosner was, by his own account, a Christian convert. He invariably attended Sunday service along with presidents of banks, insurance companies, industrial conglomerates plus a few movie company heads. Some would take in the first nine, park their golf carts discreetly in the vicinity, pray, then take in the back nine before their first Bloody Mary of the day. Oddly, though most of the parishioners could each have afforded to build his own church, this billion-dollar parish had no church of its own. But the Lord, or more specifically the Slade Grimond Banking Corporation of America had allowed its vast and marble-pillared lobby to be consecrated as a church. After business hours. Its incumbent, a bearded, dedicated, denim-shirted priest, much beloved by movie stars, golf celebrities, and a penitent sinner or two, would deliver his stern sermons against a backdrop of 'EIGHT AND A HALF PER CENT COMPOUND ON ALL DEPOSITS OVER TWO THOUSAND DOLLARS'. God and Mammon were never more effectively contrasted. But it was prayer. And Rosner delivered his hushed ' amens' as devoutly as the next millionaire.

Rosner and the chosen few had knelt in worship. All had been by the book. The performers' voices had been rich and resonant. The sermon had been modest occasionally enriched by a deft theological reference. But, gazing in boredom, beyond the temporarily erected altar at the glass wall and the great drum

of the strongroom door beyond, polished steel guarding much
rubbed gold, Paul Madison decided that Mammon had taken it
by a unanimous decision.

Now, riding up to Rosner's penthouse suite in the stainless steel
capsule of an elevator, Paul Madison was reminded of that setting
for a Palm Springs Sunday. It had been truly reverential. The
reverence for money having the edge. He must hang on to that.
It might help him during the next hour.

The elevator glided to a gentle halt. Its doors sidled away his
own reflection in a light-blue striped seersucker suit and open-
necked blue shirt and revealed a beige and chrome reception area.
You stepped straight from the elevator into it. He did just that
toward a smiling secretary who did not hold the job because of
youth or figure.

'Mr Madison,' she said. 'If you'd like to go right through. Mr
Rosner will be with you right away.'

'Thank you.' He smiled his best smile.

He stepped in the direction she had indicated and pushed open
the twin-leafed velour-covered doors. He went on in to an office
just nicely calculated enough to prevent a newcomer such as
himself guffawing outright at the pretensions of its size.

It was done in brown and grey. Apart from the carpet and the
two walls that were not all ceiling-to-floor windows, the basic
texture was suede. The desk, centre in front of the facing long
wall of smoked windows, was covered in mid-brown suede with
grey borders a foot wide. The desk-chair behind matched the
brown as did a solitary straight-backed chair in front and a suite
of armchairs arranged in a self-consciously introverted cluster
off to the right. The two non-window walls were panelled in the
black, brown and red of rosewood. The carpet was dark brown
and as thick almost as the LA phone book. It was purpose-laid
there to induce a sinking feeling.

The office was, of course, empty. He had expected that. Princi-
pals, whether of high schools or international conglomerates are
prone to making the errant stew that vital few minutes longer
than they have nerved themselves for. Screw that! Not to be
wrong-footed or nonplussed he walked swiftly to behind the desk
and, seeking diversion in the view, had his back good and ready
for anybody entering.

It was ironic. He had cancelled his call to Oates or Leonard.
Knowing what the rap would be, he would fight this one out for
himself. But now, as he looked westward along Wilshire from
nineteen storeys high, it would not have taken him too much of

an exaggerated effort to piss upon Oates's office. It was only two
short blocks away. He found himself trying to check out the
parked cars to see if any was Oates's Rolls. Pissing over that
would be more – fun. More poetic somehow. But it would be off
the street and in its personalised slot. Maybe that's why Rosner
had chosen this location. Because it allowed him to look down on
the premises of Oates, Becker and Rimmer. It certainly did not
permit him to directly supervise the running of any studio. On a
clear day you might make out Culver City somewhere out there
in the long sprawling fall-off to the south where maybe they still
made a film or two. But you couldn't see the Thalberg building.
And Rosner's office had firmly set its own back to the Burbank
studios where, at 7.30 sharp, a chauffeur would set him down next
Monday. Perhaps even Wilshire marked a concession. It was big
of Rosner not to have set up his offices downtown next to all the
other stock manipulators. Well, maybe not. Maybe Hollywood
still exerted a ghostly touch of its long-lost mystique and a
Wilshire address still had clout when clacked out on Wall Street
telexes . . . One thing had worked out for Monday. At least now
he'd be spared the presence on the set of little miss—

'Paul! So sorry to have kept you.'

Rosner had entered the room from a side door. Paul Madison
turned a half-second later than natural and smiling his second
best smile went to meet him halfway.

'No sweat, Milton. How are you? Good to see you.'

They shook hands. Rosner was wearing a dark blue suit.

'Always good to see you, Paul. I'm fine, thanks. I'd have been
here right away but I just had London come through. Evening
over there. All closing down. Believe me, Paul, there are more
crappy production decisions rushed through on account of that
eight-hour time-slip than there are stars in the firmament.'

It was possible, Paul Madison decided, he actually had been
talking down a transatlantic line.

'It's good of you to spare me your time,' said the man who had
commanded it, 'especially on the eve of battle, so to speak. I appreciate it. And I appreciate you've got a lot on the front burner at
a time like this. But . . . Paul . . . I need advice . . . and right now
I've a hunch or, better, I'm making this educated guess that you
can help me . . . Look, let's sit down and make ourselves – no,
let's make it here at the desk. I may need to dictate a note or two.'

And I, quite certainly, will have to look full towards the windows, Paul Madison continued silently.

'Wherever's just fine,' he said out loud.

'Oh, forgive me – would you like a drink? Scotch, vod—'

'Thanks, but no. A little early for me. I'll take a rain-check.'

He'd been ready to field that one from the outset.

'Coffee?'

'Thanks – I just had some.'

'Fine, if you're happy. The business always gets in the way of business, if you follow me.'

He moved around the desk to assume the more grandly inquisitorial position his chair would grant him. Paul Madison had already sat down in the surprisingly comfortable straight-backed chair. He's a little like a Wendell Corey version of Jose Ferrer, Rosner, he thought; he's got just a little too much cutting edge to give him the total anonymity he tries for and not quite enough class to do the gentlemanly bit without a hint of strain.

Rosner took an audible breath.

'Paul,' he said. 'If you'll excuse the pun. I'd like to talk a little turkey. This is in confidence, of course, but between these four walls, I have to tell you this Christie Roberts going lame on us is just one hell of a note.'

'I was staggered,' Paul Madison lied.

'To put it mildly. Between us, I always had my reservations about casting her. I'd heard word, you know, she was as neurotic as all get out and I had my doubts about her performance-wise. What works for one director – or doesn't, as the case may be – doesn't necessarily work for anybody else. But Frank swore he could deliver a performance and when he does that – well, you don't argue. Now we'll never know. But I've certainly been vindicated on the weirdo thing. Much satisfaction it gives me.'

He twisted in the chair as if undecided what next to say and for an instant presented his unremarkable profile for inspection.

'We have to replace her, of course,' he went on. 'And like yesterday. And we will. Don't mistake me. But I'll level with you Paul. We don't have anybody so much as in the bull-pen as of this moment in time. Paul, you can help us. Any thoughts? It's you that's hanging in there with whoever it turns out to be. Who'd you like to see get it now?'

He had stressed the personal pronoun. Paul Madison hesitated. He'd anticipated there would be small-talk first but not this kind of feint.

'Not easy,' he stalled. 'The part's sort of, well, in-between . . . Mia Farrow, maybe, if she'd—'

'Right!' Rosner darted him an approving nod. My thinking too. But I struck out. That was part of my call from London. Seems she's more interested these days in their legit. theatre and not straying too far from hearth and home.'

'Too bad . . . Lauren Hayworth?'

'Tried there too. Tied up. Not bad, again, with a little de-glamourising.'

'Hmmm . . . Gretchen Whosherface. You know, the girl with a semi-steady—'

'Ah! hadn't considered her. And I see what you're getting at. Yes . . .'

Rosner tilted back in his chair and brought the tips of the extended fingers of both hands together like a fastidious Pope. He gave an appearance of thinking.

'Interesting choice,' he said.

With a decisive grace he lunged forward and somehow had opened a drawer in his desk. He took out a small, brown suede notebook and a tobacco-coloured fountain pen. He wrote down the name.

'You know, Paul,' he said with a look that seemed to be mid-way between total honesty and shrewd appraisal, 'levelling with you again, I'd be prepared to say privately between the two of us that I consider you so big I'd almost be prepared to go along with some total unknown. Granted the talent, naturally. Even though you do only have one major credit under your belt.'

He smiled nicely. Paul Madison tried to smile and shrug his shoulders like a man in the presence of a major compliment rather than a threat.

'Any ideas there?'

He stayed silent. A thin cloud hung raggedly motionless in the filtered sky. If Rosner was angling to have him come up with Sam's name first, well, he had two more denials before any cock would crow.

'None, Paul?' Rosner asked gently. 'I mean, you get around town more than I do.'

'None that would suit,' Paul Madison said for the voice's own sake. But as deftly as before Rosner had flipped a copy of *The National Enquirer* from out of the same drawer. The copy. It lay fluttered upon the suede, looking cheap and nasty.

'Have you seen this?' he asked.

Paul Madison nodded.

'Bad scene,' he said.

'A bad photograph. A very bad photograph. It fails to do you justice, Paul. The whole episode fails to do you justice.'

Madison shrugged.

'Coincidence,' he said. 'A bad break. Sooner or later in a town like this you can't help treading in the edge of something.'

'Oh but you can, Paul. This is a scene you shouldn't be making in the first place. Not if you've a sense of responsibility to your image and what becomes you.'

'Don't you mean to your stockholders?'

Stung by Rosner's Dean of Morals manner he had lost his cool and launched off a hay-maker. He tried to recoup the tactical loss.

'Come on, Milton,' he said. 'Going out to a fashionable restaurant with my best date. What's so . . . so reprehensible about that?'

'About the place? Or about her?' Rosner mildly asked.

'About either!'

Rosner tilted back, swivelled and profiled, put fingertips together. He swivelled and tiled round again and leaning forward put his forearms on the desk.

'Paul,' he said, 'the paper uses the word radical in their spiel three times. I don't think that it's in anyone's best interests that you should go with her.'

He said it with such a deferential finality, Paul Madison decided to quit playing games.

'And just what the hell is that supposed to mean?' he said. Thickness, as always, had crept up to his throat to tell his anger. Rosner amiably shrugged.

'I should have thought that was obvious,' he said. 'On two levels. At least. One, I don't think you can afford the publicity. This garbage is on sale at the check-outs of supermarkets right across the country. Two, I—'

'Milton! For Jesus Christ's sake!'

Rosner frowned perceptibly but Paul Madison had committed himself to headlong indignation.

'You don't seriously believe,' he said, 'that because I'm seen going places with some black chick the holy sacred gross of *Turkey* or any other movie I'm in is going to bomb. Milton, really! In this day and age!

'Look Milton. This isn't *Guess Who's Coming to Dinner* time. We've come way past that. This isn't Harry Cohn busting a gut over his new sex-symbols playtime with a black singer. We're in the, "black is beautiful" business . . . and screw who's coming to dinner!'

Rosner studied Madison carefully. 'I don't need lectures, Paul,' he said quietly. 'We're not talking about a black girl. We're talk-

ing about this black girl. The right girl and we could go to town
on it. You're quite right. The right girl and we could sweep up the
second-class vote.'

He had allowed his cynicism one open joke.

'So—'

'You don't have the right girl, Paul. You didn't have her in the
right place at the right time the other night when this paparazzi
creep was laying for you.'

'What the hell did she—'

'Her. That place. They go together. It's a place where, well,
your leftist wave-makers hang out. They're anarchic, divisive and
dangerous. Oh, I know it's considered chic by some to go down
and be seen rubbing shoulders but—'

'It's a restaurant, for Christ's sake! People go there to eat!'

'Don't insult me by being disingenuous, Paul, please. You
know what I mean. We're not talking about your way-out,
flower-power-cum-Manson syndrome. They're a pain but they're
easily identifiable. They're powerless. But these people. They know
how to organise, infiltrate. I doubt the ones who really count are
ever out in public anyway. They've been getting to you through
her and you've been hob-nobbing with their front of house men.'

'I've not been hob-nobbing with—'

He stormed up out of the chair and then checked his excess.
Again, he sought to redress the balance. Stay standing – that was
one. He'd play the scene better away from the third degree glare
from the windows. He attacked harder on his feet and moving.

'Milton,' he said, 'you're the last person on earth I'd have
tagged for a paranoid.'

Rosner flipped an unimpressed shoulder.

'I'm not,' he said with a more open finality. 'We can handle
them.'

Madison's pacing seemed not to annoy him. He leaned even
further forward and held up his right hand, thumb and index
finger a millimeter apart.

'There are times,' he said, 'when I know – I absolutely know –
this country's just so far away from having a West German situation from those types. That's why it's bad for you, Paul. You
don't remember the days of the McCarthy witch-hunting out here.
The talents that were halted right then and there in their tracks.
But I—'

Paul Madison had opted to go for the big aria.

'That's right!' he interrupted, 'I don't! Ancient history is not my scene! Now listen! You say you don't take to being insulted. Fine! Neither do I! And I don't like being brought up here and being led through that pantomime about "Who do I think would stack up as Christie Roberts's pinch-hitter" and having it hinted way out loud that maybe I don't pull quite as much clout as some, star-wise, and, like maybe if I just don't step back into Magnum's party line, you'd not be too sorry to just let me go!'

Milton Rosner looked gently up to the ceiling li e a country house host whose guest has just perpetrated an outstandingly avoidable grossness. He sighed.

'Now who's being paranoid?' he said. 'I could under certain circumstances sever your connection with this picture but—'

'Like what? Well, okay, fine! You go right ahead and do that!'

But other than pausing Rosner ignored him.

'—but have you any conception of what sort of an impression of myself as a businessman I would then have? At this stage as you know, it would be the most costly proceeding. Though not, of course, as expensive as cutting losses at a later date. I wasn't trying to bluff or blackmail, Paul. Far from it. You have a tremendous quality on the screen and, frankly, there's nobody I can begin to think of who could get anywhere near doing the job on *Turkey* you will do. I'm not paid to throttle talent. If I was oblique when you first came in – I apologise. This is not an easy situation for me. I wasn't angry. I was concerned. If you are honest, you will recall that I have always scrupulously avoided the slightest mention of that previous incident when you irresponsibly – if I may insist, Paul! – injured yourself in that car accident and cost Magnum in excess of a million dollars through, well, let's call it re-scheduling and so forth. I repeat though, that I'm not angry. Only, I like to believe, a little wiser. I had no wish to upset you just before shooting, I assure you. I merely ask that in future, with your own best interests in mind, you try to behave a little more thoughtfully – and, for everyone's sake, choose with whom you associate on a more responsible basis.'

But Paul Madison could not allow Rosner so long and so apparently gracious a final word.

'Got you,' he said. 'Now listen to me, again. You'd better roll on those "certain circumstances" because I don't care, see. I'll tell you something. The other day somebody very big indeed paid me the greatest compliment of my life. He called me a "one-man clan". And he was exactly right. I'm my own man, right. I do what I, alone, choose to do and I choose my own friends. Right?

Damn right. Damn fucking right. You don't own me. No-one owns me.'

Rosner sighed again. He stretched his arms out wide, the palms of his hands turned upwards.

'How can you be so naive, Paul?' he said. 'A man of your intelligence. What makes you think I even begin to own myself?'

Paul Madison's jaw dropped and of a sudden he conformed to the tabloid photograph on the desk.

'I . . . I . . . I don't . . .' he began. For the first time the sheets of window glass reminded him of Christie Roberts's pad by the Pacific.

'You'll have to learn this, Paul. In our world everybody is answerable to somebody. It's only a difference of scale. And the penalties.' Rosner smiled wearily. 'Don't think that because you don't see the threats they're not there. Sure everybody wants to be his own man. It's when he wants to eat the best, drive the best, live the best and lay the best that the problem starts.'

Rosner let his hands fall on the desk.

'We'd better call it a day,' he said. 'Think about it. See you Monday on the set.'

He made no effort to get up or to shake hands. Paul Madison gathered he had been dismissed. Less than stylishly he side-stepped towards the door, turned to approach it directly, turned again. The consuming need to avoid anti-climax had made his mind a blank.

'The photograph,' he heard himself say, 'there are more of them?'

Rosner this time had not moved a muscle.

'Of course,' he said. 'But don't worry. It'll be taken care of. What we're here for.'

Madison had doubled the anti-climax. He went out.

Rosner did not move immediately. He stared at the closed door knowing that the interview had left him with a sour after-taste. He reran the episode through his mind. Madison had balls, no doubt about it. But there was danger to him. Rosner slowly shook his head. It was the kind of danger he could not permit. He pressed a button on his desk.

'Yes Mr Rosner?'

'Has my next appointment arrived yet?'

'Father Monroe has been here for only a minute or two.'

Damn that Madison! 'Ask Father Monroe if he would be kind enough to wait just a moment longer and . . . get me Mr Martelli on the phone.'

The call was swift in coming. Frank Martelli who had long handed over his general legal work to subordinates in order to concentrate on the more delicate requirements of the powerful, was always available to Mr Rosner.

'Yes Milton?'

'We've got Paul Madison trouble, Frank, and I don't like it.'

'I saw the picture in the papers, Milton.'

'That's the first thing. It's already had wide circulation around the town. If it gets syndicated world-wide, that's very bad publicity for us, for Madison, and the movie.'

'You want that stopped, Milton?'

'I'd be happier, Frank.'

'No problem. Anything else bothering you?'

'Well Frank...'

'There's also the question of the girl.' Martelli was ahead of him.

'Yes, that's the other thing. There's some political dynamite in that situation we could well do without.'

'I'll have to lean on...'

'Frank, you and I have always had an understanding. You never have to tell me how. I trust you. And count on you. I just like to sleep peacefully at nights.'

'It's done Milton. Forget it.'

'Thanks, Frank. Take care now. Goodbye.'

He pressed the button again. 'Please ask Father Monroe to come in.'

The priest, middle-aged, silver-grey hair at the temples, his tan squarely locating him in California, smiled and rustled forward in his long black cassock with an outstretched hand.

'Good of you to find time to see me, Mr Rosner. I know the calls upon you for charitable works must be very heavy indeed.'

Rosner smiled humbly. 'I try to be human, Father,' he said.

He paused delicately for some sign of ecclesiastical acknowledgement of his best intentions. And received it.

chapter eleven

... Principal shooting commences today on Milton Rosner's *Cold Turkey*. This is the third production initiated by Rosner to go before the cameras this year ...

The Hollywood Reporter

In the last twelve years the high-rise buildings with their wall-to-wall office rentals had stretched up and along the less fashionable stretch of Sunset just west of Vine. They were beginning to march southward down the narrower, faded cross-streets. But they had not encroached that far yet. Stu Sandford was still able to rent a small single-storey, thirties, frame house two blocks south of Sunset on Seward. It was as close as he could reasonably afford to live to where his action was. There was a good print house nearby on La Brea; a greasy spoon next to a cleaners and a barbers up around the corner on Sunset. He could make downtown in ten minutes, Bel Air in fifteen. Until he struck oil with the glossies, here was fine.

He had one regular fixed habit in his otherwise ad-libbed existence. Every morning he would round the corner to the spoon and eat their bacon, eggs over-easy, hash-brown breakfast. Two cups of coffee later he would amble down the north, sunny side of Sunset past the big Catholic church and into the offices of *The Hollywood Reporter*. There, in person, he would purchase the day's issue.

It would have made life simpler to have it mailed. But to be a day late in this town with freelance photographers cutting each others balls off for the top assignments was bad business. Also there was something therapeutic in that stroll which put him in the mood for work, set him up for the day. This morning he felt particularly good. He'd finally hit the jackpot. Page One. With luck the cheque from *The Enquirer* would be through this morning and, who knew, it just could be the start of something big. It would certainly get him the hi-fi system he'd been eyeing in the discount Sony house he was now passing. A fat little butter-ball of a still-young man with curly, sandy hair, he turned the corner back on to Seward wondering vaguely whether there might be any grist to his mill in the *Reporter* today. He got most of his poop from the odd extras or assistant directors or hairdressers who would shoot him a quick bit of information for a quick price or, sometimes, by reading between the small-talk of the unknowns for whom he knocked out the occasional portfolio. But the 'Ins' and 'Outs' of the trade paper sometimes alerted him to a possibility – sent him posthaste down to LAX or, at more leisurely pace, off for a long night's stakeout across from the latest talked-of chop house.

Now, approaching his white-paint-peeling house, he checked abruptly. There was a man on the verandah-porch trying his bell. He ran a quick computer-check. He owned his car, was paid up on the rent. He had just mailed his Master Charge billing off. Was it just typical of LA or something about the man himself that had given the first glimpse of him a hint of menace.

Stu Sandford crossed his small patchy lawn on a diagonal.

'Looking for someone?' he said. The man faced him.

'I'm looking for Stu Sandford,' he said easily. He hadn't consulted any kind of note or card. He was about forty, a little above average height and solidly built. He wore a mid-grey business suit. Insurance? The tanned face and close-cropped en brosse hair somehow did not suggest it.

'Can I help you?'

The man smiled pleasantly. 'Ah, fine,' he said. 'It was about a photograph.'

Business.

'Ah,' Stu Sandford parrotted. 'Something you'd like me to take?'

The man continued to smile. In profile he had a nose like Victor Mature. Photographing him, it would be a bitch to lose the shadow.

'Something you already took,' he said.

'I don't quite follow.'

'Could we go inside?'

Somehow Stu Sandford found himself on the porch next to the man and opening his own front door.

'If you'd like to step in, Mr er—' he said.

The man seemed to impel him through the door first. He did it without speaking.

The street door opened directly on the one large room in the house. In the far corner Stu Sandford had a large desk and two ancient non-matching steel filing cabinets. Examples of photographs he'd done to please himself, quite a way back now, it seemed, hung on the walls and rested on the mantel-shelf above the big old fireplace.

Stu Sandford had gravitated naturally, unthinkingly, towards his desk so as to lay the *Reporter* down on it. The man was in the lounge area of the room between him and the door. He was looking at a colour print of oil on water, an abstract really, he had taken down at San Pedro as a student.

'Your work?' the man said.

'Yes.'

'Nice. Good sense of densities.'

'What exactly—'

'You took some pictures a few days back outside a restaurant called The Silver Peso.'

'I . . . er . . .'

'One of them made the *Enquirer*.'

'Er . . . maybe. What did you say your name was?'

'My understanding is that you still have possession of the negative of that picture.'

'Now listen, mister! I'm not sure I like this whole line of yours . . .'

'That's right, you don't. I would like to buy that negative and the negatives of all the other pictures you popped off that evening. And in return I'm perfectly happy to pay you the sum of twenty dollars.'

'Twenty dollars! Are you kidding? What are you, crazy or something! I pulled in two and a half grand just for first crack at that baby. I got the world rights.'

The man had never quite stopped smiling but now his grin broadened.

'Two and a half, eh?' he said. 'They short-changed you, sonny. And no, I'm not kidding. Sometimes, though, I have to admit I do go a little crazy . . . Twenty dollars.'

'We're talking about my living!'

The smile went now. The man slowly shook his head. His face had become mean – more mean that just the loss of a smile should have made possible.

'Wrong,' he said. 'Your life.'

The menace was fulfilled. At the same moment that Paul Madison was stepping before the camera on a Burbank stage for his first set-up in the latest movie, Stu Sandford licked his lips once and swallowed.

'All right,' he said in a thick, hoarse tone.

By the time Paul Madison had earned a quick, conspiratorial grin of approval from the director, Frank Slater, on the successful completion of take three, the man was smiling again too as, a buff envelope in his hand, he crossed Seward Street towards a parked LTD. Stu Sandford watched him go through the narrow gap in the door he held almost closed. He watched him go and shivered. There was sunshine in the street but the day had turned cold and strangely distant. The engine fired. After what seemed a long time the car moved off. Sandford closed the door. He turned and leaned back against it. He felt diminished. He should have done something. He looked round the untouched room and found it changed. It and all it housed seemed dirtied. Something, though, was different, catching his eye on the corner of his desk. Sick to his stomach he realised what it was. A twenty-dollar bill. He was sick too because he knew he wouldn't tear it up. He began to replay the meeting in his mind coming out a winner every time. The first time he threw the man off his porch. The third time he stabbed him with a steak knife. Between the sixth and seventh replay he felt better. 'It's only a frigging picture,' he told himself as he put some coffee on the stove. It occurred to him that maybe he was being sort of hasty. His photographic eye, however, noticed that his hands were shaking.

At the same moment that Paul Madison was stepping before the camera on a Burbank stage for an early set-up in his latest movie, Christie Roberts, drawing a deep breath, stepped inside her primal therapy room. Her eyes were blank with apprehension recollected, anticipated. Her bruised face was rigid with the in-held tension of forcing herself to obey her will, deny her instincts. Her hair was drawn straight back flat against her skull as though it had been allowed to dry untended after a swim. She wore white cotton pyjamas of a cross-over Oriental style. Their pallor matched her own.

She closed the door shut after her. She began to speak out loud.

'It happened,' she said. 'It happened. It's an event in the past that happened and it's over. It hurt. I'm still sore. But it didn't touch me. It didn't touch me because I took no part in it. I didn't give myself. It was as impersonal as an accident. My integrity has not been violated. Myself. It has not. No! It has not!'

Unconvinced, she had started to cry. Without comfort, she threw back her head and, in the padded box of a room, howled like a young wolf. Between the howls her sobbing grew louder and her breath began chokingly to come and go.

'Kitten!' she moaned to only herself.

'Kitten!' she cried out loud.

'Kitten!' she screamed at the full sustained bent of her lungs and with a cadence that rose raucous into shrillness.

She began to beat with her forearms on the wall of the cell as if it were the chest of a man holding her against her will. Her forehead snapped hard into the padding as she let her head jerk forward-back with the same furious, accelerating rhythm of her fists.

'Kitten!' she hollered. 'I want to go with kitten!'

At the core of her frenzy she was as forlorn as a neglected little girl. As much gripped, as helpless, as a few nights before.

'Clean!' she hissed. 'I'm clean! Baths, baths, baths! I've had baths and baths and baths! Kitten!'

She swung at the walls like a middle-weight planting body blows. She turned and charged two steps and swung great polo punches the padding blocked in mid-air. She carried on in this way for nineteen minutes.

Abruptly she stopped. Away from the walls she slumped her shoulders and chest heaving like bellows as they became aware of the prodigious effort she had just expended. Sweat stood out on her face and pulled the back of her pyjamas tight across her shoulder blades.

'No use,' she said in a flat voice returning to resigned normality. She moved to the door and opened it. She stepped outside.

She stood alone in the high pine panelled room with its L-shaped gallery along two wide walls.

'Poisoned,' she said. 'He's poisoned it.'

Outside beyond the great window the grey Pacific rolled its waves relentlessly forward to the beach.

chapter twelve

. . . not visibly active on the club scene these nights Paul
Madison, since shooting started on the Rosner movie *Cold
Turkey.* Close by to help him punch his lines and so forth is
that ebony lovely Samantha Montgomery now said to be en-
joying exclusive rights up in the clouds on Mulholland where
Madison has installed . . .

Gossip International

That evening he had asked Tibor to light them a fire. For effect
rather than warmth. It wasn't that cold. But the steady crackle
of the logs burning and the flicker of fire-projected shadow about
the darkened room did more to unwind him than a pitcherful of
margaritas could have managed. It was strange. He lay full length
on his vast settee, his head cradled in Sam's lap, and it was all a
memory of childhood. And in all his childhood he had never
known a live fire in a grate.

He was wondering about the four days' shooting he'd so far put
in. He thought he'd got it about right. The director, Frank Slater,
had certainly professed satisfaction. Delight even. The thing was
that the hastily rearranged shooting schedule had kicked him off
into a time-slot in the scenario when, an addict getting a regular
supply, he was to be in a junk world of his own, indifferent to all
the everyday routines of life. The thing was to underplay each
scene without coming on like an actor underplaying. It was a lot
tougher and more demanding than freaking-out full bore. By
comparison the sequence where mistakenly thinking she had
stashed a supply, he had to tear the girl's apartment to pieces
would be something he could do as if to the manner born. But
he'd about got the low-key, withdrawn stuff right.

They'd signed Janet Cooke to replace Christie Roberts. She'd
do it differently but you could see she might be good. Well, that
was okay . . .

He moved his head sharply on Sam's lap. She reached a hand
down and stroked his forehead.

'Sssh . . .' she said.

But something had disturbed him.

'You want a drink?' he said.

'A small one. A thin gin.'

He swung his legs down to the floor and levered himself up. He moved across the Guatamalan rug, the slate flags, to the bar he'd had installed in back of an old plaster-built stone-looking altar. A props man had tipped him off it could be shaken loose from an upcoming Culver City auction of studio white elephants. He set out two glasses, got ice from the built-in refrigerator. It was too much trouble to mix margaritas. He'd drink his tequilla straight. He reached for a lemon and began to slice it.

The image of Christie Roberts sprawled legs apart in a padded cell, a hand covering her nakedness, clicked up on his mind's screen like a slide. By some freak of association he found himself viewing the scene through the aghast eyes of one of Dickens's over-gentlemanly heroes. That was absurd, of course. That was another age, another place. Dickens's villains were more interesting because that's how those old guys had really been, putting it to twelve-year-olds they'd just bought off the street. All the same, there was something troubling in the togetherness of those whiter-than-white heroes that gave him pause now for regret. They had a kind of uninterrupted integrity . . . Maybe he shouldn't have done that to her. Not because she'd talk. That'd get her no place fast. But that night, for the first time, screwed up and all as she was, she'd started to come on like somebody human. He'd kind of found himself having too much of a good, bad time to pull out.

'Shit!'

'You all right?'

'Yeah. Just cut myself a little. You don't mind a little blood in with your gin, I hope.'

'If you're out of vodka.'

He took the drinks back over to the couch. He gave Sam hers. Sucking his finger he sat down. The cut was not deep. He picked up the blue-covered script that all along had been lying on the rug and handed it to Sam.

'Just help me run those lines one more time,' he said.

Lyndon Oates had impressed upon him that apart from his studio dressing room suite, he should insist on a trailer dressing room on the actual sound stage. He had mildly protested at the potential hassle.

'I don't really feel the need, Lyndon,' he'd said. 'It's only another status symbol.'

Oates had rebuked him like the Colonel of the Eighth Hollywood Lancers.

'My boy,' he'd said, 'in this business never put the word "only" next to "status symbol". It's what it's about.'

So Oates had done the insisting, Leonard the telephoning and there it was. Virtually unused. He wasn't going to begin thinking of playing Barrymore games like in-between-take fucks and when it came to psyching himself up for the next scene he preferred to do it sitting in the time-honoured canvas chair at the set's edge while he soaked in the atmosphere of the electricians, camera and sound guys, lining up the next set-up.

This was a biggy. A key scene. The setting was a Village club and the action subtle. He would begin playing like a dream but, gently at first, the music would disintegrate into a meaningless chaos. But it must be apparent that he himself was still rapt and plainly convinced he was a performer reaching new heights. So, for the first time, it would become clear to the world that Bud Clarke was on the needle and had lost it as a piano-man. There was no dialogue. But he had the fearsome task of duplicating Hank Wells's original fingering to playback and the still harder job of suggesting a mind blown so high as to be seeing rainbows, God, infinity in a progression of building wrong notes and chords.

He sat watching as guys worked. Frank Slater was himself supervising the positioning of the tracks along which, as the take progressed, the camera would slowly dolly back. The visual effect would be to isolate a steadily diminishing hero in the one lit area of the frame. It was a nice improvement on the first-thought cliché of tracking in to emphasise the melodramatic moment of breakdown. Paul Madison approved both the concept and Slater's patient courtesy in talking it through with him.

A sudden shadow fell across his chair. He looked up and did a double, a triple take. For a second he had thought for some reason that it was Frank Martelli come back again. The lawyer had been by that morning to collect a signature for a tax-loss investment and, for once, he had used his trailer as a place to take care of business. But this visitor wasn't Martelli. The lawyer had been turned out Supreme Court style with a tie which a casual observer would swear was Harvard. This caller, dark, swarthy and Vicuna-coated had none of Martelli's finesse. But the muscle was there.

'Hi,' the man said. 'Paul Madison?'

He was smiling an easy smile in an unpleasant manner. Meanness began a millimeter beneath the easiness. When the man was asleep his face would be naturally mean and you knew that if you turned your back on him the smile would go and it would be the mean look that knifed after you. He disliked him on sight.

'It says that on the chair,' he said.

The man's smile broadened.

'Then this must be the place,' he said.

'Who the fuck are you?'

'That's unimportant,' the man said. 'I—'

'Who let you in here? Hey—'

'Now, now – don't shout. This is a message you don't want others hearing. It's not what you'd call a Candygram.'

'You'd better tell me—'

'In fact it might be a good idea to go on in to your sweat box over there.'

'You got a message, you've got thirty seconds to deliver it before I call—'

'Tsk. Tsk. Tough-guy talk.'

The smile was still broader, the lips well parted. The teeth were regular but large and slightly convex.

'The message, sonny, reads: "you wanna shoot for two?" '

'Two? Two—'

'Two balls. A movies lifetime career. Two ladies in the lake.'

'I warned you—'

'No, sonny. I'm warning you. Horse's head style. We wouldn't hurt you any place that showed – leastwise not until this joketime fairy tale was in the can. Don't harm the investment man. But her – her we'd kill. Slowly.'

'Who the hell do you . . .'

'You know who, lover, unless you're colour blind. There's been a ruling about her. She's bad, real bad for you and that means for the investment. You beginning to get the message?'

Paul Madison thrust downward on the chair's wooden arms to lever himself up the quicker. The emotion burning him was not fear or simple anger but sharp indignation. He was a star! No anonymous B-picture hood was going—

But, laughing, an old friend sharing a well-tried joke to a casual observer, the man had put a hand on his shoulder and leaned on him. He was thrust hard into the canvas of the chair's seat and back. The gesture was shocking in the force it generated from so little effort.

'I'd just as soon kill you,' the man said. 'From what I'm told, you got no gratitude. But you will have now. As of now you're going to be real grateful for what you got. Or what you got to lose.'

As stylised as a bad actor he chose now to erase all traces of the grin. Hatred came into his hardening face. He let the smile slide back over his teeth and bent forward confidentially.

'You little jerk-off artist,' he said. 'You got a lot to learn.'

Once more, contemptuously, he had pushed him hard back down. As contemptuously he had turned to walk away.

From sheer masculine reaction to the put-down of his ego, Paul Madison was on his feet to go right after him. But Frank Slater was approaching fast and smiling genuinely.

'This is touchdown time, Paul,' he said. 'We're ready when you're ready.'

Motivated by nothing but goodwill he had put his hand on the same shoulder.

'Say,' he said. 'Who was that masked man?'

'Oh, just a hit guy,' Paul laughed, 'telling me where I'm gonna get it!'

Slater grinned. 'Oh, that's okay. You could have seen him off with the piss they serve as coffee on this set. Let's go!'

With lazy unconcern Bobby Briggs tossed the ball three feet above his head and swung his racket, as lazily, it seemed, to meet it. Not flat but arcing down slightly in its flight the ball whirred deep to Billy-Jo's receiving backhand, and began to break back crowdingly in on her. But she had read it well. Her feet had side-stepped her neatly forward and to the centre and, taking Briggs's service on its early rise, she dinked it back diagonally – short but very wide.

Briggs had already ambled there. Casually, back almost to the net, he picked up the return on the half-volley. Slowly, the heavy back-spin quite apparent against the blue of the sky, the yellow ball looped high towards the base-line. Eye never leaving it, Paul Madison back-pedalled to cover it. He readied for the smash. At the last second, even as his racket was beginning to swing, he saw the spin had kept the ball afloat in the air that deceptively crucial difference longer. He tried to adjust but his stroke was too far committed. Meeting the ball half-heartedly he ballooned it far beyond the bad guys' base-line. Tom Leonard who had dropped back to cover against the smash caught it on the fly. He tossed it to his partner.

Briggs, balding at the crown of his head, carrying more weight around his middle than in the days of his classic encounters with Budge and Parker, strolled easily back to serve again.

'Forty-five,' he said as he positioned his feet. He said it in the elaborately casual tones of a man who knows it is set point in his favour and that a hundred bucks is riding on the game.

Again the fluent swing. The ball sped wide to Paul Madison's forehand and clipped the inside of the service-line four inches deeper than had first seemed likely. Sliced this time, it seemed to pick up speed and width from the bounce and he was suddenly being forced to rush his stroke. It ended up an improvised slap rather than a controlled swing. Without much sense of direction the ball flew high across the centre of the net. Moving across smoothly from the volleyer's position, Tom Leonard was able to spike it convincingly away for the set-winning point.

'Shot, Tom!' Bobby Briggs called out routinely.

'Thanks very much,' Paul Madison was lightning quick to call across to them. He smiled as boyishly as possible to hide how murderous he felt.

'Sorry,' he said to Billy-Jo.

She shrugged, bounced a loose ball over to him. Squeaks and squeals were coming from the neighbouring pool.

'Forget it,' she said. 'One service break. You got a good eye.'

But it had been his service they had dropped.

'And old Bobby,' she said with wry admiration, 'he's been around.'

All four players had made their way to the small gazebo of a pavilion set level with the net beyond where an umpire's chair would stand. On the padded garden chairs in the pavilion sat Jack Preston and Dennis Curtis. Curtis was very British in grey flannels and white shirt. Preston, a graphite racket across his knees, was wearing some four hundred dollars' worth of Head tennis gear. The court was his. They were his guests at his Bel Air house.

'Good set,' he said. 'Close, and anybody's match right to the end.'

Curtis laughed good-naturedly. He alone held a glass. He must have brought it from the house.

'I can't believe all this running about after yellow balls does you any good at all but maybe I should join in just for my financial health. At least if I were playing I couldn't sit here staking five bucks a point.'

'Well, how we going to slice it now?' Paul Madison asked. He threw it away to show he didn't care. But it was bugging him. He'd hit the ball clean and hard all afternoon. It galled him that for three successive sets with changing partners, he'd been on the losing side. Losing the bread was nothing. But it put him low man on the score board. You expected Briggs to wrong-foot you, sure, but not the pat-ball returning Leonard. If he hadn't double faulted twice to Leonard on his service game through trying too hard to—

'I guess I've done cooled off past the point of no return,' Preston said. Sweat had dried in his hair to turn it slightly spikey and, emphasising his incipient baldness, emphasised as well his tendency to rattiness.

'Seems to me,' he said, 'it's about time the bar was opened.'

'What an excellent idea!' Curtis was half on his feet.

'Sounds good from where I sit,' Briggs said.

Preston reached for the phone.

'I wouldn't mind another game,' Tom Leonard said. 'Anyone fancy a singles?'

'Alright Tom, if you want,' Paul Madison said. He'd hid his smile expertly. His heart had just zipped with glee. He could handle Leonard: out-hit him. He led the way back to the court. Across at the pool Preston's rotating crop of water nymphs were sunbathing and treading water while they waited for the tennis to finish, and the real games to start. There was class company and Preston must have put the word around. All the girls were wearing costumes, brief though these were, and keeping their language up-market. Preston stagemanaged the evenings as a matter of priapic course. Screwing was all part of the service. This was Madison's fourth or fifth time up here and he'd had as many sexual partners as games. As many foursomes. It was Leonard's first time – so the edge should be his therefore on having the feel of the court. Strange that a yes-man like Leonard should get invited—

'Call!'

'Rough!' Winning, Paul Madison elected to serve.

He steadied himself, threw ball and racquet hands up together and, rolling his right shoulder into it, let fly. The ball speared away deep and true. Tom Leonard clipped it back deep to the backhand. Paul Madison checked his impulse forwards to the net and scrambled back and sideways. Cut, the ball sat up fatly waiting to be hit. He let the swing of his backhand flow full-bloodedly through it. He got it centre racquet. The ball shot back like a flat tracer shell. On to Leonard's racquet. He met it three inches above the net and a foot beyond. With a faint 'chink' he killed the ball stone dead. It dropped dying back on Paul Madison's side of the net and scarcely bounced.

Ten minutes later Paul Madison was four games to love down. He had hit slicker and harder than ever and covered the court like a combination of skate-board champion and jai-lai star. He had pushed Leonard to some eight stroke rallies, twice made deuce. But that was the best he could manage. While he was almost immediately plastered with sweat, Leonard, always at the centre of a suspiciously shrinking court, seemed to chip, steer and pass with only occasional recourse to a speeded reaction. There was a neat, economical inevitability to every stroke and about every position he took up. Once on the base-line he responded to a bullet-like drive with the savagely cutting action of a man decapitating a flower with his cane. The ball seemed to lose shape and hang forever, a three-dimensional oval, some two feet from his racquet's face. The next instant it was crawling across the net to drop, and bouncing, break three feet inside the line.

From the pavilion Briggs applauded spontaneously and, as he took position to deliver the next service, Paul Madison saw a girl yawn, rise and disappear into the house. Leonard took that game as well. The rout turned into clear humiliation when hitting both services with exaggerated ambition, Leonard patently threw the penultimate game. Madison reddened.

'Thanks. Boy – too good for me, there!'

'Well – things went well for me.'

'Way out of my class with you. Wow!'

As they returned to the pavilion Paul Madison hated Tom Leonard without reserve and with that black ice feeling deep in his gut only social golf or tennis can impart. On bad losers. He reached for the pitcher of Sangria the houseboy had brought.

'Oh, yes, thanks Paul. Cheers.'

'Time to shower up,' Madison said.

A while later he stood towelling himself in the changing room next to the shower room next to the gymnasium, sauna and solarium Preston had ordered to be built on to his house. Leonard had joined him there. Previously, under the hissing showers, both men had stood naked before each other with the iron-willed casualness of the male locker room. It had been a point of honour not to stand wrapped in a towel. They had each scrutinised the other tacitly agreeing that honours had hung evenly divided between them. Paul Madison had found no solace for his sore feelings there. And now the sonofabitch was patronising him.

'Don't take this wrong,' Tom Leonard was saying, 'but you play a very fair game. As you gather I went through the coaching scene, the whole bit, one time. I paid you the compliment today of going flat out all the time.'

That was a lie.

'Thanks a bunch,' Paul Madison pretended to joke.

'Other things being equal,' Leonard said, 'a guy who can work the ball is always going to beat a flat hitter. If you could develop a little spin – you know, slice, top-spin – you'd be better able to break up the other guy's game. There's sure nothing wrong with your reflexes. You're close to top-spin the way you hit already. If you just worked on your forehand some you'd get a thirty per cent improvement in points won. Honest.'

Thus to injury he added good advice.

Paul Madison grinned charmingly.

'I'll do that thing,' he said. But he sought diversion.

Squeaks and squeals still came from outside. And now the 'plop' of slow ball on racquet. Someone was still playing. Paul Madison stood on the slatted bench against the wall of the changing room. In that wall, some seven feet plus up, there was a window. Now he could see out. What he saw made him grin.

Two of the girls were playing at playing tennis. The stars must have departed. Apart from sneakers both girls were nude. Both had smooth all-over tans which indicated that that was the way they usually played tennis. They were both very young. One was a little stringy. One was already inclining to the plump. Neither had any idea of how to hit a tennis ball. They scooped at its vague presence and missed more often than hit. The plump one caught the eye. Her breasts wobbled in time to her giggling as she half-heartedly chased shots that wouldn't reach her. When she bent to pick up a ball her belly hung pendulous as well as the breasts. Doing so once, she full-frontally presented Paul Madison with a view replete with every possibility.

He chuckled and saw his way of getting even.

'Hey, Tom,' he said, 'Come take a look at this.'

Tom Leonard joined him on the bench.

'Well, now,' he said pleasantly. But Paul Madison was delighted to detect him under instant stress.

'I don't like the look of yours much,' he said.

'Have them both. You're welcome,' Tom Leonard fought back with.

'You aren't planning on sticking around?' Nice and casual.

'I've done all the serving I'm capable of today.'

'Oh, that's too bad. Sure you won't – hey, look at this one down here.'

Much nearer to them, by the pool in the foreground, a third girl was sitting. She too was now naked. She had jet black, rather curly hair but a skin much whiter than the other girls'. She seemed dumb. A downtown city girl. She had acquired one of the yellow tennis balls. She lay sprawled on a raised-back sun lounger, her legs apart. The ball was wedged firmly at their junction. With a look of mindless moronic indulgence she was steadily rotating the ball against herself. Paul Madison watched fascinated by the calculated ritual. He became conscious he was about to tune into it. He must say something.

'I've heard of balling but that is something else.' He pulled on his shorts in some haste.

'Well, I guess that confirms it,' Tom Leonard said. 'Not that I ever had doubts. A few quick genuine snorts and I'll leave Jack to do his thing.'

'Or whoever else's thing.'

'Or whoever else's. With whoever else, of course.'

'I wouldn't want to include myself out,' Paul Madison said. 'From where I was standing the goods looked kind of fresh.'

Tom Leonard paused in buttoning his shirt.

'Do me a favour, Paul,' he said evenly. 'Remember the poor bastard who has to do the tidying up afterwards. For my sake as well as your own, try to keep your nose clean.'

'Oh,' said Madison easily. 'Appearances can deceive. I'm sure those beautiful little honey-pussies are all safe, sound and road-tested.'

Alone on the couch in the enormous Mexican room of his house high on Mulholland Paul Madison stared, unseeing, at the script. He was supposed to get on top of it fast but after ten pages he knew nothing was sinking in. His head was throbbing with spasms of anger, a sense of loss, and personal outrage. Alcohol, instead of deadening the effect had somehow seemed to sharpen it. How dare they push him around like this! He was a star! If he walked out on them tomorrow, eight million bucks let alone the two

hundred jobs would be in jeopardy, probably lost. Christ, he'd
show the bastards! Jesus he would . . . but it was all too late. In
fury he hurled the script across the room. It disintegrated in mid-
flight. Two pages fluttered down like tenement-dropped litter on
to his altar-shaped bar. Mother fuckers! That they should treat
him like this! She'd had class, a style that raised her out of the
ruck of legs-open bitches that you used like they were Kleenex.
And in bed, God, she was stupendous. Sam! The image of her
lying back naked, serene, swam upon an inner retina and hung
there like a mirage and, out of reach, was so much the more
potent.

Bastards! He needed the cool poise of her presence, that grace,
the incomparable slaking of his flesh in hers. He stretched down
to the phone.

And paused. Nothing he could do now. He had already written
that 'Dear John' to her, and made sure it would stick by insulting
her with the car. Fixing the goodbye note on the windshield was
brutal, humiliating, and terminal. Anything less, although she'd
never know it, could have seen her razor-slashed beyond repair.
Or worse.

So Rosner – it had to be him – was determined to get Sam out
of his orbit, even if it meant using the thick-eared tactics of some
bad mob movie. Sure he had ignored that sweaty-faced hood
who'd barged in on the set and talked like an M-Squad hit man.
Fuck 'em. They'd made him a star. That gave him privileges. And
freedom of choice.

So Paul Madison reasoned. And having convinced himself,
he enjoyed Sam with a new fervour, his appetites and versatility
given the added frisson of defiance. A week had gone by and he
had totally forgotten the caller on the set. He had picked Sam up
and they had slipped into the El Padrino bar at the Beverly Wilshire Hotel for a pre-dinner cocktail. It had thrilled him to see the
sensation she created. She wore a white, sleeveless cat suit, the
breasts softly half-mooned within the deep plunging neckline. The
velvet darkness of her skin against the sheer white silk, a flash
of gold from the slim belt at the waist, matched the haughty
black-is-beautiful tilt of her head. It was because of her, Madison
decided, that they were given one of the prime booths against the
wall to the left of the door.

It wasn't until they were seated and had ordered drinks that
Madison noticed Frank Martelli, alone on a stool at the bar.
Madison nodded a brief greeting. Martelli did not return the

gesture. He stared back without expression. Then very slowly, almost sadly, he shook his head. Madison frowned back at him, the tension between them unmistakable.

Sam's eyes followed Madison's glance.

'Who's the friend?'

'Big lawyer,' Madison said. 'Bigger than that even. He fixes things for people.' He had not taken his eyes off Martelli.

'Oh,' Sam said. 'Do we invite him over for a drink?'

'Too late. He's coming anyway.'

Martelli had left his drink at the bar. He brushed past two tables then stood looking down at them both.

'Want to join us Frank?' Madison offered.

'No thanks, I'm not staying long.'

'You know Sam Montgomery . . .?'

'I do indeed.' But he hadn't looked at her. His eyes were rivetted to Madison's.

'I hear you had a visitor on the set the other day?' The question was as casual as a piece of idle movie gossip. But it stabbed into Madison with almost surgical precision. So! Martelli was the big lieutenant. The front man for Rosner. There had been stories. Of killings. Of warning mutilations. But though the whispers linked these with this tall, suave character in Prince of Wales check, nothing stuck. And now he, Madison, had been selected as a suitable case for the treatment.

'Yep, I had a visitor,' he said carefully.

'He gave you a message.' Two ugly red blotches had suddenly appeared high on his cheekbones.

Paul Madison smiled. 'I have a feeling he did.'

'Funny, if anybody gave me a message, I'd know for sure. Well, I really only wanted to say hello. Have fun.'

Martelli still had not glanced at Sam. He turned and went back to the bar.

'What was all that about?' she asked, puzzled. 'What was so special about the message?'

Madison took her hand and kissed the fingertips. 'Business talk,' he said. 'You know what lawyers are like.'

But then, the following morning the Candygram had arrived. Tibor had taken it in for him. With an agonising clarity he saw himself again, tearing off the gift-wrapping. Inside the box was a plastic replica of a woman's breast. Dark brown in colour. A young breast, so perfectly shaped, the nipple so delicately fashioned, only touching it would reveal it as fake.

Madison did not touch it. He knew he was too angry to throw

up. He looked at the card. 'Next time it will be the real thing. A well-wisher.' His heart pounding he had raced to the phone. The contents of the package had savagely scythed her out of his life. He had grabbed the phone and punched out Sam's number. He just wanted to hear her voice. No more. He knew this was the last call he could hope to place to that number. He had heard her voice, and thanked God that it sounded normal, untroubled.

'Who is this?'

He had not replied.

'Who is this?' she had repeated sharply.

But he had put the receiver down. What kind of nightmare was he into? Did they really mean to carve into that beautiful body of hers?

The opened package with its grotesque exhibit provided an eloquent answer.

Then Martelli had phoned.

'D'you get the package, Paul?'

'Fuck you Frank!'

'You're a schmuck, Madison. They picked you from nothing and made you a big, big star. All you had to do was show a bit of loyalty. The word was out that that girl was bad for us, for you, but you wouldn't listen. We've got strength Paul, don't make us use it. Now be smart. It's all happening for you. Enjoy, Paul!'

So he had written her the note. And kissed her off with the car,

After a while he began to assemble the scattered pages of the script. The original pages were blue. The re-written ones, pink had been slotted in between. All so easy. All life could be a fucking rewrite.

Tibor brought him some coffee. He began to read.

Samantha Montgomery lay staring at the ceiling of Jerry White's bedroom, a naked arm's length away from the owner. In the remote fastness of its sadness her face was even more that of a dark goddess.

'That mother-fucker,' she said. She said it as if delivering a considered judgement, in sorrow and not at all in anger.

Jerry White scrunched his head round on the pillow. He could just make out the classic profile but nothing in his heart turned over at its beauty. Once it had, but she had ceased some months ago to exist for him as a person and so as a self-sufficient end. She and her beauty were a means. Of fulfilled pleasure. Of access. Of use. Black power had to have its beautiful face. It helped get the enemy by the balls.

'I blame myself,' he said. 'I got a pretty good idea of how you're burned inside and I blame myself. It was me sent you in there. I guess it was a pretty crude play. I thought you, me, we had our eyes open. I didn't like the thought of him . . . the thoughts I got to think. I never thought he'd out and run like that. Man, what style! A lousy three-line note.'

'On the windshield of a car. Payment in full to the hooker of the month.'

'Honey! Don't even—'

'Okay then – the season.'

'I think you ought to return the car,' he said. 'I want you to.'

Perhaps she picked up the duplicity his tone was always close to.

'He wouldn't even notice,' she said. 'He'd just turn it over to that Kraut creep he keeps to sponge his pants clean. Me – I'd notice. My old heap can still fetch maybe two-fifty. Hmmm! Quittin' pay.'

'What are you proposing to do now?' he said. He kept the relief out of his voice very neatly. So long as he steered it clear of Watts, a de-luxe European coupé could gain him points in certain quarters.

'I'll see,' she said. 'Put the word out I'm around for session singing. I don't know. Have to run a few scales, I guess, to see what I remember. It hasn't been so long. I'll go out next week and get me a half-ways decent agent before the gossip column crap is all cooled off.'

She closed her eyes a moment, a pained thought creased a wrinkle into the smoothness of her forehead.

'Shit,' she said, 'they didn't even let me collect on a screen test. There was bitterness now.

'After what I said to him,' she said, 'about the kind of actress that I'd one day like to be. Well – I had it coming, I guess. Whoever heard of a black Joan of Arc – only, now I just won't know if when I said I wanted to play, you know, Lady Macbeth, he was cracking up inside at what . . . well, shit, I don't know . . .'

She lay in silence for a while as shadows darkened in the room. He had the sense to remain quiet.

'I don't think he was,' she said at last. 'Laughing at me inside. Until it got so I was boring him, I guess he saw it my way. A little. Jerry, I don't want to hurt you . . .'

'You just keep on talking if it helps,' he said, 'don't mind me.'

'Well once, after, you know, a long night of it, I guess he thought

13

he'd peaked, tried once too often and hadn't scored. Well he kind of pushed himself back off me and said – dig this – of all the girls he'd had I was the only one so beautiful that just to look at my face and know, he, well, possessed me, could make the difference and press the button for him. Turn him on good, again.'

His cool was always as suspect as his aping of white folks' style.

'Bet he says that to all the girls,' he had to say. He felt her stiffen and thought he'd blown his evening. Sour annoyance gripped him. The images of Madison with her, Madison on her, white on black and legs intertwined, had started to arouse him.

'No,' she said quietly after a moment's reflection, 'I don't think so.'

She seemed satisfied with the thought and he had a sense of her relaxing. He did too. There was life in the evening for him yet. He reached out a hand and tentatively began to stroke her thigh. She made no answering move but neither did she say to stop. He began to make the strokes more intimate.

Minutes later he had cast the sheet aside and was fiercely on her as she twisted beneath.

'Oh, Jesus, so good! So good!' he gasped.

'Lover!' she said.

He felt himself very close. It was massing, bunching thickly at the base of his spine. He sought to sustain the anticipation, delay the loss of pleasure exquisite moments longer. He worked his arms under and around her, pulled her to him with a force only just short of painful. Conscious of his muscled back, his strength, he bit her throat like a conqueror. He moved his lips up to her ear.

'You're beautiful,' he said throatily. 'We're beautiful together. With him it was never like this now, I just know. I just know, baby. I know.'

Her eyes were focused on the ceiling, safely away from his. She made no effort to stop them transmitting the emptiness that she felt. This meant nothing to her. She had refused to demean her sense of loss by filling her mind with memories of the bedroom on Mulholland as she lay there. She had never before known a man take her and not be excited, desirous, stretching her feelings until they surged together. Or tried. She had loved the feeling. The feeling for its own sake would be enough if love or affection weren't there in the guy. But now some seed of death, some cancer, had entered her to burn out that simple, animal nerve end. Or so it seemed. To burn it down to numbness. Nothing. She stared at the ceiling and wondered if this nothing at the core of sex was final for always and symbolic too – a forecast of the nothing at the centre of her life a three-line note had made. But she should say something.

'That's so right, baby,' she said. 'He was no man like you.'

His vice-like grip relaxed with satisfaction as he heard the compliment and she was able to resume her twisting, her rotating of her hips. That way it would be over that much quicker. To speed things further she began to make the usual noises. She did it very well. He began to grunt as the finale mounted in him. What an actress they passed up in me, she thought.

'Let me stop kidding both of us,' Tom Leonard said. He pressed himself up off her and fell back into the bed. He sighed.

'I'm sorry, Celine,' he said.

He swivelled onto his side and looked at his secretary.

'It doesn't matter,' she said softly. She said it gently and he half thought that whether from kindness or boredom she might truly mean it. But he had no way of telling. He looked at her ruefully and wondered.

'Tom Thumb,' he said with a grimace.

'Forget it,' she said as softly. 'It doesn't matter.'

She reached out and held him to the long smoothness of her body. The contact seemed to amplify the noise of his too fast beating pulse. She reached up and, a touch abstractedly, as it seemed to him, began to stroke his forehead.

'There, sssh . . .' she said.

After a while she stopped stroking.

A while later he rolled away onto his back again.

'Listen,' he said, 'I don't know whether I'm trying too hard, which is likely, or whether my heart's not really in it tonight – for some reason or other not to do with you – but we both know I'm not going to make it tonight.'

'It doesn't—'

'Thing is, that being so, I guess I'd feel a – well, an imposter waking up here in the morning in a way I wouldn't if well, I'd made it properly.'

She shook her head, and slowly slid down his body. He checked her, however.

'Maybe I just don't want to open my eyes and be reminded first thing right off the bat of a failure . . . a . . . well, you know . . .'

'You want to go home?' she said. Her eyes were clear and neutral.

'I kind of think it's best right now,' he said. 'More – comfortable. For me. If you don't mind. I can tell Margot the trip had the rug pulled out from under and I ended up in some bar as per routine.'

'I don't mind,' she said in the same soft, faded voice.

'Well . . . okay, then.'

He bent forward and gently kissed her. She let him. He got off the bed and began to dress. For an ironic instant as he pulled his shorts on he seemed to sense some beginning thrill that offered possibilities but he forced the feeling down and away. It would be too pathetic to fail on a second take. He finished dressing and was standing by the bedroom door.

'Er . . . do I say "some other time" or something stupid like that?' he said.

'Of course,' she said 'and it's not stupid.'

She eased out of bed. Fair, tall, slender without being angular, she walked towards him unselfconsciously. Before him, dressed, she seemed doubly nude. The bedside lamp picked out ivory highlights on the slight swell of her belly and, as she moved, hinted halos at the curled rim of her triangle of hair. He saw and desired and was awed to helplessness.

She took his hands in hers and placed them on the fine in-curve of her waist.

'I love it,' she said. 'I love men. It's the one time I can forget myself and how lonely I am. I am lonely. Please come back.'

At once he knew he never would.

'Sure,' he said. He kissed her tenderly. Chastely.

The BMW whispered its way home on automatic pilot. As streets and intersections drifted by beyond the windshield he sat behind the wheel a prey to the sad chagrin, the hollow anger, the scalding shame of one who knows he is, irredeemably, a sad sack. Mechanically he turned the wheel and saw his street.

The house was dark. He ghosted the car into the port in case Margot was home and asleep and opened the front door as silent-ly. As he stepped over the threshold he heard voices. Or thought he did. He closed the door and all was quiet. He negotiated the lounge in darkness and reached the corridor that led towards the dismal prospect of the second bedroom when, a light snapped on. Blinded, he started and blinked away target circles of eye-stabbing light and dark. Margot was in the doorway of her bedroom. She was wearing a housecoat over nothing.

'The trip never happened,' he said. Not so untruthfully, he thought.

'Oh,' she said. 'For a minute – you know – I thought maybe

we had an intruder. What I'd've done, Jesus knows. I didn't hear the car, I guess. Well . . . goodnight.'

But with a tactless insistence maddeningly oblivious to time or place, his flesh which had failed him with Celine less than an hour ago was now pressing its urgent demands upon him, with his wife. The rare sight of Margot dressed like this, the sense of nakedness beneath the housecoat had hit the magic button. He had a sharp fierce urge to take her, to get even this once by fucking her raw. Yes, it was about time he raped the bitch he'd had the green sense to marry!

His thoughts must have shown in his face. She stepped back and her hand reached out for the door knob. At that precise moment, as if by magic, the door opened of its own volition. Not of its own volition. Wearing Tom Leonard's robe, Paul Madison stood in the doorway. He was smiling and unabashed.

'Hi,' he said.

His voice was pleasant and controlled.

'Just been doing a little practice work at the net,' he said.

Tom Leonard felt a need for the release violence might possibly bring. As hard as he could he smashed his wife about the face. She staggered backwards from the impact into Paul Madison's arms. He seemed highly gratified by it all.

To justify his cuckold's cornball response Tom Leonard began to muster mental pictures of his children sleeping further down the corridor. They brought a fine edge to his moral indignation.

She had read that they always left a note of some sort and, whatever it immediately said, however matter-of-fact its contents, the note was a reproach to those left behind. It said: you didn't love me, any of you, and that's why I've left . . . Well, she would be stoic. She would not leave a note.

Wearing white pyjamas with an oriental-style cross-over jacket, she came out of the bedroom and went into the bathroom. She stared at the dim reflection of her face for a second but then, fearful that the sight of her own image might make her alter her decision, she abruptly banished it by opening the mirrored door to the cabinet. There was a flashing gleam of silver. Her reflection seemed to vanish as if the mirror had been shivered from before her eyes by a dart of fairy-story lightning. Then, although she had not wanted to, she was obliged to turn the light on so as to be sure of getting the right bottle. She took a tooth mug and filled it to the brim with water.

She came out of the bathroom and into the large pine-panelled lounge. Outside the huge drawn-curtained window the Pacific rolled in grey and indifferent. For a moment she halted. She turned her head to glance up at the railing of the gallery some dozen feet above. For that moment it seemed to give her scope for thought but, squaring her shoulders back, she seemed to shrug whatever it might have been away. The sudden move splashed a small amount of water coldly onto her bare foot. She proceeded on her way into her Primal scream therapy box.

She closed the door after her. Entombed. She looked around. She looked at the far corner. She took a deep long breath but made no other sound. She moved to the far corner and turned round. Careful not to spill more water she slid down against the two right-angling walls until she was sitting on the floor, her back pressed against them. She drew her knees up to her breast. One by one, sipping water with each one, awkwardly, she began to swallow the pills from the selected bottle.

Less than two hundred feet from the padded tomb she had elected to die in, the grey Pacific continued to roll its breakers up on to the beach like so many reaching hands. Christie Roberts would not know it, but as she slipped into unconsciousness a white Chevvy drew up on the highway. Out of it, a mink coat wrapped around her bikini, a tall red-haired girl ran onto the sand. Behind her a short, bearded man in dark glasses followed, carrying camera equipment. The girl ran towards a single palm tree thirty feet in from the water's edge.

'Okay?'

The photographer knelt on one knee, raising the camera to his eye.

'Now! And make it sexy.'

The girl threw the mink coat off her shoulders. Tanned and topless, she put hands on hips, turned sideways on and gave the mandatory centre-fold smile.

Suitably retouched it would have upwards of five hundred outlets nationwide. Christie Roberts's obituary would have a more modest coverage.

chapter thirteen

... Out of town (but not out of mind – how could the No. 1 draw be?) – Jack Preston to Cannes for the annual Beverly Wilshire by the sea and then to Belgrade to manoeuvre with the Yugoslav army over the battle sequences on 'Von Manstein'.

'Travel Log' –
Hollywood Reporter.

There was a light but steady breeze. The smog-free Los Angeles sky was as absurdly rich a blue as an early Technicolor print. Eyes on his own shadow on the concrete, Paul Madison steadied himself, threw ball and racquet hands up together and, rolling his right shoulder into it, let his arm lean into the service. The ball sped away in the line designated by the racquet's follow-through and converting his own momentum into the first stride, he moved fluently into the net. He need scarcely have bothered. Dennis Curtis managed no more than to balloon the ball gently back straight down the middle some eight feet in the air. Relishing the anticipation of the smash and then the zapping executioner's shot, he murdered the ball unerringly away between Curtis and his plump partner.

'Shot!' Curtis called. 'Game, isn't it?'

'Right.'

'Ah. Set too?'

'Not yet,' Paul Madison winked confidently at the blonde girl partnering him.

'Oh, pity. I was rather hoping it might be. We do change ends though, don't we?'

'Yup.'

'Oh, good. I must just pause and lubricate the old right elbow a touch. Rusts up on you, you know, when you get to be my age. Maggy?'

'Thanks, I will.'

The British pair panted their way to the gazebo where the Taiwanese girl whose exquisite fragility suggested a pliant sexuality smilingly helped them to more vodka martinis from the thermos pitcher.

That was the nice thing about Dennis Curtis. He played tennis the way geriatrics screw. It was easy to dominate the court with a charm that did not appear ruthless.

Madison made no effort to join in the between-games happy hour. He strolled leisurely to the other end of the court. His partner, Ingrid, was already ahead of him and seeing her enthusiasm he smiled openly and happily. Her enthusiasm, he knew, was not for tennis. She was nearly as bad a player as the other two. Her enthusiasm was for him – or, rather, the career things he could do for her. She'd been working on him unremittingly since they'd been introduced. She had waited now, for instance, until he was quite close. Then, catching his eye as if by chance, she smiled and turned to pick up a loose ball. Her tennis dress might once have been regulation stock. But somewhere she had a cunning little woman. The hem had been taken up to the edge of parody to ensure that when she bent downwards from the waist – as now, of course, she did – she achieved the fullest effect of briefest bikini panties stretched across taut buttocks. It would have made no difference had she picked up the ball facing him. The same expert seamstress had been at work on her neck-line. She never wore a bra, and made sure he noticed. He did. He had been able to decide her right breast was fractionally the smaller. It was the sort of dress that opened doors all the way up to Hugh Hefner. Her obviousness immediately amused him even as it ultimately repelled. It confirmed that you had to think about women; the ideas in their heads were whatever men had put there. But the only mistakes he'd made on court this afternoon had been when the bounce of her breasts had taken his eyes off the ball.

He had met her a few days ago courtesy of Blake Darroll. Lyndon Oates had paved the way with a phone call.

'Listen, Paul, it could be something. Darroll wants to have a get-together with you.'

'Darroll! The hell he does now!'

'It could mean a whole lot. I said we had no objection to a meeting, informal and all that shit. He said "of course" and he wanted to do the right thing all the way from square one and that's why he'd approached me first. And all *that* shit.'

'What do you think he wants?'

'You. If he can get you for a price. A halfways reasonable price. He knows you'll be through on *Cold Turkey* pretty soon and he's got *Rat Race* out of his hair, so—'

'What about Rosner? What if he hears?'

'Well, he will. That's the idea. I figure we'll probably end by staying with Milton. But we ought to get something in the way of a Dutch auction going. Stanley and I talked and he feels the same way.'

'Okay by me, whip.'

'Fine. Real good. I gave him your number and I think you'll find he'll call you up himself.'

So he had gone along to meet Blake Darroll. In the event it had been dinner. Dinner at the Beverly Hills.

He had purposely arrived late but, from design, had let a twenty-dollar bill allow him to go a few minutes further unannounced. He had spent them at the bar letting his eyes become accustomed to the total eclipse lighting level. He had known himself exotic from the covert glances of the more typical drinkers. They were all men of middle years carrying too much weight around the middle, around the jowls and neck. An irredeemably B-picture sourness came from each and every one as if the demise of that gone forever bush-league had robbed them of their natural, their only, habitat. They would be all making out okay or would be, if it weren't for that fucking alimony. As they waited now to get stoned enough to be able to ignore their barren homes or for the hookers to make their *concours d'élégance* of an entrance, he could detect the permanent hostility of the envious in each and every one of their expressions. These were guys who'd come so near and yet missed. Even the two at the far end whose faces were so vivacious as they tried to top each other's stories, gave off an aura of spite the instant their faces lapsed into half-listening repose. B-picture people. B-picture faces. B-picture creeps.

Faces! That he had begun to read them meant his eyes had got beyond silhouettes punctured by the occasional purple-luminescent dazzle of a dress shirt. And by the looks of him, that tough-jawed Irish type a few places down had had just enough liquor to be thinking of coming across to pick a fight or, with sickening familiarity, polish his ego on the mantle of the greatness he'd missed. Time to split! Paul Madison killed off his margarita. As he had Victor lead him to Darroll's table he felt in good spirits. The delaying tactics, the drink, had put an edge on his awareness. He was stepping into the ring at his peak.

He had not tried to make out the table from the bar. As now he threaded his way towards it, he felt an instant let-down. The table was laid not for two but five. Flanking Darroll were three women who might have been the pick of the past ten years' Miss Universe competition. One was fierily Afro-black; one startlingly Swedish-blonde; one exotically Asian princess. As the producer-studio-boss had risen bluffly to meet him, Paul Madison almost broke stride and laid aside his actor's first-time-meeting charm. He felt insulted. The crass obviousness of the stratagem seemed to slap him across the face and he knew his psyching himself up for the encounter had been beside the point. Darroll, he realised, had forfeited all claim to his respect. Possibly for ever.

'Paul Madison,' the producer had warmly emoted, 'good meeting you.'

Brusquely moustached, not yet fifty, he was thicker set than the father whose famous independent mantle he had shrugged off but whose career he had emulated and surpassed.

'Likewise, sir, I'm sure.'

Corning it up, he could purge away some of his contempt. Jesus! Was this how the world saw him!

'Paul – I've been an admirer of your talent for a long while. It's been my wish to meet you. And that, sincerely, is about all. As I'm sure you're aware, I've gotten what we might call "clearance" on this meeting from Milt and Lyndon just so we can all be sure it doesn't signal that I'm trying to make some sneaky end-run play on this. Paul, I can't tell you how much respect I have for Milt. And the organisation he heads up. Okay. It's certainly my present wish that maybe a year from now, five, maybe you and I might work together on some project. As I say, I'm a devout fan. But that's as fate may decide. Tonight as far as I'm concerned is pleasure. My pleasure. I picked just about the most old-hat and open place in town to meet so you wouldn't scent the aroma of smoke-filled rooms. And just to remind us that business is strictly on the back-burner, I brought along these three most beautiful admirers of yours to grace our table. They sure beat floral arrangements I think you'll agree.'

He introduced them. Born in the right century, Marian Darling was a liberated Atlanta belle. Ingrid actually came not from Sweden or Minnesota but Norway. Thérèse was, in fact, Eurasian, born in Taiwan of a French father and the Chinese mother whom she favoured. Even by standards of a town flocked to by attractive women wishing to optimise their few brief summer years of physical potential, they were outstandingly beautiful. He found it literally impossible to decide who was the most gorgeous. Whoever he looked at had the immediate edge. But Darroll's lack of class had taken away all theirs. The crassness of his gesture had poisoned the evening's possibilities. As he made charming, Cary Grant-style small-talk, Paul Madison amused himself by wondering how each girl had described herself on her passport. They had all, he gathered, done the odd bit – a commercial, a magazine cover, a Rowan and Martin feed. But what? Actress? Model? Mistress? Hooker? No doubt on the law of averages one might make it.

The dinner wore on unremarkably enough. The staff were expert enough to make sure no glory hunter came table-hopping. Darroll did two predictable things. Over his pheasant he just happened to mention he'd been lucky enough to secure the latest Washington exposé. And once, during dessert, he excused himself to take 'an overseas call'. As Victor had pulled his chair back to help him rise, the three women had simultaneously held their breath. The pseudo Swede and the spade had looked Paul Madison directly in the eye. Thérèse with a modesty with which she intended to fool no-one, had kept her eyes cast downwards. There are different styles of playing Hollywood roulette just as there are different approaches to securing a Sultan's nightly favour. But he had not played the game. He had made it a point of honour not to rise to the crudity of Darroll's bait. He had made no date. Pleading an early morning call he had left after his first Armagnac.

Rarely, he had spent the night alone and found the experience unnerving. He had found the early-gone-to bed too large. Reading, he had realised he was triple-scanning each line. He had got up and wandered through the house. It seemed to fit his mood no better than the bed. He had wandered into the library he was having the former all-purpose den made into. The shelving would soon be complete. He had found himself making a lone disconnected entry in the calf-bound diary Lyndon Oates had presented him with months ago.

'Dinner at the Beverly Hills with Blake Darroll. Three high-class hookers (highest) to grease my palm with. Did not play ball.'

He had written almost unwittingly but seeing it before his eyes in black and white he found himself amused. Maybe he should keep notes for the *Moon's A Balloon* of his old age.

Two nights later a sour core of honesty was compelling him to add an asterisk and later entry—

'Had Tibor call Celine to chase phone numbers for Iceberg and the Slant-Eyed One.'

The Atlanta belle had pitched in the wrong game. It wasn't that he was worried by Rosner's faceless associates. So long as black was beautiful it would remind him of Sam.

Now, on the tennis court, Ingrid came forward to hand him a tennis ball and a closer look at the fjord between her boobs. Curtis and his English aristo were still quaffing their booze. A high-pitched squeal and a resounding splash came from the near-by pool. Temporary master during Preston's absence, Curtis had invited the usual crop of nymphets who worked their weekend passage around the place. They were now running a naked riot.

'Those two,' Ingrid said, 'they are a long time.'

She made no pretensions to a Garbo or Liv Ullman wish to be taken seriously. Dazzlingly white-gold sex goddess she just wanted to be taken.

'Yeah. They're not too interested. We'll just finish this set off and jack it in . . . Hey, you two. We've got limits on the pit stops in this State!'

They played three more desultory games before giving Thérèse the pleasure of pouring more drinks.

'It's been years since I pranced abou n this energetic fashion,' Lady Margaret Glendenning said, 'and now I think about it, I can see why!'

She had the piercing, tight-assed pronunciation of the English upper classes. Sipping straight Schweppes, Paul Madison looked at her covertly.

He didn't like her but she had a claim to fame of sorts.

Curtis had said she was something like seventy-second in line to the British succession.

'If the other seventy-one of them were to go out in some terrible garden party disaster,' he had said, 'we'd have our first fully authenticated nympho on the throne.'

He had let on that there had been an intermittently global thing between them since London in the 'sixties had swung her into permanent separation from her Catholic ambassador husband.

She was a few years younger than Curtis and, though considerably shorter, approximately the same poundage. A weight problem would always have prevented her being petite. In these middle years, dark, almost Arabic with her full-faced, now royally-flushed features, she had clearly long since given up trying to find a solution to it. She was a hairsbreadth from plain fat. Plastered to her body by an easily raised sweat, her white Lacoste sports shirt made very evident that her heavy-duty bra girded in earth-mother breasts.

'But splendidly vital and all that thing all the same,' she was continuing. 'We're in your debt, Paul. Now, tell us what have you got in mind before we all settle down to a grade-A Hollywood orgy and a nice no-holds-barred fuck-for all?'

Caught off her guard, Thérèse had cackled, with a laugh that suggested some coarse predatory bird, distinctly less than exquisite.

'Oh,' he answered, 'I thought we might shower up and such and sit around a while. Have another drink, maybe, smoke a little pot. Then maybe go out and eat and then, well, maybe come back . . .'

He let his voice trail off into a grin. How many girls have I known, he was wondering, who were still beautiful when they laughed?

'I hear there's a Mexican place downtown some place real good,' Thérèse said. Her hint of lisp was too good to be true.

'The Silver Peso,' Ingrid said, 'I heard that too.'

'It's overrated,' he said quickly. 'Too far to go for what you find there . . . Listen, why break up a good thing? I'll phone Chasen's and have them send something along.'

'Will they do that?' Lady Margaret asked.

He activated his charm mode.

'They will when I mention it's for you,' he lied.

'I think I'll go and make myself even more beautiful,' Dennis Curtis said.

The shower, plastering his hair to his scalp to emphasise its sparseness, had emphasised his age. As he towelled himself he looked fifteen years older – twenty-five older than that of his current screen image. His roles invariably had something of the chipper, the agile and incisive about them. The reality was far less wholesome. Legs and, above all, arms were pipe-cleaner thin, the pallid skin almost uniformly unbulged by muscle. Tone had gone from the body years ago. The chest was close to concave as the off-duty shoulders slumped. The gone-home abdominal muscles had contrived to make the belly look like a stuck-on after-thought.

Paul Madison felt his derision almost touched by pity as, working the towel about his crotch, the Englishman shuffled forward. But how could a man – any man – let himself go like that? As regards the standout performer, tonight would be just like the tennis.

'Things could get a bit, er, frantic, later on then, you think, old boy?' Curtis said.

'Well, we'll see. I was figuring maybe a little mix and match. Your barefaced Contessa or whatever seems rather looking forward to something like that?'

'Oh, it's never a case of Maggie May, with her. Always a case of Maggie Will! As often as possible, believe me!'

'Well, fine—'

'There are two things actually, Paul . . .'

'Oh?'

'You're quite sure this place is, well, safe?'

'Sure I'm sure. Why?'

'You don't think this could be one of Jack's tricks. Handin;
the keys over to you and then sneaking back for a little bit of the
old voyeur stuff. You know, cameras and such for private re-runs
to friends?'

'Oh, come on! Jack wouldn't do a thing like that. Not his style.
And as for safety – well, this place has better electronic protection
than mine. And mine, I swear, shades Fort Knox.'

'Ah . . . you see, once in London Maggie and I got rather caught
with our pants down. Another couple rolling around with us.
Famous and all that too. Sons of bitches got behind a see-through
mirror with infra-red film or whatever these cunts use.'

'Wow! Still, I guess we're used to tighter security here than in
London.'

'I suppose so. Though you never know.'

'So what happened? You buy the guy off?'

'No. Unfortunately the stuff ended up in some editor's hands.'

'Jesus!'

'They were quite decent. Never made use of it. I think Lady M.
pulls so much rank they never quite plucked up the courage.'

'That helped.'

'Well maybe. But it was not very inspiring knowing some prick
of a sub-editor might be splitting his sides watching you try to get
it up . . . That's the other thing.'

'Yes?'

'She likes it as often as possible, I said. Pre-menopausal last
fling. No. Actually, to tell the truth, she's always been like that.'

'Well, bully for you.'

'Not really. Not anymore.' Ageless masculine embarrassment
was emphasising Curtis's own age, and anxiety. His spruce, ship-
shape voice sounded hollow. It was the tone of a man forced
reluctantly to reveal secrets he'd sooner have kept under wraps.

'I'm pretty much at the stage,' he went on, 'where peniswise I
have to use my toothbrush as a splint. Between ourselves, I'm the
menopausal one. I rather think a foursome or whatever will over-
tax the machinery a bit.'

'Come on, it'll all be among friends. We'll all turn on a little
before. You know there's nothing better than sex on pot.'

'The spirit may be willing, turned on or not, but if the flesh is weak, there's—'

'Hey, listen! I once ran across a cop from the Narcotics Squad. He gave me the very stuff for you. It'll raise the dead. Just get one good sniff of that and brother! stand back!'

Curtis's worried expression brightened with interest.

I'll have Tibor run it across,' Madison said.

It was hard to breathe. He wanted to come up for air. But her urgent, writhing pressure would not let him. Her muskiness was full and cloying in his nostrils. And he was close to making it. It was his third time up to bat, his second re-take in under an hour but the other one, the Norwegian girl, was doing things with her teeth and tongue he wouldn't have thought possible. Astride his chest, knees under his armpits, Thérèse pinned him like a wrestler as she pulled his head hard into her. So much for your Eastern demureness! The steady hissing of her breathing missed a beat and then a short, gasping aspirate of a syllable broke roughly from her. It was repeated with double force as she grappled him to her. Abruptly, sinews taut, she froze. Savouring it to the lingering full, she began to shudder as if from within. And doing so clicked a switch home in his brain. He was royally burgeoned. Summoning the juices from some deep and doubly delicious reservoir he arched the small of his back from off the bed and, incredulous of the ecstasy, made his mark with Ingrid too. She feasted on him. It lasted seconds and whole years. Spent, still incredulous, he relaxed and sprawled back on the bed, his arms outstretched.

Thérèse had relaxed her hold. She stared down at him with eyes like black almonds. Her long gleaming hair hung forward down about her cheeks. She smiled and bending down kissed him with a wicked thankfulness. She had skin the colour of damp sand. She twisted and kissed him where but moments ago the taller, milkier woman had set her lips and then, straining acrobatically up into Ingrid's receiving arms, kissed her long and fully on the mouth. Limp, knowing the triumph of an emperor, he felt the circle to be complete.

Grunting broke into his floating pleasure. He turned his head on the pillow to the left. On the parallel bed Dennis Curtis was less imaginatively sprawled across the extensive, demanding body of Lady Margaret Glendenning.

Paul Madison grinned. Immersed in his own affairs he had

forgotten the two of them. Lady Margaret, stripped of her Playtex cantilevering and buttressing was an awesome spectacle in the flesh. Not tall, she bore some affinity to a bleached double bass. Her belly sloped smoothly down and forward, its well-fed contours stretching the skin drum tight. Her breasts were heavy and totally pendulous. Her haunches were meaty, her legs squat to the point of stubbiness. It was not a comfortable vision of the English aristocracy. Displayed in front of Ingrid and Thérèse it was painful. But still retaining a touch of that aristocratic 'the king can do no wrong' she had led all of them to bed. Naked she had blithely called for 'a group grope'. Lying back, feeling the vibrations of his bed increase as Thérèse and Ingrid's langour modulated swiftly up to passion Paul Madison began to wonder if turn and turnabout he might have another shot in his locker for her ladyship.

If that turn ever came, that was. They'd been going at it hammer and tongs for the length of *Gone With the Wind*. Way back, he now remembered, she had shrieked with pleasure, spouting a stream of four letter exhortations in her majestic accent. That had been within moments of Curtis going to her. She must have been packing an instant fuse. But since then nothing. Nothing but noise. Curtis was blowing and gasping like a winded boxer getting tagged by the second. He was sounding like a marathon runner matching gasp for stride, gasp for stride, with the tape still miles away. In the grim determination of their coupling, they had slewed diagonally across the bed. He seemed to be seeking better traction through a foot braced firm against the far wall. His head was over her left shoulder and his puny buttocks rose and fell beyond the bunched muscles of his shoulders. Her hands stroked with imploring desperation at his back, urging him to a faster rhythm. Now she too began to pant. It was the mating of a grampus to a sea-cow.

Paul Madison laughed. His two bedmates broke from their own embrace in surprise and then, following his lines of vision and sight, began to laugh as well. It was cruel, sure, but Jesus! And hell, he must have flipped his lid to think he'd enjoy serving that indiarubber butter-ball.

Astonishingly, Dennis Curtis joined in their laughter. At the top of another stroke he halted. He pressed himself up push-up style. A chuckle burbled deep in his throat as it struggled to escape. Then it had. And was not a chuckle. It was a rasping, strangled gasp for air that rose into one full-bore yell of agony. Lady Margaret screamed high and shrill above it. As Dennis

Curtis, his face puce, collapsed like a stricken beast across her, she scrambled frantically to disengage her visibly shuddering body from his. His mouth was fixed gasping open like that of a fish and, contagiously, both of the other girls were screaming too. It was hard therefore to tell exactly when, with the sweat still moistly warm on his brow, Dennis Curtis's last, reduced, gasps for air had ceased altogether. To Paul Madison, watching with the detachment of amazement, it seemed that something invisible yet discernible went rigid in the face.

With heavy awkwardness, Lady Margaret slid out from under. It would no doubt be a moot point in the records and her memoirs. But quite probably, for a brief moment, she had been coupled with a corpse.

Perhaps the throughput hadn't been so heavy lately. Maybe the merciless scrutiny of the strip-light above her vanity mirror had lit up the first creases in the skin across her classic bone structure. Whatever the cause Celine was figuring that she better strike it matrimonially while men were still hot for her. She'd known he'd moved out on Margot. Maybe he seemed a good prospect for place money. Against all his expectations after the embarrassment of the first time, Celine had been patient and kind with him these past weeks. Feminine, and old-fashionedly considerate.

Tom Leonard almost succeeded in suppressing the thought that she had an angle. That she was motivated by an awareness that Madison, that pleasure-happy, cock-sure, self-gratifying shit would never give her another shot. Well, he had always suspected that as well as for his own, Madison might get to be too big for a lot of people's boots. Another ten years or so, and by then a burnt-out has-been, he might come crawling to Celine begging for a night for old times' sake. Boots on and all.

− In the meantime, Celine's slow patience, the sheer beauty of her slim nakedness had made him feel he was a man again.

The phone rang. It was three in the morning. Celine groaned. She rolled over and fumbled for the light switch. It was less than an hour since they'd separated to their respective sides of the bed. A staccato voice shrilled semi-audibly to drag him back to consciousness.

'It's for you,' Celine said.

He took the receiver from her. The service charged the earth but almost earned it by operating round the clock. He'd left instructions to bridge through.

'Mr Leonard?'

'Yeah.'

'One moment, please. I have a Mr Ukinski for you.'

'Huh? Oh, yes. I'll speak to him.'

'Tom?'

'Right.'

'Tom. I'm at Jack's. I need you Tom. Something's happened.'

'Now?'

'Now.'

'Oh, for Christ's sake, not—'

'Really now, Tom. It's serious . . . Tom?'

'Yeah, still here.'

'Are you coming?'

'. . . yeah. Would you for Christ's sake just say "please". Just once!'

Twenty-five minutes later he stood next to Madison looking down at Curtis's mottled face.

'Killed in action?' he asked.

Madison nodded.

'Who else was here?'

'I sent them home.'

'For Christ's sake! If I'm going to fix this one too, I've got to fix it good. No loose ends. But none!'

Madison gave him the names. Tom Leonard considered a long slow length. He let his breath out in a sigh drawn out almost as long.

'All right,' he said. 'It could be worse at that, I guess. Just. The other two we can get to. Darroll could be the only problem. But a big one if he is. That could be big, big trouble. Those two will have been around long enough to know the value of the card they've got to bargain with. They won't come cheap. Not by light years. You just may have made co-stars out of them. Probably on to Darroll right now.'

He was striding around the room trying to see it as a cop from Homicide. It being Preston's place was the real bitch. No, there was no way it could stay here. He turned to Madison again.

'All his clothes still here?'

'Yes.'

'Why can't you stick to little two-and-twenties,' Tom Leonard said, 'with stars in their eyes and brains only between their legs. These two – you just might end up working for Darroll yet, you know!'

'Yeah. Well, if you think you can handle things, guess I'll be going.'

A small rocket of red fury exploded at the core of Tom Leonard's brain.

'That's right!' he heard himself screaming, 'you do that! Beat it! Vamoose! Walk away! Leave me to sweep it all under the mat and shove it down the garbage shoot. Put a can of Lysol in my hand and walk on out! And – I know – you don't want to know! "Fix it, Tom, will you, sport – but I don't want to know." Well you just might like to know I've been straight-arming your mother's fucking demands these past three weeks and that arm is getting mighty tired. Maybe it's about time you did it! How about that, Paul, sweetheart!'

Madison's cheeks had begun to grow red with anger. Abruptly they paled and the tensed fighter's crouch he had half assumed lost its latent force. Tom Leonard chose the luxury of driving his initiative home like a nail.

'I've got just one question to ask,' he said. 'How does it feel to know if I weren't here to wipe your ass, you'd be in shit-creek up to your eyeballs?'

Paul Madison's eyes opened wide less with anger than with shock.

'So what does that make you?' he said in a voice surprised and almost sorrowful, as if the thought had only just occurred. Tom Leonard felt his fury curiously diverted.

'We know what I am,' he said thickly.

The two men looked at each other at a loss to know what each should be feeling.

'Go on,' Tom Leonard said, 'beat it. Go back home and impress on that fascist valet of yours you've not been out all night. Got it?'

'Got it.' Meekly, Paul Madison turned and went.

Reaching for his handkerchief, Tom Leonard moved to the phone.

The Police Commissioner could consistently outdrive Lyndon Oates off the tee by forty yards. He had, however, a persistent tendency to hook. Lyndon Oates could be relied upon to slice. Like robot light relief in the unnatural landscape of a bad sci-fi movie, their golf-carts stood separated by some eighty paces and the undisturbed fairway of the tenth hole of the Bel Air Country

Club. It took seven more strokes before the two carts were parked within robot chatting distance at the edge of the close-shorn green. It took six more strokes before Lyndon Oates was able to stoop and retrieve his ball from the cup. The Commissioner, four up already, was replacing his putter in his bag.

Oates walked towards him with a crisp military step. And moustache. In the larger-than-life tartan of his golf slacks he contrived to suggest a Colonel of an historic regiment keeping open the route into Afghanistan. For a man playing off twenty-three it was a staggering achievement.

'That Dennis Curtis going like that,' he said. 'That's a helluva note.'

The Commissioner held off comment for one significant beat of time. No other golfers were pressing from behind. They could both reflect on the tragedy.

'Well, there you go,' he said. 'Or rather there he goes.' A scarlet and black streak of a cardinal flew from out of the token rough behind him toward a clump of birches beyond the hole. There had been smog earlier on but for a while the breeze from the coast had driven it further inland making the air and sunshine seem fresh-minted. The sky was of such a saturated blue the sprinkler system must have worked overtime the previous evening to keep greens and fairways in the same colouring book mode.

'One helluva note,' Lyndon Oates repeated. 'He was just bouncing back so well. We had big plans for him, Mike, I can tell you. All shot to hell.'

The Commissioner nodded sympathetically. He was a big, generous-bellied man who strode around like a benign giant. Sure, he ruthlessly applied the law. But in his book, privately, being a schmuck was the real crime. You had to expect crazy behaviour from movie stars. They were kinda freaks and though you had to sit on 'em once in a while, they were only a problem to themselves. He'd had the coroner's snap opinion that Curtis's heart had virtually exploded on orgasm. Christ, the tricks these customers go in for.

'Guess it was open and shut,' Lyndon Oates said. 'Natural causes. I don't suppose the investigation will come out any different.'

The Commissioner almost smiled as he wrote up the last score on his card. Oates wasn't doing it too well. But he would be nice to him. No reason not to.

'I heard he was doing so well, there's rumours he's almost certain to get one of those Academy nominations,' the Commissioner said.

'You can count on it. In fact if you were a betting man – which I know you are not—' Oates grinned, 'you could pick up some useful odds on that.'

The Commissioner laughed as he pocketed the information.

'Yep, it was natural causes all right,' he said. 'No question. Coronary as big as your fist. Mind you, there were a couple of little items which the sawbones didn't overlook.'

'Oh?' Lyndon Oates suddenly felt less secure in his tartans.

'Well pathology tells us there had to be some gal involved. He died on the job you know.'

'Really!'

'And how he came to be where – well, never mind. I guess there was someone sure as hell scared and, well, I guess there's no point in hurting people any more than need be. Or the memory of some-one I'm sure was a regular guy.'

He smiled a backroom politician's smile.

'We'll just let things lie,' he said.

Lyndon Oates felt silence rushing in on them.

'I'd say that would be an act of human kindness Commissioner that would be highly appreciated, very highly appreciated,' Oates said.

The Commissioner smiled placing both of his huge hands squarely on Oates's shoulders.

'You don't have to say it, Lyndon,' he beamed. 'I know you mean it.'

He was working out in the mini-gym which, influenced by Jack Preston's spread, he had built in to the room which in Stella Lang's day had housed a wall-length mirror, a bar and a sprung floor. So maybe that was kind of sad. But plus ça change and all that shit. In the past six months he'd put on as many pounds. Trying himself on for size one morning he'd been shocked to find the sixty press-ups he could smoothly knock off in his college football days had dwindled to a breathless, ear-pounding twenty. Who the hell said a good screw was the equivalent of a seven-mile walk? He'd better shape up or he'd be photographable only in wide screen. He must work at it. It was his job.

And it was coming back. He hadn't let things go too far. The taut ridges of muscle across his stomach continued to give him a basic grip on the athletic. Toes hooked behind the fourth wall bar up he levered himself up through a slow, searching series of sit-ups.

There was a knock on the door. Annoyed, he completed the series.

'Come in!'

It was Tibor. He had never needed to come here before.

'What is it? Something wrong?'

'Er, no sir. I just wanted to say how sorry I was to hear about Mr Curtis.'

'Oh. Yeah, that was too bad. I have to tell you that you sure picked a swell time to convey your condolences.'

'Yes, sir. I'm sorry. But you have your appointment for ten and it's my half-day off.'

'Oh yeah.'

'It must have happened not so very long after I brought that package over to you.'

'How do you mean?'

'I did catch sight of him at Mr Preston's that evening, didn't I? That evening you did, of course, come home early.'

'What the hell are you getting at?'

'I'm sure the news of his death came as a great shock to a lot of people.'

'He was found dead in his tub in his apartment.'

'Yes, sir. Mr Madison – it would rather suit me if I could have this coming weekend off. I wonder whether that might be possible?'

Paul Madison scrambled to his feet. Inside the sweat-suit he felt sticky as a fresh wave of perspiration seemed to break angrily over the surface of his skin.

'Listen shit face,' he said very quickly, 'I don't know what's on your mind but it had better not be what I think it is! I didn't hire you, you were wished on me, remember?'

'Mr Madison, I'm sure you got the wrong . . .'

'No, you got it wrong, my Hungarian friend! You try to pull anything like this again and you're out! Finished! Kaput. Yeah – there's a word you understand, right!'

'I was only trying . . .'

'We both know what you were trying so let's not play fucking games. One more stunt like this and you won't ever work in the town again. I personally guarantee it. You'll be pressing pants back of some two-bit Chink laundry. You're out of your league, Tibor!'

The Hungarian's regular features remained as tautly distinguished and self-contained as a senior UN diplomat's. But he had gone white.

'May I just say I am sorry to have provoked this misunderstanding, Mr Madison,' he said. 'I assure you I'm most happy in my position here. I've known some very hard times in the past. You can absolutely rely on me, I do assure you. And, of course, I'm most grateful.'

'See it stays that way. Now beat it!'

'Yes, sir.'

The gentleman's gentleman withdrew. Madison glared abstractedly at the blonde wood of his gym. The nerve of the guy! Perhaps he should let him go. The sweat on his chest and legs was beginning to congeal now but he felt flushed and oddly flustered. He stared at the horizontal grill of wall-bars. For some reason they blended in his mind with memories of a padded cell.

chapter fourteen

Milton Rosner,
Magnum Leisure Incorporated,

Dear Milton Rosner,
I am sending you by accompanying mail the latest edition of
'Pictorial Serenity Glades' which is just off the press.

This 'Pictorial' is being sent to you, not as a reminder of
Serenity Glades' reverential ambience, but of its artistic and
cultural side. So few people seem to realise that Los Angeles
has in its midst these gems of art and architecture which we
have brought from Europe through the years.

Too few who live in this community know Serenity Glades
although over a million people from every country on the globe
visit these art treasures each year. Sometimes I think that this
eternal resting place is better known worldwide than it is in the
Los Angeles area.

It may be that after you have looked at the pages of this
book, you will want to visit our art collection. I am attaching a
list of some highlights which you will find worth while.

One of my personal passes is enclosed. However, if you call
my executive assistant, she will be glad to arrange a personally
conducted tour for you, visiting only those points of art and
culture.

I also take the opportunity to enclose brochures outlining
certainly newly devised and, to high-income tax payers, very
advantageous investment schemes now made available through
Serenity Glades Mortgage and Investment.

With warmest personal regards, I am

Cordially yours . . .

Christie Roberts's body had been flown home to Rocky Mount,
North Carolina, for private interment in the family crypt. Her

father had been stunned by the gruesome discovery of her death. But had not been too dazed to use the influence his considerable private fortune gave him to keep the revelations at the inquest and the local press coverage to a minimum. He had gone along with his daughter's passion to become a star. It was difficult not to indulge a craving which, he conceded, affected thousands of girls like her. Even less lovely than she. Than she had been. The primal-scream room had come as a shock. He had never heard of this bizarre therapy, still less of his daughter's flirtation with it. As he stood, a tall, greying figure staring at the almost animal claw-marks on the padded walls, and considered what that had meant in torment to his daughter, he wept. The police lieutenant had taken his arm. 'No point hanging around here, sir,' the man had said gently. 'It's part of the scene these days.' What scene? Pressing even harder on him than the fact of his daughter's suicide was the nagging uneasy question – who, or what had driven her to it? As this year's nominee for mayor he had strong political reasons why he did not wish to make public his misgivings, his utter loathing for a profession which seemed to destroy more than it created. He had refused to be interviewed either for the newspapers or television. But through a friend, a Judge of the Los Angeles Supreme Court, he let the Santa Monica Chief of Police know that he wanted the matter probed, Christie's friends and lovers grilled by experts. But nothing could bring her back now.

He travelled with the private plane carrying her body in a bronze casket on a crisp fall morning from a sparse corner of LA airport. He shook hands with the Santa Monica police chief. 'Don't worry, sir,' the officer had promised, 'there'll be undercover enquiries. I know what you want.'

Dennis Curtis's leave-taking, on the other hand, demanded no such covert operations. Anyway, covert was not a word that fitted easily in the vocabulary of Oates, Becker and Rimmer. Not when the pickings were so promising.

There had been a brief meeting between Rosner, Oates and Leonard. Serenity Glades had come forward with an attractive package deal which Rosner decided was an offer they couldn't refuse. Though burying a dead star was a legitimate charge on the budget, no point in chucking money away. Oates, over an intimate lunch with a spruce executive of the famous mortuary, had explained the enormous publicity that could be harvested

from the affair. A generous discount on the total tab would ensure
Oates promised, that Serenity Glades would be mentioned in all
handouts, their name discreetly positioned in all TV and newspaper photo coverage.

'You can have the departed one's initials embossed on a replica
of the British Union Jack,' the official offered.

'Good thinking,' Oates said.

Alone with Tom Leonard afterwards, Oates reflected on the
good and the bad of the situation.

'Bad – we've lost the mileage we'd have got out of his personal
appearances with *Curtain* in Europe, especially England. You had
him fixed for a plugging on Parkinson – is that the guy's name?'

'Good – as we both know, dropping dead around Oscar time
earns points. We pick up the sentimental vote. What's the coverage been like over in England?'

'Terrific,' Leonard said. 'The BBC are sending a team to cover
the funeral.'

'Good.' Oates laughed. 'So Curtis finally makes it. Screws
himself into a legend. Isn't anybody claiming him, I mean the
body, over there?'

'Not a whisper. He came originally from a place called New
Malden outside London, but he's been away so long. Nobody has
come forward asking us to freight him back.'

So it was left to Serenity Glades to find an air-conditioned niche
among other cosmetised stars, appropriate to the status of the
newcomer. With it went 'eternal lighting' and round-the-clock
music selected by a temporary typist from a cassette drawer
labelled 'English'. The rites were scheduled for the most favoured
chapel at Serenity Glades – The Wee Kirk o' the Highlands.
Tartan-covered pews, a background of mournful bagpipe music,
emphasised the chapel's Scottish motif. But as the brochure stated;
Jews, Catholics, all creeds can just as serenely 'rest assured' as
those of Scottish descent.

The chief embalmer at the Glades had been carefully briefed.
This was a big one. It was a famous face. Whatever had caused
the life to drain from it, must not be visibly discernible on the day.
The choicest fluids, powders, paints and potions were selected to
ensure that on his final appearance before an admiring public,
Dennis Curtis would be putting his best face forward. Logistically
it would have been simpler to pump in the formaldehyde
there, in the embalming room at Serenity Glades. The entire
operation from the first dab of rouge to the last pounding home

of a certified piece of English turf, could all have taken place within a few hundred reverential square feet. But the stratagems worked out between Oates and the Public Relations Counsellor at the Glades required something more meaningful.

'Do you wish to maximise or minimise the rituals?' the counsellor had asked excruciatingly.

'Maximise,' Oates had replied gravely. 'No one should be denied an opportunity to pay their last tributes to a loved one.'

'Good,' the funeral man said with an involuntary lapse into good cheer. 'That means we'll prepare the corp . . . the loved one at our resting-in chapel in the Hollywood Hills, the cortège and the mourners all leaving from there.'

That arrangement was doubly convenient to Oates and the studio. Curtis's temporarily rented bungalow at Westwood was distinctly 'B' class status. If he couldn't be buried from an address on Beverly, Canon, Coldwater, or Benedict, then better off to choose a classless but consecrated spot where nobody stays for drinks.

It was to this jumping-off point on the morning of the funeral, a Saturday (maximum crowds and no need to interrupt shooting schedules), that Paul Madison went. It was from here that the cortège of mourning Cadillacs would slowly wend its way up to Serenity Glades. Paul Madison supposed that he owed his position among the chief mourners as a pall-bearer – he would this once be supporting Dennis Curtis – more to their recent professional association rather than his being a witness to and virtual bedmate of the late actor's death.

Ordered to collect him from Serenity Glades later, Tibor dropped him off before the chapel, outwardly a mixture of Church, Colonial Mansion and Pancake House. He was wearing a specially purchased Botany 500 charcoal-grey suit with a cream silk shirt and black silk tie. He appeared handsomely bereaved in them with a touch of Mafia too. It was an appropriately cold day. The sky was a thin universal grey except beyond the canyon hills to the north where a leaden blackness was bulking up in a visibly rising tower. It looked, Paul Madison thought, as if God was going to be right on time with His special effects.

He showed his invitation-pass to the two security men at the door. A third man deferentially ushered him into a large sombrely-panelled room. He had purposely timed his arrival to the last minute. The room was already quite full of other sombre mourners ignoring the creeping strains of an overly hushed organ tape

as they talked in subdued voices among themselves. Several
caught his eye as he entered and even risked discreet smiles.
Lyndon Oates, of course; a small percentage of agents; a failed
director doing his elder-statesman bit; Morton Crane standing in
for the British-in-America contingent; an Academy luminary
representing dignity. Paul Madison felt suddenly lost without a
glass in his hand. It was as if everyone had individually got the
time of one of the town's less discriminating parties wrong and
having all turned up at an hour before the opening of the bar,
found themselves flung back on their own unliquored-up re-
sources. That was it – a bad party in slow motion and the wrong
clothes. It only needed a rock idol to be standing with fly unbuttoned before that trough of lilies to complete the impression.

Ah, true to type and job specification Tom Leonard was coming
forward to help wipe the egg off his solitary face as if the other
night had never been. Ass-licking creep!

'Hi, Paul, how's the shoulder?'

'Oh, bearing up. Or about to.'

'You were looking appropriately serious standing there on your
ownsome.'

'How's Margot, Tom?'

'No better for the company she keeps.'

'And fuck you too, Tom.'

'How's the tennis, Paul?' The animosity between the two men
flashed nakedly across the closed-circuit confrontation. In that
tiny slice of time an almost feral hatred glinted in their eyes. But it
faded just as swiftly as each tacitly understood the benefits he
drew from the other. The faces reverted to a bland Hollywood
handsomeness.

'Actually, Tom, I was thinking – same old crowd, different
fancy dress. I guess about everyone's here.'

'Not really. Be ten times more at the church.'

'Give the public what they want and they'll turn out for it.'

'Red Skelton, *circa* 1957.'

'I don't think the public wanted this one,' Leonard said. 'Or
Curtis. Pity you souped him up.'

'I just gave him a boost. The poor bastard was past it, that's all.
I don't see Lady Margaret here.'

'Are you kidding? I had her out of here the next morning, like
she had cholera.'

'A more social disease, I'd guess. Back to England?'

'Caribbean. Safer. You'll find she's wired flowers.'

'Say, that guy seems to be wanting people to move. You know which car you're in?'

The funeral procession set off eastwards across the city. It moved without interruption from stop-lights. Police outriders had been arranged. The twelve matching Cadillacs might have made up the motorcade of a visiting Arabian ruler. They murmured on to Sunset. For a long ten-mile-per-hour time they wound past the well-kempt gardens and manicured lawns of houses elegantly eloquent in their silent testimony to money and their indifference to the parade going by. Only vacant window-eyes observed Dennis Curtis's last public appearance. It was not until the rise of higher buildings signalled their approaching the Strip that they began to pick up rubber-neckers. Chiefly the looks they drew were hostile. It was too early in the day for people bent on pleasure or recovering from it to have their thoughts set running on death. For all their garish invitations to the living, the countless massage parlours turned fronts to the cortège as indifferent as the other kind of expensive houses. No longer in the land of the living, Dennis Curtis was beyond their power to stimulate or revive. Raising from the dead was not their scene.

Tom Leonard was sat next to Paul Madison in the second limousine. He felt his ribs nudged. He caught Madison's eye, then saw it flick a quick glance sideways out of the window. He followed the direction of the look. They were abreast of 'The Body Shop'. All very well, he thought, but they like their leather living there, and female. He caught Madison's eye again, friendly suddenly and, in a fraternity-boy way, conspiratorial. Now the living were making common cause against the dead's over-insistence on decorum. He began to grin but checked himself. Sylvia Kilmartin, sitting up front, just might pick it up in the wide angle rear view mirror.

On Fairfax, while an old Middle-European Jew stood still from either present-day respect or a dead weight of memories, they turned left. And then right on to Hollywood. This was the object of their routing. Flags on Grauman's Chinese were, by prior arrangement, at half-mast. So were those on the Egyptian. The Egyptian's marquee bore a simple legend: 'Dennis Curtis. Thanks for the Memory.' And thanks for the plug, Tom Leonard thought. *Curtain* was to be reissued there the next day.

Once more he felt Paul Madison's elbow in his ribs. They were rolling past the Hollywood Wax Museum. People were gawpingly lining the sidewalk now so this time it was easier to keep a straight face.

The scuzziness of one area changed to the broader thorough-fare of another. Either the drivers were getting bored or they had their orders. The cavalcade gathered speed. It accomplished the final shuffle of quick turns rapidly. Then decorously it slowed again. It was motioned straight through the main gates of Serenity Glades and began to mount the long green slope at funereal pace.

The Wee Kirk O' The Highlands was not at the summit of the ascent. It was also far too small for the occasion. As he ducked out of his Cadillac close to the church porch, Paul Madison could see that the house had been way oversold. Public-address speakers had been set up outside the church to relay the benedictions for the overspill. A large number of people gathered under them. But for their sombre clothes they might have passed for an average drive-in audience. They stood blankly around while stretched black Chevrolets swelled numbers with a ferry service from the parking lot. Paul Madison shivered again. He didn't envy them. The black cloud rearing up earlier over the west of the city had now extended to the almost total extinction of the grey. It lowered toppingly over the upsweep of dark green lawns. It was obviously pregnant with immediate rain. From the thought, from the cold, Paul Madison shivered once again. He had handed his British umbrella to Tom Leonard sensing that as a pall-bearer under the coffin instead of in it, getting soaked was no hardship.

The relief of action, however, was at hand. The press at the door had been cleared. A grave official actually wearing a cutaway was motioning him to take his place with the other pall-bearers. As he scanned them curiously – two he didn't know, Morton Crane the British actor, well, yes, Celine had warned him, and Curtis's agent, sure, grieving the loss of his ten, but why on earth the twangy-voiced Bruce Denham? – it dawned on him they were a complete pick-up team. The chances of getting down the short aisle without a catastrophic fumble were probably no better than even. They would have to do it in one take with no rehearsal. But the coach was working on them.

'Our people will bring the casket to this point,' he was saying. 'You gentlemen need only carry it the length of the aisle which is quite a short and manageable distance, I assure you. The cata-falque is just before the altar. If the leading bearers will simply direct the casket on to it, those behind need only push it into position.' The man in the cutaway lined the six of them up in parallel some four feet apart. He buzzed towards the back of the line. The pros were bearing the casket towards them. It was adorned by a simple wreath. Crane intercepted his glance. Cockneys, especially this famous one, specialise in gallows humour.

'See what happens when you play with yourself,' he said. He shivered too. 'He's got the best of it today, though,' he said.

The casket slid between to block the sight of his superiorly deadpan expression. Paul Madison was glad. Throughout the wait he'd been aware of the sniping presence of the cameraman. It wouldn't do to be seen cracking a smile on CBS tonight.

'Now, gentlemen, if you'd be so kind as to step behind the bearer you're relieving. Good. Now, shoulders under. Now – take the weight. Yes? Good. Now hold it there. Now when you start to move, please remember, all start off with your left foot. Now, we'll just wait for the signal.'

It was heavy but bearable. He had the weight on his right shoulder. Shared among six it didn't seem too bad. If only they didn't have to wait around too long. Like an actor in the wings he was on the verge of panic, when, catching him by surprise after all, the cue came.

'Right, gentlemen, by the left foot, please. Now, if you please.'

Aware of the media whirring about him but feeling like an extra in a Dracula remake, he put his left foot and his most dignified demeanour forward. 'You know something?' Crane whispered to Madison, 'I got my ear glued to his balls!' Simultaneously, as pat on cue, the first fat raindrop stung hard upon his cheek and moistly disintegrated.

Their progress up the aisle past packed and standing rows of mourners was slow but reasonably sure. While it lasted his chief concern was transferred from disquiet about the corpse's dignity to worry as to his own. Skewed partially sideways as he was by the weight of the casket he had to crab his way forward. He felt a fool. Raindrops were trickling down toward his shirt collar and with his left hand up steadying the casket, he had no way of brushing them away. They felt like liquid, creeping flies. He was having to stoop a little. The effect was to send a shooting pain through the left-hand side of the small of his back. The urge to grimace was almost total. But he could not be sure that cameras had not been allowed inside as well. They had such fast fucking film, these days. In any case it felt as if all eyes were on him. It was hard to tell. Head wrenched into the oak side of the casket, left forearm up before it, he could only glimpse the house out the corner of his eye.

Thank Christ, the thing! Gingerly he helped ease the casket on to it. Bumpingly they slid it full home. With relief he stood erect. Now he could see Crane again. His expression was magnificently ironic in its emptiness. A discreet cough. A round-faced minister of some sort was anxiously nodding them towards the vacant pew that had been dealt them.

A hymn was sung. It was not 'Gather at the River'. He would have lost money. Not caring to risk giving voice he ignored the verses printed in the song-sheet and stood doing goldfish impersonations. The minister led them in a short prayer that besought the Great Electrician in the sky to shine perpetual light upon his servant. The thought had to be that this was okay for a kicked-off stand-in but less than appropriate for a star. Maybe it was right, though, ego-wise. He squinted down through half-closed eyes to read the plum-voiced, strange-accented minister's embossed name upon the pass card. Geddes Campbell, Dean of Religious Studies, Occidental College: Associated Minister attending the Wee Kirk O' The Highlands, Serenity Glades. Evidently a true son of Scotland. As the rain outside rose audibly in violence to lash at the plastic spirituality of this film-set house of God, Paul Madison had a sudden sense there had been something fractionally more honest in the service in that bank that Palm Springs Sunday morning.

The wee dean had stopped his spieling. Yes, it was time to sit down again. The main event was upon them. Milton Rosner was mounting the pulpit to deliver, as advertised, the funeral address. Dapper, self-contained, he seemed more at home than the huffing and puffing clergyman had been. Paul Madison glanced curiously to his right. Three places away Morton Crane kept his thoughts to himself with the same quizzical aplomb.

Rosner gently cleared his throat as he placed a page of notes upon the open Bible. He placed a hand on either side of the pulpit as, easily, he looked out over the congregation.

'Ladies and gentlemen,' he said. 'My fellow mourners. Friends of Dennis Curtis. I don't think I could be accused either of irreverence or of giving away a jealously guarded secret if I were to say now that Dennis Curtis – Denny, as those of us who knew and loved him will always think of him – that Denny was not somebody known for his formal observance of a religious faith. Let me say in the same breath that never was I more certain in mind that any human being more deserved the prayers and this ceremony with which we now honour his memory. There's a story

D.—I

concerning Denny and his early days which I think says it all. In my capacity as a producer – I produced one of Denn's earliest Hollywood successes as well as, I am proud to be able to say, his last – in that capacity I was privileged to hear that story a long time ago. I would like to share it with you now.

'It goes back to the early 'fifties and the time of the Korean War. In those days Denny was a very young man indeed, learning his craft in the peerless tradition of that same English vaudeville that gave us Chaplin, Stan Laurel, the great Sir Harry Lauder, so intimately connected with this picturesque reminder of his homeland. It was typical of Denny that at this moment in his young career he should take time out to join a show entertaining the British Forces then fighting alongside our boys in Korea. But not exclusively the British. Denny's company played to various US units and he told me that it was then and there that meeting Americans for the first time – among them, naturally, our own beloved Bob Hope – he began to form those deep attachments which ultimately were to make him our gain as a favourite adopted son and his native land's loss.'

Paul Madison was drawn to look at Morton Crane. His instinct had been correct. Finding it more than flesh and blood could bear the English tax-casualty was staring fixedly at his own lap while he struggled to keep his laugh stuffed up his sleeve.

'Well it seems,' Rosner was continuing, 'that one evening Denny's little troupe was playing to a group of British and Commonwealth soldiers. Some artillery battery had received the wrong co-ordinates and, well, they started to drop shells right alongside the theatre where the show was taking place.

'Well the show broke up. Everyone dived for cover. Denny found himself under some kind of cart it seems with half a dozen other guys. The shelling was getting worse. There was screaming. Cries. People had been hit and well . . . here's the point of this story . . .'

But as far as Paul Madison was concerned he had already lost his audience. He was as disappointed in Rosner as he was surprised. He had thought he knew the producer, the leisure activity executive, to be above such 'no atheist in the fox-holes' crap. Rosner would surely not have stooped to such banalities in private. Well, that was it. This was not private. The rule guiding the Tom Leonards of the world seemed to be the larger the audience, the more commonplace the cliché. It went with not saying fuck. You geared your platitudes to the lowest intelligence in the auditorium or the convention centre. So where on the scale did that put million dollar grossers?

Oh, to hell with that! Fuck it! Think about something else. For a moment, unbidden, but not for the first time, the elegantly sensuous image of Sam's face tilted back and sideways with her ecstasy rose up to taunt him. As in a photograph he clearly saw the clean line of her body as, naked, she approached his bed.

'Shit,' he muttered.

He came to at once and glanced swiftly from side to side. It was okay. The expletive hadn't carried. The service remained sacrosanct as Rosner clichéd on about English oak. Just as well he'd not been allowed to dwell on her. He'd begun to feel sex uncoiling beneath his suit of mourning. It was a little early in the day, maybe, and what a place to get it on! There were other fish in the sea. Spades in the tool shed. Later, perhaps . . .

Later, he stood one of the drenched elect in the exclusive, walled plot in which Magnum had seen fit to purchase Dennis Curtis a final earthly resting place. Substitute Cinecitta for the after-life, he thought, and it's about the same as the VIP lounge at LAX. He was wearing his raincoat now and shielding himself and Sylvia Kilmartin from the driving rain with one of the umbrellas some genius of a prop man had been distributing as they'd emerged from the service. Mercifully it had always been understood that the one pall-bearing gesture made and their names in the papers guaranteed, the casket could be left to find its own way to its long home. It had made it in one. It lay now in the arms of the hydraulic gismo that shortly would ease the very last way for Dennis Curtis. Downwards, appropriately. Rain was hammering the saturated wreaths now covering it into a forlorn flatness. It drummed sound-drowningly on the geodesic roof of umbrellas, bulleted into the rich brown earth by the gaping grave in readiness for an even prompter return whence it came than the dead man. Regardless of both umbrella and London fog, rain had gotten to trickle down Paul Madison's back. Jesus, he thought, its cliché time run to wretched excess. As if reading that thought Sylvia Kilmartin turned to mutter privately up to him.

'This rain,' she said. 'I've lost track of whether we're remaking *The Barefoot Contessa* or *The Big Sleep*.'

'I think it's the remake of *The Killers*,' he said.

She smiled quietly up at his erudition. When somehow he'd found himself obliged to offer her shelter, he had feared the worst. He'd sometimes had a sense there might be something between her and Curtis . . . But as ever, thank God, she seemed totally self-possessed.

For the umpteenth time that morning he shivered. The umbrella dropped a different pattern of raindrops from its rim. His shoulders felt damp but it was maybe only cold. It was impossible to tell which.

'Why the fuck couldn't he have asked to be cremated?' Crane had said. They had been standing in the porch and looking out at the smoking rain while waiting for cars to take them to the Garden of Remembrance.

'He probably did,' Paul Madison had said, 'but coverage-wise it's less dramatic.'

'Not as a POV shot. How did you think it went?'

'Not original enough. They need a screen in there and slide support for the preacher and guest speakers. You know, customised audio-visual modules covering the late lamented's career. They could've run highlights from his best movies.'

'Well that would've taken care of two minutes.'

'So you've come to bury Curtis not to praise him.'

'Now, now, he was in three of my epics, don't forget . . . Where are they burying him?'

'Some special plot some place up the top near their store.'

'Well, no offence regarding your last,' Morton Crane had said, 'but it'll be the first real plot he's had to do with in years.'

Now, standing a little apart and suffering the gusts and sudden slanting onslaught of the rain with the enigmatic indifference of a stoic or a reasonably proficient actor, Crane was standing obliquely opposite them in the loose circle around the grave. His presence more than any other lent to the universal scene its sense of unreality. It seemed more like a Universal scene. At any second the director would yell 'Cut!' The FX boys would turn off the hoses and a make-up girl would hurry in to touch up some pancake made streaky by the water. But this was only too real. Oblivious to his fellow creatures' discomforts, it seemed, while under an umbrella held by some lesser cleric, the round-faced Scots minister was droning on apparently happy to be exacting his own dramatic pound of flesh in conditions that evoked childish memories. Paul Madison tried to kill the time by scrutinising the inner band of soaked-through mourners. The ugly, unbeautiful person whose dated hairstyle shrieked English ordinariness must be Curtis's long-lost first wife. The second and third, both minor sex-bomb actresses now sunk without trace had decided not to come. Both must have known the red-inked look of his estate. This one had been the cause of a very early marriage. She was non-show-biz. Chances were the opportunity of a few all-paid-for days in fabled Hollywood had motivated the rebirth of her lachrymose affection. Denham looked less decent and more haggard. Whether his wilder appearance was from grief or discomfort was a toss-up. He wasn't, by some way, the youngest of men around any more, but it was well possible they might both be up for the same part one of these days. With the thought he felt his stargazing harden into the half-paranoid, professional hostility of one top acting gun for another.

At that moment Denham turned his head and looked directly at him. Their eyes locked. Envious fear of territorial invasion linked them until, feeling the more guilty as the first to stare, Madison flicked his eyes away. Goodness! That guy with the greying beard was Peter Rostinov. He hadn't noticed him before. He was standing quite respectfully still, eyes fixed on the casket but was yet somehow contriving to suggest a distaste for the entire proceedings. He may have liked the man, the message read, but his feelings as to the mise en scène were unprintable: only a certain sense of propriety had made him come, and, just, kept him there. At any second it seemed, his nose might wrinkle.

'Man that is born of woman hath but a short time to live, and is full of misery. He cometh up and is cut down, like a flower; he fleeth as it were a shadow, and never continueth in one stay.'

The minister had, after all, the best lines. The tremendous words recalled Paul Madison to the moment, the occasion. Like Rostinov he stared at the casket by the fresh wound in the earth.

'I heard a voice from heaven, saying unto me, Write. From henceforth blessed are the dead which lie in the Lord; even so saith the Spirit; for they rest from their labours.'

A signal must have been given. The wreaths had been laid aside. Like a robot from the latest *Star Wars* rip-off the complicated machine began to lower the casket into the hole in the ground. Ultimate reality for each one of us. For a moment Paul Madison had an X-ray like impression of the corpse lying waxen within the fancy box. Curtis! He'd helped him out at his first big party once, the time he nearly got into a fight over Stella Lang. She'd been sprawled out like a Bowery wino and that bald ugly guy with a face like an ape had soiled her dress and been looking to get one. Then Curtis had stepped suavely, a little drunkenly, rather charmingly, between. Maybe in the end that counted for more than the countless re-takes on the set as his shot nerve failed to hold together a performance. Poor bastard! He hadn't been that old. And what a way to go! At a moment when you could hardly call your dong your own! The remembrance of the interminable bar-scene take in *Curtain* was clicked from his mind as the image of a terrified Lady Margaret Glendenning scrambling her seismic jelly flesh out from under Curtis, flashed up to replace it. Jesus! Well the guy had died happy you could have said.

The casket had sunk quite out of sight. There was the sound of a squelching jolt. As mysterious as life itself, the machine was able to extract its freshly dirtied tapes.

'O God, the Father of our Lord Jesus Christ, vouchsafe we beseech thee . . .'

And forever immortalised on a few hundred feet of blue actuality film in some safe in some London newspaper's office as he tried to screw the woman who, to a degree, had fatally screwed him. And somewhere in another hole was the girl who had gone, fellatio style, to eternity. Somewhere in an Orange Country pauper's grave were the bones of his old man. And that was all. Win a little in life, or lose, or box a draw, when they put you down there it was the end. For ever and ever amen. So get it, baby, while the getting was still good!

Another signal. A man in a black oil-slicker came to the edge of the grave and threw into its insistent, eye-drawing openness the ritual handful of earth. Heavy with the rain it landed on the casket with a dull thud no sound man would have wished to improve upon. While it hung in the air it was the rap of Death on the door of all their lives. While it lasted all several million dollars worth of them were frightened children once again. Paul Madison wondered that split second if, just possibly, his view of life was wrong. Then, praise the Lord, the hiss of rain had washed the ugly heaviness from their ears.

It was a wrap. Rather aimlessly the minister was shaking such hand as were offered to him. Paul Madison looked down at Sylvia Kilmartin.

'I've got a car waiting for me,' he said. 'Want to come find a drink some place?'

She nodded.

'So long as it's dry,' she said, 'and I can start thinking again. Just consider – I edited him into a nomination and now he's home free. There won't be a dry seat in the house.'

'It's a hell of a way to make sure of collecting.'

They made for the gilded barred gate in the wall enclosing the Garden of Remembrance. There were few other graves. One was surmounted by a female angel that could have won points in a Pacific Coast pornography play-off.

Well, Sylvia Kilmartin would do to talk to a while. She was always good for a laugh or two. He'd think of somebody to rescue the weekend with in due course. Maybe call Jack. Sylvia slipped. She grabbed his arm in steadying herself. And not surprising. The sodden grass was thickly treacherous underfoot. He steered towards the white-edged security of the central gravel path.

It was funny, but for some reason, the person he really felt like seeing at that moment was Stella Lang.

chapter fifteen

And the nominations for Best Supporting Performance by an Actor are:

Desi Lopez Jnr. in *The Palomino*
Dennis Curtis in *Curtain*
Maurice Critchley in *The Rat Race*
Michael McCarthy in *Flashpoint 2000 Rising*
Jack Warden in *Washington Post*

> Beth Naylor: *Academy of*
> *Motion Picture Arts and*
> *Sciences Annual Award Ceremony.*

'May I have the envelope, please,' Miss Naylor said. It was placed in her hands by the suitably subservient functionary. The crowd of fifteen hundred held their breaths as if they had indeed arrived at the Civic Centre in full evening dress for the sole purpose of watching the earthquake, and it was now about to happen. The boring awards for editors and costume designers for the best black and white foreign entry made south of the Falkland Islands had finally come to their interminable end. This was where the money was. The television cameramen bringing the event to the world tightened their framing and agents grew nearer to coronaries from the effort of keeping the dials of their faces set at nonchalance.

Not imitating her dress, the volatile, still-beautiful Beth Naylor eschewed cheap theatrical effect up front and opened the envelope slickly, as if she'd had practice at doing it before. As adroitly she removed the card. Her eyes flicked over it as she exacted her ostensible privilege of being the first to know.

'And the winner is . . .'

Her voice caught and card and envelope shook uncertainly in her hands. She did it well up to her superstar form.

'May I just, er, as somebody who's paid her dues – may I just say I think this is the most beautiful thing the industry has ever done.'

A dramatic pause.

'The winner is – the late Dennis Curtis for *Cur*—'

She'd been wise to impose her moment upon the occasion first. A roar of swelling applause, cheering overtopping clapping, seemed to crash forward and overwhelm the stage, with an almost physical presence. It was slightly reminiscent, perhaps, of a wild Pacific breaker surging to its foamy disintegration at Malibu. And very like a Republican Convention. For a moment the crescendo totally drowned the sound of the orchestra which, on the drop of the name, and with the prescience afforded the musicians on all such Academy gigs, had launched at once into the main theme from *Curtain*, the current number four in the album lists. It was perhaps the follow-spot beaming on to rake the audience that began to temper the scene of wild enthusiasm. Curiosity began to abate the cheering. Who would step up to collect the dingus?

Barbara Lemerle by all accounts was a shoe-in for the biggy so they wouldn't be pre-empting her. Or would they? They just might – no, of course! It was obvious.

The follow-spot had come to rest on Paul Madison. Or rather, modest to a fault, he had anticipated its blindingly silver arrival by a split second on the empty seat next to his assigned date for the evening. It was obliged to overtake him with its time-serving bath of limelight halfway down the aisle. Applause had diminished now to a steadily reverent awe as if the Ark of the Covenant were getting a hand. As athletically, far less ungraciously than most who'd stumbingly gone before, he climbed the steps to the stage, the applause fluttered up slightly. Perhaps the increase came in acknowledgement that he was stuck with a somewhat delicate job. Perhaps it came from those fashion setters aware that the word was already out he'd be back up there for real next time around.

A nice entrance, he thought, clean-cut, efficient but dignified, respectful. He'd come through the flash of press bulbs and spot-lights outside, the flash of partying, first night foyer style smiles on the same wave length. He slowed down as he approached the regally over-grave Beth. A nice decision now – no-one had briefed him on this. In the event he inclined to give her a chaste, polite kiss on her much visited cheek. From the funtionary, via her, he took the Oscar. He had been warned in advance of the weight (embodying the dated design). Its heaviness still nearly took him by surprise. With professionally heightened instinct he smoothly translated the incipient slump of his shoulders into a half bow of acceptance. Beth Naylor thus had no place to go but off. To a renewed ripple of applause that managed to sound, he was glad to think, like charity slightly begrudged she sailed away. He humbly adjusted his 'seriously though folks' face as he waited for the last spatter of clapping to die completely down. He took a pace forward to the microphone. Silence. Now! No, wait. Stretch it out until the expectancy, the tension is at the breaking point. Let it build. It's your job. Now.

'Members of the Academy, Ladies and Gentlemen,' he said, 'I have no need to tell you or, indeed, anybody in the whole world why I should receive this ultimate award here tonight and not the distinguished performer whose name you just heard linked to it forever by your vote. Words, of course, are inadequate to the situation. But if this is the ultimate trophy, then it is so because it is bestowed by your collective professional judgement on one of your working fellows. I just hope that right now Dennis is taking time off from sharing a jar and a joke up there to look down and observe this final declaration that he had what I'm sure he's known he possessed for years —your highest affection and regard. On his behalf – thank you very much.'

It had been a real bitch getting his tongue around that lot. He'd been willing to bet Tom Leonard had overdone the po-faced convolutions, and maybe been setting him up for a pratfall in front of millions. But as, after a long respectful hush, the tumult of applause broke exactly as he orchestrated it with his own move from stillness into walk-away, he knew Leonard had played it straight. There was nothing like a little cock-sucking literacy to flatter idiots into thinking they'd witnessed the real thing.

He walked into the wings past a winking Morton Crane. Somebody wasn't the least bit fooled then. He offloaded the tawdry, vulgar and please-can-I-have-one trophy with the security guy. As he turned back, Crane was still looking at him. He bent his right arm and mimed downing a fast one. That was right – Crane had done his bit.

Paul Madison grinned. One more round of the PR-fest and Madame would be tripping up the stairs. That he could do without. If he was there when she was getting hers it wouldn't have anything to do with Oscars. He nodded to the Englishman. They beat it to the bar upstairs.

Already there to prop it up was Sylvia Kilmartin. By her standards she was very drunk. She had not been nominated that year.

chapter sixteen

. . . number two or three or six or wherever he's now at that makes Paul Madison try harder. Clearly the youngest of the world's handful of superstars, he is evidently the busiest. With *Cold Turkey* everybody's idea of this year's main dish at the Academy Awards, Paul already has no less than two more blockbusters in the cutting rooms and post-production stages already – *Twice Upon a Midnight* and *Incident at Kent State*. Word is quantity is having no effect whatsoever on his quality. Blake Darroll who has just succeeded in signing him for *Pastimes* says: 'Paul puts me in mind of the great names in the heydays of the studios. He eats up work, thrives on it. Reason? He likes to work and knows it's as good for him as he is for the Industry. Maybe it's Number One the boy is at after all! . . .'

Daily Variety

The buzzer sounded. Lyndon Oates picked up his phone.

'Yes, Celine.'

'I have Mr Markham for you now, Mr Oates.'

'Who?'

'Mr Markham. At the Franklin Hotel. You told me to try—'

'Oh, yeah. Right. Okay put him through. I'll talk to him . . . Robert, how are you, my friend? Good to hear that good old Queen's English of yours again . . . How's the jet lag, then? . . . Good, good. It's always day two that's the killer. Better this way round, though, than going over in your direction. . . sure, sure, of course I appreciate that. I've been giving that list of yours quite a lot of thought . . . Yeah, well, I think I can save you a lot of fruitless labour in that quarter. Paul, well Paul has sat back and toyed with those charming rogue types for so long now, I think he's getting kind of wary of the whole interview scene. . . . Yeah but he says the way his interviews come out, they always end up looking like a paste-and-scissors job . . . Else he does his bit about there are no decent writers in the world and he's knee-deep in

scripts that stink . . . I guess so. I guess so. My guess is he's burn
ing more and more about not getting some real man-size parts
head on before he goes distinguished grey. I just don't know if
Steve is seeing anyone these days. I guess his one thing is burning
up Baja on two wheels. Kind of dropping out of sight, too . . .
that's true, Robert, very true. No argument when you put it that
way . . . But take a little well-intentioned advice. Fellow you
should promote to number one on that line-up of yours is Paul
Madison . . . Yes, really . . . Robert, I have to tell you, Paul
Madison is just the hottest thing in town since, Christ, you name
it. He's got more producers phoning him up all hours than . . .
Well that's where you strike oil. He's learned to be discriminating
and right now he's out of town. He's just finished *Kent State* –
that's going to be a smash by the way – and went down to
Acapulco to unwind a whiles . . . Hey, Robert, hey! Hold your
horses! He happens to be a very close personal friend, as I think
you already know, so you're in there, believe me. I said I'd go
pick him up at LA airport when he gets in tomorrow . . . Right.
Tomorrow. Now, listen, Robert, there's no-one more approach-
able. So here's my plan. Why don't you – if it's okay by your
schedule – why don't you just tag along with me for the ride . . .
Sure, sure. No sweat. You can meet and talk in general and get
up an agenda for your interview and a firm date for your cameras.
It's good for you he's between pictures . . . Robert, my friend,
that's what I'm here for! And listen. I'm tied tonight on something
I just can't shake loose from but tomorrow evening we'll go some
place and eat and catch up on the gossip. Quid pro quo. You
give me your dirt, I'll give you mine . . . Right. I think I just might
be able to find a place that serves some of that fine old English
Ale of yours . . . You betcha! I'll call you back just as soon as I
know . . . Of course. My pleasure entirely . . . Ciao!'

Mission accomplished. Among the cunningly veneered pieces
of his sedately furnished room, Lyndon Oates cradled his phone.
Two arms seemed to move as he did so. The rich bloom of the
table's surface reflected an image that seemed to lose nothing by
way of definition. Perhaps it was the white three-quarters of an
inch of impeccable shirt-cuff beyond the black and white fine
check of his sleeve that this time caught his eye. This time among
hundreds he noticed the twin motion. On impulse he bent forward
to study his own features. They reflected back from the surfacing
an assured satisfaction. Spruce. Confident. Dignified. For a man,
a face at the prime of life. The face of a senior Presidential adviser.
It beamed its congratulations up at him.

Hmm. The prime of life. His current wife was over twenty years younger than he. As a starlet she had been considered one of the town's great beauties. And last year he had caused her to be voted one of its ten best dressed women. But women aged far faster than men. At last night's premiere he had noticed a distinct come-to-stayness about the two horizontal creases in her neck. The cheeks were maybe a little heavier, her upper arms certainly were. Her tits . . . well, it was hard to remember just what her tits had first looked like. But there had been a moment afterwards when standing next to Universal's Maureen O'Malley – okay in soft light, sure, but even so – his wife had looked the same age as the former star. And that single-minded, up-yours-unless-we-do-it-my-way, shanty Irish star was even older than himself.

He frowned and a dozen wrinkles leapt into well-worn place across his forehead. Fortunately for his peace of mind, though not for his wife, he had sat back by now. His brain was dealing with his thoughts and not a reflection directly under his nose. Hmmmn . . .

Lyndon Oates hated to enter a room with a woman less than the evening's most desirable upon his arm. It demeaned his image to go through a doorway with the second best. Yes . . . women aged faster. It would be cheaper, of course, to send her along to Eichler. That would win her back a good five years and no-one would ever know . . . But he would know . . . Hmmmn . . . it had cost but he had been divorced more than once before and he was still here at his table effortlessly promoting his stars their interviews. He went into his oak-panelled washroom to check his appearance. He studied his reflection in the gilt mirror. Shit, what face am I supposed to have on this morning . . . ?

chapter seventeen

. . . And if you've got tears, folks, prepare to shed them tomorrow. The low-pressure area off Santa Barbara will mean a
heavy smog count over the entire city area tomorrow. Looks
like a good one to stay home on. Wish I could . . .

CBS Weather Channel 2, Los Angeles

The gag had not been very funny to begin with. Six months of it
filtering down from directors and producers to agents' runners,
to mail room boys, to the press, had worn it threadbare. Okay so
he'd been busy. He was the hottest thing in town, for sure. So
what? All he felt was he'd been working his ass off without being
able to call it his own. 'Did you hear, they're renaming Mulholland Madison Avenue?' Funny! Not even logical, somehow.
Well, it didn't do a thing for him one way or the other. He wasn't
flattered. He wasn't mad. But face it – he wouldn't have cared
enough to sign a residents' protest petition if they'd renamed it
Polanski Promenade.

High on Mulholland he looked out through his south-facing
picture window across a city in which, forget the savings and loans
bosses and those repositories of everyone's bad secrets, the
shrinks, and he probably had as much clout as anyone. This season. Oh, forget the Mob, as well. Without their money skimmed
off into Europe and returned as a laundered, legitimate investment, there would doubtless be no Paul Madison, superstar.
Because no Magnum. No Rosner. No Darroll able to offer him a
cool three million for twelve days' work on *The General*. Well,
earn at the rate of a quarter of a million a day for shovelling shit
and who the fuck cared if they named a street after you? He
sipped his margarita and stared out over the city.

It was evening. But no soft westering sun made the air gentle
and full of memories. No-one would be snapping the first beer
open and wandering out in the yard to sip its cool sharpness and
watch the sky's golds and lilacs redden as night moved closer.
Even at Mulholland's height, the sun was barely visible. Its sole

effect was to pervade through the amalgam of thin cloud and thick smog that covered the city a white, piercing glare that shrilled at the eyeball and, for all its diffuseness, seemed to lance through the brain like a laser beam. The smog was of a special effects density. It had delayed his flight's landing. As Oates's Rolls had whispered them along Santa Monica, the towers of Century City had for once been topless in their wreath of nicotine-stained mist. Grey, straight-sided masses they had loomed up submarinely like outposts to the city of Atlantis. The palm trees had looked like giant stalks of asparagus over-boiled in dirty water, or the less than erect phalluses of some dying, throw-back species.

With sudden malevolence, Paul Madison grinned. He sipped at his drink with added zest as a gleeful memory overlook him. He'd got shot of that self-important Limey fast enough. Oates had not liked it one little bit but the little prick could take what he didn't like and put it with that phoney smudge of a moustache and go stick it up his prostate. Meeting him, stale and tired off the plane with a mealy-mouthing parasite like that in tow! He'd had his fucking nerve! Some homecoming! Smog and Oates PR! It was about time that sawn-off little shit of a pimp got it through his mahogany head, familiarity breeds has-beens. Over-exposure proved the law of diminishing returns. From now on playing hard to get was going to be his scene. If you're exclusive don't flaunt it!

Yeah, some homecoming. Smog and Oates! And Acapulco had been a bust. The smart places had been Bel Air with mariachi singers and fat brown people trying to get their photographs taken with him while the Angel dust lay around set out in bowls like pretzels. He could have got the same set-up five minutes' drive away. As for the slum side of the place . . . it had been to get as far away from that as possible he was up here.

Yeah. Up here. Home. With nothing to do. He should've tele-phoned ahead.

For a moment he thought of Sam and the ghost of her fine-boned beauty was a presence in the room. He was so big now there was no way association with her could dent his image. He'd even heard Jerry White had turned pure hundred per cent Wasp since making the City Council. Another one who'd rather switch than fight. So why not? Why not? Well . . . it had been awhiles. She'd been great. Different. Special. But maybe just a hint a loser . . .

His mind worked on at the rationalising while his spirit shrank from confronting his past disloyalty.

He should've phoned. Well, fuck it! He would phone now! If not Sam, who? He set his phone down and, checking the number first, whistled Dixie on the buttons. Philip Grayson would help him out.

Philip Grayson had two professions. The minor one was portrait photographer. Studies of the great ones, Chaplin through Dietrich, hung on the walls of his office, each affectionately, effusively, dedicated and autographed. The major profession was pimp. Not metaphorical pimp like Oates but literal pimp. Pimp pimp. Need a high-class hooker? Grayson would provide. His pudgy hands would reach for his index of models. He was an underground bye-word with out-of-town producers, agents, big shots. Due to visit they would phone Grayson even while their secretaries were contacting Pan-Am. Which way they swung was immaterial. And if they really got stuck or unexpectedly lucky, Grayson provided another service. He made his own place immediately available while he drove the night hours away or holed up in the Sunset Holiday Inn. Legend had it with no doubt more accuracy than usual that Wilder had used him, scaled down, as prototype for *The Apartment*.

'Hello?'

'Phil? Paul. Paul Madison.'

'Paul sweetheart! Nice to hear your voice. Where you calling from?'

'Up the street.'

'How about that! I heard you'd followed the birds south.'

'The birds south are for the birds. Think you could do better for me?'

'Well, now . . . I think we might go so far as to promise that. Any particular packaging?'

'I trust you, Phil. Surprise me.'

'I'll do that. Pleasantly, I hope. Er, where did you have . . . ?'

'Why don't we meet for a drink?'

'Certainly. Somewhere dark and silly. How about the Mou Ling? Know it?'

'Yeah. Sure. Nine o'clock?'

'Nine will be fine. I'll look forward to it.'

'Me too. See you there, then. Nine.'

'Right. 'Bye Paul.'

'Ciao.'

He floored the receiver-rest, punched up another number.

'Hello?'

'Kurt? Paul. Paul Madison.'

'Oh, hello, Mr Madison. Welcome back. Nice trip?'

'Pretty good, thanks. Kurt, I need you.'

'Yes, of course, Mr Madison. When did you have—'

'Like in about thirty minutes.'

'Oh, Mr Madison, I don't think that's going to be possible. I've – well I've another—'

'Kurt – I need you really bad. I went to some Jap assassin down in Acapulco and he's turned me into the fag of the year. When I went out on the street the boys came around singing Rock of Ages.'

'But Mr Mad—'

'When I saw what he'd done I asked him to fall on his scissors. It was that bad. So if you'd just—'

'But I—'

'Kurt – I pay you a big retainer. When I lift the phone I expect you to come. And come running.'

'. . . I'll be there as soon as I can, Mr Madison.'

He replaced the receiver, picked up his drink. It had grown tepid and he made a small face of disgust. There was disgust somewhere in his head now, too. Or was it his gut? Why the hell go to all this trouble and the lowering of yourself just for a quickie. Because you liked it, right? Needed it. Okay next year he'd stay at home and read more books and listen to music that wasn't syruped out of Coldwater Canyon.

All the same, he had wandered into his library. The books sprang smartly to attention as he flipped the light. They had their own confidence. If he didn't get around to reading them some day, it was his loss: elsewhere somebody already was. Well, there was no point in starting something he most certainly wouldn't be finishing the first chapter of tonight.

He went to his desk. He took out his fat diary from a drawer and briefly added to the many short bursts of black squiggle breaking its cream pages up. The old-fashioned fountain pen was like another finger, he thought, and the ink flowing from it was a black tell-tale bodily excretion. He completed his entry with sour amusement. It was as if he had wanted someone, a different self, perhaps, to be looking over his shoulder as he wrote.

Two hours later he had the direct, unalloyed pleasure of sliding once more behind the wheel of his Porsche 928. His accountants and his inclination had combined to have him upgrade his auto lifestyle. The Fiat X1.9 he still kept as a backup and runaround for Tibor, but the Porsche had been designed with him in mind. Letting the engine idle while the oil was properly warmed, he let his eye run over the clusters of dials and controls with an almost sensual satisfaction. The press of the body-holding seat into the small of his back seemed more of an affirmation of his arrival in a world of quality than a dozen requests for overseas TV interviews. Screw Oates! He checked Geisler's work in the mirror. Yes, okay. From resentment at being called away from whichever little boy he was shellacking, Geisler had kept his lips faggotly pursed in silence most of the session. But that was a plus, in any case. And he'd done a good job. The cut and restyle had restored to his hair its familiar off-hand chicness. And he'd had his revenge. As Geisler was packing his things into that impossibly impressive case, he'd casually thrown out a question.

'Kurt, can a man in your position afford to allow himself to get as thick in the middle as you've let yourself become?'

Geisler's face had whitened in gay fury and his best shot for reply had only been a pretence not to have heard.

In the privacy of his own Porsche, Paul Madison laughed loudly at the memory, and letting the clutch out, gunned the car away. It slithered huggingly round the sweep of bends down to the entrance to his grounds and as it neared the gate he reached out to the dash to flick the sonic cue. Instant erection. The pole rose clearingly up through the twilight to let him pass and, flicking the switch again, he shot underneath without a check in speed.

Three seconds later he was braking like a maniac. For every sane reason. Arms flapping like a windmill trying to flag down a Boeing, a maniac had jumped yelling out on to the pavement straight between his sights. Tyres screeched. The safety belt bit into his shoulder as he all but whiplashed from the waist. He'd been accelerating to change up. A less good car would never have emergency stopped in such short distance in so straight a line. A less good driver would not have reacted so fast in the half-light. Even so it had been a damn near run thing. The man was standing less than eighteen inches from the bumper. Head craned to one side, hand shielding his eyes, he was peering awkwardly as if unable to penetrate beyond the curved windshield's tinted-glass reflection. He brought the hand down across his face and just for a second Paul Madison's heart had leapt into his mouth with angry surprise. For that moment he had thought the man was Jack Preston.

But it was not. There was something of the actor in the rattily receding hair and in the over-compensating moustache that looked false, but otherwise there was a sagging heaviness about the unshaven lower half of the man's face. A seedy dustiness about his too-loud chain-store sports coat which made certain this was no elaborate Hollywood gag but some kook or drunk. And yes, bulging on jacket pocket was the flat outline of a bottle of hooch. Paul Madison slipped the gear-lever back into first and revved the engine hard. If he couldn't go round the guy, this time he'd go on through him. But disconcertingly, hugging tight against the side of the car, the guy was edging forward. The game was either break both his legs for him or reach for the police special clipped beneath the dash and, thank you, officer, licensed by your very accommodating superior. Paul Madison took the cold, cross-hatched butt of the gun into his hand. The metallic weight felt baleful. One peep out of you, buster, and you're going to get it right between the eyebrows. But no point in ruining good glass. With his left hand he whooshed the window down four or five inches.

The man rested a forearm on the windshield. Slowly he stooped. He looked cautiously, cunningly in. The scrutiny was shrewd with a peasant's servile belligerence. Paul Madison brought the gun up into prominence. The man's course pores, the blackheads on his skin-flaked nose, the yellowing teeth all came at him from out of a childhood past where people smiled a little self-consciously before they smashed you across the face.

'Reckon, yeah, that's it, you're Madison alright,' the man said. He had a twanging, nasal intonation as no-good as his face. Paul Madison slipped the safety off the gun. As he had ignored the weapon, the man ignored the gesture. His breath was directing a stale stink of liquor into the car.

'Hell of a job finding you,' he said. 'I guess you don't figure any need of being in the phone book.'

In spite of being on full guard, Paul Madison blinked. If he were in danger it was from an idiot. Nobody, but nobody would be simple-minded enough to—

'Paid a fella for one of them maps with all the stars like yous' homes marked out. But I guess it was out of date. I went back and told him that he'd ripped me off and I didn't take kindly to being—'

'What do you want?' Paul Madison asked.

'Well you ain't no Paul Madison,' the man said with a sudden confidential leer. 'Your name's Ukinski. I know that for certain because I'm kin of your'n. I'm married to your ma, my little Norma.'

A car whined by out of and on to nowhere. Its brake-lights blazed doubly brightly through the dusk as it cornered out of sight. Another light was redly pulsing inside Paul Madison's head. The man's words were juddering at his brain like so many stabs on the low strings of a cello. Kin, he had said. Kin! This yellow-faced combination of cringer and bully, this hick smart-alec had—

'I guess Norma's pretty riled at you for never remembering who your ma is. I guess she figures you ain't been looking after her the way you should if you was a good son to your mother. She knows how much them movie people pay you for being in their shows and we both of us saw you that time on Johnny Carson . . .'

It was incredible but he believed it without question. The man's irredeemable fifth-class citizenship made him his mother's partner. The stench of his breath, the insinuating whine of his words as he wheedled and threatened on confirmed his identity beyond any need for papers. These were the sort of men who laughing too easily, cock-sure, had come out to the filling station and given him a quarter—

'Get away from my car,' Paul Madison said. 'Get your hand off of my window.'

The man ignored him. Eyes crinkling up in a parody of reasonableness, he continued like any pan-handler convinced he'd be paid to go away.

'. . . bear you any grudge or malice,' he was saying, 'so she sent me on out here from Tucson to kind of talk things over personal, man to man and all, and maybe get from you right here and now as showing you don't feel—'

Paul Madison sent the car's electric window shooting upward. The man was too slow in reacting to move his hand away in time. He screamed in pain as the edge of glass jammed his knuckles hard against the door frame.

Hey! Hey! You're hurting—'

Paul Madison was shocked. Reaching for the steering wheel he found a gun in his right hand. He threw it, safety still off, on to the passenger seat. He let out the clutch. The car darted forward and the voice of the man from all his bad childhood rose in shrill animal panic as he was pulled totteringly off his feet. And dragged onwards by the car.

Gas pedal, brake! Gas pedal, brake! Serve left, swerve right!

Change up! Swerve left! Brake! Gun it! Swerve right! Stick it to him good! Break him for her! Let her have it too!

Paul Madison's Porsche had travelled some forty erratic yards before the agonised hysterical screeching of the man was able to stab into some last corner of his sanity. He released the hand. The body crashed down out of sight. Paul Madison accelerated on.

Another fifty yards on he stopped. He sat staring in his rear-view mirror. A crumpled piece of sacking lay motionless in the middle of the pavement. It was that piece of sacking you see from time to time and your knees go weak because just for that tiny, questioning, endless moment you thought it was a body. This time, he knew, it was. He sat hypnotised, too paralysed to think or drive away. After a minute, an eternity, he saw the sack stirring in the wind. It was crawling. Now the man was slowly kneeling up. As he did so, a strange thing happened. A second man, shorter, stout came from somewhere and crossed into the centre of the road. He was nothing but a shape against the fast darkening western sky. He bent to the man on his knees and seemed to talk to him. The son of a bitch could not be too bad. He'd just about had the lesson he deserved. Paul Madison drove on. A sweet relief flowed through all his veins.

And yet it did not. Within less than a mile of Mulholland's ridge-following twists that final image had returned to hang sinisterly in his mind. A strange staggering pair of silhouettes dark in the dusk. A scarecrow buckled at the knees, one arm raised out against the sky. A smaller, rounder shape. But not Quixote and Sancho Panza. Something meaner and Los Angeles and heavy with a vague yet not to be mistaken menace.

He was all the way to the Mou Ling and parking before he remembered the gun. Jesus! A dead dog in the road, less good suspension and Darroll would have had his re-scheduling problems. He put the safety back on and the gun away.

He looked but on the outside of the car there was not so much as a single solitary scratch.

Tom Leonard had elected to take the schmuck to eat at Musso and Franks. That meant he'd get a decent lunch himself and the tired brown furniture and walls, the churlish snappiness of the waiters, would make him pleasantly homesick by his second martini for New York and the East. At the same time, if he had any soul at all – though that was dubious – the fat nervous little man might get the message that he wasn't ever going to ride first-class when Oates, Becker and Rimmer were picking up the tab. For once Tom Leonard felt he could safely enjoy the luxury of letting some of his contempt out of the bottle that he kept so tightly corked. A sticky little opportunist who'd grown fat by buying up the copyright of a dead genius's work. A parasite sucking the dead blood of the delicatest of screen talents. And this one opposite! What had he but a fraternity boy's swotting stubbornness in litigation.

'Okay Howard,' Tom Leonard said. He weighed out his politeness with scrupulous, ironic care. 'You're certain – maybe – you've got access to some of Langdon's "lost" movies. Fine. I don't exactly see – in fact I don't begin to see – where we come in.'

The little man's fat face was comic in its efforts not to give away the address of the gold-egg-laying goose. He smiled nervously and swallowed. He did some goldfish business with his mouth.

'Well . . .' he began.

He was rescued. Elegant pepper and salt slacks were close against the table. Even as he raised his head, Tom Leonard saw people at other booths nodding and nudging and trying not to look.

It was Paul Madison. He was wearing heavy shades. They may have helped in the great outdoors but here, emphasising rather than disguising stardom, they fooled no-one.

'Tom, I got to talk to you,' he said.

'Well, Paul, bring up a chair and—'

'Alone.'

'But, Paul, I have a guest.'

'It's important, Tom. Yes?'

The dark lenses had not deviated a millimeter to acknowledge anybody's else's presence. Tom Leonard threw his napkin down upon the table and rose.

'Excuse us, Howard,' he said. 'Be right back.'

'Oh, yes, sure. Certainly. Go right ahead.'

The creep had smirked. Tom Leonard followed his star along the narrow corridor between the booths toward the rear door and the parking lot beyond. By rights he should be furious at Madison's discourtesy. At any other time, whatever his reaction, he privately would have been. This time he was delighted. The interruption might have been pre-planned to show the little creep his place in the scheme of things. To think he actually put his name up there with Langdon's!

They went out through the door, turned right along the narrow corridor and negotiated the steps to go outside. The sun smashed at them like a fist. Tom Leonard winced and shaded his eyes with his hand. He had no sun-glasses.

In the small, crowded car park, just beyond midday, they appeared as two flawlessly dressed men standing and casually talking in the blazing sun.

'What is it, Paul?' he said.

Madison seemed oddly at a loss for words. When they at length came they were strangely low-key and without the arrogant glitter that had increasingly been their hall-mark.

'I don't know,' he said. 'Last night – evening – I was driving out of my place and this guy flags me down. Damn near threw himself under my car. I had to stop. He came on like some East Texas grifter. Said he was married to my mother. Said he was kin. I believed him.' Leonard said nothing.

'Tom,' Paul Madison said, 'you're supposed to run interference on things like that for me. Warn me. Keep them off.'

He said it not in anger or hostility but with a kind of deflated helplessness.

'Try to shake you down?' Tom Leonard said.

'I guess. I drove off before he was through.'

'That figures,' Tom Leonard drew a deep breath.

'The reason you didn't know,' he went on, 'is that you always ask not to be allowed to know. If you're right and it was your step – the guy married to your mother – then it's no surprise he tried to shake you down. She kicked him out of the house some weeks back. I guess he's so smart he knows all lawyers screw you. You didn't give him anything, then?'

'Nothing.'

'If you had, she'd never have seen it, that's for sure. Oh, home by the way is Tucson, Arizona.'

'He said something about Tucson.'

'She wanted to move back West. I was thinking that was too close to home and considered stopping her selling up in Texas. Then I thought maybe that's a two-edged sword. She's nearer but it's easier for us to keep tabs on her. So I didn't put a block on it.'

'What if I do a movie out there?'

Tom Leonard shrugged.

'You're above that league for ten years straight,' he said. 'We'll worry about it then. How'd he track you down?'

'Christ knows. Said he began with the phone book.'

Tom Leonard grinned with the same Hollywood incredulity.

'He knew my name, you see.'

'Okay, well, I'll put some security guys on your gate for a few days. How'd that be?'

'Yeah ... thanks. I'd appreciate that ... I wish to fuck she'd drop dead.'

'Just forget her. It's easier.'

Fatuous, slick-talk, Tom Leonard thought hearing himself. Whatever she once did to him is built right into the wiring down his backbone. He decided, for a moment, that he almost liked Paul Madison.

'I guess,' Paul Madison said uncertainly.

'Okay then?' Tom Leonard asked.

'Yeah, okay. I just wanted to talk, I guess.'

'Sure. I suppose I ought to think about getting back to that creep I'm with.'

'Be a gesture. Who is he?'

'Nobody you need bother knowing. A nobody.'

'Well, fine ... oh, Tom – I guess I kind of roughed the guy up a bit last night. Nothing heavy. But there might be some follow through. You know, static.'

Ill disguising his exasperation, Tom Leonard squared his shoulders. He gave Paul Madison a sideways look.

'Is this another fine mess you've gotten me into?' he said.

chapter eighteen

. . . Carl Robertson for *Chief Executive* and Clint Walters for *The Undefeated.*

UPI

There was no ostensible reason for the party whatsoever. The stiff white cards with their pretentious, deckled edges had merely announced in the over-elaboration of silver italic that the Lyndon Oateses would be 'at home'. In reality two clear-cut and universally recognised purposes attached to the evening. The first was to commence the public humiliation of Mrs Lyndon Oates. The second was to begin promoting the ground-swell of PR that would help sweep the newly nominated Paul Madison to his Oscar.

Home was not quite in Pasadena but adjacent San Marino. Some two hundred paces behind high, road-fronting hedges it lay built on a slight rise in Cotswold brick and style. A rigorously informal English garden began right at the hedge and ran up to the house in a series of ascending modulations marked by sundials, a herb-garden, a goldfish pond and an assymetrical series of low mellowed-brick walls. A few yards from the house the lawn abruptly braked to a halt more cleanly cut than the invitation cards. It was as if it possibly shrank from closer association with the reinforced steel and high aluminium cement behind the large-stoned yellow facing. The guests gracing the evening were, for the most part, of the same order of genuineness as the house.

A select ninety or so they had disposed themselves comfortably in loose-knit but not isolated groups in the large single room that with the doors unfolded took almost the entire first floor. They stretched via tea-rose sofas and an authentic Lawrence from the panelled ingle-nook fireplace wall to the Chippendale-cabinetted Zenith. And they all sucked, Paul Madison was thinking.

He had been charming for well past an hour now, receiving congratulations on his nomination like a modest bridegroom with some of the material Tom Leonard had supplied him with. 'I'll never replace Elvis,' had been the best choice for those with the "Vacant" sign most obviously nailed between their eyes. It allowed them to crack back to a man and woman with 'Who would want to?' Then he could smile and they could feel themselves fine fellows.

But that had passed and palled. The gathering was getting down to the seen-it-all-before smallnesses of bitchery and proposition. And to a degree of business. Oates was continuing studiously to ignore his wife as he lavished attention and attendance on the slim ash-blonde unknown he had just taken into his stable. His wife, Paula, had full raven black hair and a pouting, sultry sexuality of face that exactly matched the slightly perverse promises of her figure. She was the sort of woman for whom, in another age, heads would have turned and in some cases rolled. Now, not bothering to play diplomat, she was amusing most people present by the balefully basilisk looks she was directing towards her receding husband. He, meanwhile, maintained a posture of sweet indifference to her murderous visual bombardment. The elfin Indiana ingenue who, he was proclaiming, held pole position in the race for the, by some, coveted Mrs Oates IV Grand Prix was his sole concern. Paul Madison had talked to her and found her as big a turn-off as Peter Pan.

'Oh, thanks,' he had said. 'I'll never replace Elvis, though.'

'Who'd ever want to?' she had quipped.

He had decided then she must have a sphincter in her vagina but watching the two of them now across the room it belatedly occurred to him that she owed her being singled out to no more than a Chaplinesque yen for child-brides. In fact, forget the heads and Oates's physique was identical to the comedian's in middle-age.

But what to do? He had made the excuse of needing a leak to get away from the tired wisecracking but now, returned as far as the threshold of the room, had to decide which group among the babble of voices to approach as the least of all conversational evils. Maybe Tom Leonard was . . . But Tom was doing business. He was earnestly talking in a corner to that acne-faced journalist who did a column for a women's magazine. It was a simple trade-off. Milton Rosner would advance her ten grand as script development and option money on an idea she had once thrown out over her third vodka martini. It return, it was tacitly understood, it might just happen she would care to puff Paul Madison as an Oscar shoo-in. Well, yeah. A bribe by any other name still comes as sweet.

'Excuse me . . . excuse me, please . . .'

There was a shuffle, a peristalsis in the group standing close to him and he experienced a strong feeling of déja vu. At how many other boring parties had he . . . ? The feeling was well justified. Emerging to stand directly before him was Alex Eichler.

'Hi, Alex,' he said as pleasantly as possible. 'How's the old skin game?'

They had both been present at public occasions but it was months since they had spoken. Not since—

'Paul. Nice to see you,' Eichler said.

The pale blue eyes in the potato face stared earnestly at him for a long moment while they tried to determine what other expression they should adopt. Then slowly a broad, knowing, peasant grin spread over the plastic surgeon's features. He stepped forward and, being careful of the empty glasses he held in either hand, clapped Paul Madison on either arm.

'Paul,' he said, 'I forgive you. You are an ass-hole, still, and no doubt always will be and I will never trust you again. But I forgive you. You know why? Because you are successful and because you got away with it. We're two of a kind.'

He's drunk Paul Madison thought. Drunk but right.

'That's the first thing I heard tonight that didn't make we want to puke,' a third voice growled.

Paul Madison looked down and to his right. Eichler to his left. From a leather wing armchair pushed hard against the wall an old, old man was leaning forward into view. Wizened, shrivelled, bald all but for a few wisps of white hair he had liver-like blemishes blotching his sunken cheeks and a skull shrunk tight enough to reveal the knitting together of its bony plates. The shoulders were thin and stooped so that the scrawny neck protruding from a too large dress-shirt collar lent the beaked nose, thin-lipped features inescapable resemblance to the old dry head of a giant turtle. Eichler, looking, saw probably no more than a Feiffer caricature of a capitalist and an old man so close to death as to make his personal rejuvenating skills irrelevant. Paul Madison, astounded, saw Sean Flaherty. Part of his astonishment was that so vigorous a voice could have proceeded from so frail a frame.

He looked at Eichler wondering whether, how best, to essay introductions, but the surgeon embarrassed to the point of fear at having been overheard was transferring his weight from foot to foot like a boy needing the bathroom.

'Well, Paul,' he said, holding the glasses higher, 'I guess I must go to the bar and be a gentleman. Catch you later, yes?'

'Okay. Be a gentleman,' Paul Madison said. He side-stepped

to let Eichler by. But the clown inside the surgeon could not deny him an exit line. He turned in the doorway, holding a glass nipple-high in each hand.

'Low score today,' he said. 'Only four.'

He took the out he had been wanting. Paul Madison swallowed and turned to Sean Flaherty, an old old man and an eternal legend in a high-backed armchair. He sat there staring through bottle-glass thick lenses at what could have been infinity.

'Er, Mr Flaherty,' Paul Madison began.

'Yes, I know,' the voice growled, 'you've always admired my work and it's a great privilege and honour for you to meet me. That about it?'

The head had not even turned.

'Er, pretty much.'

Now the head turned.

'Son, I just don't have the time,' it said. Paul Madison did as fast a bit of type-casting as he had ever risked.

'I was also going to ask,' he said, 'what the fuck's an old bastard like you doing at a place like this?'

The eyes glittered. The lips might have stretched even thinner.

'Don't be promiscuous with the word "fuck" son,' the old man said. 'Save your best ammunition until you need it.'

He looked hard at Paul Madison. It was ironic. In extreme old age the director of four or five of the world's classic Westerns had taken on the predatory, hawk-like look of a fabled Eastern potentate.

'You might have amounted to something, son, in my day,' he said. 'Today you've got no chance.'

'You haven't answered my question.'

'I spend what's left of my life now turning down invitations. What do I want to go anywhere for? They ask me because I'm like the Pope. I can bestow a blessing on whatever game of crap it is. They don't ask me for me. But once in a while I get intrigued to see if it all stinks as much as I remember it. I sneaked in here twenty minutes ago and found it's gotten twice as bad.'

With a skeletal hand he indicated the whole room.

'Look at them,' he said, 'not a person here who doesn't think each time he craps he's shitting pearls.'

His hands braced themselves on the ends of the chair arms. Now he was a Venetian Doge or a Death from the Middle Ages.

'Glad I came,' he said. 'It'll make kicking off easier. Not much. But some. Who wants to stay around for this? Now, if you'll excuse me or equally if you won't, I'll go get me a taxi-cab to come.'

'Why don't I give you a ride?' Paul Madison was suddenly no longer at a loss through boredom. You'd offer a reincarnated Mark Twain a ride, wouldn't you, Madison, a returned W. C. Fields? You bet – and pray that they'd say yes.

The old man's suspicious eyes tightened behind the thick lenses.

'Be quicker,' Sean Flaherty said. 'Way back on Wilshire out in Westwood, though.'

'Hell. Further the better. Further it is, further away from here.'

The old man nodded.

'Okay,' he said tersely.

He struggled to rise. It plainly cost him dear. Paul Madison had the tact to let him do it alone. He did. On his feet at last, he reached for a stick. He must once have been a robust man but now loose skin made the phrase 'a bag of bones' apply with a near literal grisliness. And yet surprisingly stiff-backed. There was dignity and determination in his stance as confronting the scene he was choosing to leave to its own thin amusements. More reptilian than ever, he cocked his head enquiringly at Paul Madison.

'Okay?' he said.

But Paul Madison had a problem. He had just recalled that he had come straight on to the party from the Pacific Coast tennis at the LA club. Tom Leonard had driven him.

'One second,' he said, 'one quick goodbye.'

He threaded a dancing way through the groups of cliché exchanges.

'She's having a fight with a man she thinks may be her husband,' he heard.

Good! Tom Leonard was still feeding the journalist's captive mind. While she was there, he'd be home free. He tapped Leonard on the shoulder as he smiled his little boy special at her.

'Hi again,' he said, 'hey, Tom. A quick favour. Sean Flaherty's feeling kind of pooped. I said I'd lift him. Could you let me have my keys back, pal.'

Leonard didn't even look as if he'd fumble.

'Oh, sure,' he said. 'Mea culpa. I just plain forgot. I used a little gas so maybe check it, huh?'

He grinned at Paul Madison a look of cheerful, covert malice. Paul Madison snatched the keys out of his hand, tossed them just the salt-rubbing-in once.

'Anytime,' he said. 'Back soon.'

As he left he heard Tom Leonard saying how typical it was of

D.—K

his sense of the older Hollywood traditions that he would dee da, dee da, dee dum.

Flaherty meanwhile had made it to the door and received his coat from the Oates's house boy.

'Please convey my thanks to Mr Oates for his hospitality,' he was growling. 'He seems to have his hands full at the moment. Tell him it was everything I expected.'

The Japanese bow of deference was beautifully alloyed by faithful reception of the contempt. He let them out.

Flaherty made it to the car with more despatch than Paul Madison had expected. Seeing it he muttered in his throat.

'Low-down foreign junk,' he said. 'Checker cab's the best design for people grown as old as me.'

The large door seemed to mollify his old man's ire a little. He got into the front seat by himself and he did it very well.

'Used to like Jeeps, though, too,' he said. 'Know what I hate most in all the world?'

'What?'

'The expression "senior citizen".'

Paul Madison smiled tacit agreement and let out the clutch carefully. The car purred away.

He went up on to the Ventura Freeway and kept the speed way down as they headed due west. The old man sat without speaking but his eyes were open and alert.

'Always get the feeling when I'm out now it might be the last time,' he said at last. 'Adds a spice to things, you know. Even in this town.'

He lapsed back into silence. At the interchange with the San Diego Freeway Paul Madison headed south. Speedily they were cruising down the Wiltshire off-ramp.

'Left,' the old man said. ' 'Bout seven furlongs. Just a Futurity away.'

They cruised past the shadowy outline of large houses set back from the road and distant sweeps of lawn curving down to it.

'In here.'

An entrance between high, untidy hedges. A half-moon driveway. Paul Madison halted the BMW before a house not small, but less large than those they had just ghosted by. More compact in its four-square way, it seemed better set down into the earth.

'You'll have a drink with me,' Sean Flaherty stated.

Not easily but by himself he got out of the car. Paul Madison gave him pride of place as they moved to the door. The old man produced a key-chain.

'Nobody in, tonight,' he said. 'Come in.'

Paul Madison followed him inside. Flaherty turned a light on and the wall of a small hallway loomed out. Panelling ran up the wall to a height of five feet. There was a comfortable clutter of unmatching chairs, a barley-sugar legged black table, a vast mirrored hall-stand. Flaherty threw his stick clatteringly into a tall chine umbrella stand already bristling with as many others as a top pro's golf bag.

'This way,' he said.

He pushed open a door to the right and this time ushered Paul Madison into a room which, as the lights came on, revealed itself as a study-den. It was wood-panelled too but from floor to ceiling. The wood was a somber oak worked in large rectangles delineated by raised strips. It succeeded in looking American and proud of it, not an English transplant self-consciously out of place and sulking at having been untimely ripped from its mother room. As at Oates's house its run was interrupted by a fireplace. On the high mantelshelf four Oscars gleamed softly in the light.

'Let's see,' Flaherty said. He moved to a large Spanish chest, wood again and black and carved with a sort of heavy intricacy. The massive looking lid rose up with an ease suggesting constant use. The tops of many bottles became visible.

'No fancy cocktails,' Flaherty said. 'Too crafty to make. Not worth it when you have. Some of whatever you like that comes straight from a bottle.'

'Scotch,' Paul Madison said. 'As it comes.'

He had noticed another Oscar keeping guard over a stack of papers on the big dark knee-hole desk. Yet another stood at attention on the floor close to the door they'd entered by. Down there it had not caught his eye as readily as the others. The not-large room was as tightly packed with antiques and momentoes as a dealer's showroom. Six Oscars! Six! Or was it more? The director read his thoughts.

'If it matters to you, seven.'

'Damn!' Flaherty muttered. He shuffled toward Paul holding a huge slug of Scotch. The proportionately vast glass was just adequate against the shaking of his hand. The other hand held an empty bottle. A tray of used cigar-butts lay alongside it.

'Sit down,' he said. 'Be right back.' He left the room.

Paul Madison ignored the gesture toward a worn Chesterfield. He began to prowl the museum of a room.

It was a treasure-trove of associations. Some were spectacular. Alongside the desk a wooden frame stood some four feet high from the floor. Slung across it was a magnificent Western saddle, its cherry-black leather almost invisible beneath the riot of silver studding that adorned it. A plate on the pommel was inscribed to Flaherty 'with the gratitude of the Mexican Government and People'. Casual and yet spectacular, too, was a framed photograph on the wall of an ear-to-ear grinning Harry Truman. There was a long inscription and a first-name signature. Next to it hung a second photograph. It showed Flaherty, big-chested, standing in Marine fatigues upon the deck of a warship. In his hand he held a hefty-looking movie-camera and a small man stood next to him reaching his arm up to put it around the director's wide shoulders. The man was Halsey. He too had chosen to be on first-name terms. The photo, Paul Madison knew, must date from Flaherty's legendary facing of strafing Zeros with no more than a view-finder between himself and their scything tracers.

He worked along the wall. An early Winchester hung there without a speck of dust qualifying the somber gleam of its barrel. On the dark polished stock a brass plate indicated the affectionate friend and donor – John Wayne. Beneath it hung a framed membership certificate to a Kenyan Safari Club. Flaherty had been proposed by William Holden and seconded by Howard Hawks. On a corner of the mental-shelf a touchingly young Clark Gable grinned muggingly over Carole Lombard's shoulder. The adjacent, nearest Oscar seemed to date from the mid-thirties. Paul Madison picked its heavy weight up. Ah, yes, 'Wild Rose of—'

'Seven of them,' Sean Flaherty's voice said interrupting him. 'And not one of them for a Western although there should have been.' He had in his hand a full bottle of Bushmill's. He carried it over to Paul Madison.

'Be kind enough to unscrew this, please,' he said gruffly. 'Thank you.'

As Paul Madison sat down he went to the chest and carefully poured himself a small measure.

'No director will ever get seven again,' he said. 'They just don't make enough movies anymore for anyone to have the chance.' For chrissakes I don't even hear the word movie these days. It's product, property. I read you're up for an Oscar. Don't let it fool you son. Most it'll ever get you is a ten cent discount on a cup of coffee. If you're good, you'll work. If you're in it just for what you can get, they'll eat you. You've had my speech. Now drink up. I run out of steam pretty fast.'

He slowly shuffled across the room and sat down in the wide editor's chair behind the desk.

He looked hard at Paul Madison. A drum desk-light had been among the lights springing on. It side-lit Flaherty now and in the momentary silence of the room he seemed so old as to have outlasted Time.

'I don't know what to tell you, son,' he said, 'except maybe "quit" and that sounds like old man's talk. Though I believe it isn't. I saw part of a movie you were in. Didn't stay too long, to tell the truth. You know its problem? It had one idea to the set-up. Each new idea – a new set-up. It was like reading a book all in italics. I used to get six, eight, a dozen ideas, thoughts, into every set-up and let them work on folks without they'd know that they were there. I used to trust my audiences. I'd let the storyline carry things along and say what I wanted to say underneath it.'

He paused to drink again. Paul Madison did not wish to interrupt him.

'I used to carry a shape in my head of what the finished film would come to. And all the time in my head I'd keep rolling that shape down a hill to see if anything inside was rattling around and anything outside breaking off. Whatever broke off, I just left to let lay. What rattled, I bolted down. I don't think they do too much of those things now.

'Idiots used to come out and interview me, but I didn't like it. I always used to tell them I worked at a factory – that I just showed up at the studio on a Monday and picked up a script and went right out and started to try to get it done in the time I'd just been given.'

He paused. He was reminiscing but not talking to himself.

'But it wasn't like that,' he went on. 'I used to work at getting each film so if you prodded any part hard, you'd feel it in every other part all the way up and down.'

'Like Dickens,' Paul Madison heard his voice saying.

Flaherty's thick lenses glinted reflected light inquisitorially at him as the old head sharply jerked.

'I know the stuff,' he said. 'I wanted to do *Our Mutual Friend* once. But I was going to ignore the social satire and all that tomfoolery and tell the main drive of the story just like a mystery – which it is.'

'You never did it?'

'They wouldn't trust me by that time. The studio system had crumbled. The city was full of middle-men – publicity types, financiers, agents – who suddenly found that when they'd worked up to what they'd always wanted – the top – they were afraid to make a decision. They had no craft, no knowledge. They turned all the talent in Hollywood into inventory – great artists and technicians waited on the shelf like props in a warehouse.'

He had been speaking with the clairvoyant privilege of his years but suddenly grinned with an old pirate's wickedness and fleetingly the vigour of the byegone times elbowed old age aside.

'Something in that factory idea,' he continued. 'Work did get done. The machine was running and people had to make up their mind to help steer it or jump off. I made four movies in '36 and the last was the best. It's true enough – deadlines do concentrate the mind. When I went independent – after the war – I was never quite the same man.'

Now reverie had bested him. He sat for a moment contemplating something with an air of regret and distaste. Quiet stole back into the room from out of the long past. The shadows grew denser in the dark room's corners.

'I only had one son,' Flaherty said abruptly. 'He was killed on Bataan. I think that was the best thing for him as things have turned out.'

The old man had put a foot wrong. Paul Madison felt constrained to speak.

'He might not agree with you,' he said, 'if he could hear.'

The colourless seam of Sean Flaherty's lips compressed to the point of disappearance. Their tightening seemed to lend his head a rigidity independent of the rest of his frail body.

'Yes,' he said, 'he would have agreed.'

The head moved slightly.

'I'm boring you,' Flaherty said.

'No. Not at all.'

'Well, I'm boring myself. And I've run out of gas. When you're my age and all your friends are dead, communication's a pain. Thank you for the ride, son. I'm tired now. I must go to bed.'

Paul Madison stood up. He stepped toward the desk.

'It was a privilege,' he said, 'and thank you for the drink. I'd like to ask you one last thing, if I may. I'd like to ask if before I go I could shake your hand.'

That same hostile rigidity returned to the posture of the head.

'I've no wish to seem discourteous,' Flaherty said, 'but I think you know what I mean when I say you haven't earned the right to. I told you: I don't think you'll ever get the opportunity. If you ever do, though, you'll have to dig eight feet down to find my hand. Goodnight, son. I'll ask you to let yourself out.'

Flaherty made no move to rise from out of the circle of desk light that had turned him into a late Rembrandt.

Dismissed, Paul Madison nodded just once, with a curtness that came from bruised feelings swelling at that moment into pain.

'Good night, sir,' he said. He turned and side-stepping an occasional table bearing a small bronze of a mounted Apache, made for the door. The voice of the old man pulled him up short and brought his head back round.

'If I'd've had a grandson, I'd've talked to him,' Sean Flaherty said. 'There would have been some life in that. Maybe. Everything between is spoiled.'

That had been out loud but for himself. Paul Madison continue out of the room and, softly, out of the house.

Five hours later a black fury possessed Paul Madison. He had not returned to the party. He had not returned Tom Leonard's car. Instead, drifting down to the no-man's-land around the Coliseum, he had gone the rounds of the bars on Pico, Adams, Figueroa. Not wanting to be recognised, he had kept his head down and hadn't been. The car had fared less well. Somewhere in its small-hour travels it had collected a long uneven pair of envy stripes. And fuck you too, chum.

He was driving it north and homewards now up Western. Despite the copiousness of his program he had not succeeded in getting obliviously drunk. A sour hard bolus of reality was stuck somewhere at the centre of his being and neither tequila nor beer had had much success in washing or dissolving it away. He felt cheapened, soft, a fool. Like a bright-eyed sophomore he had pushed himself into a cap-in-hand position where Flaherty had had no choice but to put him down. And yet it had not been truly personal. For Flaherty, dying as the world knew, of a hopeless cancer, it had all been utterly impersonal. The hell of it was that given the old fart's body of work, there was nothing he had said you'd want to quarrel with. The rejection of the handshake had not been animus against Paul Madison but indifference to the fate or feelings of a whole shoddy generation. So why this black bile towards himself and to the world?

He turned the car left on to a virtually deserted Hollywood.

Was it because for a second or so he had seemed to be on the threshold of a personal, a son-father relationship with the old man? Had he been on the edge of acknowledging to himself that Flaherty could be a surrogate for the crude, rough man who'd been the sole source of kindness in that doomed early childhood. Hardly. Flaherty was a grandfather figure, physically repellant if viewed in cold blood. But he had lost a son.

And he had seemed a repository of objective wisdom. His remarks had carried that clairvoyant stamp of authority. Was the sourness at his own stomach's core born of the awareness that there was nothing he could do tomorrow to alter structure or stench of the midden he found himself topping – the shit-pile that found in his success some kind of rationalisation for its own fetid being?

Or was it worse than that? Was the disgust not outward at his impotence to change the system but inward at his unwillingness to try. Didn't the bitterness come from the knowledge that he too much enjoyed the luxury to which he'd grown accustomed? He had it made, all the smart money said. Didn't he agree? Tomorrow he would be unwilling to lift one well manicured little finger if it meant risking his status, his possessions or in any other way make waves for his personal pleasure cruise. Flaherty had hinted that his own work might be better than the frame Hollywood was able to supply for it. So to save his soul he should find new framemakers. But there were none beyond the people who'd made him. And to invest his own time, effort and, of course, money in finding a new setting for himself involved tremendous career risks with no guarantee of success. And guts.

He drew his lips in and against his teeth in a manner he abruptly realised was copied directly from Flaherty.

'Shit,' he said out loud. 'Damn the old fart to hell!'

A signal went red on him at his lack of charity but, quite safely, at that hour he ran it. He'd been pushing up the speed. Beneath the flux of all his conscious foreground thoughts had been the added irritation of an urgent need to pee. His bladder was pressing down through his flesh to make the teasing, bursting itch there almost more than he could bear.

He'd got as far as ghosting the car along past Pickwick on the rubberneckers' stretch of Hollywood Boulevard, Not far enough. He'd never hold out the several miles to home. But with that realisation came a thought. He steered sharply to the curb and braked. As he slid from the car and crossed to Grauman's

Chinese, he was smiling. He had devised a manner of obtaining two-fold relief.

Alone under the moon eclipsed by the street's sodium lights, he passed under the long covered walkway and hand going to his fly stared down at the famous forecourt. There sterilely, futilely, set in a temporary eternity were the illiterate scrawls and marks of those from a previous Hollywood who'd gone down on their knees to cement their remembrances in the affections of the public. Or had it been, he wondered, to placate the arbitrary god inside the house of adoration. He fumbled his prick free from his shorts.

As soon as it sensed the cool air it began to spout. It curved out in a stream made curiously colourless by the unnatural light. It steamed in mid-fall and far more so as it splattered spashingly on the flagstones touched by greatness. Initially it cascaded down on Joe E. Brown, filling the lower scoop of the big B and running bubblingly by, frothily over and on to the parody caricature of a smile publicity had insisted that he sketch.

It was a beginning. Primed for a sustained outpouring, Paul Madison shook that thing. Urine hosed snakingly through the air, falling like sudden rain upon such unsuspecting victims as Natalie Wood and Elizabeth Taylor. He whirled about in a semi-circle, a complete turn. Other celebrated imprints of the living and the dead were baptised anew in the piss of him whose star had more lately risen over Hollywood.

Ah, a slight hiccough! He concentrated his fire full on Valentino. The urine coursed along the letters with an effect animated credits. It began to fail at source. Drops fell upon his shoes and trouser cuffs, but such sacrifices were rewarded. Petering out, he was still able to deliver a prolonged coup de grace to Shirley Temple.

He began to smile. To chortle. Hollywood? Piss on it, Jack. He had been revenged upon the whole pack of them!

'Hey, bud! What you think you're doing?'

An LAPD patrol-car shark had slid to a silent halt opposite the theatre's walk-way. A cop had his head questioningly out the window. Seeing the obvious, he was quickly out of the car and, more warily, coming forward.

In another sense, Paul Madison was still standing petered out. He was quite leisurely in tucking it away and zipping the fly closed again. He put on a locker-room, conspiratorial smile. This one was a cinch. Thanks to his name and image, a couple of jokes and he'd be out of this one before you could say 'kiss my ass'. He wouldn't even need Tom Leonard.

chapter nineteen

... last night not two feet away from this year's and surely next year's as well No. 1 Superstar – Paul Madison. Honestly – those shoulders which have no right to be so wide above that pinched-in waist, those light blue eyes that look right into the back of your mind. This morning I'm still trying to uncurl my toes ...

The Morning Show

Jack Preston had not troubled to equip his Los Angeles home with an all-systems movie theatre. He had one in Palm Springs, but in LA had limited himself to a projection booth at one end of his Larry Rivers lounge. Most of its working life was confined to providing a substantial tax write-off but occasionally it was pressed into the actual running of a movie. At such times its flawless sound-proofing unquestionably enhanced the viewing of whatever was on offer. The screen dropped down from the ceiling on the touch of a Hollywood button. There were both 35 mm and 16 mm projectors together with conversion lenses for 'scope but this print was plain old 16 mm black and white. Jack Preston had threaded it himself.

Because of the good sound-proofing and because there was no sound track, it had been quite impossible to detect the first girl's distress as she abruptly fled the room and, some moments later, a second girl's attempt to hide her retching. Other of the girls were made of sterner stuff although they too, for a while, were given to the low, private mutters of the utterly appalled. Towards the end however of the quite short work – a Guatamalan or Panama City, possibly, import – the rivetting attention of the living upon those about to die on the screen bound the room in a common, unblinking, breath-baited tension. They had become a jury viewing the last exit from the courtroom of the woman whose life they had just declared forfeit.

She was a short girl, squat, a little inclined to flabbiness. Her formless breasts were widespread and indifferent going on small and there was already a rippling over-heaviness about her naked thighs. She had far more of Indian in her than Spanish and for that reason, her slick hair stupidly waved, cheap make-up, even in black and white, obviously glazing her face, she had reminded Paul Madison of the man gunned to death at The Silver Peso. He doubted if she had made herself up especially for her big chance of breaking into the movies. That would be the everyday work-paint of all the cheap hookers working whatever town it was for the navy's or the oil-riggers' or whoever's benefit.

At the outset she had obviously had no idea of the scenario. Solemn-moon-faced, blinking a lot from the point-them-all-at-her lighting, she had allowed herself to be bound wrists and ankles to the cross with a dumb cow-like resignation and she must have believed she was acting. Several times, however, she made direct eye-contact with the somewhat shaky lens to destroy utterly any gesture towards fiction. Her leading man was negro and apparently seven feet tall. He wore an abbreviated mask and, voodoo-fashion, white paint skeletally exteriorised the bones helping to give him his Boston Celtic frame. He wore nothing else. He was a giant making her look almost pygmy. It would have been an act of sadism for him to have made conventional love. That was not his intention as the girl's bound-together ankles made clear.

What followed, sickeningly emphasising the movie's over-kill, needed neither the victim's screams nor the imagination, to fathom. Branding irons and finally a kitchen knife were brought into the ritual. The coup de grace, like all the preceding scenes lacked all finesse. The director, in the manner of a bad bullfighter had savaged his subject. Real, not simulated murder had been played out on the screen. Incompetence rather than any feeling of revulsion had thrown the closing sequences out of focus. As they blurred into shadow Madison allowed his thoughts, locked shut during the filming, to flow again. He had heard about this kind of movie, and had laughed in uneasy disbelief. He had heard about it, been invited to it, because once in that inner circle of status and of wealth, acceptance of invitations to these secret rites is tacitly expected. Approval and silence are assumed. So he watched and heard the gasps, saw the sudden movements of sil-houetted figures stumbling towards the exits. And before the reel had disgorged the last strands of film, he too hauled himself to his feet. Preston stirred, shone a silver pen-torch into Madison's face.

'You okay?'

Madison squeezed past him looking for a door. 'How the hell do you get out of this sewer?'

'You want a drink, Paul?' Preston's smile, visible now in the raised lights, was a shade too bright.

'It would help.'

'That's all folks,' Preston announced one arm loosely around Madison's shoulder. 'It's playtime now. Cindy, Grace . . . stay by the house-phone. Paul and I may have work for you soon.'

Madison looked back at the faces and felt nausea rising inside him. And a sudden weariness. His knees sagged. 'Christ, did I really see all that, Jack?'

Preston gave no answer. Instead he piloted him to a guest room, pulled back the yak-haired coverlet on the King-sized bed. Madison kicked off his shoes and slumped down. Preston pulled a curtain cord shutting out the phantom greenness of the spot-lit foliage around the mansions opposite. He poured Madison a quarter of a tumbler of Bourbon. Madison sank it at a gulp. Then Preston said. 'Take this.'

Madison looked at the pill. 'I don't need it. I'm pooped, wrung out.'

Preston studied him seriously. 'You want to nail the shutters up real good? I mean you want to wake up your mind a clean slate?'

'And this will do it?'

'Better than a cart-load of shrinks,' Preston said.

And so he had fallen asleep, or maybe not completely. He felt himself borne across a heaving, primeval landscape. Then raised up to a racing vermillion sky flaked with lurid purple and blinding violet. Paroxysms of colours swept past him like clouds against a fast-descending aircraft. Now he too was conscious of soaring movement . . . and suddenly of horses' hooves . . . he is in a carriage but the interior is of his car, the dials clean, luminous and reassuring . . . beyond the windshield the horses' heads, black and nobly carved like chess pieces, are turned around . . . their silver-ornamented blinkers conceal not eyes but sockets . . . and there is laughter, a woman's laughter . . . it rises shrilly over yet another change of scene . . . a theatre . . . they are giving prizes . . . and he is in his seat, Preston is holding one arm, Tom Leonard the other . . . Christie Roberts is on the stage . . . her face bears no expression . . . a voice announces . . . 'The Oscar for the best actor . . .' and Christie Roberts tears open the envelope from which blood drips

... 'It's you, Paul ...' Preston says, but he cannot move from his seat ... paralysed he tries to scream, tell them he cannot move, but now it is his mother who holds the envelope ... and her laughter is obscene as he had once heard it, 'Ladies and Gentlemen,' she croaks, 'the name is ... Ukinski ... Ukinski ... Ukinski ...' ... the light is pale green now from a lamp suspended over a couch ... the man in the white coat is saying, 'it is mainly a problem of identity ...' but it is Tom Leonard's face ... 'take my picture Paul,' he says ... 'look through this lens and you will see two images ... you turn the focus until one image is superimposed on the other ... then you have a perfect picture ... that's your trouble Paul, you're out of focus ... two images Paul and that makes for a lousy portrait ... look at you Paul, you've wet yourself, at your age ... The face of the Mexican zooms into his like a colliding planet ... 'you gonna shut your mouth son or do we ...' and there is more blood ... his mother is pleading to him from her bed ... but her face is that of the swarthy girl in the snuff movie ... then all fades into oblivion. Three hours later Madison awakens feels well-rested, almost buoyant. The Preston house is like a grave. He and his guests lie around, single or paired corpses. Madison pulls up the collar of his suede jacket and slips out into the dawn light. With total clarity now he can assess the events of the dark preceding hours. It had been loathesome. Shit though, he'd only been a spectator. Then to his sudden annoyance he felt guilt. He wasn't supposed to. He'd been ordered to move around with the top seeds in the trade. He was programmed to enjoy the action. Not self-destruct. But in the crisp, clean dawn air he felt guilt alright, and anger, and a sudden sharp compulsion to exorcise last night's screeching ghost. He understood, only God knew why, he must go to Tucson and see his mother.

chapter twenty

... Undoubtedly the 'in' Unisex shampoo-parlour whether it's a
simple repeat cut you're after or an entire re-evaluation of your
current styling. Presiding genius – and the word is not used
lightly – is Kurt Geisler who promises to be personally active
in Scissors Incorporated just as often as 'my other obligations
permit'. Those other obligations include the various crowning
glories, natural and otherwise, of half the stars in town. He
certainly worked wonders for this old wordsmith and I emerged
if not a new person, one ten years younger. Take the tip and
nip in for a snip. You'll find it ...

Minna Halliday *Who's Where?*

The white highway-dividing line wound him steadily onward
through the night. The Porsche's headlights strove stabbingly to
overreach it but always there was more streaming zappingly at
him from the darkness. The tyres zapped too. He had the window
open in case he fell asleep. The tyres whirred zappingly on the
pavement and, released by the night desert, hot wind came buffet-
ing at his face. A curve. The hi-beams lanced into a landscape of
dunes, undulating eerily like waves of a frozen lunar sea. Then
the darting white line again and the hot breath of the night. He
must be close to Yuma. The elemental spirit of the old peniten-
tiary seemed abroad. It seemed to be homing darkly on him riding
at his shoulder a few inches outside the car as though urging him
to some act of destruction whisperingly above the drumming of
the tyres. But what sort? Or was it the friendless spirits of un-
buried Indians? He must be close to reservation territory here.
Or was what rode at his left ear the sum of every bad memory
from the past, every bad fear for the future?

There was nothing else in sight. He put the window up and his
foot down. The line sped at him even faster. He let the onrushing
night engulf his power to think until the very act of motion
seemed an end and purpose in itself.

It had happened. For three weeks he had wanted it to happen

and not wanted it to happen and then, as if it had made the decision for him, he had found himself leaving Palm Springs not west on 10 but south on 111.

He had been sitting by the free-form coffee-table-shaped pool of the Springs Racquet Club drinking and talking to Dino Silvestri. Dino was top brass. Had more movies going than anyone else in town. But Madison was not in good shape. His hair felt too long, too sloppy. Despite repeated messages with an answering agency he had been unable to get hold of that neutered fat-cat faggot. The queen was obviously not bothering to call him back. Perhaps he should set about finding someone else.

That was small stuff. A surface irritation, throwing him momentarily off-balance. Undermining every thought and plan and half-made wish was the sound of a girl he could not put a face to, whimpering with pain. The pool before him shimmered with a hard-edged, chemical brilliance and he saw suspended in it the image of a swarthy, writhing body. It hung in his mind like an intended screen dissolve obstinately refusing to fade.

He had expected to be unaffected by Preston's grisly substitute for a home movie. In the event he had been uneasily aware of a lack of clinical detachment. It had got to him, maybe not as savagely as it had struck its sacrificial victim. But the vision and the screams had invaded his mind, refusing to shift. Still, he had moved around being charming and dutiful in the name of *Cold Turkey* and his Oscar. Yet the ritual smiles and selective back-slapping could not pull the curtains across his sub-conscious, behind which, in hideous relief, laughed the vulgar features of his mother. It hurt to think about it so he turned to choicer thoughts. He found himself wondering if Preston had type-cast his handful of disposable one-nighters to provide willing meat to follow the film. They had not discussed it. On the one subsequent occasion of their meeting at The Walt Disney Memorial Charity Banquet, he had not felt able to question Preston out-right. Both men had smiled their public smiles and, letting the subject lie, got on with repeating their supply of ad-lib throwaways . . .

'Naturally, my friend, I should not expect you to make up your mind on the strength of a few casual words now. I will leave you the script, eh?'

Tanned, short, stocky, Dino Silvestri was smiling at him affably from across the table. The low sun glistened off the brown dome of his cranium and the distinguished grey side-hair positively glittered alongside the black side-arms of the Godfather sun-glasses.

'I'd certainly like to take the script home and take my time on reading it,' he saw his twin reflections say. A girl desperate to impress dived inexpertly into the pool and from beneath the brightly coloured safety of the umbrella'd tables several people laughed out loud. At one of them, keeping a profile so low on this one as to be below sea-level, sat Lyndon Oates with his new public mistress.

'Of course, of course,' Dino was saying. 'I'll have one sent round to you before you leave town. You're staying at Alex's, yes?'

'Right!'

'When you've read it, my friend – you'll want it bad enough to eat.'

So as to be able to vomit it back down the john. It was a story, the producer had intimated, about a Grand Prix driver who discovers he has leukaemia. His ten-minute verbal synopsis of the plot had been cursed with such a sense of déja vu, it seemed to have been made six times already. Its one faint plus was it would require long weeks of European location. But Europe, it was fair to assume, would be no more than a pallid reproduction of the holographic slides at Barbara Lemerle's. Silvestri's chief concern was to get his signature before the Oscar award allowed Oates and Markovitch to double his asking price. At least Dino hadn't come at him with girls.

Having allowed the water to tighten her too small bikini and thus make her design even more transparent, the girl was taking her time in clambering out of the pool. It was the wrong time and the wrong place to be pulling tired stunts like that and there was far too much of the cocktail waitress in her to make it worth even trying. Breasts to the fore, she levered herself laboriously up over the pool's side.

Well, he would get the script with its yellow first-draft pages and its blue rewrite pages and he would stack it on top of the pile of other blue-yellow paged scripts that were all the same story with different names and, maybe, one rainy Sunday, he would let his fingers do the filming. Because he wouldn't. Not crap like that. The next one up, he'd chose.

On the screen of his mind's eye he saw the unbidden head of Sean Flaherty resolve itself into a clear-cut image. The old-hawk features of the dying man still stonily ignored him as beneath serious consideration.

Then it happened. He knew suddenly he did not want to spend

the evening dividing his attention between Oates's strategising out loud on the Dino Silvestri scene, Caroline Ross whom he was vaguely supposed to meet and whichever B-girls Eichler by now had in tow. Nor did he want to drive home to an empty house and a choice between cruising the Strip, telephoning Philip Grayson for a lay or sitting down opposite that pile of commercial script crud. He didn't want to play poker, read Dickens or get married. Dormant in his mind these three off-balanced weeks, the compulsion was informing him the time, if only by default, was ripe.

He stood up.

'Dino,' he said, 'I've got to go. Send it over – it goes straight to the top of my list.'

He stretched out a hand.

'Ciao,' he said.

'Ciao,' Silvestri said and flashed a final smile of radiantly Latin inscrutability. He matched the smile with equal insincerity and flicked a hand in long-distance farewell to Oates. He would not go over. He would not be seen running over to report like some White House field man. Oates could well have had their table bugged in any case . . .

He walked by the most exotic feature of the entire oasis, the green, green grass of the genuine lawn-tennis courts, and came to the car port. A jockey exchanged his Porsche back to him for a tip. He tooled easily down the curving, several-hundred-yards-long private road and then out into an instant residential area too discreet ever to allow a citizen to stare the profit-motive squarely in the eye. On the scuzzy edge of East LA was the town of Commerce. It had a main street, factories, stores, accountants' offices. The Springs had none of this. Not even signs. To buy a shirt or tennis racket meant invading the privacy of one of these apparent homes he was now passing where salesmen would appear from out the plastic with an arrogantly omniscient sub-serviency. The stores were as anonymously genteel as high-class whorehouses in a bogusly respectable rich town. And the comparison was apt. No industry, perhaps. But the Springs cash-flow was many times over that of Commerce.

Pastel cabanas, bungalows, all the colours of cassatta. He drew up outside the one rented by Eichler, the one with the lime-green concrete-latticed walls. He crossed the vestigial patio front yard and let himself into the inevitable ranch-style through lounge.

'Alex?'

No-one was in. One way or another Eichler must be out scoring. He marched over to the telephone.

It took him a long time and many calls. Tom Leonard was not at home. Nor was Celine. The answering services kept telling him no-one had checked in. But his purpose didn't waver. A mood of washed, faded fatalism held him and he, in turn, held himself still, not moving, not turning, at its centre. He rationed his drinks and his calls by the half-hour.

Darkness thickened in the room even as light still clung to the garden-yard outside and the whispering of the air-conditioner became over-insistent. He got up and switched it off. The patio doors, eight paces wide, might have framed a depthless view across the pale sage desert to the mauve mountains of the distance but its prospect fell immediately upon stoney walls. Pink, they divided the yard from that of the rose-coloured bungalow beyond. The glass framed a view of an uncertain yucca tree, a prickly pear and a sheet of sky which, bleached by heat at noon, slid down the scale in consort with the sun through a rich blue to twilight grey-lavender.

No-one called him back. The dark chocolate of the upholstery had lost its outlines to the encroaching darkness. The blond wood of the furniture gleamed through with enhanced brightness. As he got up to fix another drink the tumble-twist pile rugs under his feet felt like the skins of poodles. God, he thought, a town without a past, where everything is new. A town where everything is in the present tense. What future have I other than aging? Still the phone did not ring but, isolated in his cocoon of fatalism, he was preternaturally calm.

It was close to midnight when it did and the room was in blackness. But he could see. He made the phone in two chirps. It proved to be Bergman, Leonard's all-purpose gumshoe. From him he got it – the Tucson address. Five minutes later he was shifting up through the Porsche's syncromesh.

The straightforward thing would have been to head himself due East on Highway 10 and run direct to Phoenix. But sitting in the darkness of the sterile room he had decided not to go that route. If he was going to reach down into the past, if he was going to confront the woman and the part of his mind he had so long been at pains to avoid considering, then he would psych himself into the right mood. He would head South on 86, using the minor road to link him with Highway 8. That way he would be cutting down behind the desert wasteland of his childhood years, the time spent in that filling-station store upon the edge of no-man's land. Out of the desert, out of the darkness, might come a vibration triggering . . . what he did not know. A flood of understanding, peace and reconciliation. A burning flame of confirmed hatred and contempt scorching the past into ashes he could rightly leave oblivion to tend. The hot wind off the desert past might blow into the arid landscape of his mind and there deposit some sort of healing seed, some clue as to how he might look openly upon the picture memories he carried locked away in screaming silence; how he might look upon them and not feel they demanded revenge for his father, vengeance on his mother, expiation on himself. So, the hot air breathing a thousand voices at his ear, the white line darting at him, he had headed East on 8.

The last stretch after he'd linked back with 10 was rough. He blinked once to find that he had come to and at the wheel of a speeding car not knowing if he'd slept for one second or ten. But the great drop in the desert temperature throughout the night worked for him. He remained stitched to the white line. Through flat blackness to his right and left he came into Tucson just as the dawn's early light was making the horizon brighten further eastward yet.

And needing sleep. Three minutes off the freeway, still trying to adjust to city speeds and halts he saw, rounding a wide traffic island, the haven of a motel. He pulled into its darkened forecourt and then trod the brake. Parked in shadow was the high bulk of a movie generator truck. Of course! He should have thought! The Tucson Studios! There'd be some series, some low-budget feature shooting there and all the guys would be stashed here at night drinking themselves fat, screwing themselves thin. Recognition he did not need. He put the car in motion and stopped again. He was over-reacting. If he slept now, they'd be out at work when he awoke. Nowhere else in town would there begin to be a night-clerk.

He parked the car in a dark corner, hefted his grip into the lobby past signs announcing the Mad Greek was in cabaret. The night-clerk was in a similar league but by going into the room in back of the counter, he found and woke him. A twenty did the rest. Past whirring ice and hazily glowing Coke machines, he was led down long low-ceilinged corridors. The room was large, pleasantly ersatz Mexican, and held two beds. He crashed down on to one of them. For a considerable while the rhythms and the noises of the speeding roadways pushed through his veins and back along his nerves. The lines still shot towards his brain. But after a time they faded and he began to sleep.

The second twenty that along with an afterthought he slipped the clerk was a well considered investment. Not only was his own room left undisturbed, no noise came to waken him from its neighbours. When he awoke his Rolex told him it was afternoon.

The house was still another anti-climax. It had all been too easy. He had surfaced slowly to full consciousness showering the last taste of the drive away. He had eaten two eggs over-easy in the coffee-shop without falling foul of any stray character actor or technician. Checking out he had discovered Wilmington was only a moment's drive away. Seeing the bills in his hand the girl had not thought to question his false registration. So she had spared herself the agony of deciding whether to keel over in an 'oh-my' swoon or bust a blasé gut-feigning disinterest. Unhampered by emotion her directions had been impeccable. He slowed the Porsche to a standstill outside the house he knew to be his mother's.

Someone was home. A Chevrolet parked in the driveway indicated that much. At first glance, there was no clue as to what he'd find inside to add to or subtract from his memories. The house was middle-class America (South West). Part, obviously, of some development it was a little too large, a little too close to the verge of individuality to make the phrase 'tract housing' what you'd think of first. It was low with wide frontage faced in a more modern facsimile of adobe. In beige. The roof was partly flat, hinting that it had its uses, partly pitched and red-tiled in the Spanish fashion. The houses to its left and right were identical.

Or were they? Perhaps a second glance did suggest a clue: suggest that things might not have changed. The Chevy, though new, carried a scrape down its off side and a dent in its rear-end. It was less than clean. A screen hung just visibly awry outside one window. A tile was missing. Beyond a midget pink concrete wall the pocket handkerchief of front yard was flattened mud. It was as if by playing the part of a private eye, being the camera tracking in on the opening set-up of a sequence, he insulated his feelings once again as he crossed the quiet street. The mailbox simply bore the number. He went past it up the cement pathway to the door. He drew in a breath. Breathing it out he reached up and pressed the buzzer. It sounded. Surprising him by the speed of her response a woman was opening the inner door and, peering at him as she did so, the screen door too.

'We don't want – Oh.'

He had removed his shades as she began to speak and she had recognised him at once.

'My God!' she said simply. 'My God!'

Blinking at the brilliance of the outdoor light she retreated two paces backward into the house. Her hand had gone to the edge of the inner door and it seemed to him she was about to slam it in his face. He began to slide a Gucci casual across the threshold to anticipate her but even as his foot moved she stood completely aside.

'You'd better come in,' she said.

He went on in to momentary darkness and a strangely cool and air-conditioned mustiness. Mouse dirt seemed to dispute possession of the atmosphere with stale tobacco fumes and gin. He heard the door close behind him and the removal of the sharp, thin slant of sunshine on the wall to his lefthand helped his eyes begin to open to a new f-stop.

'In on the right,' she said.

He took three paces along a token hallway then stepped through a wide-shouldered archway of an opening into a not small room. The smell was stronger here and the things brought together in the way of furniture and fittings had the same air of irreconcilable individuality. The basic Mexican wrought-iron, carved-wood feel of coffee table and settee was dominatingly countered by the huge, square glaucous eye of a television suspended in mid-air by a floor-to-ceiling pole. Its lead trailed in an unplugged coil to nowhere and a smaller, portable set sat on the glass-topped coffee table next to an overflowing ashtray. There were no glasses or bottles on the table top but sticky, opaque circles and crescents showed that, recently or not, there had been. A glass was lying on its side by the creamy, pretzel-textured wall on a carpet beige and whorled like a beach after the tide's retreat. Three or four stains spread randomly about managed to suggest the sand still had some drying out to do. An ornamental spoon lay near the glass and above it, at eye-height on the wall, a cheap display cabinet housed a dozen or so others spaced thinly in two tiers. There should have been perhaps in excess of thirty as the spoons commemorated Presidents of the United States. The monthly subscriptions seemed not to have been kept up. There were just enough spoons to suggest the last few good teeth in a diseased mouth.

'Well,' his mother said, 'it finally arrived. Big money from the West. My superstar himself.'

She'd had time to collect herself and the scraps of smart-talk together. Tension was evident in her from the stiffness with which she was holding herself but if she felt guilt or anything more tender, it manifested itself in a brittle, challenging belligerency. She moved self-consciously about the room gathering sections, pages, of strewn-everywhichway paper.

'You want to sit down?' she said.

'I guess I'll stand,' he said. It sounded hostile. 'I've been driving,' he added but it came too much an afterthought to serve as a passable excuse. She moved to the mantel shelf and rummaged for a cigarette in a long carton of Kools. He made no effort to light it for her. She picked up a statuette of a medieval knight and on the fourth time of trying a flame shot up from the helmet top. There was an over-yellow reproduction on the chimney breast of a Remington stage-coach. She turned and looked at him.

'So, why?' she said.

Neither her voice nor the cigarette in her fingers was quite as controlled as she would have liked them to be. He shrugged slightly.

'I don't know,' he said.

'Hmmn . . .' she said. 'Guess I should be asking for your autograph seeing as how you're so famous a big-shot and all.'

Words failed both of them. He shrugged and pulled a face. He'd been surprised from the outset how . . . trim she was. She was quite without any excess weight. She was wearing tight black toreador pants and a green-blue, faintly irridescent mohair sweater. Its neckline was quite conservative but there was a worrying definition of brassiere beneath it, just as the line of her panties was more than hinted at through the tight slacks. Like her auburn-red, semi-bouffant hair, there was something artificially worked at in her figure but she was surely, leaner, less fleshy than he remembered her. A flash of insight came penetratingly upon him: she was desperately trying to figure out just what he did remember. That, more than anything, was making her uptight. The answer, both for the night, the morning after, was everything. He felt his stomach contract with fear and disgust but he sensed a gain. Here, in front of her, at any rate, he could take those dirty pictures out from the tin box in his mind and look at them.

'You want some coffee?' she was asking.

'Er, yes. Fine. Please,' he said.

'Okay,' she said. She disappeared out through the wide, round-shouldered arch and surprisingly, along with a clink of cups or something, he heard muffled voices. As surprisingly empty-handed, she was right back.

'Be right with us,' she said.

There was something more positive, an initiative of malice, in her manner now and something of a private grin dormant in her sharp, sun-dried face.

'A guy showed up on my doorstep a while back,' he said. 'Said he was your husband. Tried to shake me down. Said you'd sent him.'

'What did he look like?' She spoke with sudden harshness. A kind of foxy indignation had brought her chin enquiringly up.

'Had a Texan accent.'

'Him! I never sent him. I kicked him out of here. Way back.'

'So I found out.'

'Shit-ass,' she muttered.

'Which number was he?'

She looked at him sharply.

'What's it to you?' she said.

'Just like to know where my money's going.'

'Just like to know nobody else knows where it's going!'

She must have felt she'd gone too far.

'The last,' she said. 'I swear to God the last. Four-time loser's four times too many for this girl.'

She corrected the dive toward self-pity.

'Give him anything?' she said.

He shook his head. She laughed. The laugh made his blood shiver. Raucous, the sound had sent his emotions whirling back to his yelled-at lonely childhood in the stale heat and dust, the fly-blown wooden rooms of that sad, doomed, pointless wasting of three lives beyond the back of nowhere. She had laughed like that whenever she was starting to get drunk. It meant an hour or so and she'd be screaming like an animal and lashing out at him until his tears of pain matched hers of incoherent rage and frustration . . . Yes, if you looked now, you could make out the fine broken lines of a juicer redly veining her tan. But he was so much bigger than she now when before she had seemed like a . . .

'They never found them, did they?' He had to interrupt his thoughts with words. She shook her head this time.

'After a week, maybe, they didn't even try,' she said. 'They weren't old. Kids. They're still walking around now, free as air. I had no money to put pressure on some captain or City Hall big-shot to keep on with it. I didn't count. They just let it die and lie there. And . . . well . . . so what . . . ?'

She spoke with resignation and not rancour as if neglect had been a deserved penalty for being poor. But he was less convinced.

'Maybe you were happy it should be that way,' he said. Again the jut upward and forward of her chin.

'Just what—'

A rattle of cups on a tray cut off her counter-attack. He saw the ghost of triumph steal onto her face again. He turned his head. Standing framed motionless in the arch was a girl, tall, long, dark-haired. Sexy. She held a tray with two cups of coffee. Steam rose gently from the cups as, unsure where to set them down, she hesitated.

'Put them right here, Cathy,' his mother said.

She yanked the portable TV down off the table to the floor and stacked the overflowing ashtray messily on top of it. It sat there at an angle. He saw ash tumble finely down into the set's interior.

'Big one's on the blink again,' his mother said inconsequentially.

The girl came forward. She was wearing cut-down jeans faded, it seemed, by genuine old age. Her legs were long, slender and, besides tanned, dirty. Her man's work shirt was an even more faded blue than her jeans. She wore it with the tail out at the back, the front cross-tied to give a glimpse of belly. It was mostly unbuttoned otherwise. As she stooped to set down the tray he had easily obtained opportunity to see that, unlike her employer, she wore no bra. The fullness of the relaxed breast suggested that she either needed to or didn't – depending how you liked them. From where he sat—

Still stooped over as she transferred the cups from tray to table, she turned her head sideways and looked straight up at him. Her face was enigmatic, deadpan. But he knew at once she'd intercepted his line of vision and had read his thoughts exactly. She began to straighten up.

'Cathy – meet your big brother,' his mother said.

'Hi,' the girl said tonelessly.

'Hi,' he said. Ridiculously. 'Half-brother,' he said.

The girl nodded. Unimpressed, it seemed, either by the relationship or his status she stood holding the tray before her thighs at the stretch of both arms. There was neither hero-worship nor envious resentment in the unblinking, unselfconscious way she stared at him. He felt himself being assessed: found himself unnerved. Expressionless though the scrutiny was, it compelled him to stoop down for the coffee and so escape it.

'I guess I already put sugar in,' the girl said.

And cream too. But as it was only some kind of instant piss it made little matter. It hadn't come in mugs and she hadn't slopped it but there were no cookies to camouflage the taste. Ugh. The second sip was worse than the first. He bent forward and replaced the cup on its saucer. The tray with its Wisconsin lake and tall can of Hamms was cheap and tinny and stolen, obviously, from some bar. And she was his half-sister! He used all his acquired actor's skills to mask the series of shock-waves jolting through his belly and his brain. No wonder the bitch had worn that faint, smug look of malicious triumph on her face! She had waited, giving him time to run a stud's eye over the girl before she'd sprung it on him. Well, so fucking what! There wasn't a brother born who wouldn't look at his sister in that way if she gave out the same vibrations as this one.

'Great coffee,' he said sarcastically as he looked at her again. Dark-eyed, long faced, high cheekboned and full-lipped, she reminded him of someone. She had a gypsy take-it-or-leave-it sexuality. I can do it pretty good, her loose, sullen pose seemed to be saying but you've got to come to me and I don't make no promises about liking you. There was a touch of Indian about her, not Apache or Navajo but . . . Jesus Christ! Could the father be . . .! He tried to judge her age and do the arithmetic and it didn't seem impossible. Her colour made sense of it. Was that why the bitch had got that inward smirk. Well he'd soon wipe it off the ass-side of her face for her!

He looked at his mother.

' 'case you were wondering,' he said, 'I remember alright.

Too fucking well, he thought, but as he saw alarm flash brightly in her eyes he felt a simultaneous surge of getting-even pleasure.

'Cathy,' his mother said. 'leave us alone for a moment, will you, please? Your big, rich, famous brother and I have got things to talk about.'

Things, he thought. Yes, things. Not money. I'll be fucked if I'm going to buy a phoney peace between us with my money.

'Yeah, sure thing,' the girl said just as lifelessly. She turned and walked away. Nice Geneva movement his mind automatically registered even as another part of it began to ask just why he'd come, what he was doing here.

'Okay,' his mother said, 'so you remember. So?'

'So I don't like what I remember.'

She shrugged.

'Tough. I saved your skin, I guess you'd have to say. I saved both our skins.

'You didn't save his!'

'How could I?'

As if to point her exclamation, someone outside fired off a light shot-gun. A missed heartbeat later he realised it was the front screen door slamming on its spring and that its plunger arm needed attention. Like everything else in the house. He tried not to let it phase him, as he kept on after her.

'You could have tried!' he half-shouted.

'How could I, for Christ's sake . . . And for Christ's sake, why should I!'

'He . . . he was your—'

'My husband? Don't make me laugh! You think I didn't know that every first second every morning I opened my eyes. I married him because of you and he sentenced me to a living death out in that dump! What life was that!'

She stared challengingly at him. The vividness of that bitter remembrance, those million petty defeats to each frustrated day, had made her defiant.

'I was going to leave you,' she went on, 'the both of you. I'd made up my mind. It was just a question of time. It was always the two of you. Against me. The way . . .'

'You didn't want for someone to go to! I remember that as well!'

'Christ, I should hope not! A worn out old wreck . . . he was old enough to be my father, remember! Christ, that lousy San Diego! The gallant sailors home from the sea!'

The vehemence of her defence was pushing her towards self-pity once again. Again she was faithful to a more central hardness in her make-up.

'The way it happened,' she said, 'it was all clearer-cut.'

'So you were glad!'

'Yes,' she said, 'why not?'

'And afterwards, in that motel, you enjoyed it!'

'You saw?'

'And heard!' His laugh was out of hell. 'The whole play.'

'You always were a little smart-ass of a peeper . . . Okay so I enjoyed it. At first I pretended to because I thought it was the only way to stay alive. And then I didn't have to any more because as a matter of your actual fact I was. Enjoying it. And the reason? The reason is I'm a woman – full and complete and I liked having a man inside me, right, and I still do! And that night I had three. Young men. And often! If you really want to know that was the first decent fucking I'd had since Christ knows and the longer it went on, the better it got!'

So she had a hooker's slattern honesty. In that strident refusal to ask pardon he could detect the dark, the wilfully indifferent side of his own nature. Even as she stood unrepentant trying to out-face him and he sought to find the most wounding thing possible to say to her, some part of him had to offer her respect of a soiled, much-handled kind.

'Christ knows what they saw in you,' he said.

Knowing she had him, about to enjoy her own joke, she coarsely grinned.

'It's not what they see,' she said, 'it's what they feel.'

'Bitch!'

'Maybe. Okay, yes! So what! That why you come? To tell me what you've thought for years?'

'Not when you've known it as long.'

'Ha!'

'He was kind to me. You never were.'

'And why in God's name should I be kind to the whining brat who wrecked my life.'

He gestured largely about the room with a wide sweep of his arm.

'Better than the back of nowhere,' he said, 'If you had any class. Class to fix it up. It's one thousand times better than you've got any right to deserve. So ask your bitch mind this: what kind of wrecker pays for this?'

'It sure ain't Beverly Hills,' she snapped

'Damn fucking right!' he said. 'And don't—'

'I don't want your charity!'

'Too proud to beg, huh? With me. Doesn't stop you begging with the others, does it? Looking out at the end of each month to see if what scares you shitless is this time, yes, this time, going to happen for real. The mail-man carrying that big fat cheque walking straight on by and, when you rush out calling after him, turning around and holding up to you his two big empty hands. What exactly would you call that cheque now, mother dear? Money from home, now, would you? Huh?'

'I never begged for it,' she said. 'I did a deal. I sold something. I sold staying away. I sold keeping off your back, staying away from all those gossip writers, newspapers and such.'

He heard himself bark out a sharp, high laugh.

'Too proud to beg!' he said,

'Not proud, smart,' she said. 'Begging gets you nothing the third time, And you don't owe me any favours.'

Asking neither quarter nor concession she gave him back as hard a stare as he gave her.

'Christ knows where you got your looks,' she said.

'You couldn't be sure,' he countered. Then the thought struck him again. 'The kid,' he said, 'the girl – she a bastard by your husband's murderer?'

She laughed again.

'Something you didn't remember, after all,' she said. 'You forgot what the bed looked like the next day.'

He moved across and knocked her down. He didn't slap her but threw the same short punch he'd throw at any guy in a bar. She gasped and went down like a falling tree. But not unconsciously. As blood curled from her split lower lip her hand went up to it. She levered herself up on her other arm and shook her head. She looked at him,

'Bastard!' she said.

'You should know.'

'No such luck, superstar. You're still stuck with that fuck-up.'

Beneath the tan she was pallid with pain, but she was not afraid. She still had the courage of her bitchery.

'You didn't come to take me to your Bel Air rose garden,' she said. 'So why? Curious? To remind yourself what trash you're sprung from?'

'Pretty much,' he said. Was that true? Why had he come? If it had been in search of some kind of peace, he had only found a confirmed hardness in her and in himself.

'You hit me five hundred times,' he said.

A spurt of swallowed blood converted her laugh into a choking cough. She swallowed harder and, as she wiped her chin, succeeded in clearing her throat.

'Hero!' she sneered. 'Superstar! It should've been a thousand!' Wincing with the movement, she jerked her head. 'Her,' she said. 'Her I can take. She's no brat and she's no superstar.'

He let that ride. Instead he asked her the question that, because it implied a need to follow through, he had never in all the years quite bothered to ask himself. It conjured a picture of bare brown earth humped slightly in a cracked mound with a small numbered stick stuck into it like gardener's use to tag their plants.

'Where's he buried?' he said.

She looked at him.

'He wasn't buried,' she said finally. 'He was, er, what you call it, er, burn—'

'Cremated.'

'Right.'

So he was denied a further search for a better self – the mourning figure in a pauper's graveyard, shot in long shot with the sun atmospherically low and a nice long, lingering fade out. Or was he?

'So where are they?' he said. 'The ashes. Who has them?'

She was slow this time replying. He saw her look at him consideringly. Then resolution came into her face, along with the whore's honour she must have sensed was her last talisman against the cancerous wasting of self-disgust.

'I had them,' she said. 'They gave them to me. I had to sign for them. They were in a kind of fancy tin thing.'

'Had? Had!'

'Well, you know. Moving all the time. Inglewood, El Centro – Texas, for Christ's sake. I guess I lost—'

'What do you mean "you know"?'

'Oh for Christ's sake! They were something too much to tote. They were just ashes for Christ's sake. I flushed them down the john!'

He closed on her, the animal in him geared for gutter violence. She drew her knees up, half turning, expecting to be kicked.

Instead he spat at her and headed for the door.

But she was tough. Her voice stopped him, turned him, as he reached the arch.

'I don't know why you came,' she gasped, 'but let me tell you this for free. Me, you think I don't remember that night, too? When they came at me and I thought it was the end. What he looked like, the poor bastard, when they brought him in? Whatever you remember, I remember twice as good. But also I forget it. Understand? I remember but I forget it too. If you've got brains, there's no other fucking way.'

'Mother-fucker,' he said. 'There's no deal you can do with that kind of memory.'

'Sonny, you don't have no choice.'

He took one final look. Yes, he was his mother's son.

'I won't be back,' he said.

'You going to pay for the damage?'

He fished his billfold up from his hip pocket and blindly tore from it what notes were there. He hurled them scatteringly about the room. As he turned from it a grey cat went scampering in after them.

The sun pierced his brain like a sword. As he fumbled for his shades the screen door cracked like a car back-fire behind him.

Period, he thought. Finish. The End. He found that he was trembling. Of its own volition, despite his will, the inside of his gut was quivering, dissolving into liquid. Bitch! Whore! Hooker! But above all, bitch! His whole painstaking pilgrimage had been a bust. A bummer! She'd taught him nothing but bad news!

He shook his head. It must be the spearing of the sun's rays at his eyes that made them water so.

He drew in deep, deep breaths and braced himself. Now all that fucking way to drive. Well, first a bar. A well-stocked bar. A bar on the roughest side of town.

Reaching in his pocket for his keys, he crossed the narrow suburban street. He bent down to the car door and was brought up short, frozen in mid-motion. He must have left the car unlocked. Sitting in the passenger seat was the girl – the girl who, whatever her father, shared a mother with himself.

Now she anticipated him. She leant across and opened the driver's door. She looked up at him. Some prudery made him look into her eyes and not down into the shirt he knew instinctively she hadn't buttoned higher. For the first time in their brief acquaintance, expression, a look of pleading urgency, had come into her somber, sullen face.

'Take me with you,' she said in a rapid mutter. 'Away from here. Please. Take me away from that bitch!'

At the back of his mind a red alert flashed, a warning-bell rang. There was her age . . . a state line . . . But she had been lucky in the wording of her plea. She had used the one word most bound to win his sympathy, trigger a positive reaction.

'One bitch-rescue coming up,' he said.

He ducked into the car. As he turned the ignition and revved her, he felt his spirits surge in concert with the engine. Revenge was a dish best eaten cold.

'Her I can take,' she'd said. Well now sirs, now he'd do some taking. Far from being a drag, the drive back was going to be a gas.

chapter twenty-one

Coca-Cola – an intellectual beverage.

Advertising copy

On the long drive back to LA she had sat for mile after mile without offering to talk. When he had started on something she had responded naturally enough but not once had their exchanges opened out. She had seemed uninterested in pursuing any topic, thinking aloud. He had thought her shy, then guarded, then, finally, dumb. The drive had become a bummer after all. The Inter-state had streamed at and by them with a monotonous daylight unremarkableness. No Indian ghosts had ridden alongside.

Only once did their brief forays into talk remotely approach significance.

'So you're called Cathy,' he had said early on.

'Janice,' she had said.

'Your mother calls you Cathy.'

'That's why I call myself Janice.'

At the cross back over into California, the guy had been all eyes for the movie star and for the Porsche. The girl was not Ann-Margret and with that his interest died.

He had blasted straight by the Springs and on to LA. He had installed her in one of the never-used guest rooms. As he'd shown it to her he had already been feeling bored with his caprice.

'I've nothing to wear,' she'd muttered the next morning.

He had given her two thousand bucks and had Tibor drive her down to Wilshire. Tibor had returned in a car weighed down with Chemin de Fer denim. She had returned riding a tiny Honda runaround.

'Anything else?' he had said that evening as she watched Kurt Geisler do his nails.

'Yes,' she had said. 'Get me into movies.'

He had laughed.

'We'll see,' he said.

That had been more than three weeks ago. In that time no phone had rung with lawyers on the end. No Feds had showed up. His mother had not come pounding on the door to scream for the girl's return or sue for her fat lip. No schoolboard official had waited outside and grabbed him. So, if only by default, going her own way, scarcely showing herself around, she had stayed. She said she was eighteen. But she also said her name was Janice. Looking at his half-sister's rangy, coltish figure, her ugly-attractive face he had a couple of times tried to fix her age. It was impossible. Within minutes he had gone on idly to consider what it might be like to make her.

That evening she had not split to the Strip or some place on Laurel Canyon or wherever else in town she seemed so easily to have dropped in. Unusually she had come wandering in on him as he sat dismissing yet another nothing script from his life. Jesus! Sweet Jesus! . . . The stuff they were feeding him, the Silvestri lemon might win out yet. But he'd serve time before he agreed.

'What's it like being famous?' The question, posed with her back to him as she looked through the window at the band-box acreage, had a fan-club banality to it. 'All this yours?'

'It comes with the package, like the free extra pair of pants with the new suit.' He picked up a script.

'But being a star . . .' her interest was genuine and it bugged him. 'I mean what does it really feel like?'

Christ he was going to have to give her an answer. But what? He'd never thought about it. Painless rape? An ego jerk-off they paid you for? He was about to say . . . 'well for openers I'm my own man' but stubbed that out while it was still burning knowing that Oates, Leonard and Rosner would have laughed fit to be put away. Sure, it meant his own fag hairdresser coming in on call to blow-wave him on the premises. Bullshit, Madison.

'Well I'll tell you,' he said lightly. 'There's this old lady who sits out around Sunset and Baroda selling these maps showing where the movie stars live. The out-of-town suckers pick 'em up for a couple of bucks apiece then take the bus tour to gawp at the inmates. Had 'em outside here the other morning. "Ladies and gentlemen," this broad says, "some of the most famous Hollywood stars have lived in that house. Lately it was the legendary Stella Lang. And . . ." get this . . . "as of right now Paul Madison lives there." Do you read me, Cathy called Janice? As of right now I'm famous, only you gotta be quick! Now do me a sweet favour go sit in that chair there and relax.'

Curling herself into the soft squishy leather of the vast square armchair, she did as he suggested. He settled back himself and looked at her. Jeans, still another workshirt. There was something boyish about her every move and pose. There was something of a young, moody punk from off the street corner, out the pool-room, Juvenile Division, in her not quite co-ordinated sullenness. Making it with her would be like going with a guy. He wondered if she'd ever had it. She must have – the buttons she left undone to show what she didn't wear. He wondered if she was into some special tricks. There was something perverse about the not caring dumbness she brought to every topic and—

'You haven't got me into movies,' she said abruptly.

'I'm too busy trying to get myself out,' he said on reflex. He looked at his watch.

'Listen,' he said truthfully, 'there's someone I'm expecting. It might be an idea if you split.'

If Mephistopheles ever returned to earth with the redundant aim of capturing the souls of a fraternity house, Paul Madison thought, this is what he would look like. As he smiled and chuckled appreciatively at the man's small talk, he tried to gauge the depths of disingenuousness chinese-boxed away behind the frank, open, all-things-to-all-men face. The not quite young man's name was Wilson. You could, he'd said, call him Jimmy. If it hadn't been for the conservative three-piece, tight herring-boned pattern suit he was wearing in defiance of the Los Angeles heat and habit, he could have been an up-and-coming pro on the golf circuit. He had the same kind of easy show-biz smile on the same kind of totally even features – the wide mouth, the straight nose, the firmly defined chin. He almost had the same tan. His hair was neither redneck short nor freak-out long. It was light brown. The sunlamp that had induced that touch of orange to his complexion had given the slight hint of curls around his forehead a suggestion of true blonde.

He might have been a golf pro but he wasn't, he was a lawyer. He was flown in from Washington. He did not practise law there directly. He worked on the staff of the Junior Senator for California. You might guess that, Paul Madison was thinking: you might guess that from the way his smile slid in and out like a lizard's tongue, from the apparent absence of all depth beneath the shining surface of professionally bright eyes and, above all, from the distinct crow's feet already whitely evident where the anti-UV goggles had prevented the tan becoming total. He should wear tinted glasses to hide that, Paul Madison thought, even if he doesn't need them.

'Well you've certainly caught us at a good time in one respect,' Lyndon Oates was saying, 'because we're clear between projects at this moment in time.'

Oates was the inevitable PR spectre at their lunchtime *Ma Maison* feast. The 'we' referred not to an ascendancy to any throne but conventionally made clear his meal-ticket interest in Paul Madison. The tone of his voice meant he was in favour of complying with James Wilson's request.

Wilson looked across the table with a totally engaging display of candour that deceived no-one. The phoniness of power was in his frankness. He had a need. But not for people. It was just that the game was played this way. Sooner or later he'd get what he was after.

'I guess that leaves it to the man who'd have to do it,' he said. 'Paul – do you feel you can give us a yea or nay right here this minute?'

Deliberately, Paul Madison said nothing. He toyed actorishly with his demi-tasse. James Wilson's smile broadened. More than ever you would run to him for counselling – if you were eighteen.

'Or could it be this really quite excellent meal has blunted your appetite for making decisions?' Wilson picked up.

Paul Madison drank some coffee.

'I guess I would like to give it a little thought at that,' he said.

'We'd love to have you aboard,' Wilson said.

'You know,' Paul Madison said, 'I've often wondered why politicians should care so much more about the opinions of Wayne or Newman or Sinatra or MacLaine and all than they do about the views of George R. Hardaker.'

'I don't believe I've ever heard of George R. Hardaker.'

'Exactly.'

For an instant Wilson was a kid who'd been caught smoking his first cigarette behind the gym. His eyes lost their sparkle as they narrowed in wariness and fear. But not knowing when you're beat is the hall-mark of the American gofer. He returned to his pitch.

'Oh, come on,' he said, 'surely it's only natural that people should take seriously the opinions of talented individuals they've come to know well and respect in other fields. Why—'

'Jesus! I hope to fuck they don't know me well,' Paul Madison said.

Lyndon Oates laughed heartily at the pleasantry and a half-second too late, this time, James Wilson joined in

'Seriously though,' Oates said, 'you think your man is going far?'

His talent for unconscious parody had been undiminished by his fourth marriage.

'All the way,' James Wilson snapped out with automatic reflex from the steel-trap of his mind.

'. . . admired a long time,' Wilson was doggedly repeating. 'And he's not blind to the advantages of having his campaign endorsed by the man who's on everybody's lips as the one most likely to succeed Oscar-wise this time around.'

'People like a winner. Winners should stick together to win more,' Oates said. 'It's very simple, really. It's a kind of power-incest.'

'Well I don't know,' something in Paul Madison insisted on insisting, 'I wasn't too happy on the line your man took over that last Rizzo thing.'

Some freak of memory – an actor's ability to hack a fast study? – had sprung something into the forefront of his mind.

'The Senator has since made it very clear for the record how he was misquoted on that issue,' Wilson snapped again. Once more the dead, inhuman timbre of his voice betokened the automatic PR pilot. Sensing his error he tried smiling his way back on to his fraternity row course. With his right forefinger he stabbed at his digital watch. He looked down at the punched-up display.

'Gentlemen,' he said, 'I know you'll excuse me for a couple of minutes. I must place a call to Washington before everyone starts heading for the bars.'

He upped and temporarily left them. Paul Madison watched his confident, decisive walk toward the restaurant's entrance.

'Come back John Dean – we forgive and love you,' he said.

But Oates was turning to him. A beetroot colouring had suffused itself above the dark tan of his cheeks. He all but choked, all but hissed from the violence of his self-righteous indignation.

'Listen,' he said in a fast low monotone. 'Listen fucking good. I told you once that when I told you when to shit or who to fuck you would! And I told you if I said "No", you wouldn't shit or breathe until I said you could. That was when you were nothing and I could have decided right then and there that was what you were going to stay – nothing! But I didn't! Let me ask you one thing! Who do you think put you right up there with Redford and De Niro and Pacino and—'

'Why, you did, cunt-head.'

'And it's not too late for me to change all that – let me tell you that! I can do that right whenever I choose! Right now I'm telling

you you're going to bed with that US Senator because you on his
platform endorsing him entering the primaries is going—'

'To lose me the under-thirty vote.'

'Give you A-Class status!'

'I got me a status all of my own!'

'Now, listen, you jumped-up mother-fucking jerk! Listen good!
I've seen a dozen like you who got so big and then thought—'

'Lyndon, fuck-face, baby. Your voice doesn't go with your
classy English blazer and all these fancy perks. And you're wrong.
You know you're wrong. It's way past the time for you to even
begin considering throwing me out of your office. That'd mean
throwing me out of your income column. And there's no way
any more you're going to tell me who I'm getting into bed with –
literally or any other way. It's certainly not going to be an asshole
like your buddy when he needs you, the Junior Senator. A guy
who hires guys who get up from the table with summa cum maxi-
ma ostentation to give me time to see things his way while he calls
up the next guy on his shopping list – a guy like that I can do
without. You'd be surprised who I can do without, Lyndon,
sweetheart.'

Now Oates had blanched under his tan. His eyes flicked a look
about the white-linened elegance of the restaurant to see if their
exchange had carried. But they had both stayed on duty. They
had kept their vehemence low, their postures casual, as they'd
flashed their knives. Assured of that, Oates flushed the apprehension out of his eyes at once. As he turned them back on to Paul
Madison they transmitted a hostility shocking in its naked discarding of all pretence to PR veiling.

'If you don't take the trip to Washington, sonny,' he said with a
slow, even delivery, thick from hatred, 'I promise you I'll work
every angle at my disposal in the town to see you don't collect
that Oscar.'

He leaned forward to add yet greater emphasis to his ugly
intensity.

'And that means you won't,' he said. 'Come Oscar handout
time you know what you'll end up holding!'

A scene projected itself upon Paul Madison's inner vision –
Sean Flaherty's den: the Oscars lined up like so many holy senti-
nels. Or used as a doorstop. He recalled the old man's hawk-like
profile and knew that he would have rasped out nothing but
contempt for anyone who had felt the sharp, instant pang that
Oates's words had just caused him. He had at once been filled by
an awareness of potential loss as painful as any on-the-night-also-

ran reality could be. In that instant he had known from deep
down in his gut he wanted that award. He wanted it like he was
starving, it was food. But the old man . . . He wouldn't rasp contempt – he'd just disdain to speak. And yet . . . seven, he had.
What were they to him? Holy Grails? Cynical jokes at his own
cop-out expense? Doorstops?

'Just remember – when you thank the members of the Academy – if you ever do – you'll really be thanking me.'

Oates again. And he had timed his thrust well. Threading his
way back through the tables toward them was the formally
dressed, informally smiling, friend to all his fellow Americans.

'Hi, again,' James Wilson said, 'sorry to have kept you.'

'You didn't do that, Jimmy,' Oates said.

Wilson put on his best scrubbed behind the ears and bright-
eyed and bushy-tailed look.

'How'd the caucus go?' he said. 'Now don't tell me you didn't
talk some . . . Well, am I going to have the pleasure of seeing more
of you guys?'

Paul Madison opened his mouth to tell him to go piss up a rope.
As he opened his mouth that had seemed to be his intention. The
words, however, came out as somewhat different.

'Looks like hail-to-the-next-chief time,' he said. 'I've just never
been to Washington before.'

Relief a prime constituent, the wide beam of the newly successful dog-robber spread across Wilson's face. Still standing he
extended his hand. To his own disgust, Paul Madison grinned
easily and took it.

'Welcome aboard,' James Wilson said.

That evening, Paul Madison added two and a half pages to his
journal. Five paragraphs of his neat handwriting dealt with the
substance of his lunchtime meeting and his feelings about it and
his decision. The first of the last two paragraphs dealt with his
feelings for Lyndon Oates. The final paragraph sketched out a
contingency plan to be implemented 'one of these days' for how
Oates might be separated from his cojones. And not necessarily
painlessly.

chapter twenty-two

When you first talk about going out to Hollywood, your friends all advise you against it. 'You'll be swallowed up,' they say, 'vanish from sight. It's like invading China.' But you go anyway. And after a while, to your astonished delight, it seems like you've proved them wrong. You're talking with people, doing some kind of work. It seems you've established a bridgehead. Then one day you realise something. You're talking Chinese.

Attributed to Joseph Mankiewicz

Washington was tomorrow. He'd said 'yes' so why the fuck not go? It couldn't be worse than how he'd spent the last few weeks – exhausting himself doing nothing . . . Some nights, of course, he'd been on tours of super-star duty. There'd be the mandatory appearance to show he was a nice guy. Mandatory – except that he was getting picky now. He took in a couple of premieres because you did somewhere, incidentally, get to see the movies. He went out to a Can-Am meet at Riverside. Cars turned him on and it might just be good background material if it should happen that he'd go for Dino Silvestri's two-hundred-mile-an-hour soap-opera. But many, now, he ducked. Tacitly pretending that their deviation into a true show of feelings had not happened, he and Oates had settled for something between a Cold War and a Mexican Stand-off in their relationship. Over the phone their voices were never more resonant with good fellowship. But they had begun to keep their social distance. As it happened, distance to everyone was the name of the latest game plan anyway. As he waited for the Oscar to up his asking rate and the new tax year to make it marginally significant, he was playing harder and harder to get. Interviews of any kind were out. With Oates's approval he ducked a Merv Griffin, a USC Cinema seminar. As Oates had programmed for him back in the dim days beyond recall, exclusivity was now the name of his game. PR having set him within sight of the summit, he had made the final climb himself. God-like, he should be enveloped in Garboesque clouds of mystery. He was there. Exposure now could only devalue the currency.

At one rare coming together in what he liked to call a 'ways-and-means committee meeting' (though it had been at *The Bistro*), Oates had hinted it might do his image a service were he to get married.

'You know, Paul,' he'd said, 'to stop those foul-mouthed fucking rumours.'

'That are true about everyone else?'

'Well, exactly.'

But marriage meant a permanent woman about the house. Or a running financial sore. And he could detect a personal malice in Oates's voice. He had choked him off as brusquely as his status now allowed.

'Funny how inmates are always inviting people into the asylum.'

'Personally, Lyndon,' he'd added, 'guided as I am in everything by you, I'd have to say you're not doing me a favour. You've proved yourself weddings are for guys with pricks longer than their memories. Thanks but no thanks. I guess I just won't follow your several examples.'

Oates had once more reddened beneath his tan but this time decided to take it.

Which left Paul Madison, nights he was not out personally appearing or impersonally banging, at home and alone.

Classically, he would wander from room to room, not settling in any place, with any activity, for more than half-an-hour. Janice was out doing her own thing most every night. The rare occasions she condescended to stick around he found her presence unsettling. He had tried establishing her as a chess opponent. But bad as his game was, hers with its inane vacancy of any concentration, was worse. And she disturbed him. She would sit across from him with her shirt open to inspection and dark face as sullenly enigmatic as ever seeming to invite him to less cerebral games. She reminded him of an on-heat Mona Lisa. Well it continued to be a thought. The vision of having his mother's daughter fluttered somewhere in the back of his mind like a black moth. But it would not be cool. It would be asking for all kinds of trouble, of course, but, beyond that, when he finally got around to kicking the girl out he would not want to give that bitch in Tucson the satisfaction of knowing that he'd done so un-chic a thing as that.

He must kick her out pretty soon though. Her weekly 'get me in the movies' number was becoming a big bore.

When he heard the whine of her bike high-pitching its way

down and out of his drive-way, he increasingly felt relief. An alien element was out of the house and, if he were not about to call for a quick lay, he could resume his room-to-room roaming free from constraint. Yeah, right, it was time she left. He'd see to it first thing he was back from Washington.

It was now, sometimes, that he'd reach for the pile of script garbage that had passed through the outer filter rings to reach his desk. Always his feelings charted the same course: disbelief that anything so crass should be taken seriously by anyone from its writers on; amusement that it should be so, and at its ineptitude; a hot-sour indignation that anyone should expect him to begin to want to associate himself with such crap. He found himself asking the question he asked more and more: was that how they saw him? The sour answer had to be a 'yes.' In fact he was inseparable in people's minds from the junk heap of scripts – indivisible. Despite his brave boasts of a few months back that he was his own man, both he and the scripts were filed in the money men's minds as 'properties'. That said it all. And so had Sean Flaherty. It explained why intelligence, wit, originality, imagination were all rigorously excluded from the pile. They were carbon copies of lowest common denominators. They bore the same relationship to art as tract housing to architecture. They were commodities. Things. They lacked humanity. 'Property' with its impersonal weight was the perfect word to label them. But if it said it all for them, what was it saying for him?

Only one script began remotely to interest him. A political corruption thriller set in Finland. He mentioned it to Oates and Frankovich to learn that though 'personally we both find it very interesting' it was a mistake that it had landed on his desk. It was too 'parochial'. Even his name would scarcely make it bankable . . .

Skipping pages, he never completed the reading of a single other script. He would toss them aside, reach for the remote control to the nearest TV. In mid-evening that would last him maybe twenty minutes. Then the sense of modular, pre-digested, off-the-shelf plots or the laid-on laughs would get to him. He'd stroll listlessly to his altar-bar and then, glass in his hand, on to his study. He was trying George Eliot, now. Slowly. The weight of words strained him and in the constant theme of people needing to find themselves within an occupation he found something as directly disquieting as the sight of his half-sister with her shirt undone across from him or, lithe and brown, stretched out naked sunning on the diving board.

Daniel Deronda was his latest bow to quality. But, a few pages at a time, he kept at it with a self-conscious sense of duty. It was good, he knew: was he? was the question it raised. Well who the fuck cared? For the thirtieth time he laid it aside. He yawned. For the lightest diversion, for something to do, he unthinkingly punched up the cameras on the monitor to his security TV system. Like riffled postcards the grey pictures flipped by. But then, abruptly, no longer feeling half asleep, he was sitting forward in his chair. He back-tracked in sequence. Yes! The camera covering his front lawns was showing something moving. It was dusk outside. The image was not clear. But something blurred yet not quite shapeless was mysteriously undulating amongst the trees out there. The faint, thin contrastless picture made whatever it was a ghost.

He reached into the desk and took out a small Walther pistol. He loaded it. He passed through the house and out into his grounds. Cautiously, he began to cross the lawn.

A dozen paces taken and he had relaxed. He pocketed the gun. The camera had not lied. It was a ghost. Slowly pirouetting in the darkening air, oblivious of him, perhaps of everything in present time, was Stella Lang. She was crooning huskily, he could just detect some sad little tune from her bright times way back. He stood in silence watching her.

Not all magic had gone from her. No doubt to hide her booze-fed weight, she was wearing a long, light-coloured kaftan. As she turned, it swirled fully, solemnly, visual echo of a hundred ball-gowns, a dozen movies almost lost to memory. More than once she tottered as her footing all but went, yet in the stylised grace of a sudden, sweeping, straightening of her arm, the arching backward of her neck, a sudden effortless change of direction, he saw the shadow of her legendary elegance. Was it that which held him spell-bound? Or the pathos? The sad sense of the forever-lost vainly trying to find itself as the darkness settled nearer on an air feeling its first chill. The attempt, sweet and gentle somehow, for all the ridiculousness inherent in the too-fat body seeking for its gilded youth, was doomed to failure. And yet – in that turn now, that quickly adroit glide between two trees, there lurked, if only for a second, the hint of an impression that time could after all be tricked and early summer made to come again.

The moon, he realised, had appeared and stars were out. He did not think they mocked. But now, the steps, the rhythm were altering. She was no longer swaying on the lost dream of a solo but returning to the arms of the partner – it had to be Astaire –

who had set her floating off upon her arabesque. Now she was advancing back on him to resume the perfect pairing of their talents, meeting of their steps. Advancing on a tree.

'Hello, my lost and one true love, my silent lovely hero, how about taking—'

That was too embarrassing. Too cruel. He stepped forward into her line of vision and cut her soliloquy short. No longer a dancer but a person surprised, she swayed uncertainly. He had a sense of her eyes struggling to focus.

'Hi,' she said. 'Just re-visiting the scene of the crime!'

'Hi.' Then inanely but he could think of nothing else. 'How'd you get in?'

As if puzzled to know herself, she seemed to ponder the question gravely.

'A girl let me in,' she said at last. 'A girl on a bike. I was outside looking in and she asked me what I was doing and I said I was a friend of yours. I hope you don't mind.'

'Your coming in? No—'

'My saying I was a friend.'

Her voice was thick about the tongue this time as well as from the throat.

'Why should I mind what's true,' he had the style to say. Something relaxed in her and he stepped in closer to her. It was an error. The dim light did not aid her at such short a distance and the blotches, the paunches of her face were uncomfortably visible. The magic evaporated instantly. And yet . . . it was as if a secondary, a genuine ghost was waiting to step out of her late-show past and, lovely, stand looking over her shoulder.

'I told her my name,' she said. 'But that was a mistake. She didn't recognise it.'

'She's just a kid.'

'Another little ego bruise nevertheless, kind sir . . . You're cradle-snatching somewhat, are you not, these days? Or if it's not too indelicate, perhaps I should say cradle-snatch-snatching.'

'She's my sister.'

'La de da dee da . . . I'll believe you, gallant sir, but millions wouldn't . . . This used to be my house.'

'Yes, I know. I bought it from you, remember.'

'Yes. I know. It had to be done. You were better than most. I wandered around, finally found, it had to be you. To coin a phrase.'

'A song. Would you like to come inside and take—'

'No!' Suddenly her voice was very firm.

'I don't think I could bear that,' she went on. 'I'll still keep on getting back in by the memory door. I dream about my time here all the time. Those are my good dreams. My good dreams are always about here . . . If I saw the inside now, all changed you know, it would make my poor dreaming so sad and confused.'

'I haven't changed it so much.'

'Inside, it's the little things. The fruit bowl where you used to keep your car keys . . . But I would thank you for not altering the outside.'

'It's pretty dark. How can you be sure I—'

'I've been by here many times. It's a soft spot that's turned into a bruise. I can't stop fingering it.' She shivered. The sub-tropical night had strode in with its usual lack of subtlety.

'Hey, you're cold. Let me go get you something.'

She shook her head.

'No,' she said, 'I must be going now. I have a car still.'

'You should've called – the times you were here before.'

'Oh – I could see. Even after you turned it into Stalag Hollywood, I could still see . . . the police never mention me to you?'

'No.'

'Ah. They have longer memories . . . I wanted to come in, this time, though 'specially, so I was glad when she came out. Hey, oh my! I hope I wasn't making a fool of myself just then when you were watching! How long did—'

'You were never lovelier,' he said.

'Oh yes I was, smart mouth. And more sober too.'

'What's so special about tonight?'

'I'm going away.'

'Oh? Not for good, I hope.'

'I don't know. I'm going way back East to a place. It's a place, you know, where they dry you out. Upstate New York. They have a distinguished list of past successes I have been most faithfully assured. Half those other famous, once-famous lushes the papers like to drool over. Politicos . . .'

'What do I say now?' he said.

'What is to say? . . . I've tried before. Not there. Other places. I couldn't make it stick. They're supposed to be better. I told myself I had to try it one more time. One last stand before the slashed wrists finale. I sold my last few oil shares and what-all. So, California here I go.'

She shivered. Instinctively he knew this time it was not the night.

'I saw your picture,' she went on. 'About the jazz man. It was okay. But it wasn't real. This will be worse because it will be real . . . It's going to be terrible. I don't know if I'll be able to hack it. I may not. I may not be back. That's why I wanted to see the house again. For a last time, maybe. You never know.'

Her words had been coming slower and slower as the prospect before her took on substance in her mind. On his part he was short of words.

'You're not working on anything now, are you?' she said.

So she still kept up.

'No,' he said. 'I guess I've got some problems too.'

'You think you have problems!'

'Well . . . from inside here. Everything they put my way seems crap . . . I guess I'd rather spend my time screwing, getting a little high—'

'Don't!' she said. There was urgency, fear for him in her voice.

'And beat up on girls,' he said.

There! He had said it. It had just come out. Hiding their expressions from each other, the darkness had created a dangerous intimacy between them and created in her a confidante. He could have bitten off his tongue. And yet . . . if anybody he respected had to know, it was she he would have chosen.

'Are you shrinking about it?' she asked. Her voice seemed a lot sharper, a lot less dreamy, now. Was that so? Or was it just his alarm that he had dropped his guard listening on a different frequency? He shook his head, then wondered if she'd made that out.

'I don't want an exorcist,' he said. 'I run me. Nobody else.'

She said nothing but he seemed to hear her snort. Even while he had a sense of skirting the edge of sheer and fearful revelations he must step back from, he detected she was staying silent as a grown-up before a pressing child. Older, sadder, maybe wiser, she was, he realised, holding her peace because she knew no words would serve to anticipate what he would learn the longer, harder way. So who was right?

She had turned. Her back three-quarters to him she was staring in that direction where a gap in the trees and hedge gave a glimpse of the lights of Los Angeles spread out like paste jewels on a velvet less than black. It was the orange sodium-light scuzz gathering in the sky above, that conveyed, perhaps, the irredeemable cheapness.

'You ever hear Joe Mankiewicz's story about Chinatown?' she asked.

'Where you end up talking Chinese?' he said. 'Sure. Who hasn't?'

'It's true, goddamit, truer than Hades. Someone tells you "Personally I think you're great" and right away you dig the translation: the whole town thinks you stink. Only . . .'

'Only?'

She turned to him. And now he would have sworn there was beseechment in her voice and the set of her stance.

'Only once you're in,' she said, 'a native, you have to make your justification from inside. Don't you? I should have thought so. I guess after a while I didn't . . .'

He waited to see where she was going.

'A guy made a figure of me once,' she went on. 'What do you call those cross things they build up all the clay around?'

'Er . . . er . . . oh, I—'

'Well you know what I mean?'

'Yes. Sure.'

'Well work's like one of those. A job. Armature! That's the word! Armature . . . Work's an armature. Unless you've got something very special in your head, you need work to hold your life together. And that's the truth – believe me.'

'Even when the work is crap?'

'Maybe particularly so, then . . . I used to have a stand-in. A regular. Her name was Connie. My build, my colouring, of course, but a lot older. Vaudeville, bands, she'd been in show-biz all her life following the dream. Never made it. I was the nearest she got. When she first started working for me I nearly got her canned to tell you the truth. She was too beat-up, too tacky. Too much like a death's head at the feast saying "one day you too chum".'

She broke off, laughed sourly.

'Guess I was right at that,' she said, 'wherever she is now, I swear to God she's in better shape than I am . . . I used to look at her and think "Ugh!" Ugly, over the hill, a piece of furniture for the cameraman to order around, why does she do it? What's in it for her?'

'Needed the bread, I guess.'

'That was irrelevant. She wasn't dumb. She could've earned as much, more, in a less grinding job. A regular job. Instead – endless hours, the heat from all the lights I mustn't be allowed to wilt under, the seven o'clock morning studio calls. When I came back to the set, she'd tell me to the half-inch where I had to stand. She'd tell me what my eye-line was. Between takes she'd have a chair there for me at the first sign of delay. Coffee, cigarettes – she'd get them. Never bother me for change . . . Gradually I saw what she was doing and I stopped despising her. She was winning something back from a no-count life by just being a pro. It was all she had. And therefore it was a tremendous victory. Then I saw something else. I saw that underneath the ranch minks and the emeralds I was just the same as her. That's when I tried getting out. Getting married, getting out. That didn't work, I came back. But I didn't have her class. I couldn't keep on trucking when to keep on trucking is the only reason there is for doing it.'

Her voice came to him disembodied. He could scarcely see her now. As if realising it, she had drawn close and taken his hand.

'Don't be like me,' she said. She let his hand go.

'Sorry to turn preacher of the year,' she said. 'I'd better go.'

'Wait—'

Now he took her hand.

'Can I ask you a favour?' he said.

'Me? Well you can always ask.'

'For this place you're going. Can I wish you good luck? Could I kiss you?'

He felt the hand grow tense, then she had removed it from his again.

'I need all the luck and good wishes going,' she said. 'Thanks. But – no. No kiss. Kiss the memory of me on the late-show if you want to but don't let what I've turned into in real life spoil the effect.'

'Well . . . okay. You want to give me the address of this place you're going.'

He was just able to discern another shake of the head.

'I guess not. It's me and them, ace. Show-down time for one.'

Silence hung between them with the darkness.

'I'd better go,' she said.

'I'll walk you to your car.'

'No. Thanks – but I'll go alone. I'll start the treatment as of right now. And I'd like to just pretend it's still my place I'm leaving from.'

'Sure,' he said. Her shape began to drift away.

He waited a beat to give his last words as much off-beat weight as his timing could impart.

'Ya'll come back and see us now some time,' he said.

Perhaps the departing ghost hovered still for a few beats of its heart. Then its voice came back.

'I can't promise. I'd be happy to,' it said.

A little unevenly, it continued to glide away. Then, like all ghosts, it had vanished.

He was left alone. And shivering. The cold in the air was getting to him too. He gave the lights below a parting look as he prepared to go inside. The sodium glare was stronger now, the halo of some pervasive disease. Overhead the stars were thick and brilliant in a night sky free of clouds. For a second he was tempted to read in their cold eyes the future of all lives.

Fuck it, he then thought, they're dead: what do they know?

Isolated by black incalculable emptinesses they were no wiser, no surer of their destiny than people. And less bored. At a loss, irresolute as to what to do next, he hesitated. The empty house was uninviting. He began to stroll. After a few paces he halted again. To walk around his property was to head in no direction. He shivered again and the chill made up his mind. The house won by default. He turned about to walk back up to it. It was because there were no clouds that the night had turned cold so rapidly.

chapter twenty-three

Just remember that once the toothpaste is out of the tube, it's going to be very tough to get it back in.

H. R. Haldeman

It had not just been a conversational gambit. He had been speaking the truth when he had told James Wilson that he had never been to Washington. What he had so far seen of it, he didn't like. It had still been daylight when his flight had touched down at National. Seen from the air the capital had seemed clean, green, gracious. Not even Wilson's whiz-kid presence overseeing his exit to the Lincoln limousine could quite dissipate that initial impression . . . as seen from seat 1A in the first-class cabin.

'It's great having you on our bench,' Wilson had said.

Paul Madison had smiled with becoming modesty and settled back to wonder just who was picking up the tab for this chauffered leather armchair that motored with the sound of falling leaves.

They had crossed the Potomac and the nearing city had still conveyed a civilised spaciousness. But the closer guided tour of inspection that Wilson was now politic enough to suggest speedily completed what his college-try-but-the-game-can-be-fixed personality had begun.

The official heart of Washington, Paul Madison decided, lacked a human scale. The too-broad avenues were structured for the convenience of automobiles and not pedestrians. The great slabs of buildings, for all their thousands of windows, seemed blind and inward facing, uncaring. The older, pseudo-classical buildings seemed phoney. Monolithic as they appeared their porticos and pediments had in reality been made of plaster, two by-fours, by the studio workmen. They were only two dimensional and nobody ever went behind their indifferent façades to work. Then the limousine would turn a corner and he could see there, at the FBI building, for example, that, to a point, he had been mistaken. The film-set did have depth. The question now became

– what sort of people went inside to work? Did they leave their feelings behind wherever they lived and shopped? Well, okay, it was the nation's City Hall, so what did you expect? Something better than a block-house Palm Springs, maybe.

'That's the Senate Office Building across there,' Wilson was saying. 'Can't you just feel the dynamism, though! The sense of power just comes right out and grabs you.'

'I gues that in LA we try to be a little more oblique,' Paul Madison said. 'Are we heading for the hotel this way?'

'Sure,' James Wilson had said. 'Coming right up.'

The paste-on smile had vanished. He had turned his head away as if anticipating more up-coming points of interest. But Paul Madison had seen the self-doubting chagrin come into his eyes and knew the turn away had been to hide vexation at so naïve a tipping of his hand.

They had reserved him a suite at the Savoy Carlton. The manager himself had come forward to greet him personally, all dapperly moustached.

'Welcome to Washington, Mr Madison,' he said, 'it's a privilege to have you staying with us.'

He had gone along with it. The creep had to earn a living. But the suite had come as a relief – or would have had it not come as more of a surprise.

It was routinely enormous and probably the usual and ubiquitous example of contemporary vinyl at its level best but it was hard to tell. It looked at first glance more of a collision between a fruit market and a liquor store. Champagne was on ice, compliments of the hotel. Fruit of most varieties was vastly basketed, compliments of the hotel. The near commercial-size bar was stocked like the Waldorf Astoria's and a dozen Cos d'Estournel '66 were racked nearby, the dust upon them still in the main ostentatiously intact.

'Compliments of the Senator,' Wilson redundantly confirmed. 'As I said, he's real sorry not to have been able to meet you personally but you probably know how it is on these Sub-Comimttee go-looksees.'

'Intimately.'

'I do know he's most anxious to have breakfast with you tomorrow morning and get to know you then. If that'll be possible for you . . .'

'Oh. Oh sure. Fine.'

'You'll find the Senator's formal invitation in with his personal letter to you there on the table. I'll come by in the morning and take you on down.'

'Great.'

For the second time that late afternoon, Wilson was unable to sustain his eager-beaver eyeball-to-eyeball contact. In his grey flannel suit with double-breasted vest he should have been able to win friends and influence people for ever. But for an uneasy, curiously embarrassing moment he had forgotten his lines. Then some memory of the day or week before must have prompted him.

'Er, I, er, didn't make any arrangements for this evening because I figured you might, well, be a little tuckered out from the flight in—'

Paul Madison recognised he was back in Chinatown. The translation was: each of us loathes the other and speaking for myself I'd much rather spend the night as far from you as possible.

'—on the other hand I have kept the evening open if you feel you'd like to take in a little night life. *The Empress*—'

'Well that's very thoughtful of you, Jimmy, and much appreciated. I guess I am—'

'On the other hand and again, if a change of pace and, er, maybe, gender might hit the spot – well, just say the word and I guess we could rustle up something in that direction too.'

The superficial eyes had tightened to the mean focus of somebody who feels sure that everyone has his price and he's just establishing yours. Part of Paul Madison hated giving the little rat-fucker the satisfaction, but he had finally gotten to some sort of point.

'Please don't misunderstand my meaning,' he was saying now in some alarm, 'I was—'

'Why don't you just send her up,' he said. 'Around eight.'

Wilson had nodded. Then grinned. He had not bothered to conceal his delight. He had been further vindicated in his cheap evaluation of his fellows. He's second-rate, Paul Madison had thought, he lets far too much of it hang out to make it to the top. He's a bad advertisement for his boss's judgement . . .

The girl had arrived in due course. Wilson had not read him too well. She was not his type. She was blonde and lush in an educated cocktail waitress sort of way. A Washington way, he decided, set by jolly Jack. But she had all the usual equipment and he had made use of it. In working fact the whole thing had seemed like one time too many pretty early on and he had thought for a moment of rolling off and paying her to go home. Then a sense of his image as a star had whispered in his ear. Coitus interruptus is bad news PR-wise for a superstar. He had persisted until convinced her sharp cry and soft moans were genuine.

The morning after he had met the Senator in the Mayflower coffee-shop. Newspaper photographs and television clips had alerted him not to expect too much from the living flesh but an eight a.m. start to the day made clear why the would-be Governor needed all the charisma support going. He was not Henry Fonda. He was Al Capone. Three-quarter scale. Even at that crack-of doom hour he seemed to have five o'clock shadow. One glance at his bovine thrust of fleshy features, his shifty eyes and it was not a case of not wanting to buy a used car from him; it was not wanting to sell him yours. They had shaken hands, hail fellowed and well met each other. As he had diminished his short stack with the unhesitating perpetual jaw-motion of a steel-worker, the Senator had mouthed platitudes about his hopes for the Golden State and the people of America that even a Lyndon Oates must have blanched at. Tom Leonard had provided some adequate feed lines for the few isolated moments when the Senator flagged or bit off a little more than he could comfortably chew.

They had adjourned to a room especially taken for the purpose of a ways-and-means briefing where, all the better to be propped up, the Senator had been joined straight from the airport by a cardinal from San Francisco and an athlete from Oakland. Actor, prelate and ball-player all had in this the identical, smiling support role. They were to make themselves visible at the Senator's right hand during the formal announcement of his candidacy at a brief Press Conference scheduled for mid-morning as thus being assured of coast-to-coast coverage that evening. They themselves that evening were to participate in a grand banquet and amid the whooping and hollering say a few words encapsulating the unshakeable rationale of their allegiance. James Wilson had these to hand. Paul Madison's four paragraphs touched on the importance to California of its movie economy as if the profits actually ended up there. They also spoke of a lengthy past acquaintanceship marked by mutual respect. But what the fuck?

In one of the hotel's smaller conference rooms before a somewhat meagre conglomeration of newsmen and unaffiliated cameras – the Senator seemed not to rate the first team – he had smiled and been a villain. The Senator, on camera, had presented a slicker image with some intimations of intelligence. But there had still been the broadest generalisations, the most pious homilies and in their midst the nakedness of his stereotype ego had been painful to behold. There had been one sticky moment for Paul Madison. A sharp-jawed reporter had asked permission to address him directly and then without waiting to be vouchsafed an answer slipped in the obvious question.

'Mr Madison,' he had asked, 'why do you consider it should be necessary for a movie star such as yourself to lend the Senator public support?'

James Wilson had been scrambling to his feet and clearing his throat but knowing that to have interference so blatantly run for him would blow the whole credibility game in the first quarter, Paul Madison had risen to anticipate him.

'I don't consider it at all necessary,' he had said, 'I consider it desirable. I happen to be that rare thing, a native-born Los Angelino. I also happen to work in the movie industry. With apologies to the States of New York and New Mexico, I've come to regard California as still the centre of our film and television industries, still, in fact, the world's. Historically it has always been so and I want to see it kept so for the future. Let's not forget that Hollywood represents a tremendous forum for free public debate – direct or oblique. I know the Senator is keenly aware of this and as I support this particular stance of his – which is obviously, I admit, in my own interest – so I support his views on the wider issues confronting California and America today.'

In a pig's fucking eye, he thought, as he sat down, up yours Senator for making me do that to myself. Up mine. He felt furious. Yet there was a strange satisfaction not in Wilson's quick smile of thanks as he scrambled up again, but in the slower smile, a pure distillation of cynically disbelieving admiration, which spread across the reporter's face as he dutifully made a note and the odd flash-bulb popped.

Wilson headed off any chance of a free-for-all with a brief wind-up announcement and the news that refreshments had been provided in the adjacent room: that drinks were on the house.

'Nice kick-off return,' he said to Paul Madison over the first round.

'Jimmy, I guess I've got a headache. Not used to the cameras and lights, I guess. I think I'm going to duck lunch, if you don't mind and take five in my room.'

'Oh. Well, sure. Sure thing. You'll be okay for tonight, though, won't you? I mean—'

'Oh, sure. No problem. Oh – and Jimmy, see if she's not working now. Would you do that for me?'

A room-service club sandwich and several Jack Daniels later

he lay staring moodily up at the pebble-dash ceiling of the suite's bedroom. Nobody as yet was on top of him. He had circled the television dial in seconds and rejected everything in sight. From where he was lying the evening's dinner seemed like the far side of eternity. He would have liked to sleep but he knew that at that hour he didn't have sleep in him. Only ill-will. It irked him that a too-predictable response had made him ask Wilson to set him up with a girl who'd bore him a second time. Well, it would get him through the afternoon a mite less demandingly than a tramp around the Smithsonian.

The door-buzzer sounded. Zero hour. He swung himself off the bed and walked the quarter mile through the lounge area to open the door. It was not the girl. It was a middle-aged woman, her face flushed, who had mistaken the room.

'I – er . . . can I help you?' he said warily. Maybe she wasn't mistaken but some kind of screwball fan.

'I have to talk with you,' she said. 'Are you alone?'

'As it happens—'

But in a sweep of cheap melodrama she had somehow pushed by him to walk to the centre of the room. He caught her breath as she went past and he realised the hectic look to her face and about her manner had as much to do with liquor as embarrassment. He closed the door. As he turned back into the room she was turning to face him.

'We weren't introduced this morning,' she said, 'but I'm Mrs Burton Mills.'

Before she got the name out his mind had got there first. She was one of those partners who resembling their spouses make you believe that marriages are not made in heaven but by human egos rushing narcissistically into the arms of their own mirror image. Before she had reached the proper name he recognised her as the Senator's wife.

'How do you do?' he said.

'I know who you are, of course,' she said. 'It's all part of their politicking we weren't allowed to meet this morning. I wasn't allowed to meet you.'

Resembling the Senator, she was an ugly woman. She had the same downward, forward thrust of features that projected a bulky emphasis about her pouchy cheeks, her weighty jaw. She had never been pretty. She just might have once been sexy. Even allowing for a certain girdling, her figure still had a straight-backed, full-breasted trimness beneath the grey tailored, somewhat rumpled suit she wore.

'Sorry?' he said. 'I guess I didn't quite get that.'

'They try to keep me out of it all. They don't want to risk me making waves or ruining his image.'

Her left hand went up to brush abstractedly at hair of the same colour, the same order of disarray, as her suit. Like it, she seemed in need of valet service. He wondered what the minimum time allowable before he could decently sling her out.

'Well, we've met now,' he said. 'And it's nice of you—'

'Oh forget all that,' she said.

She looked at him.

'My husband's a complete son of a bitch,' she said. 'The completest. The reason they don't like me around is because I'm apt to forget my party manners – ha! – and tell people. Also to get drunk.'

She gestured toward the shooting gallery of a bar.

'Having done one,' she said, 'mind if I continue about the second.'

'What would you like?'

'To help myself – if that's okay by you.'

'Sure.'

Scotch was her poison. He watched as she poured enough into her glass to keep her flush stoked for the rest of the day.

'You can pour me a Jack Daniels,' he said. 'Your measure's making me thirsty.'

'It's his, isn't it?' she said. 'His lush fund. No point in being cheese-paring.'

She poured as generous a drink for him. Something caught her eye.

'Oh,' she said, 'you haven't opened his letter to you. Well that, I'd have to say, suggests you are a man possessing a certain style. a certain sense of taste.'

'So he's a louse and I'm not. Did you just come up here to get a few proxy licks in?'

'No.'

She walked over to him and handed him his drink. He could see that his first impression of fluster had been correct. Any poise the business at the bar had given her was possessed very precariously.

'I— er—'

'Cheers.'

'Cheers. I'd better be quick, I guess. That little skunk of a gofer is probably tearing the place down right at this moment looking for me.'

'Wilson?'

'Yes.'

'Well I'll drink to that – that he's a skunk. Not such an efficient one.'

'All part and parcel . . . Mr Madison, I came up here to ask you not to appear at this dinner thing tonight. In fact, not to support my husband at all. Not politically not—'

'Why the hell should you ask this?'

'Because of what he is. A . . . a shit. A lying, deceiving, ambitious, self-seeking—'

'Hey! Hold it! You're his wife!'

'My God don't I know that!'

'Then why should you of all people – even if—'

'Because I've had enough! Because I'm getting out from under his slimy presence like I should've done twenty-five years ago!'

'Aren't you kind of over-reacting?'

'No! Well, yes – but only because I'm late reacting at all . . . Mr Madison, may I ask you – why did you come up here today to do this thing?'

To clinch an Oscar? To show the six producers able to afford him he represented a blue-chip investment? To get laid in another town? He sipped at his whisky and discovered that he hadn't really wanted it. There was an edge to it that seemed to set his mind awry and for a moment the room was less than real and it was all a dream, an improv. in some drama class. But the woman – the wife – was real enough. Head set to one side as she waited for an answer there was a kind of grotesque earnestness about her that threatened to flare up at any second into full bore hysteria, collapse into a welter of tears for a lost and wasted past.

'I don't really know,' he said.

She seized on that.

'You can't have any real commitment!' she said.

'Well now – I couldn't honestly say I have.'

'Who could! What is it? Some kind of a deal? If you give him a helping hand on his way up now, he'll return the favour in due course, you bet?'

'Well, I wouldn't put it—'

'Let me tell you something about that son of a bitch. Right now this very minute he's got money in the Bahamas put there for him by the Arabs to represent their interests against the Israeli Mafia. Three guesses who gave him the money he's got in Switzerland to see the Arabs get the short straw in the Middle

East. Tobacco, oil, banking – so many interests look after him for looking after them he draws his Washington salary in dimes for the parking meters! I mean these are the sort of things I know. What he's done in the way of bugging, smearing – all the Watergate spectrum – I just can't begin to speculate. But he has. I don't care but I wouldn't be at all surprised if he had this room bugged right now. When the San Bernardino County Sheriff—'

'Mrs Mills, if this is the way you feel, why don't you just up and say so? Or up and leave him? Why?'

'Oh, don't worry, I'm twenty years too late but I'm going to do exactly that. And soon. In the one way that . . .'

Her voice trailed away.

'Why me?'

She hesitated. The larger than life indignation slowly went as she looked at him and she had ceased to seem ridiculous. She became forlorn and vulnerable. Her eyes had lost the sharp focus of anger. She was looking in his direction but staring across the prospect of twenty barren years and estimating how her used-up time might otherwise have run.

'You're very handsome,' she said irrelevantly and, realising the import, got herself in gear again and steered towards correction and his question.

'Partly because you're a big star,' she said. 'Just because you're pretty, people will vote for him to make themselves feel close to you. People – they're such fools. I tried to head you off at the pass this morning before the announcement but – that's the other thing. I'm walking out on him today, I swear. But he and that skunk of his have got some of the Press Corps nicely tamed, thank you – they've got the word around. I'm kind of a foolish hysterical old bat, don't you just know. You don't pay much attention to what she says, fellas. And you'll print even less if you want to do the decent thing . . .'

A strangely tense tremor passed across her face, and, quite visibly, she gulped.

'I do a pretty good job,' she said, 'of helping him out on that one. Making it all seem very reasonable. "Oh, she's a juicer, too, you know, but you've got to be kind, fellas, understanding, because of her son." '

Again the wincing up of that plain face.

'My elder boy was killed in Viet Nam,' she said. 'He'd be maybe a little older than you. His daddy thought it would catch a lot of votes for a Congressman if he was seen to be a patriot who'd risk the thing that he held dearest! Jesus! He hadn't talked to Jeff since the boy went off to school.

'And David – the other one – how many special schools and institutions do you think that he's been to, trying to come to terms with a brother whom he worshipped being fried to death and a father who doesn't know what colour his eyes are!'

He thought she was going to cry but she didn't.

'Oh, Jesus . . .' she said. 'I'll go.'

But he had decided that he liked her.

'No, wait,' he said. 'I'll get you another drink.'

He took the nearly empty glass from her shaking hand and went to the bar. He looked for the Chivas Regal.

'I guess I never took to him way back,' he said, 'when he was a Congressman and trying to stick it to the grape-pickers.'

He finished pouring and took the drink back over. Her head had come up at his words and a questioning sort of hope was trying to establish itself in her eyes.

'I didn't like him this morning either,' he said. 'I guess I wish you had got to me. It's all kind of a bore – right?'

Her disbelief began to evaporate.

'I'm not asking you for a big heroic gesture,' she said, 'a whadycallit – messenger speech. Just don't show up.'

He smiled. The heroic speech had flicked the back of his mind: the respectful applause as he stood up, the outraged, incredulous silence as he compared the circus of the Senator's campaign to a Hollywood front office . . .

'I guess that would be overplaying the scene a little too much for my style,' he said.

'But you won't show up?' The question expected an affirmative reply.

He paused. Another idea had flicked his mind. It was outrageous. Therefore he must do it.

'The Senator does deals, right?' he said.

'Does he ever.'

'I'll do a deal with you.'

Wariness qualified the optimism she had been allowing to show on that heavy face.

'How old are you?' he asked sharply.

'Forty nine. A genuine forty-nine.'

'How many women of forty-nine do you know who have spent an afternoon in bed with the world's number three box-office attraction?'

She drew in a deep breath, and he saw that, though it was from shock, it was also to help her believe that she had not misheard this staggeringly pleasurable, totally unlooked for offer.

'Scratch my back, I'll scratch yours,' he said.

The door buzzer went.

'We'll ignore that, shall we?' he said smiling.

Wide-eyed, a little afraid now, she nodded.

He had only brought with him a fold-over two-suiter and he packed it now and carried it to the elevator himself. As the first floor doors opened he saw that he was out of luck. The first figure the slide-back of the doors revealed was Senator Mills. He was the centre of an admiring crowd of blue-rinsed daughters of America. Buttons shone whitely on their collars and lapels to make them appear like oversized and so curiously irresponsible school-children. Whoever they were they carried enough clout for Wilson the rat-fucker to have laid on three or four photographers to immortalise their fervid adoration of the Senator. Paul Madison's first thought was that he had timed it badly. He stayed without moving in the elevator. Then the dark angel of his psyche gained the upper hand. He stepped boldly out in full view.

Wilson was lurking on the fringes of the happy throng just out of the cameras' fields of view. He frowned with a justified apprehension as he saw the well-filled over-nighter in Paul Madison's grip. But smiling reassuringly and throwing him a quick circle of his thumb and index finger, Paul Madison set down the case. Quickly, to a moment of silence, then of squeaky 'oohs' and 'ahhs' he stepped into the throng of palpitating matrons and to the Senator's side.

Mills knew a good thing when he saw it coming on down his pike.

'Ladies,' he said heartily. 'I'd like you to meet a good friend of mine in whose company I'm sure you'd have much rather spent the last hour than my humble own. But I hope I'm at least a good enough politician to know when I'm being outgunned at the box office so I can take a back seat gracefully. What do you say, Paul?'

Paul Madison took Senator Mills' hand and shook it enthusiastically. He smiled at his proximity to the corridors of senatorial power. Still smiling he leaned forward and seemed to share a private joke in the Senator's ear.

'I say you suck, Senator,' he was saying. 'And your wife sucks too. I know. I've just had two hours of her upstairs in my room. You shouldn't neglect her so. She gets real juicy once you've primed her pump.'

He continued to smile as, all around, the flash-bulbs continued popping.

It was past midnight. He was in some bar. He had bailed the Porsche out of parking hock at LAX and driven just long enough to get away from the ersatz overnighter traps along Century. He put on shades and switched off and went unrecognised. It was a good place to drink – small, dark, a comfortably muted gleam coming from off the long narrow counter, a darkly illuminated Schlitz feature. It was more empty than full and the barman did not try to talk. A radio was turned to a station playing good small-hours-of-the-morning jazz, slow and bluesy and from far enough back to make you think of sweetly-sad memories however old you were.

He sat and listened and tried to think what memories he had to think of.

A deeply lilting saxophone was faded down to nothing far too abruptly. A voice cut in.

'We've just received this news flash. On the same day that Senator Burton Mills declared his intention of running for the Governorship of California, police answering a call from neighbours went tonight to his Washington apartment. Their grim finding was the body of the Senator's wife, Mrs Diane Mills. Cause of death was a head wound from a small calibre hand-gun and was described as certainly instantaneous. A gun was found close to the body and what is believed is a suicide note. A police spokesman is quoted as saying that as of this moment in time other parties are not being sought in connection with the death. At the time of the slaying Senator Mills was attending a Washington function.'

Just that. The tenor sax resumed a bar after its crude interruption. It played a lament now and he had no trouble wondering what to think about.

He waved his hand.

'Yes, sir. Same again?'

'No. Make it a Chivas Regal. A large one.'

It was past three a.m. With the measured deliberation of the half-drunk, he wound the Porsche up Laurel Canyon towards Mulholland. The bends were coming faster than the speed of the car seemed to warrant but a distant part of his mind steered him through them safely enough.

Hanging in the rest of his mind were the ugly close-up features of the last woman he had made love to. Flushed for reasons other than alcohol, they floated suspended on the huge screen of some darkened movie-house, an image that refused to fade to black. Had it been his affection or his condescension that had made her cry in his arms and so bring something softer to that slant of stiffened face? He would never know. Had it been knowledge of what she had predetermined for herself that made her cry? Or had his gesture, his offer to transport her back across those two decades of desert for one afternoon, had that given her the final push over the edge? In clichés, in the predictable after-the-act talk of any woman, she had murmured it had never been like that. Had he helped her go out on a high? She had said she was going to, if he had had the ears to hear. Or had the confirmation in his bed of what she must thereafter be deprived of, reinforced her death-wish? He would never know that either. Yet if she had not died that self-same day he would not have asked these questions. He would not have asked these questions because he would not have given her a second thought.

The growling change-down of the engine alerted him that he was home. The barrier rose in electronic obedience to his approach. He swept up his curve of driveway. And stopped. His house was a blaze of window-lights. Even as he watched in sobering-up shock a gaunt silhouette flitted in some shadow-play across a blind.

He dowsed the car's headlights and inched it steadily forward. He took out from the glove compartment the hand-gun he was licensed to carry. Careful in anticipation, he locked the car. On foot he approached the house.

He had his key. But the front door seemed too obvious. Tibor's annexe was pitch dark. The rear door might be unlocked or, better, the french windows to his study. Staying wide of the luminous up-thrust of blue light from the pool he moved stealthily towards the back of the house. Adrenalin was beginning to revive the former athlete in him. If he was breathing through his mouth for silence and speed, if there was a film of excited sweat breaking from his skin, it was to the high-powered good. His reflexes were psyching themselves up to hair-trigger touch. In mid-stride he stopped. The cool night breeze, chilling the sweat across his back, had also sent something rippling out from concealment toward the centre of the pool. Fear ghosted across the back of his neck. But no. Far too small. Even to be a child. It was no more than a discarded pair of denim cut-downs. He could move on. Silently, he made the french windows.

They were open. And the lights inside were on. He sidled alongside the wall like a B-picture hero. He risked a look in. The study was empty. Of people. But not of a despoilment bringing the pulse of a red fury to his temples.

Urine reeked in his nostrils and something solidly worse. Somebody had used the room as an untrained animal would. There had been a fight of some kind or a thieves' hunt. Spines broken, pages ripped and lying singly in awry sheaves, his books had been hurled to the four corners of the room. His grip tightened on the gun as he took in the vandalism. The violation of the one corner of his life aspiring to quality was a brutality not far short of rape. But it did not end with the books. The gilt mirror was slanted in a drunken diagonal shivered across the wall. A third of its surface had crashed to the floor. The remainder crazily reflected the thrown-down lamp standard, the spread of down-feathers from the gutted cushions, the welter of shattered ornaments from the broken-backed whatnot cast down in the centre of the floor. And from the desk. Its surface had been swept clear of the antique writing set, the miniaturised TV, the crystal horse and rider. Instead, a residual spread of white dust as if a search for fingerprints had already been instituted, covered the best part of the tooled leather top.

He moved swiftly to the desk and opened the top drawer. Beneath his dairy and journal his other pistol was still there untouched. So much the better!

Over his shock, beyond it, he had been hearing noises, shouts, calls. Party noises. Tripped out noises. He began to move in the direction they were coming from. Upstairs. He gained the corridor and found it empty, undisturbed. As he gumshoed down it a left-field thought came at him. This was Tom Leonard returning home early. This was how many hundred guys that night in LA? How many thousand? But Tom Leonard did not live in Benedict Canyon and upstairs . . . His heart hammering at him now but with anticipation and pent-up anger rather than fear, he reached the bottom of the stairs. Nothing. Lightly, quickly so as not to be taken at a disadvantage, he climbed their two right-angled ascent. Nothing. Nothing except the excited call from his own bedroom. He began to move toward it. On the first floor the phone began to ring.

He froze again. But with an immediacy that was ridiculous the door of his own bathroom opened and a man came out. He was like Manson, dark, young, bearded. He wore a black tee-shirt and nothing else. And was spaced out. Seeing what was perhaps a movement against irridescent lights his head went sideways in a grin of amiable idiocy. His hands rose like a preacher's, wide as they conferred a blessing. Paul Madison moved swiftly between them and using the gun like a hatchet knocked him unconscious with a vicious, controlled violence. As the phone kept ringing, the man, the kid, the punk, slumped back against the wall and slid greasily down to thud on to the floor with a noise not negligible.

Caution was no longer the play. Paul Madison made it to the bedroom door in six quick strides.

He saw no dangling or transfixed corpses. There were no mutilations to confuse him. The tableau had been arranged with a more subtle sadism. A girl was on a bed. Her long brown legs were wrapped around the straining back her hands beat frenziedly upon. As a sour, artful fate would have it, two other men, grinning naked and oblivious to him were standing swaying by the bed.

'Oh, God! Yes, yes!' the girl panted. Her hands beat on the bed now. With a grunting sound deep in his throat the man began to match her.

Paul Madison stood bemused and displaced in time. Like mother, like daughter. The girl on the bed in temporary ecstasy was his half-sister. The phone was continuing to ring downstairs.

It was past four a.m. He crashed without ceremony into the bathroom. A towel in her hand.

'For Christ's sake take a bath and do it properly,' he said.

Her head came round and looked at him dopily. He saw the effort to register meaning straining behind her blank, dilated eyes.

'Oh,' she said at last. 'Right.'

She made no effort to cover her ultra-nakedness. She was in no way abashed. But a working realisation of her whereabouts was returning to her consciousness.

'It was good of you not to call the fuzz,' she slowly said. 'I appreciate that . . . I'll leave too. Right away. I won't even wait for tomorrow. It's what you want, I know.'

He knew what he wanted. She had the flat, sinewy lines of a boy athlete and classic high, firm, rounded breasts. But he had made a gigantic effort of his will. He had succeeded in subduing the raging onslaught that had swept over him in the bedroom doorway. Somehow he had managed to remind himself that revenge was a dish best eaten cold.

'That won't be necessary,' he said now. 'The way I see it, every dog is allowed one bite.'

But not a bitch, he thought.

'We'll talk about it in the morning,' he said, 'I guess I've been neglecting you.'

He was after all an actor.

Perhaps, though, she was reading his thoughts after all. She had become self-conscious. She drew the towel about her.

'Where's Tibor?' he said.

'He asked if he could have the night off. I guess I said it would be all right.'

He nodded. Tibor would go. But a little later.

'I guess I'll run that tub,' she said. 'I'll clear up tomorrow – everything.'

'Okay.'

The phone began to ring. It was the fourth time in the hour. This time he answered it. He picked up the extension that the first man, kid, punk, could have found at his right hand.

'Yes?'

'Paul! For Christ's sake where you been? What in hell's fucking name went on back there in Washington? Who the hell—'

He hung up. He had more important things to think of than exchange epithets with Lyndon Oates.

chapter twenty-four

... while cocaine is not, like heroin, physically addicting, its regular use can lead to psychological dependence. It can be the direct cause of irreversible psychological damage. Protracted usage will inevitably destroy the inner nose, eating away the septum. Large doses may induce paralysis of the respiratory centres in the brain thus causing breathing failure and death. In the case of heavy users resorting to injection so as to obtain a 'faster high', the risk of serum hepatitis is demonstrably very considerable ...

National Drug Abuse Institute

Catching the sunlight, briefly heliographing a multitude of signals in the battery of facing mirrors, the scissors snipped away. The comb soothed a fractionally straying hair back to the straight and narrow. Paul Madison felt relaxed. When all else fails, he told himself, nothing beats a haircut, there's sovereign therapy in it. He flashed himself a split screen series of quick grins in the mirror. Almost nothing, he corrected.

His pleasure this morning was considerably enhanced. If there is always something pleasing in the misfortunes of our friends, he was thinking, the shit those we don't like step into leaves us busting a gut laughing. For a considerable while now he had been of the opinion that he did not like Kurt Geisler. The hair-stylist's present whey-faced and pre-occupied reaction to the shit that had just hit his faggot fan was giving him as satisfyingly a gleeful prod on his mirth button as he'd known in weeks of starting the day. A few well-chosen words of malicious sympathising now would be the thing. They would draw out the pleasure to a finer length and so enhance its savour.

'I do appreciate your finding time for me at a time like this, Kurt,' he said. 'I want you to know that. With all this hanging over you. I mean – well, that's one hell of a note.'

The scissors executed a particularly vicious snip and flourish. 'It's not the drugs at all. It's pure discrimination.'

Paul Madison was impressed in spite of himself. Despite his persistently outrageous camp overkill – he was dressed now in a powder blue cheesecloth shirt and red and white striped yachting pants – Geisler had never before 'fessed up in just so many words to being homosexual. Indignation now had made him suspend work. But even at this moment, as he stood by the chair to talk person to person with the mirror's image, the hand holding his comb was limply on his jutting hip in overt arch-faggot cliché.

'I've taken the whole thing to the ACLU,' he continued. 'I mean, it's a clear case of invasion of my privacy and home and I don't know what all.'

'But Jesus, Kurt. A year ago you were walking around with crosses and madalas and stuff slung round your neck. Now you're toting a goddam silver spoon and a blade. And, Jesus, Kurt, you've got them on now! I mean if you go around advertising you can't start yelling "foul" if a customer or two comes to call. Even in this town you've got to expect it.'

Geisler pursed his lips.

'It wasn't the coke,' he insisted. 'It's because of who we are. I mean, we weren't doing anything, you understand – but we were all prepared to stand up and be counted and—'

'I guess you maybe regret that now.'

'Well, yes, I do rather to be candid. I mean I'm glad I did but, oh Mr Madison – it's my boutique! Whatever happens now and if I have to go away or something, well, I'll just be ruined. Financially ruin—'

'Hey, hey! Relax a little. These things have a way—'

'It's so unfair! Everywhere you go you see people snorting. Openly. I mean, you do it! I mean at parties it comes with the canapes and caviar. Just everywhere. Not just show-business. Why Stuart – I do him, you know, did you know that? Very fly-away for a man – he just has this huge brandy snifter always topped up for guests in his living room and it's always but the purest. I swear there's a half a million dollar's worth just sitting there each time you call around.'

Paul Madison felt a twinge of envy.

'Okay. So he's got more money than he knows how to sniff,' he said. 'Pretty soon he'll have two holes in his face to sing from.'

But Geisler was in full blinkered spate by now.

'And everyone wears coke jewellery these days,' he said. 'Everyone who counts. It happens to be chic. They didn't bust me on account of that.'

Vindictiveness flowed through his body and, with the same tensing effect, out into his voice.

'I know why I was singled out. I know all right. I know which cat picked up a phone and called those rotten, grinning narcs. They don't like us, you know. The police. Whatever department.'

'Well, it was kind of unfortunate you had a full house. I mean, antique dealers, a boutique owner if I remember correctly and, er, was it—'

'Yes, I know! I know! Anyone who likes fine things and cleans his nails has to be a faggot. Well I am a faggot! So what! That's no reason to pick on me for sniffing coke like I'm sure the Chief of Police is doing right this very minute.'

Distractedly, his heart not in it, Geisler shaped up for a few more token snips. But Paul Madison was having too good a time to let the matter drop so easily.

'Gee, Kurt,' he said, close to overdoing the musing effect, 'I just wish there was some way I could help. But it sure seems so open and shut—'

'Well, actually, Mr Madison, there maybe is.'

This time the scissors had come away before fully closing.

'Oh?'

'I mean, when you were doing your drug film, Mr Madison, the one where you—'

'*Cold Turkey?*'

'Yes. Well, I mean, doing that you did some research, didn't you?'

'Oh, sure.'

'With the police, I mean. I mean, my recollection is that you met some pretty big wheels down there in the Drug Squad and so on . . . er, is that right?'

'Why, yes. Yes, of course.'

'So I was wondering, well, if there might be someone, someone with a clout, you know, influence, who you would maybe pick up a phone to or maybe even have a drink with, and sort of tell them, well, that I'm a, well, friend or at least a responsible—'

'Sure! Of course! Why, I can think of two guys with some pull right off the bat.'

'Oh, could you—'

'I'd be happy to. I'll get right on it.'

He wouldn't. But Geisler would never know.

'I'd be so grateful.'

'And I'm glad you thought of a way I could help.'

'Thank you, Mr Madison.'

For nothing. Geisler's outrageousness had been tiresome for too long. Lately he didn't seem to style hair so good, either. If he had to take a little trip then the need to replace him would be neatly imposed by circumstances. He could find somebody better. Maybe a girl. Hey! That could be a real bright start to every day . . . And maybe if his parlour was going to go under it would be a nice little side-bet of a tax-loss investment. He could slam somebody in there as a manager . . . he must talk to the accountants about that. There's be a lot of actual money passing through the till which could be good but could be bad news if . . . In the meantime there was one more twist of the immediate knife he could administer.

'Kurt,' he said reflectingly. Again the hair-stylist dropped his hands.

'Kurt – if it's, well, your image that the fuzz are really beating up on, maybe that's the area we ought to change. Look, I'm having a few chicks and such around tonight for a little, you know, ball game. If you could maybe bring yourself to swing the other way a little – we could get you high and stuff – then maybe we could take some pictures or whatever and produce them later to the fuzz or the DA or who the hell else ever as evidence—'

But raising his scissors rapidly, Geisler cut him short with a glittering threatening motion. His mouth tightened even more primly like the closing of an old lady's drawstring purse.

'Thank you for the thought,' he said, 'but I really don't think it's me.'

chapter twenty-five

His scheme had been simple. First he had talked to her. She herself had put it in his mind.

'Listen,' he had said, 'you keep saying you want me to fix you some kind of movie break. And I've been meaning to. Only – well, you know how it is. But now I've got something in mind. Here's my plan.'

'Yes?'

They were sitting across from each other at the coffee table in the barn-size living room. He had waited for her generous snorting to begin to get to her.

'I figured the best route to travel would be to jump in several notches up the tree,' he said. 'There's no point in my just happening to say to some producer that I just happen to know this chick and all that kind of shit. He hears that ten times a day. But if I walk in there with you in a can of film under my arm – well that's a different ball game. He can take a look and judge for himself. You want to remember I got my break through being spotted in a commercial.'

'You mean—'

'Right. We'll shoot ourselves a little screen test. Right here in this house.'

'Wow!'

'Personally I think you'll photograph real well.'

He doubted that. Her sullen scowling 'they buried my heart at Wounded Knee' look would be fine as one cut away, fine for a cameo of a tough whore in a doorway. But she lacked animation in her features. The ability to convey feeling, not so much across the face but a few millimetres below its surface, she would never have. And that was the hallmark of the great movie actors. It was his own prime talent. Sam almost certainly would have . . .

'Now look,' he said quickly, 'I've an idea of how it should go. I would have suggested this if it hadn't been for that scene the other night.'

And that, of course, was true.

'I really am—'

' 's okay,' he said. 'But here's my thinking. This is a pretty raunchy age movie-wise. If we're going to show you off, it's – well, frankly, we're going to have to show you off. What I had in mind was a bedroom scene. Now – how would you feel about that? How'd that be?'

She looked hard at him. For a long moment he thought she wouldn't want to play.

'I've seen you out there by the pool – hell, I've seen you in a bedroom scene. I mean it's like, er, something that would show all kinds of your talents. And I'd play opposite you myself. There aren't many unknowns get to test opposite a top ten grosser. That in itself will make the money look at you. And with me, well maybe you'll feel more . . . relaxed.'

Maybe he was wrong about her. She wasn't all wooden Indian. A hint of perverse anticipation that he read as to do with sex rather than ambition had entered her dark and no longer opaque eyes. It had hovered about the ghost of a smile on her wide mouth. Well, she would get hers. More than she bargained for.

She had nodded.

'Okay,' she had said.

'Great.'

He had leaned forward as he began to outline his scenario.

The next day he had phoned Philip Grayson.

'Paul, sweetheart. I'd given up expecting to hear from you again.'

The photographer-pimp was as arch as ever.

'I'd heard you were coping admirably yourself, these days,' he was saying. 'For yourself, that is. Not by. And a little bird about town was telling me that what you couldn't garner on your own Jack Preston was supplying for you gratis.'

'Not to mention free, Phil. But you know me – I like to spread my business around. Good for society.'

'I know the sex. What shape and size did you have in mind? Or did you need a venue?'

'Phil, it's photographic.'

'Really? This is your day for surprising me.'

'I need a 16 mm. movie cameraman who can light and who

knows where they process without asking questions.'

'Or getting hands on. Moving into production are we?'

'It's kind of a birthday gag kind of stunt I want to pull.'

'Oh yes . . .'

'I was wondering if maybe you'd like to handle it.'

'Paul, baby, I don't know one end of those things that whirr-away like coffee-grinders from the other. Me – I'm strictly from stills. You know, where the art is.'

'Oh.'

'But I think I can help you. There are several guys. How much are you paying?'

'Five hundred for one night.'

'I'm sure I can help you. Fats German is a distinct—'

'And Phil – I need some guys.'

'Studs?'

'Well they've got to be able to get it up!'

'What a fun birthday someone's going to have. Fee ?'

'Two hundred a piece. And a bonus for the one who can make the most trips to the well.'

'We're talking straight are we?'

'Oh yeah. Sure!'

'Okay. Fine. Leave it with me. I'll get back to you.'

'Oh, Phil—'

'Yes?'

'The guys. They've got to be different colours.'

The blinds were down and the bedroom was a blaze of white light from the four Color-Tran heads which with all the finesse of a hack Fats German had set up in a circle. Big-bellied, dark-moustached, he had a cheap greasy-knowingness about his slight-ly bulbous eyes that suggested he was a bad barber or bar-tender rather than a bad cameraman. He had said he'd prefer to work alone and Paul Madison had recognised that the nervousness he'd shown on his arrival was not due to the nature of the upcoming movie-making – that was obviously his stock-in-trade – but to his finding himself at long last in the presence of a name.

Paul Madison had given him only two instructions. To go on the zoom and wing it. And not to be surprised, to go on turning, when the door burst open and the other guys came in. He had left Tibor to intercept them at the gate and hole them up in his own bungalow. The 'star' meanwhile sat waiting on the bed. She wore one of his work-shirts in lieu of pyjamas. With her tan, he had told her, and the sensitivity of modern film, she would not need make-up.

'Okay,' he said, 'let's just walk through the opening. Fats, you watch this and see if it gives you problems.'

The cameraman grunted as she rose with such indifference he knew it must be feigned.

The outline he'd given her was outrageous. They didn't have sound so they would have to make it very melodramatic. She was to imagine that he was one of identical twins. They were a Jekyll and Hyde pair. She was in love with the good one and to think that she was taking him to her bed. On the verge of making love she would discover that it was the evil brother she was embracing and as her feelings switched from tenderness to revulsion learn from him that he had just come from murdering the other. Horror-struck she was to offer slight resistance when he bound her. They would then move in for close-ups while she acted being raped. That was where the brief scene would end. He would explain the 'plot' to any studio chief so they would know the reasons for her wide range of emoting. He would have the film edited so they could go over stuff and re-take to get it right. For the initial master-shot they'd go right through until the point where he started to tie her. Then, to save film, he'd cut.

Nearing the end of the walk-through, she sank down on the bed, her arms up to pull him down after her. He was only wearing a robe. He didn't want to get to ahead of himself.

'Okay,' he said, 'we'll cool it there. Fine. How was it for you, Fats?'

'Fine.'

They could have turned orange halfway through and the grunt would still have come back the same.

'Well let's try one. Why not? Tell you what you do, Janice, just relax and treat this as a rehearsal on film.'

'Okay Fats?'

'All set.'

'We can go without slates – action!'

The camera began to whirr. It was burning up film but when, for his amusement, he ran it, he would want the preposterous spuriousness of her 'acting' as the appetising preliminary to her genuine reactions when the main event hit her.

Awkwardly, self-consciously now that the camera noise was in her ears, she came stiffly towards him as they had rehearsed. The smile was straight from a family snapshot that had been posed too long. The arms had the rigidity of any novice actress uncertain what her hands should be doing.

'Darling,' she remembered she must say.

They embraced. As her arms came round him he could sense the tension softening out of her. Within his arms was a haven where she might relax. He was literally something she could cling to – something, you bet, she felt at home with. As rehearsed, her profile to the camera in the corner, they kissed. He could sense the uncertainty return to her as she wondered how much of her mouth to give to him. Plenty was her fast enough decision and as the lips became more pliant and her tongue probed he felt a different kind of tension flow into the lean, leggy body she was thrusting against his. A thin, sour, natural scent was coming off the skin about her neck. It carried that common, dirtied sense he'd known and sought in girls like her since he was her age. But this was his half-sister! A dark excitement filled him at the thought and he began to feel his flesh move. Once again he broke things off. He brought his lips away from hers.

'Now the bed,' he said as if whispering endearments.

Leading him, she backed towards it. Awkward again, she settled down, swung the long legs round and up. Yes, sex was familiar territory. The look she gave him now was unequivocally that of a woman inviting a man. He wondered how much that kiss had got to her and how much the potential for sex now promised in her eyes was fuelled from knowing his portrait was postered on the bedroom walls of a million teenage-girls: how much from knowing that they shared a parent. She twisted toward him. Her arms lifted up. He slid down to sit on the edge of the bed between them, then leant forward and across her.

'Now recognize the bad brother,' he said.

She did so in a transition so sudden and crude he all but laughed in her face. If there'd been lingering doubt, that was where she'd blown the screen test. He'd enjoy those frames later and Jack Preston would wet himself laughing. Right now, as not without violence she began to buffet screamingly at him, he pushed her back with his left hand and reached into the pocket of his robe for the lengths of torn cloth. He fished one out and seizing her left wrist carried the strip up to it.

'Cut!' he called out. 'How was it, Fats?'

'Fine.'

'How about me?' she asked.

'You were very good,' he lied, 'very natural. Now—'

'I didn't think so. I felt all kind of stiff. I didn't think I was very good at all.'

'You were just—'

'Can we do it over? You said this was just a rehearsal on—'

'We'll do it again from the top again later from a different angle. When we've been through the whole thing once and know pretty much what we need to cover a second time. That way we'll be giving the editor more to play with.'

She nodded.

'Now just lie back again and we'll get you all tied down.'

She did as she was asked without a second thought.

'Who is going to edit it?' she said.

'A guy – the name wouldn't mean anything to you.'

'Can I come watch?'

He enjoyed the joke a moment before replying.

'Sure,' he said. 'If you feel you want to.'

'Why shouldn't—'

'Here, we'll leave these long so there's plenty of play in them and you can squirm and move around. But we'll make them tight like the real thing so you've got something to play against.'

'Ouch!'

'Sorry. There.'

It was done. Feet and legs she was spread-eagled to the bed's four corners.

'Okay,' he said and stood back up. For a moment he stood quite still contemplating not only her but the fine prospect of revenge on her and, once again, on all like her. Everyone, including himself. Then, quite leisurely, he stooped forward and grasped the shirt she wore where, deep between her breasts, it was top buttoned.

'Is it—'

His eyes never leaving hers, he ripped the shirt open its remaining length. The gasp she gave, the combination that he read in those eyes of surprise, confirmation and dawning helplessness was royal to him. She gasped again, pulled with either arms. But he had kept his promise to bind her tightly. He tore savagely at the front halves of the shirt and she grunted with the shock upon her back and shoulders. Just because her arms were bound it would have been necessary to cut the shirt to remove it completely but that he did not do. Having it spread in torn sections either side of her tanned, straining body enhanced the overall effect.

She was wearing the briefest of bikini panties. As she bucked and twisted he ripped them from her with the ferocity he had once visited on Christie Roberts. He stifled the comparison as swiftly as it came to him. Well, he was supposed to be the bad brother, so let him be just that! . . . The width of the bed was making her look irresistibly vulnerable. Her breasts were parted to the flatness almost of a boy's.

He stood back again and slipped his arms free from his robe. Slowly, milking the moment to full effect, he let it slide to the floor. Her tongue flicked out to lick her lips.

She said, 'You don't have to do all this. It's what I want. Whatever you want – whatever way – you can do it.'

'I bet I can, you little whore,' he said. 'I know it. Well this is my way. It's the way I'm going to teach you that when I take someone into my house I don't have her turning it into the same buck-fifty cat house her mother would make of it.'

'That bitch and—'

'That bitch and you are out of the same stinking mould! I'm going to send you out of here so hammered you'll think twice before you even so much as look at another man!'

A flare of rage had come from out of nowhere to make him border on incoherence. Furious at himself he strode to the door and flung it open. As instructed, the men were waiting there.

'Okay.'

They came cautiously, sheepishly, grinningly into the room. As instructed they were already naked.

'Okay. Line up along this wall. Don't stand in front of the lights.'

The girl got the message at once. Her head had been straining up on its neck the better to see but now it sank back on to the pillowless mattress. Realisation had made her go limp with despair.

As the camera turned over, he climbed on to the bed. He had slumped a little. He looked at her tanned, sinewy length of body with a gathering, gloating sense of power. Then he was ready for her.

As he leaned down towards her, she spat into his face. He flinched, wiped himself. Someone behind had laughed. He slapped her about the face. She groaned and, expecting more blows, closed her eyes in a face averted as best she could manage.

Savagely, frenetically, trapped by his own furies, he rutted into action. To his own detriment. He had scarcely pinned the whole weight of his body down on hers, scarcely sought for her breast with hands before he felt the old, old, elemental sweetness coursing adolescently upward. He tried to stay it. He knew, eyes closed, she was deliberately making herself limp, offering nothing in return. The bitch! Bitch! Oh, Christ, Christ! Not yet!

Desolately, it ended for him.

'Do I keep turning or what?'

'Yeah, yeah! Next!'

He rolled over and off her. Grinning, brutish, the first of the defensive ends came forward. There was a broken ugliness about his face suggesting a life spent down back alley-ways.

'She's all yours.'

Snatching up his robe Paul Madison moved to behind the camera. Some kind of last shred of an instinct for fastidiousness had made him dissociate himself from the other participants. He shrugged the robe back on and turned to watch.

'Oh, my God!'

He was just in time to hear the girl call out, see her shudder as the man lowered himself on to her. The girl's eyes opened. They flicked about the room. They found what they were seeking – Paul Madison's face. They looked at him. Slowly, triumphantly, their owner, the girl, began to smile.

In the event it took maybe ten minutes. The bastard knew when he was on to a good thing. The film ran out and picking up a fresh magazine Fats looked the obvious question. Paul Madison shook his head.

'Hold your fire,' he said.

And now a cry broke from her thrashing head. It strained back and the sinews of her neck were rigidly apparent. She began to whimper, cried out again.

'Yes! Oh God! God! Yes!'

'Yes baby, yes! Go! Go!'

Gutturally, gasping from deep in his own throat, the man had found his own release through hers.

'Oh, baby,' the man had the basic worth to say in retrospect.

'Next!'

She had had her moment. Now it was his. Paul Madison again disrobed. In spite of herself she tightened about him and it was only by a sharp exercise of will that he held still. He saw the fight had ebbed out of her. She would not struggle. She was powerless.

He took his time. Slow and easy. He saw annoyance brighten her eyes. He heard her breath hiss out as he stroked the vital nerve that took her past the point of returning. The flat belly he was grappling to his own began to undulate.

'Bastard!' she hissed. 'You mother-fucking bastard!'

There was a crash of a door opening. A crash and the abrupt arcing change of a light lamp falling. There were yells, cries of alarm and the dull report of a globe imploding. Cheated on the threshold of pleasure he had no choice but slew around toward the door. It was crowded.

Geisler stood there and Pal. And two other men. For a hopeful second that he did not really believe in, he thought, he tried to think that Geisler had come to take him up on the taunting invitation to prove his manhood with a girl. But the preening unalloyed spite written across the hair stylist's face took the forlorn hope and made it stillborn. Pal's face read money. The faces of the two other and strange men said police. In an agony of chilling belief it all was really inexorably, happening, he twisted round (and out of the girl) and looked to Fats German. With trembling fingers he was reaching for the side of the film magazine. But the cop with a face like a snowplough had anticipated his own look and the cameraman's fumbling movements. He was crossing the bedroom to the camera, delivering a short, sharp professional blow. German had cried out and slumped away against the wall. And the other cop had advanced to stare down on to the bed.

'Okay superstar,' he was saying, 'haul yourself right out of there.'

A scalding flood of total humiliation swept through Paul Madison and he felt the girl beneath him twitch with delight. The other cop was talking to Kurt Geisler.

'You're prepared to testify to what you've witnessed here?' he was saying.

'It will be my pleasure, officer,' was the vicious response.

And still the scalding shame. At its core the ice chill that shrivels the nerve of all men who know that it is their own folly that has brought about their ruin.

chapter twenty-six

PAUL MADISON IN ROMAN ORGY.
Headline in LA Times

'It's a silver Ford Futura just round to the left,' Tom Leonard said. 'Hold it there a second while I check outside.'

He was gone. Paul Madison rested his head wearily back against the dank wall of the stale-smelling corridor that lead to a service entrance of the Santa Monica Court House. He was bushed and triple bushed. He needed a shave. His skin felt as if it were crawling the length of his frame. He felt as if the same lice had got into his brain.

From far, far away he heard shouts. It meant that Tom Leonard's plan might be working. With the Assistant DA's agreement, co-operation, he had arranged to smuggle Max Hamilton his own screen double into the Court House in a paddy wagon. Inside Max had dressed in expensive clothes and face-mask shades. He was making a run for it now to draw the fire of the popping flash-bulbs, the sun-guns, the lens staring like ray guns about to jet forth lasers and the microphones thrust out like stick grenades. Laurence Behrman would plough a path through the entire mass of the bastards of the press and, God willing, it would be his car that they would pursue to see where their best hottest break since Polanski, Pearl Harbor, you name it, was set on holing up.

It was dark outside. He was unutterably tired because he had been there all the stretched-out, humiliating hours of the daylight working day. And then some. Behrman had had bail fixed for him by mid-afternoon but to date his most positive piece of legal counselling had been to wait for nightfall before making a run for it.

Leonard was taking his time! He slapped his jacket pocket to find the cigarettes that were the best relief to his lurching mind he might dare here.

The past day was a blurred montage of shaming confrontations, questions, allegations. He had tried to act possession of a hurt and patient dignity in the face of a buzz-saw of circumstances that anyone might have walked into. But the seriousness of his position was matched by its degree of farce. Dignity, however low-profile, had been hard to come by, let alone project with any credibility when he had been caught with his pants down on top of a girl who was not only his half-sister but, as Putnam, the DA, had let him know with visibly savoured malice, was also a fifteen-year-old minor. Degradation had been piled on humiliation. The cops had taken his prints with an extra relish. They had had broad leering grins on their faces as they had tossed him in the tank with the drunks, a hop head and a black kid, who unable to believe his proximity with greatness, had admitted in a reeking breathed whisper that he was on a charge of soliciting as a male prostitute. The cops had displayed a different attitude to their brush with fame. 'Get much?' those grins had sneered. 'Well here's where we get you and serve you fucking right you fucking son of a bitch for being rich and famous and fucking women who aren't like our wives could ever be, and not being ordinary and on a monthly pay-slip when we fucking are.' Wanting a shower, his insides feeling like they'd been washed out in detergent, he had looked hazily at those cops and remembered there is no smile so blood-chillingly exultant as that of a mean, stupid man in a uniform who has you over a barrel.

And no impersonal authority so wounding personally as that of a black-robed judge in outwardly blameless pursuit of justice. The judge before whom he'd been arraigned, fifth in the stumble-bum morning parade, had, straight-faced and paper-shuffling insisted, almost inaudibly, that he be charged in the name of Ukinski. He had had the sense to make no statement either then or later when first confronted by a DA trying to sneak a solo run. In Putnam's case the attempt to humiliate had been less subtle, part of the greater aim to intimidate. But for all the wash of fear and shame, anger and remorse making much of his mind—

'Okay. Let's go! There was some guy there but he's gone!'

Leonard was back. Glad only to obey mechanically, he followed him out through the door into a night that, after a day spent in a buzzing world of run-down air-conditioning, breathed into his face with a hot moistness which seemed alive. It seemed alive and, in glee, to be mocking his downfall with an animal malignancy. It made him falter.

'Come on!' Leonard hissed.

They crossed the small parking zone through pools of soiled orange light.

'There! She's open.'

The car's courtesy-light seemed to pick him out with the intensity of ten-thousand kilowatts as he slipped into the front passenger seat. Leonard was only a split second behind him. He had the key in the ignition and was turning it.

The seat-belt warning buzzer sounded more loudly than the last trumpet calling 'Time'.

'Shit! Do it up! Quick!'

Fumbling, his dirtied hands sweaty, slippery, he got the fucking tongue the right way round and in the third time of asking. Leonard had the car in motion and, like a puppet, he was jerked forward, back, forward, until he braced himself into some kind of harmony with the suspension's action.

Leonard spun the wheel hard. They went south on Fourth Street turned left up Pacific.

'Not so godammned fast, for Christ's sake,' Paul Madison was able to think to say.

Leonard slowed. He drove a long block east up Pacific, then hung another left. Cruising he worked around back down to Fourth and – oh Jesus, what sweet relief! – up on to the Santa Monica Freeway. It had taken maybe three minutes. And no-one had followed them.

Drained, numb to all feeling beyond a dull sense of shock, he stared out at the commonplace on-rush of cement and tail-lights as the Futura picked up speed. He was groping for a cigarette when his brain managed a first precise thought.

'You wouldn't by any sublime chance have a joint on you?' he said to Tom Leonard.

'Are you kidding? Have you forgotten already where we've just been all day?'

'Oh. I thought maybe in the glove compartment or—'

'Car's rented.'

'Oh. Where you taking me anyway?'

It had just reoccurred to him that with ten thousand news hounds baying at his gates there was no way he could go home to Mulholland.

'I've got the use of a beach-house down near San Juan Capistrano. We'll head there.'

'Oh. Okay.'

Had there been a hint of malicious satisfaction glinting through

Leonard's undercover agent delivery? Sure. The smooth son of a bitch wouldn't have been human if there hadn't been. In the misfortunes of friends . . . Maybe he should head straight for LAX and be another to hop the first plane to Paris. But he didn't have the ace in a hole of a French passport up his sleeve and into a lifetime of culture-shock was no way to fly . . . He resumed his search for cigarettes. His hand closed on a piece of paper. Even as he drew it from the jacket pocket he recollected what it was. He looked down now to confirm his remembrance.

About four inches long, two and a half wide, it was a religious tract, as cheap and shoddy in its thinking as its presentation. He could just make out its catchpenny type in the coming, receding of the freeway lights.

WHAT GOD WANTS TO KNOW.
My dear Friend – I am asking you the MOST important question of life. Your JOY or SORROW for ALL ETERNITY DEPENDS UPON YOUR ANSWER. The question is: ARE YOU SAVED? It is not how good you are, BUT ARE YOU SAVED? It is not if you are a member of some church but ARE YOU SAVED? If you are not . . .

After Behrman had arrived to start the bail wheeling and dealing his status as a detainee had improved. He had been allowed to use a private john instead of the bespeckled crock of shit down in the tank. It had still been rank, foul-smelling, enough. As he had loosened his belt he had felt his guts shrink as they instinctively recoiled from contact with God alone knew what rested on the smeared surface of the cracked plastic seat. He had reached for some toilet tissue to wipe the seat clean. The fixture was bare. The roll stood on the floor and, as he'd reached for it, he had seen a piece of something wedged loosely into the central core. For a moment he had thought it a contraceptive but it had been this crude attempt to put words into God's mouth. He had read it while he crapped.

My Friend:
  Think seriously about this, don't put it off. Tomorrow may be too late. We read in the Bible of the man who had plenty, who said to his soul 'thou hast much goods laid up for years; take thine ease, drink and be merry.' BUT LISTEN: 'But GOD said unto him, Thou fool, this night thy soul shall be required of thee: then whose shall those things be . . .'

Crap! He had no memory of pocketing the thing. If you'd've asked him he would have said he flushed it. He should have! He worked the window down and as the humid night roared in at their ears, cast the paper to the streaming wind. Crap! The world was a whorehouse – a game with a stacked deck. Whatever dealer there might be was crooked. He knew you wouldn't get out of the game alive and it gave him his kicks watching you screw up what time you had as you twisted and squirmed and misplayed the few cards you had. You were on your own in this world and there was no next. The only Last Judgement was your own on yourself. Salvation was what you gave or witheld from yourself and God could keep His favours.

It was so trivial. Therefore so impossible. You had to judge your performance in a crap game!

As if uppercut his heart was kicked into his mouth. God the mother! He certainly knew when to play his 'Got you!' cards! He must wear a Rolex – His timing was that accurate.

The Freeway was running high up above the nothing-nothing world of a tract housing suburb. The great square shark-fin of a drive-in movie screen stared down on the worshipping windshields bowed down in rows about it. And on the screen, soundless, ghostly, huger than anything in the flat landscape, the face that dreams were made of – his. From the speeding car he stared out at himself going through the simulated convulsions of withdrawal pains. As if vibrating out from some hollow core at the centre of his own being, his mute, empty pretence of another's agony was being projected up against the sky in a phoniness the size of a tennis court. The ranged cars were cast down in obeisance before a plastic crucifixion, predestined within the hour to fade to nothingness.

A great and terrible sense of loss drove in upon his spirit. He was weighted with the knowledge of his uselessness. He was a star and he was nothing. That was all. It was that simple. Unwrap him, wind him up and he was nothing. Something purer than pity gushed through him. The great longing of all with ashen hearts to be held, no longer bereft, in loving arms, gazed on by eyes softly compassionate and not asking explanation burned the emptiness within him like a thirst. He wanted nothing more than to lose himself in the warmth and wonder of another's tenderness and understanding.

And there was no-one. At this very moment the one person he might turn to was a continent away experiencing in the innermost cells of her body those depthless pains that, obscenely it now seemed, his image had fleetingly pinned upon the concrete screen. Her padded room would have four walls not three and a camera crew. Her paroxysms of nerve-wracked reaction – terrifying because beyond the mind's control – would not have the safety net of knowing a score of technicians recorded and admired the player's virtuosity. Total solitude would be her audience and not one tortured cell would cease to convulse the moment a man called 'Cut!' Cell! Unbidden, inexorably, the image of a whimpering and pleading Christie Roberts rose up in his mind. What he had forced on her had killed her. There was a kind of justice in the world. Now he was getting his and she would be revenged. Much good would it do her that he acknowledged it now but what he had inflicted on her had been worse than wrong. It had been an absence of all . . . right. There had been a moment when something within him had been made to resonate by something about her. He could have allowed himself to be moved or touched . . . Then he could perhaps right now have her to turn to and ask . . . But he had turned that resonance to another, cruder, frequency and henceforth each drive-in screen that he should see would be a faceless stone marking her death and the still-births of all the roles she might have played . . .

He lit the cigarette. Fatigue was washing through him with his blood. The car was straining on to the elaborate interchange with the San Diego Freeway. Sean Flaherty would read of him, of course, and he would simply be dismissed from thought. The motion of the pavement and the whirling lights was giddying him. He leant back and closed his eyes.

Then he had opened them and was, of a sudden, sitting forward. Some kind of a last prospect fluttered in his heart; some kind of an infant hope pulsed along his veins. Sam!

'Tom,' he said, 'drop me out at the airport, will you?'

Leonard threw him a fast glance of derisive suspicion.

'Oh, Tom, for Christ's sake! I'm not going to hop a plane. I just want to rent another car.'

Leonard was silent. He had to take the San Diego Freeway south in any case.

'You're all stretched and freaked out, Paul,' he said. 'You've been through the meat-grinder today. You don't know where you're at.'

'You mean you got orders not to let me out of your sight!'

'Paul. It's common sense. You can't know—'

'To hell with common-fucking sense! I know! I know! I know

where I want to go and it's nowhere bad or going to make trouble.'

Leonard was slanting the car across to the interchange exit.

'You're out on bail, for Christ's sake, Paul!' he said. 'Now just for once in your life play it smart and be reasonable! Don't—'

'You want me to wrestle that fucking wheel out of your hand!'

He lunged wildly across. But this once Leonard had anticipated him. A stinging back-hand volley of a blow smashed him back against the door as the car snake-hipped dangerously toward the fencing inside of the slow lane. He started back at Leonard as the driver fought the wheel with both hands and was obliged to watch the road.

'For Christ's sake!' Leonard shouted. 'You'll kill us!'

'You going to take me to a car?'

'. . . Okay.'

They drove in silence another five minutes.

'Where you want to get to anyway?' Tom Leonard said.

'What's it to you?'

'Suppose I drive you there myself . . . How would that be?'

'. . . Get to Silver Lake and I'll tell you just where.'

'Couldn't you have told me when we were still on the Santa Monica?'

Tom Leonard got off the San Diego Freeway and worked round to a northbound ramp. Twenty minutes later they were skirting Silver Lake's dark glide of waters as the random scatter of lights above defined the steep rise into the night of the surrounding hillsides.

'She won't want to see you, you know,' Tom Leonard said.

'Shut up. Here. Earl Street.'

She had lived in a tiny house pushed into the side of a street narrow and on so steep a hill Leonard was obliged now to kick the transmission into a whirring low.

'Keep going. There! Stop here. There's a place a little higher up where you can turn. Run it back down and wait.'

'Yes'm Mister Mad'son, suh.'

'Okay, Tom, I'm sorry . . .'

'Yeah, well . . . Look's like no one's home.'

'We'll see. Be right back.'

The car gurgled further on up the incline its tail-lights bright against the ill-lit darkness of the thinly housed street. The brake lights glowed especially ferociously as Leonard found the turning plateau. From the house there shone no lights at all.

Jesus, it was steep! Paul Madison had to brace himself against the slope even though walking at right angles to it. He had forgotten how severe it was. But he had been here only – what? – two, three times. She had always come to him . . . Ah yes, the little gate, so, and, careful, three steps, no four, up to the door.

He pushed at the buzzer. Nothing. No sound. No light. He was about to press a second time when a light jumped on inside. Then, blindingly, an outer light was beating fiercely down on him from right overhead and he felt looked at. Silence again. Again nothing. Then a scrabbling just inside the door at a security chain. He took a deep breath. Had she heard yet? She just might not have and he might have to tell her. Would that be better or worse? If she'd been locked in some studio all day she just might not have heard – if she was still acting. If—

The inner door was opening. A shape stood there.

'Sam?'

The screen door was opening. The shape was a man. Jerry White. He was wearing a bathrobe.

'No admission, whitey,' he said. His voice was vibrant with pleasure. 'It's standing room only in there, dig? You take your trouble and bad news some other place.'

There was a noise, movement in the tiny hall. A shape with the gentle outline of long hair was in back of White.

'Yeah. Beat it,' Sam said. Her voice was as low and softly thick as ever. But that was underneath. It was the foreground animosity that counted. He turned at once and walked away. She too had worn a robe.

He closed the gate behind him and the close of the house door was its echo. The slope making him limp, he crossed to where Tom Leonard had coasted the car.

'Moved away,' he said. 'No forwarding address.'

As he completed the lie he reached to open the car door. He affected unconcern. Badly. He was defeated. He had been rejected by someone, herself a reject. He had tried to soften the kiss-off by the studio heavies and been royally stomped for his pains. Coming from Sam the insult had an edge. Is this how far he'd come since he took those vows of obedience centuries ago in Oates's office? He looked into Leonard's half-smiling face and saw instead, himself. He felt a sudden urgent need to scream into the night. Too big a gift to Leonard. Instead he looked up at the sky. Free from the cigarette glow of the city's mass of lights, the scattered profusion of the stars had opportunity to glitter down like frozen teardrops. He wondered what terrible griefs could have caused them to be shed.

chapter twenty-seven

Get caught in bed with the wife of the man who invented a
better mouse-trap and the world will beat a path to your door.

Tom Leonard

No comment.

Lyndon Oates

'If it were just you and me,' Lyndon Oates said, 'I'd walk away
and leave you hanging there to collect everything you deserve.'

'But it aint just you and me, is it, baby?' Paul Madison said,
'It's you, me and the money.'

Oates' tan purpled into beetroot with the rush of blood.

'You ungrateful little snot-assed prick,' he said, 'I showed you
the world, spread it out at your feet, and all—'

'Gentlemen, gentlemen,' Laurence Behrman interrupted
smoothly. 'We're on the same team remember.'

He laughed with a rich, vibrant unconvincingness.

'We aren't in court and on opposite sides,' he went on. 'This is
my office and we're here to discuss how best to extricate Paul from
this shit-hole he's dug for himself and present him to the world
still smelling like a rose. Easy it's not going to be. But it's going
to be a fucking sight harder if you all choose to treat the occasion
as an excuse for evening old scores or solo ego trips.'

A tall handsomely open-faced man with a head closely covered
in tight, prematurely grey curls, he laughed once again.

'As for the money,' he said, 'you'll find that by the time I'm
through that's going to be a problem weighing a good deal lighter
on your wallet.'

'That's right, his wallet,' Oates muttered vehemently.

'Oh come on Lyndon,' Tom Leonard said, 'the blood is all
under the bridge now. I'm no happier about—'

'Since when do you have the fucking gall to tell me just how I
should think?' Oates snapped. He eyed his lieutenant with the
righteous umbrage of a paymaster.

'He just pisses me off,' he said. 'He's never learned. He's never shown any gratitude. He's just gone from one ass-in-a-sling fuck-up to another. A worse other. Look at that Curtis—'

'As I should damn well know!' Tom Leonard yelled. 'I'm the lucky guy who's got to run around after him each time. I'm the one—'

'For Christ's sake, you guys!' Laurence Behrman said. He got up from behind his large chrome-and-rosewood desk and moved to the smoked glass of his floor-to-ceiling penthouse windows. Paul Madison knew instantly the lawyer had made the move to exert his presence and command the more respect. He was reminded of Milton Rosner's executive-suite games. But Behrman's office was high in the rarer air on Sunset – an easy ride to the Hollywood Freeway and City Hall. And where Rosner's walls had been decorated with a shrieking restraint in suede, two of Behrman's were lined with range upon range of law and reference books. Yet, rather than industry, they too suggested image. They had an air of stiff-backed military virginity hardly suggesting constant thumbing. But Behrman was in no measure a man assailed by intimations of his own inadequacy.

'Look,' he was saying in his lawyer's voice, 'if the four of you just want to hire a room and yell and scream and pull each other to bits, that's fine by me. But it was my impression that you'd come to see me because I'm the best goddam defence attorney West of Rhode Island and I can give you my categorical assurance that for so long as you use my office for your hatefest it'll be reflected in my billing.'

He had been pacing before the dark-paned window as if delivering a court-room summation to a patently hostile jury. Now, seeing that he had them, he relaxed his eagle-eyed indignation. A winning smile spread over his actorish face.

'Okay,' he said, 'we know it ain't no bed of roses. Let's see just what we've got and what we haven't.'

He moved back to behind the awesome stretch of desk and, a temporary judge, surveying the court, sat himself down. Paul Madison was sitting sideways to the desk at one end of the leather chesterfield and along from Tom Leonard. Lyndon Oates sat in the matching wing-chair angled more centrally before the desk. The brown and studded upholstery conveyed a considerable and, Paul Madison was convinced, calculated hint of legal clubland and he found himself wondering exactly which preparation Behrman used to bring out the highlights in those tight grey curls. It was a head of hair, he suddenly realised, such as the Greek god Pan was often depicted possessing.

Forty-eight hours after the door had been closed in his face, he was beginning to find himself under control again. His panic, ironically, was over. He had a sense of the system beginning to go to bat for him. He was in deep, Christ knew, but ranks were closing, money was starting to talk. That morning, shaving in Tom Leonard's bathroom he was staying at Leonard's apartment to avoid the pack of reporters taked out up on Mulholland) he had even felt a moment or two of enhanced ego. He had elected himself to one of Hollywood's more select clubs after all. And yet . . .

'Right,' Behrman was saying, 'we got some not so good news and some downright shitty news. Let's take the first kind first.'

'The Mann Act stuff, the minor across a state line, I think we can side-step. We've got the time lag between her entering California and the incident. And we've got the relationship. We've got to be careful over that one and see we don't dig our own grave but I think we can make the fact she's your half-sister work for us there. My information is that she is, by the way, in case you were wondering otherwise. Now, what we've also got going here is the mother's non-action in the first place – from the first moment the girl quit the reservation. I'll come back to this later but if I can get the mother – your mother, that is – on—'

'The mother.'

'Okay. Her. If I can get her on the stand she's going to step down looking like a cross between Messalina and Snow White's stepmother.

'The coke – possession thereof and inducing a minor to partake – I think we can slide by on that one too. Maybe the possession we contest – I don't know yet and, understand, I'm going to circle back shortly and spend the rest of the day asking you more questions, Paul, than you thought possible . . . Capisce?'

'Capisce.'

'Maybe, though, we cop a guilty plea here as part of our horse-trading strategy. Coke, today, I mean – I do it, you do it, he does it. The judge probably does it and I'm damned sure the DA does. I think we can low-profile this one on the day.

'Now we get into the sex and the going gets rougher. The girl being a minor, we can't ignore. We can't ignore it but there's no way a jury's going to expect you to have thought that piece of ass was fifteen. They can use every make-up and dress-up trick in the book – she's still going to come on like twenty on the stand.

'The intercourse charge – roughsville. It isn't so long ago, remember, we had another household Hollywood name copping a sentence in this area and the fact he skipped the good old US on the eve of serving it doesn't do too much for your dice. And you've got all them Appalachian incest trimmings. That's a ball-breaker. What I aim to go for is to enter pleas, one way or the other, right away and then ask for postponement pending psychiatric examination. Ours for sure. Then I may hand you over to their guys – when you know what to tell them. Tom, here, tells me you got scads of broken-blossom childhood you can lay down. That so?'

'Er ... right. Yes.'

'The goddam film is another disaster area. I'll move more heaven and earth than the San Andreas flaw to try preventing it being cited as prosecution evidence, but I probably won't make it. Even in this area, though, we'll have something going for us. I mean what's a skin-flick between friends in the post *Deep Throat* era? If I can work the right kind of jury in – well, we got chances of a sort. How'll she figure on it?'

'In the beginning, with me – just like you say, another Linda Lovelace. Having a ball, in fact—'

'Hey – get out of the wisecrack habit. You don't win friends on the jury that way.'

'Later, when the guys came in – well, like I had in mind. Of course, in between – well, I roughed her up a little.'

'Yeah ... well. So we'll run the goddam thing backwards. 'I'll go talk with Putnam on all this, of course. But what I think we really do here is work on the girl's credibility. Tell me, this gang-bang – you're saying you hit her out of nowhere with it? Right?'

'... right.'

'If you'd told her in advance – you think she'd have gone along with it anyhow?'

'Told her it was for a movie ... quite likely. Yes, sure. Yeah, given time to think about it she'd have sailed for it no question.'

'Good. That's our line, I think.'

Behrman had been talking rapidly, his elbows resting on the desk and his forearms forming an arch just below the level of his face. Now he thrust himself back into his high-backed swivel chair and hands on its arms assumed the more contemplative pose of an expert moving from charted territories on into the unknown. The technician in Paul Madison was not totally reassured. I hope he does his shifts of gear more smoothly in the courtroom, he thought.

'We'll trade,' Behrman said. 'Have to. They'll drop some

charges. It'll be win some, lose some. But we'll win most. It may not look like that to you from there right now, but we will, I promise. Except . . .'

He looked hard at Paul Madison.

'You beat somebody up once outside your home, right?' he said.

'Outside my home? Not me. Not guilty, your honour.'

'Now don't fool with the facts. Not with me. You never stuck it to your stepfather, there?'

'My stepfather . . .? Oh. Oh, right . . . But that was sort of with my car. I thought you meant—'

'It seems you got an enemy, Paul. A real mean enemy.'

'How d'you mean?'

Behrman stretched right back in his chair.

'Ever wonder why they never came hollering on your door the moment you upped and ran off with you – that girl?'

'Some.'

'Reason is that by that time your ma, the mother, had someone else to go running to besides the Missing Persons Bureau, or the Schools Board . . . I've had a couple of inquiry agents working overtime. Seems there's a wealthy industrialist – real wealthy – named Clay Roberts. Mean anything to you?'

Paul Madison shook his head.

'Uh-uh,' he said.

'Comes from North Carolina.'

'Still uh-uh.'

'Father of one Christie Roberts. The late Christie Roberts.'

Oh. Paul Madison forced puzzled nonchalance on to his face with all the skill that he knew how.

'That means something,' he said. 'Quite a lot.'

'Seems the father considered there was something not quite kosher about the way she died.'

Paul Madison shrugged.

'Suicide,' he said. 'They were a while finding her.'

'I remember. Seems Clay Roberts got it into his head you might be responsible for or connected with her death.'

Paul Madison made himself not shrug.

'I dated her a couple of times,' he said. He gestured toward Lyndon Oates as he rediscovered a good measure of his animus.

'She was one of the assignments devised for my image by the miracle worker here.'

Oates bridled like a colonel justly cursed at by a private.

'Now get this one thing—'

But Behrman had cut him short.

'Guys, we don't have the time,' he said.

He came forward to dominate the desk and thus the room again.

'My man with a friend out at the Santa Monica police headquarters tells me that Roberts put a tail on you Paul. After you dusted down your stepfather this tail picked him up. That way he got to your mother. That way Roberts did too. And he got back in to Geisler. Hell hath no fury like a fag hairdresser, Paul – never take them for granted. He didn't only blow the whistle on you with the police. He called North Carolina, too.'

'That pant-shitting queen. He was scared shitless by what they had on him.'

Behrman smiled with a cynical enjoyment.

'Well I've no doubt those particular charges are all going to get lost in a fast shuffle now,' he said. 'You've been like the US cavalry to him, Paul.'

'That—'

'But it's Roberts we've got to watch. The reason no-one pounded down your door to get the girl back was it was him that your mother picked the phone up to. Has to be. I've no doubt he had Pal and Geisler monitoring your domestic scene like the CIA kibitzing on Castro. Now – once again it works both ways. It's bad you don't have all the bankrolls in the game, bad there's a vested enemy in the form of a vengeful father who can afford to indulge himself by coming after you. But mainly it's good. If I bring all this out – when I do, that is – that they've been playing games, biding their time and so on, they're the ones who're going to come out labelled hood. I'll tear your mother to pieces on this more than anything. Your beloved, helpless daughter gets abducted – well, you don't call up businessmen the other side of the country.'

Oates was stirring restlessly in the wing chair. He squirmed forward.

'Are you holding out chances he's going to be walking around free in six month's time?' he said.

Paul Madison felt the stab of something hard and pointed jab between his ribs. At that moment he apprehended for the first time and concretely, as it were, the prospect of a jail, a cell, rising on order at six-thirty. Even sessions with a shrink would have the edge on that. But Behrman was still in the plushly accoutred world of wheeler-dealers. Once more he was smiling knowingly.

'Well I wouldn't exactly go scheduling on that kind of premise myself,' he said. 'We're into a stalling situation here. We'll be asking for postponements while those four inch headlines die down. There's going to be the psychiatric square dancing, all their Chino diagnostic shit – that takes time. We'll almost certainly be into appeals . . . If you want my best guess as of this moment in time, I'd say that at the end of the day we're going to end up with some kind of a day-release situation. But, er, don't quote me.'

'Jesus!' Oates spat out.

'I'd just like to write it into somebody's record,' he said, 'that this cowboy teenage-tail-chaser has just blown an Academy Award—'

'Up theirs!'

'—and for a chaser the absolute best three picture deal I've ever helped put together.'

He had been facing Behrman as he spoke and ostensibly addressing him but no-one had been deceived.

'There's no record for that old news,' Paul Madison said. 'All there is is that money-warped ego of yours you can't ever put back in the outhouse it comes from. With the possible exception of good old Senator Mills in today's *Times*, I don't think there's anyone who's doing a better job of bad-mouthing me than you. With a friend like you, I don't need enemies – I need decontamination.'

Oates had bounced to his feet but Behrman had had a lifetime of turning necessities into virtues.

'That's right,' he said quickly, 'If that's what you clowns are going to insist on doing, the best thing you can do is beat it. Go on, scram, you too. Don't phone us . . . Paul, come sit up at the desk here.'

Oates let out his breath in a hiss of 'I wash my hands' pique. A pouter-pigeon he strode to the door which the good servant Leonard had already employed his ear-splitting tact in opening. The two of them went out. Victor in the brief exchange, Paul Madison sat still and expressionless trying to silence the small core of awareness in his gut that was telling him that underneath his virulence Oates was right: he was a schmuck.

Behrman cracked a grin.

'Oliver Hardy could do those exits better,' he said. 'Hold everything a minute while I organise some coffee. This is going to take all day.'

He flipped a switch on his intercom.

His name was Shurwood Forrest and that was possibly why he had become a psychiatrist. A middle-aged Perry Como with an air of well-groomed circumspection he stared from the penumbra behind the desk-lamp's downcast cone of light towards Paul Madison.

'I'll just go through the nuts-and-bolts questions first,' he said. 'You were born—'

'Let me ask the first questions,' Paul Madison said. 'They sent you a fact-sheet on me?'

'Right. I have it.'

'Good. And you've been technical advisor on two major features in the last couple of years?'

'Yes, I was asked—'

'And you got well paid. Well you've got those facts and you know what you're supposed to end up discovering about me. I'll tell you what you do. You bridge the gap and put it all down on paper and send me a copy. Then we'll meet and you can brief me on whatever I might need to know. That'll work just fine.'

'I can't possibly begin—'

Paul Madison rose to his feet.

'I'm sure you just love working in the movies,' he said.

chapter twenty-eight

He was alone in the house now, of course. Pilar still came in the mornings to polish and clean but without Tibor's constant tidying presence, the job was too much for one person. The rooms he had collected around himself were showing the first signs of a perhaps terminal entropy. The bed went unmade day to day. He simply hauled the sheets – the same sheets – off him or over him according to the time. His laundry piled high in the utility room. It was easier to work his way through the tightly packed racks in his closets. When that supply ran short he could have more sent in. He ate in the kitchen. Although Pilar did the dishes each morning and, snacking at random intervals, he ate fewer meals, at the end of the day there was always an untidy litter of plates and skillets and cups beyond numbering taking up every horizontal surface within eyesore sight. Those times that he fixed himself something hot – ham and eggs, spaghetti – he often as not ended by eating direct from the skillet or saucepan. He drank a lot. Each night he promised himself that, with nothing to do but wait around, he'd get an early night. Always he'd find himself staring at an old-time movie, grey and nostalgic in the small hours. It would be ten in the morning before he woke: nearer eleven before he kicked the rumpled sheets aside.

He was bored but did nothing. He did not work out in his gym. He seemed too mentally tired to get down to that. He scarcely read. He seemed too physically tired. The books in his library seemed to be tired too. As they gathered dust they had lost the confidence they were worth reading. Sex hardly entered his thoughts. Violence seemed to have been lobotomised from his mind. In the hot afternoons, never entering the water, he would sit, drink at his side, in the umbrella'd shade, staring at the stabbing ripples of light snaking across his pool. Even as he ignored them, they were compelling, mesmerising. The pool was a screen upon which shimmered unconnected flashbacks from his past. Lizards darting like quicksilver as he and Charley Twomoons catapulted after them. Rosner telling him to lay off Sam. Sylvia Kilmartin's face the night he picked up Dennis Curtis's Oscar.

His father being carried face downwards into the store. His mother with her legs . . .

From time to time he would stir himself to freshen up his drink.

Twice he went into his library and took out his diary and the notebook he had twinned with it. The desk lamp made a small, intense circle of light and all else in the room was twilight with the shadows of his past, his thoughts and with the silence. He updated neither book. There was embarrassment he could not face in the confrontation with the facts his pen would have to write. He closed the books both times and returned them to their drawer.

His mail he ignored. Pilar brought it up but he left it untouched. The phone after the first screaming, hate-ridden calls, he had left off the hook. If Leonard or Schwarz wanted to get to him and it was that important, they could come out and see him. He switched the gate buzzer through to his stale-aired, too-large lounge and kept the security TV in operation. After the first couple of days the vindictive, meanly justified faces of the demonstrators who'd crawled out from under the Hollywood rocks to keep snarling vigil at his gate had disappeared, put paid to by a police force anxious to protect and serve its own image. He had stared at the brandished fists, the straining lips pulled taut across bad teeth and felt no connection between the manic, hateful expressions and himself. They were from some Peyton Place of a soap opera about the White House. There was only one judge, one jury, whose opinions he cared for and right now it seemed too much of an effort to consider a verdict on himself.

One evening the buzzer went. He got up from his eggs and looked in the kitchen security monitor. A shape was there, a woman. But she was like a ghost – grey in the thin image, with a scarf over her head and the eyeless sockets of huge sunglasses. He almost didn't care to use the squawk box but a faint inclination for something – relief, a change of pace – saw finally to it that he did. He pressed the button.

'Yes?' he said.

'So you are home,' a voice said. Hearing its sad huskiness he could put identity to the faded picture a split-second before it was proffered.

'Stella Lang,' the voice and image said. 'I'm keeping my promise. Want to buy me a glass of water?'

She was the one person it seemed absolutely right to see. He released the gate.

'I'll meet you halfway,' he said.

'You sure you know what you're saying?' he heard. 'I don't get many offers like that these days.'

He went out through the kitchen door and round the side of the house. The twilight air was soft and warm and pleasingly sad memories hovered in it just beyond the edge of vision. It was an evening, he knew, to take stock regretfully of all the things you've never done. But for a man young and known on five continents that is a task not so easily performed. Flowers scented the air. He walked on and the downward slope lengthened his stride a little jarringly and forced his legs on, one beyond the other almost despite his will. He rounded a bend piled high with rhododendron and found that, at a quarter of his speed, she too was walking. She paused and waited until he came down to her.

'Hi,' she said.

'Hi.'

'Not intruding am I?' she said.

He shook his head. Suddenly happy, it seemed, she removed the sunglasses.

'You're the only one who bothered to find out,' he said.

'Ah, well, you have to remember I've a sort of proprietorial interest in the house.'

'In kind of a mess at the moment. Like me, I guess.'

'Well it's used to reflecting the vagaries of its owners.'

Instinctively, naturally, they had begun to walk back up towards one of the things they had in common.

'You haven't told me how well I'm looking,' she said. It was true. She was. She must have lost better than twenty pounds. The puffiness had gone. He reached out and took the silk scarf from around her head and she shook the rich chestnut redness of her hair thickly, loosely, free. Yes. The bone structure of that face from the past once again sharply defined its claims to classic beauty. Who could have objected if she had once found herself a princess?

'You don't look well,' he said. 'You look great. You look beautiful.'

And for a moment, as she heard the compliment she'd grown unaccustomed to hearing once more on a man's lips, she was a young girl again. Embarrassed pleasure made her flick her gaze over his shoulder before worldliness came to rescue her.

'At my age great will do just fine,' she said. She darted a different kind of look at him. Then dared to voice what even to speak of maybe put at risk.

'I guess it might just have worked,' she said. 'There was a golf-course next to the place and last time round I shot an eighty-nine.'

'Easy as that, huh?'

She grabbed out at his arm as memories clawed at her.

'Don't ever say it's easy,' she said.

The fierce grip relaxed, was released.

'No not easy,' she said softly. 'So bad this time I think the horror of it may make it stick. I couldn't go back again knowing what I know now. Ever been in a padded cell?'

'. . . no,' he said.

They walked on a way in silence.

'And I've got a part,' she said.

'You have!'

'And in a real movie. A comedy, no less. I'm teamed with Betty Bacall and Celeste Holm. We go to some class reunion, get stoned – yes, ouch! – and head straight on to Europe with the credit cards. The husbands and kids like you we leave behind.'

'Fantastic,' he said. He realised this was the first time in days, no, weeks, he'd felt enthusiasm for anything quicken along his nerves.

'It's fantastic they should even make a comedy these days,' she said. 'I got clinched for it yesterday. I've only been back in town three days. How about that!'

She looked at him.

'I read about . . . you . . . in the home,' she said. 'I'd have come out here right away but you can see that a thing like a part might be just a little bit important to a girl in my, er, delicate condition.'

He reached out and took her hand. They walked round the final bend and the house was there before them. She halted. He felt the hand go rigid.

'Oh God,' she said, 'I hope I can do it still.'

He squeezed the hand hard.

'Better than anyone,' he said. 'Let's go talk to the trees.'

The warm air seemed their element. This was a time out of Time. The seconds and minutes would start scampering squeakingly by again if they went inside. Outside was peace and magic. Slowly, perhaps to hold the magic in, they walked a circle about the house. She looked up at it.

'I was twenty-four when he built it for me,' she said. 'It's still the only house in LA for me that looks as though it has a past. When it was new it had that.'

She was right. The verandahs, tiles, thick walls and narrow, shuttered windows conjured thoughts of Albuquerque, Santa Fe. It reminded you of conquistadores who might have known the Escorial, travelled to Rome, traded in Bruges. It was a house, he realised, that had a place in a long stream of culture and he realised it was an attribute quite independent of his occupancy.

'Who was the architect?' he thought to ask for the first time in his life.

'I forget. Some Mexican. A nice man . . . the best I ever knew for listening to all that Herman had to say and then charmingly ignoring every last and every thing.'

She grinned at him wryly.

'I should have asked him what the trick to it was,' she said.

Her face darkened again.

'I miss the house,' she said. 'Of all the thousand places I've lived in, this was the only one I was happy in. But if someone else had to have it, I'm glad it was you. You're not some fat banker pig of a producer. You have talent. And however much you freak out, you understood what I just said then. The house means something to you for its own sake too.'

They had come to a halt again. The soft dusk was thickening around them. Her face was faint now as in one of her early movies late upon TV. A sulphurous yellow glow was beginning to corode the sky above the town but that was lower down and ten thousand miles away. Here, high above and in their enchanted circle, the stillness of the evening air was sacrosanct.

'Please hold me,' she said.

He took her in his arms. He had expected to find her trembling but there was something resolute in the press, gentle but firm, she met with him. She was a little shorter than he'd thought and he realised she'd never lost a superb dancer's carriage. Very slowly, warm, her arms moved about his back.

'And kiss me.'

He kissed a mouth the image of whose perfection men had carried into war and women, trying to match, had found cause for despair. Like everything else in that suspended twilight it was warm and soft and rich with memory. And still, surely, possessor of an ageless cunning. A cunning which pliant and caressing, rejected all suggestion of haste and force. We have world enough and time, the kiss said, to savour the last sweet-sad deliciousness and then, if we wish, begin again. It was a long while before she stole her mouth away. She put her head against his chest and the scent of her hair was like that second kiss. She moved her head and looked up at him. Her eyes were bright and un-blinking from a confidence he'd never seen in them before.

'You know why I came tonight, don't you?' she said.

'Tell me.'

'To find out how long it's been since you slept with someone old enough to be your mother.'

Later, he lay back next to her in his bed and miraculously the magic and softness had not gone. They had wavered when he'd shown her round. The library, where they'd started, had enchant-ed her. In her presence the books had suddenly appeared august and dignified, reverend senators chivalrous before beauty old enough to meet them on equal terms. Then she had run her fingers across the top of one of the Thackerays. It had come away dusty.

'I remember that,' she had said. 'You end up selling the Degas. Whatever they do to you, don't let it happen here a second time.'

It was the first time she'd made any direct reference to what Oates had called his 'little local difficulty image-wise', but he found he was more mortified by the dust on her finger.

'Oh I guess they're working out some sort of deal,' he said purposely vague.

'They used to make lovely, stylish films in this town,' she said, 'now all they make is deals.'

'Your new one will change all that.'

'I wish I could believe that, I so truly do.'

'Come and see what else I've done.'

But the next item on the tour was his sauna-gym complex where once she'd had a wall-length mirror and her dancer's bar. She had stood in the middle of the room looking around. Then she had turned to him with a quick pain in her eyes.

'Let's skip the tour, please,' she said. 'I was right last time I came. I should have realised.'

'So should I,' he said. 'I'm sorry.'

On the threshold to his bedroom door she had paused and once more he had felt her hand grow tense in his.

'It's been a long time between drinks,' she said.

'Be all the better for it.'

Then she had been brave. She had made no attempt to slip into the bed still half-clothed. She had slowly and unhurriedly un-dressed in full upright view. He had been lying down waiting be-fore she was through. It was from this low-angle approach that he saw her approach and arms spread slightly wide in appeal offer herself up for inspection.

'No strings,' she said. 'If you don't want to, we don't have to try bridging the generation gap.'

He looked at her. Her body had not had the same powers of near instant recovery those bones had bestowed upon the face. The thighs, hips, and belly had surrendered to the years. The breasts, never huge in later screen fashion, had lost the high fine firmness of their youth. And yet, in the half-light, in the final simplicity with which she offered herself, there was a beauty that caught at his throat.

'I want to,' he had said.

'I hope I remember how it goes.'

'Let's find out.'

'Slowly,' she said. 'You don't have to worry. You don't have to think. Just remember I started this because I'm a little old and pretty stupid and I just want you to come here against me and hold me.'

So she had come to his bed. And it had all been one with the evening and her kiss. Making him wait, she had stroked him, kissed his mouth, his closed eyes, his shoulders. Her hands had soothed at his brow. When she moved to him and lay body against body it had still been with gentleness and not passion. It had been the soft, passive, touching together of people strayed and lost, finding in each other's tenderness that universal comfort and response.

'Sssh . . . wait . . .' she had whispered. 'Oh but you're so warm.'

He had found, suddenly, he was content and so naturally at peace. It could happen soon or late but until whichever of those certain moments it might be, he was at rest and floating. Before the act it was like the most perfect aftermath of sex. When at last her hand swept lower with unmistakeable intent, he was surprised.

'Now,' she said.

It was still so langorously slow. She sought nothing for herself and her repose, the soft smoothness of her skin, the dark warmth she had introduced him to as if for the first time, brought him a fullness that was imperceptible in increase until, welling up of its own without movement to alloy it, the sweetness gathered itself in a moment of fulfilled ecstasy.

'Ah!' she said softly.

She held him to her and, not speaking, he stayed with her for minutes.

'And you?' he had said at last.

'Later. Rest now.'

Floating again, he had been lying on his back next to her for a long time. Or perhaps a short time.

'I lied to you,' he heard somebody say. It seemed to be him and he seemed to have spoken out loud.

'Oh? About what?'

'About . . . about never having been inside a padded cell.'

'Oh?'

With his eyes held fast on the even pattern of his cedared ceiling, sparing neither her nor himself the smallest detail, he told her about Christie Roberts. He spoke in a dry, flat, even voice. When it chose finally to come to a halt, he saw that two long glistening trails of silent tears were catching the last gleaming of the light.

'Are you crying for her?' he said.

She nodded.

'For her,' she said. 'And for you. Because you were able to tell me.'

She took him in her arms again and held him with compassion, that other side of love.

chapter twenty-nine

Hate California – it's cold and it's damp.

Lorenz Hart

It had been grey and overcast all day. And cold. Late in the afternoon it could still have been early morning. It could have been Maine not Malibu. The great glaucous eye of sea rolling its swell monotonously forward to cover, re-cover, the wet-dark sand in an uneven creamy lace might more readily have been the Atlantic.

They had driven down in her new VW. They had the whole beach to themselves. The tide was retreating and they walked where the sand was still half moist and flat and did not make them stumble through its dry and heaped unevenness. The wind blew stiffly at them with a cold and damp moroseness and she sensed that their positions had reversed. Today she was the one with a present and a future: he was the one with a past. He was half her age but he was the one for whom the wind came freighted down with memories and whispers. It was for him it blew remembrance of things done or not done and the decisions, the balance and commitment never quite as it had felt they should be.

The damp air was heavy with the tang of salt as they walked on and did not speak. Then he turned to her.

'There are a couple of favours I'd like to ask of you,' Paul Madison said.

'Of course.'

'Could you arrange for a wreath to be sent in my – a wreath be sent to Sean Flaherty's funeral for me.'

'Sure.'

'Better just say "from an admirer".'

'Can I say it's from two ?' Stella Lang asked.

'Yes. Of course. Better.'

'I wonder what a man like that's last conscious thoughts are. A great artist, you know.'

'Rage, I imagine, he didn't have the time to square away those last ideas he still had in his head.'

'What else?'

'Hmmn?'

'What other favours?'

'You won't be annoyed?'

'I don't know. How can I tell? I shouldn't think so.'

'I want to give you your house back. I want you to promise me you'll go and live there.'

She stopped in her tracks and stared at him in a silent wide-eyed amazement. She was wearing a chunky, beige wrap-around cardigan with bold horizontal stripes in chocolate and dark green. She was still silent.

'Please,' he said. 'It's always been yours, really. It hasn't been happy while you've been away.'

A saving irony crept into the grateful disbelief with which she had fixed him.

'They haven't written lines like that since my day,' she said.

'Perhaps that's why it came out that way.'

'I couldn't,' she said. 'Thanks from the bottom—'

'Why not?'

She looked at him as if he might have forgotten who he was.

'You don't just have raps to beat,' she said, 'you have half the world suing you from here to Tennessee.'

'There's money. Have you seen what my movies have been grossing since I made the front pages?'

'Yeah, people! All the same—'

'I'm having Bratby and Finer do an audit for me on all my movies. That will be from here to Tennessee. They're going to find more money of mine that somehow didn't quite reach me than I've so far received.'

'Are you sure?'

He didn't smile so often these days but now he did.

'Positive. It's in their own best interests.'

She resumed their walking.

'So you've decided that you're . . . you're not going to be able to be there yourself?' she said.

He shrugged.

'I won't win them all,' he said. He paused but, leaning into the wind a little, she kept on up the beach. Then she had turned to face him and the wind was whipping her hair forward about her forehead.

'I'll offer you a compromise,' she said.

His head came up.

'Yes?'

'I'll go back and live there while you can't. And I'll look after it and keep it warm for you. And I'll think about you while I do and you're not there.'

'I'd really like for you to have it.'

She hesitated.

'Maybe later,' she said. 'Let's see just what you're going to need.'

'I don't need anything.'

'Everybody does.'

'I'm sorry. I didn't mean to sound ungracious . . . Okay, lady, you got yourself a deal.'

She smiled in a way that no-one in the world could quite have matched.

'Thank you,' she said.

They walked on a ways.

'I shall never need a house in Hollywood again, you see,' he suddenly said.

'. . . What are you going to do, then?'

'I don't know. You know what I'd like to do?'

'No?'

'Be a landscape gardener. That's clean dirt.'

'Oh, that must be so wonderful,' she burst spontaneously out with. 'Living with the seasons and planning things to last so much longer than just one lifetime.'

'Or one movie-time. You'd have to go and live where they have seasons, of course . . . I'd like to ask you something else, as well.'

She tried to hold herself as casually as possible. There was no way that she would hamper him by saying she would marry him.

'Yes?'

'You're shivering. Would you mind going back to the car and waiting for me while I walk on out to the headland?'

'I'll wait. But I'll wait here.'

'You'll freeze.'

'I'm okay. This is warm. I want to watch you.'

'Okay.'

She watched him move away. While they had been talking she had not been conscious of the waves' broken murmuring. But now she heard the coldly indifferent outpouring of breath they gave as their long run in to the shore was finally done. She raised her eyes up from the confusion of the foam and stared out at the distant point where the two greys of sky and sea met in a long straight line. It was from beyond there that the waves rocked endlessly in, swelling unceasingly like cold grey hopes feeding onwards off each other. When they ran up upon the shore and found themselves dashed to nothing, their long expectations fruit-less, they still clutched at the sand with pointless fingers – tried to cling with fingers become so puny they dissolved away between the shifting grains.

She turned her eyes toward Paul Madison. He had found a low rock to stand on, one stride into the water, and might have been a statue. She had never seen him rest so motionless before. She wondered if for all its immensity the sea was big enough a surface to reflect back to him his thoughts; whether it was no more to him than a clouded mirror, the surface visible, all else hidden beneath.

Not only from the cold, she shivered. Perhaps the empty deserts of his own wasting that he contemplated, were ultimately no different from those she had known and would never be sure she might not know again. But it was a landscape of the mind which everybody fashioned for themselves. And in the end there was still no guarantee a greater wisdom would come.

She shivered again. It was cold. But to leave him now must seem like a betrayal. God knew her body had acquired capacities for enduring pain. She stood her ground as the wind came on more bleakly.

At last he turned, stepped down, retraced his steps. Freed into motion by his own, she advanced to meet him along the line of his footprints in the sand. Her own face felt flushed by the cold but his seemed pale. The animal vitality that he always exuded even when in repose seemed subdued for the first time of her knowing him.

'Hi,' she said.

'Hi, yourself.'

They began to trudge back to the car.

'One last favour,' he said.

'Last until the next,' she laughed.

'When they re-run my movies to get their kicks reminding themselves that this is what a dirty degenerate freak looks like and they always had me figured—'

'They won't do that.'

'They already are. It doesn't matter. But when you see one of my movies again – if you do or want to – will you remember that just because I was a star didn't mean I couldn't act a little.'

She reached her own hand out for his and grasped it tightly.

'It's easy to remember what you can't ever forget,' she said.

In the morning when she woke he was no longer next to her. A towelling robe, blue with red trim was on the back of a cane chair and she slid out of bed to put it on. Easily, as if the house were still her own she made her way downstairs in search of him. She could bear to look upon the thousand changes now: the night had made them shared. The great central room was empty and the kitchen too. She found him in his study crouched before the big square Mexican hearth. He had lit a flimsy kind of fire. Paper was its sole fuel. Intact but totally charred leaves fluttered in the upward draught their own heat made like damned souls or the wings of tortured birds. Then giving up the struggle they drifted disintegratingly down again, black, aimless, untidy snowflakes rising thicker and thicker.

He was feeding the central blaze with pages torn in twos and threes from a black-bound exercise book. The paper he tore was white but covered in the ink of a neat, even handwriting.

'What is it you're burning?'

'Old flames.'

'On my account?'

'Of course.'

'I am flattered. Or is it the book that says where the bodies are buried?'

'Something like that,' he said.

chapter thirty

Magnum Re-issue of *Turkey* is proving no turkey in a hot first week eyeing million plus from 57 sites.

Variety

They had holed him up for the night before his first day of the trial at a motel out near the airport. Tom Leonard had made the reservations in a couple of nothing names and production managed all the other details. He had no more to do himself than count Jumbos to help send himself to sleep and, that not working, read *Bleak House* deep into the small hours.

Sprawling his tanned, vital and shirt-sleeved presence on one bed, a bathroom glass of malt whisky in his hand, Behrman had earlier come to deliver his reassuring opinion as to how the opening takes would go.

'It'll all be very low-profile and pretty boring,' he said. 'You may find this pretty hard to believe right now but halfway through the afternoon you'll be so out of your head with the overwhelming lack of drama, you're going to be wanting the judge to be handing down his sentence right then and there. But whatever you feel, you stay looking bright-eyed and bushy-tailed and pleasant. But that'll be no sweat for you. I guess an actor's an ideal client.'

It takes one to know one, Paul Madison thought.

'So what is the big hang-up,' he said.

Behrman winked again. It was a habit that conveyed duplicity with each repetition.

'I'm out to get us a star-struck jury going for us in there,' he said. 'I may have a lot of challenges to throw. Selection will maybe go on quite a time.'

'Days?'

'Probably.'

'And just so's I know, where are we unofficially officially at on the horse-trading?'

'We're going to plead "guilty" on charges one and two.

Putnam's going to announce the State is not intending to prosecute on charges five, six and seven. We'll see but I'm then probably going to move for a postponement in the light of this altered situation and announce that we are going to comply with the State's wish for you to undergo diagnostic examination by their boy. Harker will grant the postponement and delay sentencing, of course, on one and two.'

He paused, took a long pull at his drink. Then, excitedly, he had winked over the top of his glass and was pushing himself up on to his feet. He paced between the beds before the imaginary jury he so often played to. Whisky slopped from his glass as he turned to sharply gesture.

'And I've got good news,' he said in a voice deepening into its courtroom resonance.

'I've found out a little something from one of the ears I keep close to the Hollywood ground. Something about your sister, Paul.'

'Half-sister.'

'The girl. Right? It's something that for obvious reasons they've intended to keep quiet but I've found out about it anyway.'

He paused to milk his fullest effect.

'So?'

'She's signed to star in a feature about what she alleges happened that night. How'd you like them apples?'

'It did happen.'

'For Christ's sake! We just may be bugged!'

Paul Madison shrugged. He looked across at Tom Leonard.

'You know what I'm thinking?' he said.

Tom Leonard shook his head.

'If it's Lyndon, it's nothing I ever heard about,' he said. 'This is pure news to me.'

He looked up at Behrman.

'Who's she signed with?' he said.

'Aw, some sexploitation Mexican schmuck,' Behrman said. 'It'll be the turkey of the year.'

'No it won't,' Paul Madison said. 'It'll get its money back and plenty more besides.'

'You don't seem very impressed by what we've come up with here, Paul,' Behrman said. He was clearly miffed that his little theatrical coup had not been granted more acclaim. Paul Madison shrugged.

'You want me to say I'm glad my sister is maintaining the family tradition of movie stardom – I'm glad. Whoopee.'

'Now, Paul. Don't let me have you clamming up into some fake indifference on account of you've got stage fright. I don't want you as a smart-mouth but I do want you with charm.'

'Okay, Laurence, I didn't—'

'Don't you see what this means? I can crucify her on the stand with this! I can rip her open. This is supposed to be the great gang-bang trauma that's blighted her body and psychic integrity for all eternity and she's just signed to re-live it before the cameras for a piece of the action! The jury we've got us in there are going to end by urging Harker to sentence her.'

Paul Madison had shrugged a second time.

'Maybe we can share a cell,' he said.

Behrman had laughed.

'One way or another I don't think that's such a likely eventuality,' he said. He reached for his shot silk lined jacket and as he slipped it on, glanced around the room.

'If you do have to take a little vacation,' he said, 'I promise you something better than this. . . . Okay, I'll let myself out. Sleep fast, now.'

'See you in court,' Paul Madison had said as another plane roared overhead.

Though he had not slept well, he had felt fine the next morning. The tightening of nerves as he shaved was no more acute than he had known as a student actor. Less, in fact. He knew by now he had a predestined role and none of the complex speeches. There was tranquillity in that. Sunglassed in the coffee shop, the condemned eating the traditional hearty meal, he had breakfasted with a casually good appetite. The wardrobe they had selected for his return before the cameras amused him but he had gone back to the room and dressed with a good grace. He could have taken odds on its predictability: a discreet, charcoal-grey two-piece suit, a dark blue silk tie with a faint diagonal ochre stripe and a lawn shirt in a pale blue chosen because its colour would look innocent yet not dazzle under the hand-held TV lights outside the Court House and along the mad, bawling rat-race of its corridors. Similarly, the car, a Ford Galaxie, had been chosen for its becoming modesty. A man chauffeured to court in one of Detroit's finest could not be patricianly and un-Americanly above the people. The chauffeur, yet again, would be Tom Leonard. This time they would take Manchester and turn north on Lincoln Boulevard as that stretch of Highway One was known.

It was a bright morning with a feeling of spring about it beyond the glass and the air-conditioning. For a while Paul Madison was content to sit and stare through the windshield as the cheap pastel facias of southern California swam regularly by. The colours, he realised – pink, powder blue, pale green, lilac – were the same cosmetic range applied with the same heavy-handedness, an in-experienced and unsubtle chick would use in making up. To seek refinement from an LA power-base was like pursuing a life of denial in Nieman-Marcus. And talking of unsubtle chicks . . .

'Tom,' he said, 'a couple of things before the world goes bananas – that night you found me and old Margot in the sack . . . there was never anything personal in that . . .'

Tom Leonard took his eyes off the road a second to look side-ways at him.

'As I recall it,' he said, 'it looked pretty damn personal to me.' He was less than amused but not, it seemed, unrelaxed.

'Between her and me, it wasn't. I was just getting back at you because I was as sore as hell you'd whopped the lid off me at tennis.'

'Yeah, well, I guess I'd figured that much. But that's some retribution, humping the wife of the winner!'

'A point. You did the right thing quitting Margot.'

'I think so. Even with the kid . . . As a matter of fact I'm teeter-ing on getting married again.'

'Oh? Do I—'

'To Celine.'

'Oh. Congratulations, Tom. I hope it goes very well for you. I'm sure it will.'

But surprised, he had spoken a split-moment too late and too flatly. He saw Tom Leonard's hands tighten on the wheel and this time his look stayed squarely on the road. It was a mutual acknowledgement that marrying Celine was courting certain disaster.

The silence persisted for the rest of the journey. Paul Madison killed the interval by conjuring up memories of Celine knelt be-fore him, not in worship, her eyes drunk with sex. He began to imagine her and Leonard making it. But he found he did not enjoy the projection.

Then, amid a scurry of flailing arms and rushing men, of cameras bumping against the windows of the very car, of flash-bulbs blinding and of two dozen voices yapping, cursing, plead-ing, they were gliding to a halt. He braced himself a second, then forced the door open on the most significant photo call of his entire career with the sheet-lightning of the press bulbs already beginning to flash.

chapter thirty-one

There was no deal on President Nixon's pardon, period.
President Gerald R. Ford to House
Judiciary Subcommittee, 17 *October* 1975

After the bedlam of the Court House corridors, the mêlée of sheer
bodily contact as Behrman's hired hands literally ran interference
through the scrimmaging jabber of the Press, they had fetched up
in the haven of a small ante-room. A cop of some sort stood outside the door to the corridor. Inside, light wooden panelling, a
polished darker table suggested scholarship and honourable
tradition. Even peace.

The fierce jostling and elbowing had partially served to unite
Leonard back with him again. They had, after all, a sort of
common cause. Leonard looked at him now and smiled uneasily.

'Kind of waiting to see the Dean of Studies,' he said, 'Or going
for your first job interview.'

Paul Madison found the remark embarrassingly revealing and
he was still seeking the best reply to it when the door opened and
Behrman's entry provided a dubious rescue.

'Hi,' Behrman said, 'nice day for a lynching, huh.'

He winked.

Radiating good health and confidence, it was Behrman who
looked the actor. He wore a dark blue suit whose red stripe was
just loud enough in colour to suggest inside the sober man of the
community there was a swinger sometimes willing to come out.
The wearer of this suit was responsible but cared. Catch him
Sunday barbecuing in the back yard for his family and dog and
he would understand your problem better than yourself, more
sympathetically than your best friend. If you were female and
under forty – well, forty-five, maybe – and your thoughts ran
that way, the suggestion somehow lingered about his distinguish-
edly grey hair that he would take you to his bed with more charm
than you were used to in that department too.

'Okay,' he said. 'They'll be knocking on the door for us in less
than five minutes. No more instructions, Paul. Let's talk about

the Dodgers or some such, huh. Seen any good movies, lately, Tom?'

'They don't make them that way any more.'

It didn't work. The room seemed only colder.

'Larry,' Paul Madison said, 'I owe you an apology.'

'Don't owe me apologies. Owe me money.'

'Larry – I don't want to trade pleas with Putnam.'

'Paul – I have to tell you, there's no way you can plead "not guilty" right across the board and come away without getting badly burned. There's publicity on this a mile high. The DA's office will want—'

'You misunderstand. I want to plead "guilty".'

'What!'

'I want to plead "guilty". On all counts. All charges.'

'Paul, for Christ's sake! What are you saying? We've got us a deal! I've got Putnam's word—'

'You had a deal with him. Now you don't have one with me.'

'Yes, we have. I have—'

'We don't! We don't at this end. We don't because I'm not playing.'

He looked Behrman straight between the eyes and knew even dry-mouthed, now that he'd said it, heart-pounding, hands gone clammy, that what was already troubling the lawyer was his own loss of face, the taking away of a chance to shine. Tom Leonard had been looking at him with the strain of a man unable to believe what he had heard stretching his face into a subtle displacement.

'Why?' he said.

'Why plead "guilty"?'

'Because I am.'

'What's that got to do with it?' Behrman rapped out.

'Everything, I decided.'

'Jesus!' The lawyer ran a hand through his expertly blow-waved hair and was suddenly dishevelled. The bounce was crumpled out of him.

'Jesus!' he repeated. 'Why wait for now, for Christ's sake? For Christ's sake! Why only tell me now?'

'I didn't want you guys to have time to gang up on me and brainwash me into changing back again – fill me with the horrors of what was in line for me.'

'But that's just what you are in for!' Behrman almost yelled. In his passion still not totally admitting to himself that this was happening, he was leaning forward across the table, his weight on his arms.

'The kind of charges stacked up against you – Putnam'll have no option but to ask for all he can get. He'll want to. The DA who stuck it to a star! It'll guarantee his re-election. I'm not joking. He won't throw the book. He'll ask the judge to throw the whole fucking Court House.'

Behrman was wide-eyed as he surrendered his last pretensions to suave trouble-shooter. Recognition of the forensic quagmire his reputation had stumbled into had penetrated his inner consciousness.

'The guys inside – the cons,' he yelled. 'They've got daughters. They don't like sex offenders. They don't like guys who got lucky and rich in the movies. Ever been gang-banged yourself? Because that's what's going to happen to you, I swear! On my mother's grave, I swear!'

'We'll have to see,' Paul Madison said.

'. . . Look . . . look, Paul. It's a kind of stage-fright, isn't it. You don't want to face them. Right now you don't think you can go—'

'No. It isn't. It isn't that. No deal. No deal and that's all.'

Aghast, Laurence Behrman stared at him. He was rarely speechless. The quagmire had sucked his last shots out of him. He straightened up. His gold cuff-links in the shape of a tiny Justice with her scales disappeared again up into his jacket sleeve.

'Well . . .' he said, '. . . you want to play hero . . . I wash my hands . . .'

It had happened quickly. Now that he had said it all Paul Madison could feel his knees beginning to grow weak. It was suddenly hot in the room and difficult to breath. His stomach felt on the point of dissolving into the icy liquid of fear. Of knowing he had made a terrible mistake. As he had stared out at the grey Pacific rolling inexorably in to confirm with every wave that, destined though it would always be to fail, it would always struggle to be free, he had felt the calmness of a resolution unalterably taken bring him purposeful tranquillity. The ocean was a measure of some kind of reality, a measure that revealed his own life was wound around a core of poisonous triviality whose own centre was hollow. But now . . . ten years, maybe, of denial of everything! His mind then had had the strength of steel to endure in its decision. Now, he felt his spirit flinch and quail.

Unwittingly, it was Behrman, rallying to make a last appeal

who put the iron back into his soul.

'Paul,' he said shaking his head pityingly, 'they'll throw away the key.'

'It's okay, Larry,' he said, 'I only lived in Hollywood anyway.'

He found he looked at Tom Leonard as he said that.

There was a knock on the door and an usher of some kind came in.

He had not given a live performance in long ages. As he entered the court room at Behrman's side the visual sense of people crowding him from every side, the assault on his ears of the rising hubbub of speculation, came near to inducing claustrophobia in him. And yet the bench, the jury self-consciously not looking at him or blatantly catching their first rubber-necking glimpse, the gate through to the two waiting tables – it was all so much a set. It was he who now felt a total disbelief that this was happening pumping through him with his life-blood. The temptation to look for the camera was almost overpowering. So too was the feeling in some deep, still-poisoned recess of his make-up, that once again the focus of all eyes, he should feel flattered.

Behrman opened the low gate for him and he sat in the chair to the left the resigned, unsmiling lawyer indicated he should take. Behrman sat down next to him and did not speak. If a man with a tan can be pale, then he had managed it. Still not speaking he shot his cuffs and looked at his watch.

Nothing happened. Floating on a level of super reality an inch above the ground Paul Madison turned to look at the jury. A dozen pairs of eyes flicked the direction of their gaze to ceiling, floor, to bench or to their owner's lap. Their collective lack of nerve had given him leave to pass the time to look them over.

It was nicely representative for California. There were five women, four blacks, two orientals. One of the negros was very young. There were two old women, one old man . . . As a group they looked overall less smart, less well-heeled than even, say, the pseudo-professional class journalists who'd bayed at his heels, snapped questions at him as he'd walked their corridor line. What did these people do for a living. Impossible to say. Well, he was retired now, obviously. Those two were housewives, most likely. But the others . . . It was too much of a cliché to suppose the black kid worked in a Car Wash, the oriental girl in a bank. That guy could have driven a hack or worked a lathe for Douglas or . . . well you couldn't say. All you could say was that it was a face that fitted with the others – a used face, a little battered even, a lot self-conscious. Give or take they were all like that. Right off the bat, without any fast shuffles from a shit-hot mouthpiece, they were probably as averagely fair a jury as you'd come to find. They were just exactly what they were supposed to be, plain folks.

And there were the people Behrman would have sorted through. He'd have tried to exclude the women, of course, on account of the sex stuff. No doubt in the hope that her pouting come-on looks suggested she would have liked being on the receiving end he'd have settled for the young oriental girl as a token female. Good news for the girl if the jury became hung. Doubly good news if they were well hung!

See – he could joke. Life was going on. He turned his head and found himself staring straight at Putnam. He was able to maintain the eye-line. With his loose brush-cut the chunkily built DA seemed rather sadly old fashioned and, perhaps knowing how he was, in a way, about to steal his thunder too, he could feel faintly sorry for this less than intimidating, unpleasant little bureaucrat. It was Putnam who looked away. He was free to return to the more interesting prospect of the jury. He did so and again a dozen pairs of eyes were abruptly otherwise engaged.

. . . yes, Behrman would have asked them other questions too.

'Remembering you are on oath, Mrs Doe, have you at any time, in your opinion, harboured prejudices against the acting profession.'

'er . . . excuse me ?'

'Do you like actors ?'

Jesus! That was a set-piece he was doing well to miss. How did the old joke go ?

'After all, actors are human too, I guess.'

'Did you ever eat lunch with one ?'

No. He wanted no special dispensation. There was one actor he knew for sure he didn't like and it would be a monstrous imposition to hold that jury in their rows of seats for weeks trying to decide whether that actor was guilty when he knew beyond any shadow of doubt, legal or otherwise, he was.

'. . . Harker, presiding.'

Behrman nudged him. Automatically he rose as, in uneven succession, everyone else in the court room seemed to as well. He was reminded of the mourners who had turned out on Hollywood parade at the Wee Kirk O' the Highlands rising to sing their ragged hymn for Dennis Curtis.

Now he must sit. But he had the judge to look at now. A pity.

The man was utterly nondescript. Take his costume back to wardrobe and he could have lost himself among the jury. There was that consolation too. In refusing to contest any of the charges, he removed from that small bespectacled man any opportunity of interfering with what had at last become most precious of all considerations to him, his own, private, self-determination. Or destruction.

'. . . please stand.'

It was his solo this time. He did as he was asked. Behrman was sitting staring with an expressionless mask at the thick folder on the table in front of him. It was not a mask. It was an expressionless wince.

'. . . plead to the charge?'

His cue. He must neither overplay, nor throw it too much away. He was giving up acting. Behrman's face was toward him now begging a last-second reprieve.

'Guilty,' he said.

He heard silence then, a moment after Putnam's dropped pencil hit the floor, a great roar of gleeful, cheated, astonished incredulity from the packed bleachers behind. The judge's gavel began to rap down steadily and each blow contending against the uproar was a loud, fateful knock on the door of Paul Madison's future.

chapter thirty-two

Madison pleads 'Guilty' on all counts. Sentencing tomorrow.

L.A. Times

He was an exclusive property again. Pending sentencing, they had explained, he would stay here alone in his small separate, solid-doored cell. Not uncomfortable in the prison blue – it was so little different from his everyday wear – he lay stretched out on its wall-fastened bunk successfully reading *Puddenhead Wilson*.

A clang at the door, a key in the lock made him start up and lay the book aside. A guard, big, blonde, young, stood in the door-way looking down at him with a crude curiosity.

'You got a visitor,' he said.

'Do I have to see him?'

'Nope. You won't be turning them away after your first month, though. Says his name's Tom Leonard.'

Oh well, one last time.

'Where?'

'Down the hall.'

He got to his feet. A second, older guard was waiting in the passageway outside. He walked easily between the pair of them towards a group of distant doors.

'I guess they really had it on you,' the younger guard said. 'I mean going for "guilty" every time. Figure it'd work out cheaper if you played their ball, huh?'

'Something like that.'

'In here.'

They waited for him to go before. He pushed open the door and entered a small, drab, institutional room in which Tom Leonard was waiting. He rose from a battered chair as they came in. He still wore the faint check suit he had put on that morning out at the motel and now, just faintly, it was his wit that rose.

'They treating you all right?' he said.

To be polite, Paul Madison smiled a little.

'I just placed a bet that's what you'd say,' he said. 'Not sure how I collect, though.'

He was remembering he'd left a copy of *Bleak House* on the motel bedroom floor. Well, sooner or later, Stella would bring him out another.

'I guess it's because I don't know what else to say,' Tom Leonard was saying, 'I really don't.'

'So – forgive me – why come?'

'Well . . . to see if there was anything you wanted, I guess. And to try and discover why, I guess, as well.'

'Why?'

'Why no deal.'

Leonard was staring at him with a pained anxiety. And just as with Behrman that morning it was easy to see – too easy – the anxiety was inner directed.

'You're a bright guy, Tom. You know why.'

One guard had remained by the door, the other gone to a corner. But they might not have existed.

'I don't believe it,' Leonard said.

'You don't want to because you don't want to. You haven't stopped selling yourself short.'

'Paul!' The intensity of both Leonard's voice and expression belied his right to a denial.

'For God's sake, Tom. You know which of us is the treble bonded, straight F loser and which of us is only maybe a loser. You'll have to power-steer yourself back to Celine in your BMW and sink five large martinis before – if you're lucky – you start being able to live with yourself.'

He smiled. The thought had only just struck him.

'Yes, that's why I did it,' he said, 'so I could start living with myself.'

'A prison is the last place—'

'And not with Lyndon Oates.'

'Paul! I do think—'

'I'll tell you a story, Tom, Okay? . . . A way back I started to keep a kind of notebook, a journal. I put into it what I thought about all the shit people I was wading through each day – the lays, the whores, the cocksuckers, the peddlers. The Oateses, the Darrolls, the Prestons, the Madisons . . . When I started to get so sick of myself and so disgusted with some of the things I'd done – and we know, don't we Tom, sweetheart, baby – when I started to think maybe the hard route for me was going to be the easy route stretched out the length of my life, well, I thought maybe that journal could be the basis for somebody, some writer, to kind of write a kind of – not exoneration – but at least, explanation of why I'd come on like the shit who had everything. Telling it how it was and is and ever will be, Hollywood without end, amen, and naming names would at least show I was only one shit among so many.

'So I thought of who I knew could write just such a thing. And naturally, familiarity made me think at once of you ... You know what, Tom? I burnt those journals. Because when I thought of you I knew you didn't have it in you to cut yourself off from your air-conditioned meal-ticket and name names or tell it like it is, not in a thousand years. Let's face it. You're not even a writer, are you, Tom? You're in PR.

'That's your reason why, Tom, if you like. I didn't want to end up feeling about me what you feel about you. You've got some style, Tom, but you've got no class.'

Leonard had stood still taking it. He had coloured up and then gone very pale. On his deathbed he would still look Brooks Brothers.

'Well, fuck you too,' he said.

'Too late, Tom ... Don't cry all the way in to the office tomorrow ... wasn't all personal. Fingering Oates and you wouldn't have deodorised me. I finally found out. Revenge corrodes everything else around.'

'Still – you'll understand all the same, now, if I don't shake hands.'

'That won't do you any good, either.'

Leonard was suddenly possessed by a naked emotion. It was shocking, obscene. It was disturbingly against all tradition and propriety it was so elemental. And yet so complex. Regret was in it, admiration. It was subtly much more than a raw envy and a sad shame that at the very end he had been proved what he had always been and always would remain – the perpetual inferior.

'I hope it's twenty years! I hope you end up chalking up the hours.'

'You asked why. I told you.'

'Screw you, Paul. I have a last commission. There's a reporter outside. He—'

'I told them, no reporters. No interviews.'

'He doesn't want an interview. He wanted me to pass a message on to you. I wasn't going to but you just made it possible.'

'Message?'

'He said he met you once in hospital. That time you were losing the marks you picked up putting the little lady you know where. I guess you conned him pretty good then. He said to you that meeting you had been a "pleasure and a privilege". He says now to say that he was wrong.'

A suede jacket, jeans, young – Paul Madison remembered. He wasn't in the least fazed.

'There is an answer, boy,' he said. 'Go tell him he was wrong both times.'

He waited one long beat then turning to the blonde guard by the door cut Tom Leonard out of his world.

'If it's okay with you,' he said, 'I'd like to go on back.'

chapter thirty-three

For a period not less than three years and not exceeding ten.
Judge Joseph K. Harker

For a moment his steps faltered and the breaths he took were conscious and deep. A fist pushed at the small of his back to keep him going. It was done, he sensed, impersonally, routinely. That made it the more disturbing. Until that instant he had been doing well. Now, although he speeded up the pace of his clanging footsteps again it was with a cold hollowness invading his belly, knees that felt remote and beyond control.

It was not the sight of the jail's main block that had stabbed at him. It was the sudden piercing awareness that, in jail or not, he might be condemned to pass the rest of his life in a world made up of movie stereotypes, of responses already prefabricated for him by the Hollywood whose darker side he had discovered. Whatever he had begun to look for in the world or in himself would not be found at the far end of a Panavision lens.

Knowing that in his case the clustered-round guards had found an extra grinning relish in the indignities their low authority allowed them to inflict on newly-arrived prisoners, he assumed the role of puppet. He had suffered the undressing, the body-search, the showering, the issue of a used and no longer tailored workshirt impassively. The actor in him had given him the ability not to react. That way he robbed them of their mindless fun.

But when, finally, after a short walk down a corridor, a climb of sounding steel stairs, they had clanked doors open and motioned him through, he had been assailed by this first almost physical doubt.

High on the latticed steel cat-walk, he was on a movie-set again. One where they'd gone to town. It took up the entire length of the studio's biggest sound-stage and reached clear to the roof. He and the two extras behind him had come in on the third tier of gantries running a long quadrilateral about an open central well. Not totally open. The set designer had gone for broke on the budget to achieve authenticity. As if for a high-wire act a safety-net was strung tautly to the four edges of the lowest walkways. Its mesh provided the one impression of squares. All else was a flicker at the eyes of strobing horizontal lines. The light, shade, light, shade of the cell bars that in undeviating order climbed up from the first floor and blurred at his left eye as, footsteps ringing flatly, he walked on before the guards. There was something else making those blurs as well. Men. The assistant-director had done his job well too. A great metallic buzz droned up to the meshed sky-lighted roof and, trapped, hung there reverberating.

He sensed the blurs close to his left hand stirring with interest – caged animals intrigued by an exotic visitor. He sensed odd cries above the general hum directed straight to him. But for this moment while apprehension knotted its tight fist inside his gut and he increasingly remembered that there was no camera craning alongside in the space to his right hand, no Hackman or Pacino waiting up ahead to climax the shot's end, he found himself unable quite to look in any direction other than ahead.

'Hold it there.'

He stopped. One of the guards came past him reaching up keys on a long chain. He was a wide and thick-set man, middle-aged, not especially photogenic if you looked beyond his uniform. but he had his uniform. He placed a large, comically old-fashioned key into the lock set centrally into the grill door.

And now there was no option. Paul Madison was obliged to raise his eyes up from the close-up of the lock to look into the cell beyond. He caught a swift glimpse of a low and seatless toilet and two mean and sallow faces looking up, turning round enquiringly. It was as much as he could take first time. He looked back quickly at the key.

The guard had not turned it. He was turning himself to look at Paul Madison. For a man of such total power he seemed strangely at a loss.

'Er . . . er, Mr Madison,' he said. 'I – er – wonder if maybe you could let me have your autograph.' He was bringing a ballpoint and creased fold of paper out from the pocket of his shirt. The deference was, somehow, appalling. Jesus, isn't anybody getting the message!

'Sure,' Paul Madison said.

'Er, you can press on my note-book.'

Awkwardly he signed his famous name. As he did so the feeling he had known on stepping through the door engulfed him ten times more strongly. It could be he knew, that Hollywood was too subtly disseminated through his body for any gesture of amputation to succeed.

'Er, thanks, Mr Madison.'

Embarrassed by his use of the title, the guard spoke gruffly. But as he now turned the key and pushed open the barred door, he still did so with the action of a hireling.

Paul Madison stepped into the cell. The grill door swung harshly to behind him to hold him as inexorably fast as his own past would until his labour made the future different.

*　　*　　*

Press Release: At a reception at the Beverley Hills Hotel last night Lyndon Oates announced the signing by Milton Rosner of the young New York actor, Clive Massey. 'We're all tremendously excited about this one,' he said. 'The first project will be a . . .'

NEL BESTSELLERS

T046 133	HOW GREEN WAS MY VALLEY	*Richard Llewellyn*	£1.00
T039 560	I BOUGHT A MOUNTAIN	*Thomas Firbank*	95p
T033 988	IN THE TEETH OF THE EVIDENCE	*Dorothy L. Sayers*	90p
T038 149	THE CARPETBAGGERS	*Harold Robbins*	£1.50
T040 917	TO SIR WITH LOVE	*E.R. Braithwaite*	75p
T041 719	HOW TO LIVE WITH A NEUROTIC DOG	*Stephen Baker*	75p
T040 925	THE PRIZE	*Irving Wallace*	£1.65
T034 755	THE CITADEL	*A.J. Cronin*	£1.10
T042 189	STRANGER IN A STRANGE LAND	*Robert Heinlein*	£1.25
T037 053	79 PARK AVENUE	*Harold Robbins*	£1.25
T042 308	DUNE	*Frank Herbert*	£1.50
T045 137	THE MOON IS A HARSH MISTRESS	*Robert Heinlein*	£1.25
T040 933	THE SEVEN MINUTES	*Irving Wallace*	£1.50
T038 130	THE INHERITORS	*Harold Robbins*	£1.25
T035 689	RICH MAN, POOR MAN	*Irwin Shaw*	£1.50
T037 134	EDGE 27: DEATH DRIVE	*George G. Gilman*	75p
T037 541	DEVIL'S GUARD	*Robert Elford*	£1.25
T042 774	THE RATS	*James Herbert*	80p
T042 340	CARRIE	*Stephen King*	80p
T042 782	THE FOG	*James Herbert*	90p
T033 740	THE MIXED BLESSING	*Helen Van Slyke*	£1.25
T037 061	BLOOD AND MONEY	*Thomas Thompson*	£1.50
T038 629	THIN AIR	*Simpson & Burger*	95p
T038 602	THE APOCALYPSE	*Jeffrey Konvitz*	95p

NEL P.O. BOX 11, FALMOUTH TR10 9EN, CORNWALL

Postage charge:
U.K. Customers. Please allow 25p for the first book plus 10p per copy for each additional book ordered to a maximum charge of £1.05 to cover the cost of postage and packing, in addition to cover price.

B.F.P.O. & Eire. Please allow 25p for the first book plus 10p per copy for the next 8 books, thereafter 5p per book, in addition to cover price.

Overseas Customers. Please allow 40p for the first book plus 12p per copy for each additional book, in addition to cover price.

Please send cheque or postal order (no currency).

Name ....

Address ....

....

Title ....

While every effort is made to keep prices steady, it is sometimes necessary to increase prices at short notice. New English Library reserve the right to show on covers and charge new retail prices which may differ from those advertised in the text or elsewhere.